ALSO BY SHIRLEY HAZZARD

COLLECTED STORIES

COLLECTED STORIES

SHIRLEY HAZZARD

EDITED BY BRIGITTA OLUBAS

FOREWORD BY ZOË HELLER

FARRAR, STRAUS AND GIROUX   NEW YORK

Farrar, Straus and Giroux
120 Broadway, New York 10271

Printed in the United States of America
First edition, 2020

Library of Congress Cataloging-in-Publication Data
Names: Hazzard, Shirley, 1931–2016, author. | Olubas, Brigitta, editor. | Heller, Zoë,
    writer of foreword.
Title: Collected stories / Shirley Hazzard ; edited by Brigitta Olubas ; foreword by Zoë Heller.
Other titles: Short stories
Description: First edition. | New York : Farrar, Straus and Giroux, 2020.
Identifiers: LCCN 2020025568 | ISBN 9780374126483 (hardcover)
Classification: LCC PR9619.3 .H369 2020 | DDC 823/.914—dc23
LC record available at https://lccn.loc.gov/2020025568

Designed by Abby Kagan

www.fsgbooks.com
www.twitter.com/fsgbooks • www.facebook.com/fsgbooks

10 9 8 7 6 5 4 3 2 1

CONTENTS

UNCOLLECTED / UNPUBLISHED

FOREWORD

BY ZOË HELLER

The early years of a writer's career are often a period of throat-clearing, of trying on and discarding styles, but in Shirley Hazzard's case, this awkward probationary phase seems to have been skipped: she emerged with her distinctive talents fully formed. She was twenty-eight years old when she wrote her first short story, "Harold," in 1959. For seven years, she had been toiling unhappily and without hope of advancement in the general service ranks of the UN Secretariat. ("A young woman was given a typewriter and told to shut up," she said later.) "Harold" is a fable of sorts about a group of travelers at a Tuscan guesthouse who are amazed when a gauche, apparently unaccomplished new arrival reveals himself to be a gifted artist. Within a few weeks of sending it to *The New Yorker* (together with a note indicating that the manuscript need not be returned if it proved unsuitable for publication), she received a letter from the magazine's fiction editor, William Maxwell. Of course they would publish her story, he wrote, and did she have any others they might look at? Her submission, he later recalled, was "an astonishment to the editors, because it was the work of a finished literary artist about whom they knew nothing whatever."

The stories that Hazzard went on to produce in a steady stream throughout the 1960s are not typical literary artifacts of their time. Their characters—single young women and their married lovers, adulterous suburban couples, disillusioned salarymen—are recognizably of the period, but their rigorously elegant style is less so. The stately rhythms of Hazzard's sentences, the epigrammatic precision of her observations, the decorousness of her glancing, ironic blows—have a closer affinity with the classic prose of the eighteenth and nineteenth centuries than with the frank, unbuttoned work of her contemporaries.

> The possibility of worldly success had never, by them, been entertained; they conjectured only as to the form that failure would take. ("Vittorio")

> She had a proprietary way of admiring other people's possessions, as if all good taste were in some measure a tribute to herself. ("In One's Own House")

> The three boys, now reseated, looked him over with courteous reserve, exercising that perception for affinities and failings with which public-school life had endowed them. ("Harold")

Hazzard disdained the tendency toward a conversational, plain-spoken style in modern fiction. It seemed to her a perverse rejection of art's proper aspiration to beauty. (Writers, she told *The Paris Review* in 2005, had abandoned "the power of formal language" in favor of trying "to seem casual, sassy, democratic, 'young.'") In Hazzard's work, beauty in whatever form—a sentence, or a table setting—has a moral value. Demotic idiom rarely appears in these stories, even in the mouths of her protagonists, and when someone does use ugly slang or jargon—when, for example, a woman worries an acquaintance will find her "a bit dykey," or a man says "utilize" instead of "use"—it almost always denotes a certain crudeness of character. (By the same token, caring about and quoting poetry is a reliable indicator of virtue—the equivalent of riding into town wearing a white cowboy hat.)

Much of the drama in Hazzard's work arises from the bruising interactions between those who are responsive to beauty, and those who are not. Her heroes and heroines are modern romantics who cleave to high feeling and high seriousness in a world largely hostile to their idealism. ("One said 'relationship' nowadays about those one loved," a gloomy bureaucrat muses in "Official Life.") Her villains are pragmatists and philistines who want at all costs to "keep the poetry separate." The puzzlement and condescension that Hazzard's high-minded characters inspire as they make their pilgrim's progress through twentieth-century life supply the comedy of these stories. The sufferings they endure for their romantic integrity supply the tragedy. Here is Nettie, the teenage protagonist of "A Place in the Country," responding to the news that her married lover is abandoning her.

> Nothing could convince her that this first sharing of her secret existence, more significant even than the offering of her person, represented less than it appeared to. That circumstances might oblige him to withdraw from her she perfectly understood; that he actually felt himself to be less committed appalled her. It confounded all her assumptions, that something so deeply attested should prove totally unpredictable.

This is rather how one might expect George Eliot's Dorothea Brooke to sound, were she to be spirited out of Victorian England and given contraception and an apartment. Nettie is not nearly as clever, or as reliably high-minded, as Dorothea. (In a later story, we meet her again, in early middle age, and discover that she has grown up to become a slightly silly person.) Yet in the moment of Nettie's earnest adolescent heartbreak, Hazzard endows her with something approaching nobility. Urged by her sheepish lover not to "exaggerate the importance" of her broken heart, she understands instinctively that the greater sin is to take matters of the heart lightly.

The portrait of the permissive era that emerges from these stories is a rather somber one. Eros is less the bringer of carnal fun than a dark and rather dangerous force on which men and women (but mostly women) pin their romantic hopes at their peril. Hazzard's female characters are not constrained by conventional sexual morality, inasmuch as they engage in premarital and extramarital sex without compunction or shame, but they evince none of the antic libertinism or experience-gathering curiosity of, say, Mary McCarthy's women. Sex remains for them a solemn rite, a significant act of surrender, and their inability to divorce the act from higher feeling leaves them horribly vulnerable to the emotional sadism and moral carelessness of men.

In Hazzard's later novels, her noble characters are ultimately rewarded for their integrity: they get to walk out of their soul-crushing jobs, to thumb their noses at the insufferable snobs who have oppressed them, to find enduring love with their Platonic other halves. In these stories, the pure of heart are largely denied such satisfactions. They remain chained up in their grim offices, or else they get sacked; the people they fall in love with don't requite their love, or aren't worthy of their love; the people who love them, they don't want. What few glimpses of romantic fulfillment Hazzard affords us are either in rear view, or from a distance: a woman grieving a dead husband in "Cliffs of Fall," two lovestruck Norwegian travelers seen on a ferry in "Out of Itea." ("But what will they *eat*?" "Tomatoes." "Where will they sleep?" "Together.")

To the extent that these stories withhold earthly satisfaction from their romantics, they might reasonably be described as austere, or even bleak: "*Il est plus facile de mourir que d'aimer*" is the line that one unhappy wife in "The Worst Moment of the Day" happens upon in a book of Louis Aragon's poetry. Yet, these stories insist, to be open to the difficulty and pain of love is better than to be comfortably protected from its sting. Hazzard's seekers of truth and beauty may suffer, but, as one wise character remarks, "We should remember that sorrow does produce flowers of its own. It is a misunderstanding always to look for joy."

CLIFFS OF FALL

THE PARTY

The Fergusons' door opened on a burst of light and voices, and on Evie's squeal of surprise—quite as if, Minna thought, we had turned up uninvited. Evie kissed her.

"Our shoes are a bit wet," said Theodore. He stood aside to let Minna enter. "Is that all right?"

Evie had slanting eyes, and a flushed, pretty face. She was wearing a shiny brown dress, and her hair bubbled down her back in fair, glossy curls. She had an impulsive way of embracing people, of holding them by the hand or the elbow, as though she must atone for any reticence on their part with an extra measure of her own exuberance—or as though they would attempt to escape if not taken into custody.

"Minna, what a beautiful dress. How thin you are. Theodore, you never look a day older, not a single *day*. I expect," she said to Minna, "that he is really very gray—with fair people it doesn't show. He'll get old quite suddenly and look like Somerset Maugham." She gave Minna a sympathetic, curious look from her tilted eyes. (Minna could imagine her saying later: "I never will understand why *that* keeps going, not if I live to be a hundred.") "Here's Phil."

Evie's husband came out of the living room, a silver jug in one hand and an ice bucket in the other.

"You look like an allegorical figure," Minna told him.

Phil smiled. He went through life with that sedate, modest smile. He was a corporation lawyer, and he and Evie had been very happy together for fifteen years. Long ago, however, at his own expense and to everyone's surprise he had published a small book of love poems that carried no assurance of being addressed to her. "What would you like to drink?" Phil asked. "Minna, come into the kitchen and help me with the ice. Otherwise I'll never get a chance to talk to you."

Evie was leading Theodore away. Minna looked apprehensively at his straight back as it receded toward a group of people in the living room. He will enjoy himself, she thought, and then reproach me for letting him come.

In the kitchen, Phil's eleven-year-old son was emptying ashtrays into a garbage pail.

"Hello, Ronnie," Minna said. She turned on the cold tap for Phil.

"Oh hullo," Ronnie said, intent on his work. "Alison's got the virus." Alison was his sister.

"But not badly," said Phil. "Thank you, Minna, I think that's about enough."

"I got her a card," Ronnie said.

"How nice," said Minna, breaking up a tray of ice.

"It says 'Get Well Quick.'"

"That sounds a trifle peremptory."

"I expect the sentiment counts for something," Phil observed from the sink.

"Taste is more important than sentiment," Minna decided, without reflection.

"Yes, I suppose I agree with that."

She smiled. "The combination, on the other hand, is irresistible."

"You're beginning to talk like Theodore. Ronnie, you could be handing round the peanuts."

"There aren't any peanuts."

"Shrimp, then—whatever there is. For God's sake." Phil took the ice bucket from Minna and put it on a tray with the jug. They moved toward the door. "Now," he asked her again, "what would you like?"

She would have liked to stay in the kitchen with Phil and Ronnie, although the light was too bright and there was nowhere to sit down. The kitchen chairs were covered with half-empty cartons of crackers and, in one case, with a large chalky bowl in which the dip had been mixed. Ends of celery and carrot had been left on the table, together with an open container of sour cream and two broken glasses. It was, Minna decided, like the periphery of a battlefield strewn with discarded equipment and expended ammunition. When I go into the other room, she thought, I will have to talk, and listen, and be aware of Theodore across the room.

"What can I have?" she asked Phil, as they went down the corridor.

"Anything you like. There's punch, if you want that." He paused to introduce Minna to a young man and a girl with a hat full of roses.

"Minna?" said the girl. "What a pretty name."

"Her real name is Hermione," said Ronnie, coming up with a plate of shrimp.

"Preposterous name," Minna agreed. "I don't know why parents do such things."

"We called our baby Araminta," said the girl bravely.

"'Araminta sweet and faire . . .'" Phil quoted tactfully.

Minna frowned. "That's '*Amarantha*,'" she said, and wished she hadn't. She and Phil edged past, and found themselves at a long table, beside a bony man in black and an opulent, earnest woman in purple. "Punch would be lovely," Minna said to Phil.

"A Browning revival," said the man in black. "Mark my words—I forecast a Browning revival."

The purple lady sighed. "Ah. If only you're right."

"Then you do like Browning?"

"Of course. *Pippa Passes*. And I've always adored *The Rose and the Ring*."

The bony man looked disappointed. "That's Thackeray. You mean *The Ring and the Book*."

"I mean the one with the marvelous illustrations."

"Rather weak, I'm afraid," Phil said, handing Minna a full glass. "All the ice seems to have melted." He helped someone else to punch and turned back to her. "Well, Minna—we hardly ever seem to see you. Are you very busy? Are you happy? *How* are you?"

"Oh, I'm well," she said, and could not prevent herself from looking toward Theodore. He was standing not far from her, leaning his shoulder against the wall and talking to a plump man with a beard.

The bearded man looked cross. "My dear sir," he said in a loud voice, "this is not just *any* Rembrandt. This is one of the greatest Rembrandts of all time."

"Take *Sordello*," the bony man was insisting. The woman in purple gazed at him with rapt inattention.

The girl with the roses in her hat was still standing in the doorway by her husband's side. I should go and talk to them, Minna thought; they don't seem to know anyone. All the same, they looked quite contented. She glanced round at Phil, but Evie had just come up to him with a question; she laid her hand on his arm—beseechingly and not in her public, clamorous way—and he put his head down to hers. Minna set her glass on the table. Theodore, smiling broadly, had turned away from the man with the beard. She exchanged a glance with him, and wondered what his mood would be when they were alone.

"Have you looked in the refrigerator?" Phil was saying. His head remained lowered to Evie's a moment longer. Minna looked away, as if she had seen them embrace.

The girl by the door was laughing now, the roses shaking on her hat, and the man beside her was leaning against the doorframe and smiling at her.

Minna took up her glass again and turned it in her hand, and went on watching them—with admiration, as one might watch an intricate dance executed with perfect grace; and with something like homesickness, as if she were looking at colored slides of a country in which she had once been happy.

"I behaved rather well, didn't I?" he asked. "All things considered."

She came and knelt beside his chair and kissed him. "Admirably," she said. He put his arm about her but she disengaged herself and settled on the floor, leaning against his legs. "It wasn't so bad, now, was it?"

"You sound just like my dentist." He stretched back in his chair, his palms resting on his knees and the fingers of his right hand just touching her hair.

The one lighted lamp, at his elbow, allowed them to see little more than each other and a pale semicircle of the rug on which she sat. She lowered her head and watched the bright shine of his shoe, which was half hidden by a fold of her dress. Outside their crescent of light, beyond the obscured but familiar room, the cold wind blew from time to time against the windows and the traffic sounded faintly from below. During the day there had been a brief fall of snow and, frozen at the window ledges, this now sealed them in. She tilted her head back against his knees. "It's so nice here," she said, and smiled.

He passed his hand round her throat, his extended fingers reaching from ear to ear. Her hair spread over his sleeve. "Minna dear," he said. "Minna darling."

She suddenly sat upright and raised her hand to her head. "I've lost an earring. It must be at the Fergusons'."

"No, it's here," he said. "In the other room. On the table beside the bed."

"Are you sure?"

"Positive. I remember noticing it. I meant to mention it before we went out."

"I must have looked odd at the party." She settled back again. "What was I saying?"

"How nice it was."

"Oh yes. How nice."

"Just because we haven't quarreled today."

"More than that. You've been quite . . ."

"Quite what?"

"Sweet to me."

"Not something I make a habit of, is it, these days?" His fingers were tracing the line of her jaw. "I really thought you wouldn't come today. After last week."

"We had to go to the party," she said.

"That hardly seemed sufficient reason. I thought, She won't come—why should she? There's a limit, I thought. All morning, I sat here thinking there was a limit."

"And drinking," she added, but pressed her hand, over his, against her neck.

"Well, naturally." He yawned. "God, that awful party."

"It wasn't so bad," she said again.

"The Fergusons are dull."

"I like Phil."

"Evie, then."

"Well . . . But she's a good person."

"Good? I'm beginning to wonder if it's a virtue to be good. It seems to be the cause of so much self-congratulation among our friends. The sort of people who were there tonight—who choose a convenient moment to behave well and then tell themselves how sensitive they are, how humane."

"But isn't that all one can hope for? And what *is* virtue, if not that?"

"Oh—something less conscious, I suppose; something more indiscriminate. Less egotistical, more anonymous. Like that brotherhood in Italy whose members still hide their faces under masks when they assist the poor."

"I thought that was to protect them from the Plague."

"Don't be irritating. What I mean is, our good seem to be so concerned with themselves, so clubby, not mixing with the natives. Do you think those people tonight would ever make allowances, for instance, for those who want to live differently, or more fully, or risk themselves more?"

So he, too, is only concerned with himself, she reflected.

"Why, even religion—even the law, than which, after all, *nothing* could be more unjust—takes account of extenuating circumstances. But these people exclude anyone who doesn't meet their particular definition of sensibility. I'm not sure that I don't find it as distasteful as any other form of intolerance."

"I suppose they think that anyone can be kind."

"That's like saying 'Anyone can be clean' in a city where most houses don't have running water. And in the end the well-meaning people seem to do more harm than the others, who make no pretensions. Don't you think?"

"Not entirely," she said, with faint irony.

"Now you are only thinking of yourself. That's the sort of thing that makes it impossible to have any real discussion with a woman. No matter how abstract, how impersonal the subject, they will always manage to connect it in some way to their love affairs."

They were silent for a moment. She rested her hand on one of the thick, embossed Chinese roses of the rug. "Would you rather not have gone, then, tonight?"

"Infinitely."

"You only had to say so."

"You couldn't have gone alone."

"I could."

"All right, you could—but you'd have sulked for days." He turned her face slightly to him. "You're practically crying as it is."

"I always look that way."

"When you're with me, at any rate." He let his hand drop. "There were women with hats on at the party. And young couples who talked about their children. Oh, and an old lunatic who wanted to revive Swinburne."

"Browning," she said.

"Browning—was that it? So it was. Then there was Evie, of course, feeling sorry for you because of me. Because I'm so disagreeable." He laughed. "At least, it wasn't as bad as the last party they had—someone actually *sang* at that, if you remember."

"I do remember. Yes."

"And you played the piano."

"Yes."

He smiled pleasantly at the recollection. "You were terrible," he said.

"Was I?"

"Darling, you always play so badly—didn't you know that?"

"I didn't know you thought so," she said, reflecting that the knowledge must now be with her permanently. She sighed. "Theodore, why do you have to do this?"

"Why?" He looked over her head for a moment, as if the question arose for the first time and required consideration. "For that matter, why anything? Why are you here? And why is your earring in the other room? Why, in fact, do you allow this to continue?"

"Eventually, I suppose, I won't." Her voice had taken on a conversational note. "A matter of will power, probably—of making oneself want something else."

"Perhaps you don't even know what else to want."

"I think I might rather like to come first with someone—after themselves, of course. And it does seem a waste, this love, this thing everyone needs, this precious commodity—it could be going to someone who would use it properly."

"Perhaps, then, *that's* all you want? Someone to give love to—a sort of repository?"

"Perhaps. No, something more reciprocal. Only, starting over again in love is such a journey—like needing a holiday but not wanting to be bothered with packing bags and making reservations. So much trouble—being charming and artful, finding ways to pretend less affection than one feels, and in the end not succeeding, because one doesn't really profit from experience; one merely learns to predict the next mistake. No, I just can't be bothered at present." She shifted her weight and, turning, laid her arm across his knees. He bent forward and smoothed the hair back from her forehead. "So there you are," she told him. "It's all a question of inertia. I stay because leaving would require too much effort."

"Yes, I see," he said, his hand still on her head. "Of course."

"But as I say," she continued, "it's an effort one must make eventually. Simply in order to stay alive. Like going to that silly party." She plucked a thread off her sleeve. "Darling, I think I'll go home. There's no sense in this."

"That dress picks up everything," he said.

Their eyes met. She looked away, with a slight smile. "I suppose there would be a humorous side to all this, wouldn't there, if one were not involved?"

He still watched her and did not smile. "No, there would not." He leaned back again, his hands resting on the arms of the chair.

This physical detachment made her suddenly conscious that she was kneeling. She sat back on her heels. "I'm going home," she said again. She hesitated for a moment. When he said nothing, she pressed her hands on his knees and stood up stiffly.

"You must hurt all over," he remarked, getting to his feet.

"More or less."

He switched on another lamp. The light fell on heavy curtains, and on books, chairs, and a sofa.

Standing before a mirror, she drew her hair back with her hand and watched his reflection as he moved across the room. "My earring," she said.

He came back with it in his hand, and with her coat over his arm. She refocused her eyes to her own reflection in the glass, examining her appearance uncertainly as she fixed the little gold loop to her ear.

"I suppose you're right," he said, "about the way you look. You do have a rather mournful face. Not tragic, of course—just *mournful*."

"That sounds more discreet, at least." She turned and faced him, and reached out a hand for her coat. "I must go," she said.

"And the dress doesn't help—I'm not sure that black suits you, anyway. Now you really are going to cry."

"You should be trying to build up my confidence," she said, unblinking, "instead of doing everything to demolish it."

He helped her into her coat. "Confidence is one of those things we try to instill into others and then hasten to dispel as soon as it puts in an appearance."

"Like love," she observed, turning to the door.

"Like love," he said. "Exactly."

A PLACE IN THE COUNTRY

Try to keep the poetry separate," said May. "The rest can be arranged later." She made her way around the boxes of books and china to the doorway, and called up the stairs. "Clem! When you're finished up there, you could help Nettie with the books." She had a powerful, almost insistent voice and she evidently assumed that her husband heard her, for she came back into the living room without waiting for his reply and knelt down on the rug beside Nettie. "I can make a start on the china."

"Is Shakespeare poetry?" asked Nettie, peering into a box.

"No, he belongs with the set of Elizabethan dramatists—the old leather ones. But let Clem lift the heavy books." May was uncoiling newspaper from around a jug. Her broad, tawny head was lowered over the china into a shaft of sunlight, and its brilliant color made her actions seem less businesslike than usual. "Dreadful to think this will all have to go back to town in the autumn. Still, I'm glad we came early this year, in spite of the cold. And perhaps Clem can take long weekends when the summer comes, and be less in town. It's hard on him to travel so far for just the two days. And you, too, Nettie, now that you're living in town. Don't forget—whenever you like, Clem can drive you up for the weekend."

"Thank you," the girl said. She had filled the lowest shelf of the bookcase and now sat back on her heels to survey it.

"Nettie, are you all right?"

Nettie blew some dust off *A Shropshire Lad* and looked at May over the end of the book. "Yes, of course."

"You seem a bit pale." May lowered her voice slightly. "Aren't you well? Would you like an aspirin?"

"I'm fine. Really." Nettie turned back to the shelves with a load of books. She had rolled up the sleeves of her heavy blue sweater, and her thin forearms were grubby from the books. An imprecise black pigtail dangled between her hunched shoulders.

May eyed her for a moment with determination rather than concern, but was distracted by steps on the stairs. "Here's Clem, anyway. He can fill the top shelves."

"What is it I'm supposed to do?" her husband asked—apparently as a formality, since he went straight to the books and began stacking them on upper shelves. "Why on earth Meredith? . . . And *Galsworthy*— Oh, for God's sake, darling." He turned round to May with a book in his hand.

"Dear, I'll be here for almost six months, you know. Mostly with just the children."

"No reason to lose your head completely." He placed the book alongside the others. "Who was that on the telephone?"

"Oh, the Bairds are back—that was Sarah. They opened their house last week. Sent you their love. I asked them for dinner tomorrow night."

"I thought you had to collect Matt from your mother's tomorrow." Their elder boy was spending a few days at his grandmother's, thirty miles away.

"I'll be back before dinner. And Marion can have everything ready— I've asked her to stay a little later tomorrow evening."

Clem grunted. Nettie had only completed the two lowest shelves, and he was already stooping to fill the middle of the bookcase. He was tall and light on his feet and looked less than his age, which was forty-two. He had an air of health and confidence as he handled the books, lifting them from the box, glancing at their titles, and ramming them quickly along the shelves. He, too, had rolled up his sleeves, and his arms as they moved back and forth contrasted with Nettie's fragile and ineffectual ones.

"Here's Byron," he said, handing Nettie a book. He looked down at her for the first time, and pulled on her plait of hair. "What's this floppy thing?"

Self-consciously, she put up her left hand, the book in her right. "I haven't had time to do it properly." They resumed their work.

I suppose, Nettie thought, as she made a space between two books and fitted Byron into it, that I am in love with Clem. Love is so much talked and written about, you might expect it to feel quite different; but no, it does correspond to the descriptions—it isn't commonplace. More like a concentration of all one's energies. There seems to be a lot of waiting in it, though. I am always waiting for Clem to come into a room, or for other people to go out: Clem, whom I've known all my life and who is married to my cousin May. (Her hands, patting the books into an even row, trembled.) I've been close to him a thousand times, and this is the first time it has made me tremble. Would I have discovered that I loved him, if he hadn't drawn my attention to it? And is that really only a week ago?

Now Clem, too, had to kneel, and her cheek came level with his shoulder. He smiled at her, a brief, open smile. Nettie reached up, still pushing the books into line, and the sweater rose above her skirt, showing a white, ribbed strip of her skin.

May rose, and took up a stack of plates. "There. I'll leave these in the kitchen and Marion can wash them later, with the lunch dishes." She moved across the room and out of the shaft of sunlight. Her back looked, once more, entirely businesslike. She had a slow, deliberate way of walking—as if she had once been startled into precipitate action and had regretted it. It was the walk of a woman who dealt with men in a straightforward way and must suffer the consequences. Her steps sounded down the uncarpeted corridor.

Clem got to his feet and rummaged in the last box. "What are these?" He held up a book he did not recognize.

"Those are mine. I thought I'd leave them for the summer. I'll take them up to my room." Nettie got up, wincing, and rubbed her knees.

He pulled the books out one at a time, flicking open the front covers. "Annette Bowers . . . Annette Bowers . . . A. Bowers . . . Annette Bowers." He brought them to her, stacked between his palms, and put them into her grasp without releasing them. "Annette Bowers. I love you."

"No."

"*Yes*, I tell you," he said, shaking his head and widening his eyes in imitation of her. "Did you know that—somewhere in India, I think—there are people who shake their heads as a sign of assent, instead of nodding them?" Without lowering his voice, he went on: "What have you thought about all week?"

"You," she said gravely, with her hands about the books.

He leaned forward and kissed her brow. "Now, take your books upstairs, there's a good girl," he said.

She walked past him and out of the room.

"Oh, Clem, help her," May said, coming from the kitchen and passing Nettie in the corridor.

"I can manage," said Nettie.

May came back into the living room and sat down in an easy chair. She crossed her legs and lit a cigarette. "Do you think Nettie's all right?" she asked Clem.

He was piling the abandoned wads of newspaper into an empty carton. "Why not?" he asked.

"Oh, sometimes she seems such a . . . waif. Perhaps we should do more for her, now she's living away from home."

He had fitted the empty boxes, ingeniously, one inside the other. "We have our own lives to lead," he said.

May left early in the morning. Having meticulously calculated time and distance on a piece of paper, she could tell the hour at which she would reach her mother's house, how long she must, in order not to seem hurried, linger over lunch there, and when she and Matt might reasonably be expected home. Seated neatly dressed at the wheel of the car, she gave an impression of carrying away with her all the order and assurance of the house.

Nettie, untidy in a dressing gown, received last instructions with a series of nods whose very frequency betrayed inattention. May has our day all planned, she thought, as well as her own. She has allowed for everything except what will happen. The engine started, and Nettie waved. When the car disappeared, she turned back to the house abruptly, dissociating herself from Clem.

"Can we play dominoes?" asked Kenny, the younger boy, who had been left in her charge.

"When I'm dressed," she said.

"Doesn't it seem a pity," Clem said, "to waste a day like this inside?"

"We could go for a walk along the beach," said Nettie, still addressing herself to Kenny.

"I'd rather play dominoes."

"All right, let's play dominoes first. We *could* go for a walk after lunch."

While they played dominoes, the day deteriorated. They sat down to lunch with a Sunday halfheartedness, Clem short-tempered from not having had his way and Kenny petulant from having had his. Marion, the maid, came and went between the kitchen and the dining room, as though they were, all three, fractious children who needed supervision. The cold meat that had seemed a good idea in the morning now simply contributed to the day's feeling of being left over.

After lunch, Nettie proposed again the walk that now nobody wanted, and out of sheer perverseness they walked on the deserted beach. Nettie wore a raincoat and Kenny a waterproof jacket with a broken zipper. A wind had come up, releasing little swirls from sand that had been tightly packed all winter. The sky hung over the low-lying land, huge as a sky in a Dutch painting. Clem could not light his cigarette, although he persisted in trying. Nettie struggled to fold the flapping triangle of her scarf over her hair. After she had accomplished this, Kenny put his hand in hers, but when Clem took her hand on the other side the child pulled away and ran ahead of them down the beach.

"Children know everything," Nettie said.

"Well, they have a kind of insight into fundamentals. I don't think one can call that knowledge." He would not let her withdraw her hand from his. "You look such an orphan in that raincoat."

"I always look a bit like that, apparently."

"That's what May said."

"What did she say?"

"That you looked a waif. That we should do more for you."

"What did you say?"

"I looked preoccupied and said we had our own lives to lead."

Freeing her fingers at last, she put both her hands in her pockets and they walked a little way in silence.

He looked at her, faintly amused. "What should I have said?"

"I don't know. Did you mean that when you said it? I mean, what did you feel?"

"You'd be happier if I had felt a liar and a hypocrite?"

"That, at least, would be a redeeming feature."

He shrugged. "I rather thought I'd redeemed myself by telling you about it." He was a little bored. "I see no object in hurting people unneccssarily."

"It would be all right if it were necessary?"

"You say all the wrong things," he observed. "You have no experience—you're thrown back on your intuitions, like Kenny. That's why you make these judgments on yourself and others."

She spread her hands, distending the pockets of her raincoat. "I'm afraid of this. Of not knowing what will happen next."

"Ah, well," he said, offhandedly, "you would have come to some things pretty soon in any case, if only out of curiosity. As for the other things, you simply attract them by worrying about them. What you fear most will happen to you—that is the law."

No one had spoken to her in this way before, and for a moment she actually imagined the words sternly inscribed in a statute book. Now Clem thrust his hands into his pockets, which had the effect of making Nettie, repudiated, distractedly bring out her own.

"Watch for shells!" Kenny roared from the horizon.

Neither of them replied. Presently Clem laughed and looked at her, and touched her shoulder with his. "You're a fool," he said, more kindly.

"But what have I done wrong?"

"You got born twenty years too late."

So immense and so complex did the gulf between them appear to her that it was a shock to have it simply stated as a matter of bad timing on her part. She had once been told that the earth, had it been slightly deflected on its axis, would have had no winter; and the possibility of a life shared with Clem appeared to her on the same scale of enormity and remote conjecture. Inexperienced, as he had pointed out, she had no means of knowing if his remarks were excessively unfeeling. She knew him in his daily life to be a reasonable man; from ignorance, she assumed that his conduct now would represent the same proportions of logic and compassion.

"Let's go back," he said. He cupped his hands and shouted to Kenny. Of Kenny's response, only the word "shells" could be distinguished. They retraced the pattern of their steps on the sand, the wind now at their backs.

"The Bairds are coming for dinner," Clem remarked.

"I met them once, last year."

"Vernon is rather a bore, but I like Sarah. She has the most beautiful eyes I've ever seen." He glanced round to be sure that Kenny was following.

Nettie, annoyed, said nothing. Her dim recollection of Mrs. Baird became tinged with antagonism—a plump, middle-aged woman bullied by her husband.

"I have never heard her say an unkind thing," Clem continued, "about anybody."

Nettie reflected that this, when said of a woman, made her sound totally uninteresting.

"You can entertain Vernon at dinner," Clem said.

"How?"

"Simply by listening to him, I should think. He likes shy young things. Although you're not exactly shy, are you? It's rather as though you were afraid we might all find out what you think of us." They climbed up a bank onto the road. "I wish we were alone," he said, as though their entire conversation had been irrelevant. He opened a gate and held it for her.

"There's Marion," Nettie said.

Marion had come out of the house and was standing in the drive. She put her hands to her mouth and shouted to them.

"She can't be collecting shells, too, can she?" Clem made a gesture of not hearing, and Marion shouted again. This time, as in the case of Kenny, one word only was distinct.

"The damned telephone," he said. "You bring Kenny. I'll go ahead."

Nettie waited by the gate for Kenny, who was walking—inexplicably— backward. Clem had disappeared into the house. Marion stood by the door, holding it almost closed against the wind. When Nettie came up the steps, Marion still grasped the doorknob—as if, Nettie thought, one could not enter the house without first being brought up to date on its contents.

"Matt has a temperature."

"Is that May on the phone?"

"Yes. They can't drive back today—Kenny, turn round at once or you'll fall over something—Matt has a temperature of a hundred and two."

Nettie dressed for dinner with great care. Instead of bending hurriedly before the speckled mirror above her chest of drawers, she propped the mirror by the bed, in the strongest light, and sat in front of it. She combed her hair and wound it into a circle at the back of her head and fastened it there. She brushed the shoulders of her black dress, and clasped a string of pearls around her neck, and put on high-heeled shoes. When she was quite ready, she sat once more on the bed and took her hair down, and put it up again in the same way.

As she came downstairs, the hallway was cold from the passage of night air. The Bairds had arrived. Sarah Baird had let Clem take her coat and was standing at the foot of the stairs in a dark-blue dress; her eyes, shining from the brief drive, were very fine indeed. Vernon looked up as Nettie joined them. From the slight surprise in his face, Nettie thought that she had been right, after all, to do her hair a second time.

"Ah, here she is," Clem said.

Sarah turned and, although they scarcely knew each other, kissed Nettie. So did Vernon. "Are you warm enough in that dress?" Sarah asked her.

"It's wool," said Nettie, speaking for the first time.

Clem put away Vernon's hat and shut the closet door. "There's a fire in the living room," he said. He laid his hand lightly on Nettie's shoulder as they moved away.

Clem poured out drinks, and they sat down by the fire. Clem rattled the ice in his drink and talked about Matt's temperature. He had been trying to telephone May all evening; the telephone, on a party line, was being used.

"You must tell them it's an emergency," Sarah began indignantly.

Nettie, leaning back in a deep chair as the others bent forward to the fire, reflected that Matt's temperature was, socially, a godsend to them all. Sarah, it seemed, moved with complete ease among children's temperatures, virus infections, the possibility—not to be ruled out—of measles. Briefly, she took charge of the conversation. "Try not to worry," she said, implying that one must by all means worry, though possibly not to distraction. The Bairds had four children, all of whose temperatures had, at one time or another, considerably outclassed Matt's.

She really is quite stupid, Nettie decided, believing—erroneously—that fine eyes could not atone for stupidity.

Looking away from Sarah, she was disconcerted to find Vernon watching her. If he were capable of interpreting her scrutiny of Sarah, she wondered, would he mind? Or was it just that he took an interest in other women? But his interest gave the impression of being so general that it almost amounted to fidelity. And immediately she asked herself, Is Clem like that? Has he done this before? Will he do it again? The last of these questions pained her so much that she left all of them unanswered. Of course with Clem it was not the same at all, utterly different, the comparison was meaningless. . . . But in what way different?

"I know what's different," Vernon said suddenly. "You've changed your hair since I last saw you."

"And since I last saw you," said Clem, turning a little to smile at her. She thought that his tenderness, after the day's indifference, was like a warning.

"Clem could try the telephone again," Vernon said, "before we sit down to dinner."

When Vernon pushed Nettie's chair in to the table, he rested his hand, as Clem had, briefly on her shoulder. It troubled her to sit in May's place, and for that reason she took no responsibility for the meal, allowing the dishes to pass without offering to serve them, behaving as less than a guest. She was grateful to Vernon for requiring—as Clem had predicted—nothing more than a hearer. He seemed content that she should stare down onto the polished table beside her plate so long as her head was slightly inclined toward him. Once, she looked up, and Clem, who was talking to Sarah, lifted his eyes. Studying the table again and tracing the grain of the wood with her finger, she thought there had been no intimacy in his look, only a reflection of her own preoccupation, and a sort of recalcitrance. She felt that she could not breathe properly, and she disappointed Vernon by uttering a sharp sigh. The tabletop bore the damp mark of her lifted finger.

"Of course, I'm an incurable romantic," Vernon was saying. He made it sound like a disease.

"Of course," she said.

After dinner, they went back to the fire. The living room was furnished, as rooms in summer houses often are, with the mistakes and discards of a town apartment. Unabashed, these had assumed a certain style of their own. The rug was a deep cocoa color, worn pale and thin near the door and by the sofa. The chairs, with one or two defections, tended toward dark green. There was a mosaic coffee table, made by a relative, and two ashtrays that had seemed a good idea one hot afternoon in Cuernavaca. The same rash expedition to Mexico was responsible for a black and brown painting in which a man and woman stared at each other with unmistakable resentment.

When the telephone rang, Clem put his coffee cup and saucer down on the uneven mosaic, where they rocked a little, and went into the hall. They heard him speaking loudly, as people do on a long-distance call even when the connection is good.

"He doesn't sound alarmed," said Nettie.

Sarah said: "One never knows. With these things."

Clem's voice went on, with long pauses. Instinctively they watched the doorway, but it was Marion, not Clem, who first appeared there, startling in a coat and hat. She gave a polite but meaning glance at Nettie, who with a little gasp of recollection sprang up from her chair and left the room.

In the drawer of the hall table there was an envelope that May had marked "Marion," and this Nettie now passed on stealthily. "I hope it's right," she said, having no reason to doubt it.

Marion, infinitely more assured than Nettie, put the envelope in an immense black handbag. "I'll be over tomorrow," she said. "And I hope Matt's all right."

"Yes. Thank you. Good night," said Nettie. She closed the front door. Clem, sitting on the stairs with the telephone receiver in his hand, was still talking, but with a terminal inflection. As she passed him, he reached out and touched her dress. Matt must be better, she thought.

When she came back into the living room, Vernon was leaning forward as if he had been speaking earnestly. Sarah, Nettie noted, looked confused. Nettie did not sit down, but started to assemble the empty cups on a tray.

"Let me help," Sarah said, taking up the coffeepot.

"Don't bother, really. I'll just leave them in the kitchen." Nettie was halfway to the door.

"Matt is better," said Clem, appearing in the doorway. "It's a throat infection, apparently."

"I knew it," Sarah said.

"His temperature is down."

"I'm so glad." The coffeepot waggled slightly. "Perhaps I should have spoken to May. What is she planning to do?"

"She's going to call me in the morning. It depends how he is—she may stay there a day or two."

Nettie took a firmer grip on the tray and walked on down the corridor. "Be careful," she said over her shoulder to Sarah, who at once followed her with the coffeepot. "There's a step." She pushed open the kitchen door with her elbow. "Can you find the light? On the left. Thanks." The light fell, dazzling, on aluminum saucepans and a huge white refrigerator. "Just put it anywhere. I'm not going to wash them tonight."

Sarah kept the coffeepot in her hands, but came across the room. "Nettie," she began, with as much solemnity as haste would allow. "We would be so pleased if you would come home with us."

Nettie put the tray down carefully by the sink. Taking up the sugar bowl, she walked past Sarah and put it away in a cupboard. "Because of the ants," she remarked apologetically. She returned to the sink and started to pour away the dregs from the cups. "I don't understand," she said. Blankly, she felt this to be true. It was her own stillness she did not understand.

Sarah came and stood at the sink, so that it was impossible not to look at her. She had a flushed, uncomfortable expression and Nettie noticed that her eyes were not only pretty, but even kind. "No, of course. But Vernon feels— People around here gossip so. Unprincipled, really. You shouldn't be exposed to that." Sarah grew impatient before Nettie's empty look. "And, of course, we'd love to have you." Her voice ran down.

It is really quite easy to have the advantage over people, Nettie thought— if you can be bothered. You just have to keep quiet and look at them. "I'll have to see what Clem thinks," she said at last. She finished stacking the rinsed dishes and dried her hands. She exchanged a hopeless little smile with Sarah. "You go ahead," she said. "I'll put the light out. Watch the step."

In the hall, she stopped to straighten a mirror. She felt that she had unlimited time at her disposal. She could hear voices raised in the living room, and for a moment stood still with a child's pleasurable horror in listening to a grown-up quarrel. She stared into the mirror, exasperated—as Sarah had been—by her own unresponsiveness; to see her feelings reflected in her face would have made them clearer to her. But here was, simply, a strained, alarmed expression made the more unfamiliar by the care with which it had that evening been powdered and embellished.

As she entered the room, she heard Clem's voice, cold and angry. "I'm afraid I don't understand."

"But don't you think . . ." Sarah's voice wavered anxiously. It was her fate that evening not to be understood.

Clem broke in. "Good Lord, she's like a daughter in this house. What an extraordinary idea. Perfectly extraordinary. In fact," his voice rose on a short, humorless laugh, "if we didn't know each other so well, I would say it was—downright insulting."

"Oh dear," Sarah said. Vernon had not said a word.

Nettie came further into the room and glanced at Clem. She saw that he had managed to be genuinely angry—angry in some way with her, too. She felt chilly, and walked past him to the fire.

There was an arduous silence. The fire flared and crumbled, and flared again. Resting her arm on the mantelpiece, Nettie stayed with her back to the room, in an attitude of unintended pathos.

"Oh, hell," said Clem, concedingly. He laughed, more encouragingly, and reached into his pocket for cigarettes.

"Why are things so complicated?" Sarah asked generally. Nettie looked round at her with compassion.

"Let's all sit down and have a brandy," Vernon suggested.

"That's a rather better idea," Clem said. "Sarah—never mind. No harm done."

She gave a nervous, relieved little laugh. "Oh, Clem. I can't tell you how sorry— No, Vernon, of course we can't. It's so late. Clem, we must be going." Suddenly active, she discovered her handbag beneath a cushion on the sofa. "Here it is."

"Are you really leaving?" asked Clem. He took her arm. They went into the hall. Vernon followed them, but stood back at the door to let Nettie pass. They did not look at one another.

Clem was bringing coats, and Vernon's hat, from the closet. Sarah kissed Nettie again and drew on her gloves. "Be sure to let me know how Matt is." She let Clem kiss her cheek. "I do hope it isn't anything serious," she said. "Clem, dear, do forgive—"

"No harm done," he repeated. He smiled with complete goodwill; he almost looked pleased.

Vernon took Nettie's hand briefly and released it. He followed Sarah into the garden, and Nettie stood where he had left her, behind the open door. Clem, holding the door handle, watched them go to their car. He called good night, and waved once or twice with his free hand. Sarah called out that the grass was wet. A car door, improperly closed, was banged several times before Vernon started the engine.

When the sound of the car receded, Clem closed the front door and switched off the outside lights. He linked across the lock a small gilt chain in which May had complete confidence. Now, thought Nettie, he will hesitate and smile. Instead, he turned at once with a grave, concerned face, and took her into his arms.

They stayed this way, in silence, until Nettie drew back and leaned against the door. Clem moved forward slightly, holding her with his left arm and supporting his right on the panel above her head. "Don't shake," he said at last, speaking against her hair. "It isn't complimentary." His left arm tightened. She felt him smile. "In fact, if we didn't know each other so well, I would say it was—downright insulting."

"What a summer for roses," said May. "I've never seen anything like it." She laid her sewing on her knee, and took off her glasses, and sighed. As if to make her last remark irrefutable, she closed her eyes.

Clem, in a garden chair, glanced up from the Sunday paper. "Are you tired?" Without waiting for her reply, he folded the pages in his hand and dropped them on the grass beside him. "I don't know why we read this—nothing but advertisements, and it makes one's hands black."

"I am tired, yes," May pursued. "I was gardening all afternoon."

Anyone would think gardening was a penance, Nettie observed to herself. She was sitting on the lawn, a book open in her lap. She thought that May contrived with her exhaustion to dispirit them all. The warm afternoon, the garden, the tray of empty glasses on the grass, succeeded in conveying foreboding and dissatisfaction; even the roses seemed to threaten violence, brimming over their plots of earth or arrested, scarlet, on the white wall of the house. Love, she thought, lowering her head over her book, is supposed to be enriching; instead I am poisoned (she exaggerated to hurt herself) with antagonism. Here she caught herself up—I am being an Incurable Romantic, she thought, and smiled. And yet, when I can be with him, just see him, I am happy. And I care more for him than for myself—I suppose that is enriching. I would literally die for him—only, no one wants that; they would rather you went on living and behaved reasonably. It has all happened too quickly. I keep thinking there will be a pause, I will find the place again, get back to being as I was, but that never comes. And yet the surprising part, too, is that it doesn't make more difference. I would have thought such things made one worldly; instead, one becomes more vulnerable than ever.

Lifting her eyes from the unturned page, she could see at her right Clem's legs and the side of his chair. His clothes, the wicker chair, the very newspaper he had flung down seemed involved in his personality. *He* is not vulnerable, she reflected. One can even see that from the way he sits, or moves, or reads the paper. He does not need my good opinion, as I need his. If he loves me, it is as a kind of indulgence to both of us. I cannot trust him completely—but, after all, one would not trust *anyone* completely; it would hardly be fair to them. It is the discrepancy that hurts—that I should be so aware of him, order my life, think, speak, clothe myself for him.

"Nettie, that color doesn't suit you," May remarked lazily. "If you'll forgive my saying so."

"Oh, really?" said Nettie, in an unforgiving voice.

"You should wear more blue, with your eyes. Don't you think, Clem?"

Clem looked down at the back of Nettie's head. "What color are her eyes?" he asked.

Only Nettie laughed.

"What a tiring day," May said with a certain determination. "Let's hope there won't be a storm before you get back to town."

Clem looked at his watch. "We should leave soon, if we want to arrive before dark."

"And be sure to give Nettie dinner somewhere, or she won't eat anything."

She speaks, Nettie thought, as though I were not here.

"I generally do," Clem said. "We have dinner and then I take her home."

We have dinner, Nettie repeated to herself, and then he takes me home. Every Sunday evening of this spring and summer. Occasionally they went to Nettie's small, cluttered apartment, but more often to Clem's large and empty one. Saturday's unopened mail and newspapers lay on a little table outside the front door of the apartment, and, inside, the hallway echoed as it would not have done in winter, and smelled of floor polish. Most of the windows were closed and all the blinds were drawn. There were so many doors that two people must feel slightly unsafe until they had entered one room, closed one door behind them.

"That's all right then," May said. She yawned, but resumed her sewing. "Nettie," she began again, "why don't you bring a friend next weekend? Someone your own age. Some nice young man."

"Thank you, no," replied Nettie, turning a page at last.

"You must know some."

"Well, they are stupid."

"If you are so critical," May observed comfortably, "no one will ever love you."

"And if you're so tired," said Clem, conveying disbelief, "why do you go on sewing?"

"Darling, it has to be done, and I'd rather get on with it. I don't darn your socks for amusement, after all."

I would love to darn his socks, Nettie thought. She could not tell whether this marriage was worse than other people's, although it would have gratified her to think it was. Why do men ever marry, she wondered. I can understand that women must have something of the sort—it is our nature, she thought vaguely—but why men? (She had forgotten about the socks.) Because nothing better has been worked out? But they don't even expect anything better; the limitations are flagrantly justified, like restrictions in a war, in the interests of national security. She told herself reprovingly, It is an *institution*—but this produced a mental picture of a large brick building not unlike a nineteenth-century prison. If he and I had been married, she wondered, would it have had to deteriorate into this? May and Sarah discussed their husbands as though they were precocious children—"Clem is very handy in the house," as one might say "He hardly ever cries" or "He sleeps right through the night." Let me go on believing, she asked, looking at his canvas shoe, that love isn't merely getting along with someone. She thought that once she accepted such a compromised version of love she would never reach back again to this. (She had excessive confidence in the instructive power of experience.)

Clem's foot moved. Nettie looked up. "Here's Matt," she said.

Matt came from beyond the roses, swinging a small black box camera by its strap. He was eleven, lanky and dark, with an earnest face that reflected his mother's resolute honesty and her total lack of irony. The three on the lawn watched him approach. Unnerved by their attention, he started to speak while still at a distance. "I'm going to take a picture."

"Oh God," said Clem.

"The camera was your idea," May remarked.

"*You* wanted to give him a guitar."

"I don't want to be in it," Nettie said, closing her book.

"Don't be silly," said May.

"Who'd want a picture of her?" Matt snorted foolishly. Nettie, injured, looked away.

May sighed. "Nettie, what's wrong now? He's only teasing. You should be able to ignore that, at your age."

Nettie saw no reason to expect that what had been intolerable to her in childhood should be acceptable now.

"Daddy, *smile*."

"I don't feel like smiling."

"It doesn't matter. You've *got* to smile."

"Put the tray out of sight," May said.

Immobilized, they stared into the sunshine. The camera clicked. Matt came up to them, twisting the knob to the next number. "It probably won't come out—there was too much light. And Daddy moved. And Nettie looked as if she was going to cry."

"My love," Clem said, keeping his eyes on the road and slowing to let another car pass. "You mustn't."

Nettie wiped her eyes with a shredding Kleenex. She moved along the seat away from Clem until she was propped in the corner.

"Make sure that door is closed" was all he said.

If I could only think of something else, she told herself—something that wouldn't make me cry. She attempted one or two seemingly arid subjects, but they led her back to tears. It was like trying not to be sick. Unable to stay at such a distance from him, she changed her position slightly, taking her weight off the car door. "It was so awful today," she said.

"Didn't seem any worse than usual."

"Well—I suppose it's worse for me than for you." She hoped he would contest this.

"Yes, I suppose it is," he agreed.

"I don't think I can come for weekends any more." Until she spoke, she had not considered this possibility.

"Nettie," he said, irritated into using her name, "that's something you must decide for yourself." After a moment, he added with ill-timed practicality: "What would I tell May?"

"You could always tell her," said Nettie, "that I've fallen in love. With someone my own age." Almost immediately, however, she threw away this advantage and laid her hand on his knee. "Oh, Clem, what will happen?"

"Darling, I don't *know*."

"But it can't go on and on like this." His silence seemed to ask, "Why not?," and to answer it she made a little explanatory gesture with her free hand. "Without any meaning," she said. "Anything to hope for."

"But it has been like that from the beginning," he pointed out, genuinely puzzled. His eyes were still on the road. "You knew that. I never promised you anything."

She was ashamed of him for this remark. She had not intended to charge him with obligations. It also occurred to her that an obligation was not the less incurred for being unacknowledged. She took her hand from his knee (he shifted his leg slightly, as though liberated from an uncomfortable pressure), and moved back against the door.

He glanced at her. "You aren't pleased?"

"Why should I be pleased? You're not trying to please me."

"I don't like to see you so upset."

"Why shouldn't I be upset? You want it every way. When shall I be upset if not now?"

"But, Nettie, what can I say? I *am* married, I *do* have two children. May is forty-three—she can't be asked to begin her life over again."

"I *know*, I *know*." The Kleenex had shed some flecks of white on her eyelashes. "I don't expect—I know we can't be married." (Though we might as well be, with this deplorable conversation, she thought.) "It isn't that."

"What in God's name is it, then?"

"I just want you to understand."

"Well of course I understand," he said crossly. "How could I help it?"

She had not thought of understanding as an involuntary acquisition. "I meant—to be kind."

"Damn it, I *am* kind," he responded, raising his voice. After a moment he said, less harshly: "Aren't I?"

"Not really, no." Sensing a passing relaxation of his annoyance, she struggled for words, as if speaking on a long-distance call with only moments to reach him. Giving this up, she turned her face toward the window and wiped her eyes again, this time with the back of her hand. I do cry rather a lot, she conceded.

The Sunday-evening traffic was heavy, and the road not wide, and they moved along slowly. From a car that had drawn level with them, a little girl was watching Nettie curiously. Clem drove for a while in silence. Eventually, he turned his head once more and said: "Look, pull yourself together. We can talk about it at dinner."

Nettie clasped her hands in her lap. "I want to go straight home," she told him, as she might have said: "I am going to die." "To my place."

Clem watched the traffic again, frowning. He allowed it to move past him, to the great disappointment of the child in the neighboring car, who was swept ahead and disappeared, still gazing at them, around a bend in the road. At the next intersection, he put his arm out to signal and turned the car off the main road.

"What are you doing?" Nettie asked, as aloof as curiosity would allow.

He did not reply. They passed, still slowly, through a shopping center and a housing development. Presently they came into a suburban street lined with trees and with large, unfenced gardens. Clem drew the car in to the curb, and switched off the engine. Two boys were riding bicycles down the sidewalk, and a man washing his car turned to look at them in the fading light. Nettie stared into her lap.

Clem put his arm along the back of the seat without touching her. "Now what's all this about?" he asked her.

She smiled faintly. "You sound like a policeman."

"But, darling, whatever is it? I only said the weekend seemed no worse than usual, and you tell me you never want to see me again."

What cowards men are, she thought. "It can't be *that* incomprehensible," she said.

His fingers touched the back of her neck. She inclined her head further, away from his hand. The tears returned to her eyes. An Irish terrier ran up to the car from a nearby garden and began to bark at them. The man washing his car called sharply: "Casey!"

"Don't cry." But this time it seemed that he said it for her sake and not his own.

"No," she said, apologetically, the tears now falling for his sympathy. "I'm sorry, I suppose it's the strain."

"Well, of course," he replied, quite gently. "Of course."

"You don't know how isolated one feels. You have so many—attachments."

"You make me sound like a vacuum cleaner." He smiled. With his other hand he lifted a strand of damp hair back from her cheek.

She went on. "Perhaps it is all ordinary—what one should expect. I have only this to go on, so I don't know. It seems terrible. Because you are—have lived longer," she emended gracefully, "you have a clearer idea of what will happen. I can't see anything but a disaster . . . if this were carried to its logical conclusion." Her voice trembled.

His hand moved patiently along the exposed slope of her neck. "Life," he remarked, "is not strong on logical conclusions. Perhaps fortunately. But I do forget about your age. Because you are the youngest of us, you are the most important. And May would agree with that." (Her position seems to have been completely reversed, Nettie noted.) "You have no experience to guide you. As you say, I know so much more."

She smiled again. "'I said an elder soldier, not a better.'"

He turned her toward him and drew her head against his shoulder. She did not resist or relax, and he sat with his arm around her. "Are you really going to leave me?"

She sighed. "Does it look like it?"

"On the contrary. I don't know what's going on in here." He touched her head.

"Casey! Come here!" shouted the man with the hose.

"Shall we move on before this dog loses all its illusions?" he asked her.

"But we haven't decided anything."

"We can talk about it at dinner." He released her. She sat up straight and put her hands to her hair. "You look all right," he told her, starting the engine. At the sudden sound, the dog barked again. Clem swung the car round in the middle of the street, and they returned the way they had come.

Now he is driving too fast, Nettie observed. She took a mirror out of her purse. She did not look back at the square receding gardens and white houses. We disturbed their Sunday evening, she thought, and upset their dog. When she lifted her head, they had already reached the main road. "My eyes are all red," she said.

"If you want to wash your face, we could go home first."

"We may never get there if you drive like this."

"Are you frightened?"

"No, but I suppose I don't want you to get killed," she said.

He smiled and slowed down. But when she next looked at him, his face was very serious—very sad, she realized with a little shock, Clem's sadness seeming far more incongruous, far less bearable, than her own. "What are you thinking?" she asked him.

"I was thinking," he replied, "if I died, how bad it would be for you. No one would understand that you were the person most to be comforted."

The telephone bell, which had been ringing in her sleep, woke her at last. When she lifted the receiver, it continued to vibrate indignantly in her grasp, like a baby that has been left crying in the dark. She opened her eyes. The room was scarcely light, the first sun thinly outlining the drawn blinds. She tried to think who she was—she could have been any one of a dozen people.

"Hullo," she murmured, pressing the receiver insecurely against her ear and lingering over the word.

"Nettie," said Clem.

"What's wrong?" she asked at once.

Disconcerted by this abrupt understanding, he hesitated. "I'm going up to the house," he said.

"But this is Wednesday."

"I'm not going to the office. I'm going up to the house. May telephoned me late last night."

Nettie raised herself on her elbow. Her hand, holding the telephone, shook from the awkward position. "She knows, do you mean?"

"From something she said, I think so." For a moment, neither of them spoke.

"It's serious, isn't it?" said Nettie, trying to compel her own responses. They were silent again, and then she said unhelpfully: "My dear."

"I'll call you from the country," he said. "After I've talked to May."

"What will you say to her?" Her words sounded in her own ears flat and forced. I have not realized it yet, she told herself remotely, as one who after an accident watches his own blood flow and feels no pain.

"I will have to see how it is," he said.

"Do you want me to come?"

"I think not."

"Call me as soon as you can."

"Yes. Of course."

"Remember . . ." she began.

"What?"

"About my love."

"Yes."

"No one will ever love you so much."

"No, I know," he said with slight impatience, as if this were irrelevant. After a moment he added: "Yes. It has been worth it." His tone was historic, she thought, like a farewell.

She put the telephone down and lay back on the pillow. The lengthening, reddish light was already the light of a very hot day, but she shivered and drew the sheet up to her shoulders, and could not get warm. I suppose I will realize it quite soon now, she thought with detachment. He said: "It has been worth it." What has it been worth? What is to happen to me? What am I to suffer? Calamity has a generalizing effect, and as yet she could foresee her suffering only in a monumental way and not in its inexorable, annihilating detail. She considered her resources, ranging her ideas, her secrets carefully against the unapprehended future. But ideas don't supplant feelings, she thought; rather, they prepare us for, sustain us in our feelings. If I understand why I am to be hurt, then does that really mean that it will hurt me less? I know that I risked—invited—this, wounded May. I have disturbed the balance. There is balance in life, but not fairness. The seasons, the universe give an impression of concord, but it is order, not harmony; consistency, not sympathy. We suffer because our demands are unreasonable or disorderly. But if reason is inescapable, so is humanity. We are human beings, not rational ones.

She thought of Clem with a slight surprise, her predicament now seeming a thing itself, scarcely connected with him. If she instinctively wished for deliverance, it was for deliverance of an unfamiliar and pragmatic nature—much as a sailor on a sinking ship might hope to see the Coast Guard rather than his wife and children. Clem cannot help me, she thought; we are not contending with the same elements. He was amusing himself with me, really. He did not want to be inconvenienced in this way; the inconvenience will be the greatest of his burdens. (She felt this almost with gratitude, relieved of the additional weight of Clem's grief.) They will make it up. They will be very solemn with each other, and May will use words like "relationship," and they will make it up. For a while they will hold each other's hands in public, and Clem will come home from the office on time. Once she has established her advantage, May will behave admirably toward me—she will be able to watch herself behaving admirably, like a person in a play. She will expect me to behave admirably back at her, but I have loved him too much for that. Or am at too great a disadvantage. Perhaps they will send me off somewhere, for a trip. (She even considered this possibility with a certain interest, wondering where she might go and what clothes she would need.) And Clem will manage to persuade himself that that is the best possible thing, that nothing could be better for me at this moment than to go ten thousand miles and be alone. He may miss me after a while, in the one particular way, but as long as he doesn't have to see me he will be all right. She dwelt for a moment, still painlessly—almost, in fact, with a smile—on Clem's resilience. Her eyes traveled listlessly around the room. I have nothing of his, she thought, nothing he gave me—not even a photograph, and he will look different now that he has stopped loving me. I couldn't prove, if I had to, that he ever existed for me—it's like that awful story about the walled-up hotel room in Paris. I shan't be able to say his name to anyone, not even to say that I miss him. It is just as he once said, no one will be able to sympathize with what I've lost—but that sounds like a funeral:

"Profound sympathy in your recent loss . . ." In any case, even if they knew about it, people wouldn't sympathize. With a thing like this, they don't sympathize unless you die. And that would be exceptional.

The sun was up now, although the room was still half dark because of the lowered blinds. It will be hot for him on the road, she thought. If he left immediately, he will be well on the way by now. He should arrive before lunch. It is an hour since he called me, and still I feel nothing; perhaps, after all, it need not be so terrible. These things happen all the time, and people survive them; they are exaggerated in retrospect, and in literature. She closed her eyes. I have not even wept, and I always cry so easily. Perhaps I can sleep, and when I wake it will seem more distant than ever. But why am I so cold, she wondered again. Why can't I get warm? She moved her arm, which had been rigidly clasped across her body, and felt it tremble. Beneath her, the bed was like stone.

She had not even finished dressing when he arrived. She had meant, of course, to take especial care with her appearance but had slept, instead, right through the morning—probably from the exhaustion of the last few days. When she awoke, there was barely time to take her shower and put the coffee on; not even time to make her bed. It was only because his train was a little late that she managed to get into her clothes before the doorbell rang.

He had taken a train that got him to town about noon; it was the only possible one, on Sunday. The day before, when he telephoned her from the country, he had said: "I'll leave the car with May and the children." It was one of the things she had wondered about when she put the phone down, trying to discover what position he had taken with May. It had been a short and comfortless conversation, because the telephone at his summer house was on a party line. And yet, she thought, if he had something definite to tell her he could have driven to another town, called from a drugstore. She had by then passed two days of silence and suspense since he left town on Wednesday to talk to May, and the overstated nonchalance of the telephone conversation made her frantic. "But can't you tell me anything?" she cried, as he prepared to hang up. After an admonishing silence, he had said only: "When I see you on Sunday."

She finished buttoning her dress and pushed her feet into a pair of sandals before she opened the door. Her face still glistened from the shower, her uncombed hair hung down her back, secured at the neck by a frayed ribbon; these things, absurdly, were uppermost in her mind as she turned the doorknob.

Clem, on the other hand, was neatly dressed in a light summer suit; his collar and tie had admirably withstood the long journey in a hot train. He seemed a little browner, and his eyes were bright and slightly reddened as though he had slept badly. He came in without speaking, and she closed the door after him. He was holding a brief case, which he put down in a corner of the tiny hall. When she turned from closing the door, he said her name, and put his arms around her with such intensity of feeling that she had no time to raise her own and stood within his embrace as if she did not submit to it. Love, however, was too strong for her, and she moved her cheek against the side of his head. I will have to know soon, she thought, what he has agreed to do.

"I left the coffee on," she said, unclasping his arms and stepping aside. She went into the kitchen without glancing at him, and turned the gas off. He came and stood in the doorway. She still could not look at his face, which she knew must explain everything to her. "Shall I make you some lunch?" she asked.

"Just coffee."

She was lifting down the cups and saucers. "If you take the coffee in, I'll bring the tray." He stood back to let her pass, and she went into the living room and put the tray on a table in front of the sofa. "Thanks. Oh, not there; that won't stand heat—yes, there, on the tile." Sitting on the sofa, she poured his coffee and her own, and they drank in silence.

"You haven't had breakfast, then?"

She looked at him now, over the rim of her cup. "I only just woke up." In case that should sound unfeeling, she added: "I was exhausted." She was suddenly reminded of her appearance. She put her cup down and raised her hand to her head. "I haven't even done my hair."

"It doesn't matter," he said.

"Let me do it while you have your coffee. It won't take a minute." She started to rise from the sofa.

"No, don't go," he said, taking her hand. She sat down again, still watching him. He held her hand in both of his for a moment, and then pressed it against his mouth and burst into tears.

She let him put his head on her breast, withdrawing her hand so that she could take him in her arms. She leaned back on the sofa, slightly breathless from his weight and from the pressure of his head, which was quite hard. In spite of the discrepancy in their ages, she felt protective—almost dispassionate—as she held him and moved her hand consolingly up and down his shuddering spine. She also regarded him with a certain amount of vulgar curiosity—she had never seen a man weep before, and was young enough to consider it a monument in her experience. In addition, she was unable to rid herself of the notion that he wept for what he was about to say. Relieved of speculation, she found herself invested, instead, with the kind of momentary self-possession that is summoned up in a doctor's waiting room. She breathed, through the salt smell of his hair, the steam of the coffee and even regretted that her cup had to get cold. Her eyes, uptilted by her attitude, rested on the pale-green wall opposite her. She reflected that in love one can only win by cheating and that the skill is to cheat first. (Having coveted neither the advantage nor the skill, however, she had no justification for disputing—as she did—the defeat that confronted her.)

He raised his head and shifted his position so that he too leaned back on the sofa, although his shoulder still pressed on hers. He held her right hand in his own, and with his left felt for his handkerchief and blew his nose. He closed his eyes, frowning, and she could see that he was studying how to begin. She tightened her clasp on his hand and said kindly, almost politely: "Don't worry. Just tell me."

He opened his eyes and sat up a little. "How good you are," he said.

This struck her as the sort of compliment one pays to a child, to encourage its behavior in the desired direction. It comforted her not at all that her judgment of him should remain thus pitilessly detached—that she saw him, perhaps, more clearly and with less admiration than ever before. The insight was useless to her, trapped as she was in the circumstance of love. She knew that sitting there with her hands clasped about his and her eyes on his face she represented, accurately, a spectacle of abject appeal. In any case, it was a habit of hers—possibly through the fear of loss—to appear most propitiating when she most condemned.

"Nothing has been decided," he said, putting away his handkerchief with a faint air of getting down to business. "I can only tell you what we feel about it."

At the word "we," she lowered her eyes and kept them fastened to the design of interlocking fingers in her lap. Aware of having somehow blundered, he had already lost the place in his text; it was asking too much of her that she should prompt him.

After a pause, he said abruptly: "I think I told you I no longer loved my wife."

"Yes," she said.

"I only said that once, didn't I?"

"Several times," she answered, unaccommodatingly.

"Several times, then," he agreed, with a touch of impatience. "In any case—I see now that I shouldn't have said that. I mean, that it wasn't true."

She thought that the digressions in the minds of men were endless. How many disguises were assumed before they could face themselves. How many justifications made in order that they might simply please themselves. How dangerous they were in their self-righteousness—infinitely more dangerous than women, who could never persuade themselves to the same degree of the nobility of their actions.

"What are you thinking about?" he asked her.

"Men," she said absently.

Taken aback by the plural, he stopped to assemble his thoughts once more. She was not being very encouraging, lowering her eyes and offering him monosyllables in this way. But there was no reason why she should encourage him, and he reminded himself of that; he was nothing if not fair.

"Why did you say it, then?" She looked up briefly. "If it wasn't true?"

He said slowly: "I thought it was true when I said it. I'm trying to say that I don't feel quite the same—I mean, not as I did."

She was silent, watching her fingers uncurling from his and the tiny white dots on her blue dress waver with the trembling of her knee. The words seemed so loud that she thought their echo could diminish only over a lifetime, would go on sounding within her forever: "Not as I did." "Not as I did."

"I would always care about you," he went on, now anxious to be understood, as it were, once and for all. "But it can't be as it was. . . . I'd like to think we can go on being fond of one another, that you can think of me as someone who . . ." He paused for a moment and then continued, unconscious of irony, "who showed you what love is." He withdrew his hand from her slackened grasp and lifted her chin so that she looked at him. "Darling, please. Please try to understand."

"I do understand, I do really," she said earnestly—almost in a tone of reassurance. "It's only that I cannot bear it."

He withdrew his hand and leaned forward with a little sigh, his elbows on his knees. Having been compelled to look at him, she now could not stop doing so. When he turned back to her, he was unnerved by that intent, expectant stare. Spreading one of his palms upward on his knee in an apparent appeal to common sense, he met her eyes and said, reasonably: "My dear, we have to come to terms with this."

"Yes, to terms," she said. "But whose terms—isn't that the point?"

"*Don't.*" Bending forward again, he took a sip of his cold coffee. "I hate to hear you talk like that." He did not know how to show her that she was simply adding, uselessly, to an already difficult situation. After a silence, he asked: "Do you have anything to drink?"

She got up and put the cups and saucers back on the tray: "Is Scotch all right?" She went into the kitchen, and in a few moments reappeared carrying a bottle and a glass full of ice. He saw that her hand shook as she set the glass on the table.

"You mustn't exaggerate the importance of this," he told her.

She let him take the bottle from her and fill the glass. "But it does seem rather important," she answered, apologetically. She sat down again and watched him drink, so obviously awaiting his next pronouncement that he took an extra sip of whisky to gain time.

"Yes," he went on. "It seems—*is*—dreadful, if you like. But darling,

I mean that you have everything ahead of you. At your age, this isn't a—matter of life and death."

She thought that it would, in fact, be easier to die than to get used to being without him. (But that, perhaps, was not a fair way of putting it, since it is really easier to die than to do almost anything.) The possibility of taking her own life was, however, something to be held in reserve, like a pain-relieving drug that can only be resorted to in extremity. It interested her to think that her words and actions would then assume an authority they could never command so long as there remained the possibility of their repetition; it seemed hard that one should have to go to such lengths to make one's point.

If, on the other hand—as he suggested—she was merely beginning a series of similar experiences, she could scarcely feel encouraged. She sensed that she would never learn to approach love in any way that was materially different, or have the energy to go in for more than a little halfhearted dissembling. Up to this, she had led a life sheltered not from rancor and mistrust but from intimacy; nothing could convince her that this first sharing of her secret existence, more significant even than the offering of her person, represented less than it appeared to. That circumstances might oblige him to withdraw from her she perfectly understood; that he actually felt himself to be less committed appalled her. It confounded all her assumptions, that something so deeply attested should prove totally unpredictable.

She remembered her uncombed hair. Startling him, she got up quickly from the sofa and went into the bedroom. She stood at the dressing table, releasing her hair from the knot of ribbon, and then, with her hand on the hairbrush, stared into the mirror. After a moment, forgetting what she had come for, she sat down on the side of her unmade bed, propped one elbow sidewise on the pillows, and leaned her jaw on her hand.

When he appeared in the doorway, she made a small explanatory gesture with the hairbrush, which still dangled from her right hand, then reached across and replaced it on the dressing table. He leaned for a moment against the doorframe, and when he came into the room she curled her legs up on the crumpled sheets and drew back on the pillows, allowing him to sit at the foot of the bed. They passed, in this way, some minutes of that hot afternoon. Both had the sensation of leaving behind them, simply by changing the scene, the antagonism in the living room.

At last he reached out and took her hand again, as though needing for a little longer to be in touch with her. He frowned into space, and only turned his head when she spoke.

"Tell me," she asked him, in a voice that was now shaken and fatigued, "what we are going to do."

The hand holding hers opened briefly and closed again. "There aren't many possibilities. . . . We shall see less of each other. Not meet at all, perhaps." Incongruously, he added: "I will hate that."

After a pause she repeated, as if he had not answered her: "Tell me what to do."

He lowered his troubled, abstracted look to her head. "You could go abroad for a while," he said. "That might help."

They looked at each other. Her hand grasped his convulsively. "Tell me," she insisted, almost whispering, "something that won't be hard, or lonely."

"My dear," he said. Even to him, it was inconceivable that her love should not be reciprocated. In compassion, he kneaded her fingers for a moment with his own. "What should I tell you? How happy I've been with you? How many things you've done for me? That, in a way, you've brought me back to life?" He let her hand go so that she could lie back on the pillows, and stretched himself exhaustedly along the foot of the bed with one arm beneath his head. Staring at the ceiling, he said: "I owe you everything."

This admission seemed to her to set the seal on the dissolution of their love: total indebtedness could only be acknowledged where no attempt at repayment was contemplated. She closed her eyes on some sustained crest of pain. Tears of desolation moved haltingly from the corners of her eyelids and disappeared into the hair above her ears. She was scarcely aware of shedding these tears, drawn as they were from weakness and the accessible surface of grief; no such ready means of human expression could give the real nature of sadness.

"I think I should go home," he said listlessly.

"Why?"

"We're just exhausting ourselves, like this. . . . Let's hope we can see things more clearly tomorrow."

She gave a small regretful smile, her eyes still shut. "I think I must hope to see them less clearly." She felt him sit up and lower his feet to the floor. She opened her eyes as he rose and came round the bed to stand beside her.

"If I leave," he said, "you might get some sleep."

"Stay a minute," she said, still with that faint smile. She put her hand up to the now creased edge of his jacket. "I'm going to be so unhappy when you go, and I want to postpone it."

He sat down again, on the edge of the bed. Ineptly, he smoothed back her hair, and then drew his finger along the wet mark between her eye and ear. With an air of helpless simplicity, he said to her: "I'm sorry."

"My love," she said, in the same hushed voice. "It hurts me so."

"I know, I know." His fingers passed irresolutely down her head and began to spread out the tangled hair on her shoulder. "I know," he said again, half to himself. "It isn't easy."

He looked at her with such bewilderment that she raised her hand and laid it for a moment on his shoulder before letting it fall, hopelessly, across her body. After that she lay perfectly still, with her eyes on his face. This submissiveness and the slow familiar movements of his hand only served to emphasize the constraint of their attitudes. Neither of them spoke; the stillness in the room was the passionless, critical silence of a sickroom. He lifted her hand aside and unfastened the belt of her dress as gently and carefully as if she had had a serious accident, and he was ministering to her.

VITTORIO

Vittorio stopped at Nannini's on his way home, and bought a
cake. It was almost four o'clock, and the town was coming to life
again after the siesta. The shop was already full of people; it was
divided into a café and a confectioner's, and as he pondered the display of
cakes Vittorio could hear behind him the clatter of cups and glasses at the
bar, and the exchange of voices.

Leaning on the glass counter and waiting to be served, he began to
feel foolish about the whole thing. He did not want a strange couple in
his house. The idea would never have occurred to him had it not been for
Francesco, his lawyer. It seemed to Vittorio that Francesco was interfer-
ing too much in his financial affairs. It was Francesco's suggestion that he
should let rooms for the summer, and it was Francesco who had found the
English couple who might at this moment, Vittorio thought anxiously,
be arriving at his house to be interviewed. He rapped on the counter, and
when the girl came selected a green cake with a pattern of crystalized
fruits. As he waited for it to be wrapped, he pulled out of his pocket for
the third time the piece of paper Francesco had given him, and stared at
the name: Jonathan Murray.

Holding the red and gold cakebox by its loop of string, he made his way out of the shop. The girl at the counter and the girl at the *cassa* smiled at him; so did the policeman, as he crossed the main street: *"Buona sera, Professore."* The cake, he knew, had been observed and its purpose noted. The town, which had known what to expect of him for almost sixty years, could with a little application account for his slightest deviation from habit.

The house stood nearby, at the end of a narrow street, and he never approached it without being conscious of its charm. It had once belonged to his family and was now converted into apartments. Built in the twilight of Siena's glory and not truly medieval, it was not listed with the splendid little palaces that are among the town's attractions. Still, it was an elegant building of weathered white stone, with four narrow rows of arched windows along a curved façade. The entrance, as he stepped in from the June sunshine of the street, felt cool and dim and smelled like a church. The elevator was out of commission again, according to a notice dangling on the bars of its little cage, and he set off slowly up the shallow steps.

Giuseppina was at the door before he could ring. She was wearing, he saw, her best black dress and a starched apron, and her gray hair had been carefully strained back into its bun. How ridiculous we are, he thought, handing her the cakebox. I shall tell them that I've reconsidered, that there are no rooms. He began to smile at his own panic, while Giuseppina, in a lowered voice, reproached him for his lateness. *"E già venuta, la signora,"* she whispered, letting him pass.

He stopped at the hall mirror to straighten his tie. *"Ah, sì? E com'è?"*

She hovered beside him, the cakebox in both plump hands. *"Carina. Carina e gentile. Sta nello studio."*

He ordered tea and went along the corridor to his study. The door was not quite closed, and as he pushed it open the afternoon light reached from the windows and made him pause. The woman who sat by his desk looked round and started to rise. He crossed the room quickly, murmuring in English: "Do sit down, how do you do," and she, taking his hand, replied: "I am Isabel Murray."

When she was reseated, Vittorio turned to adjust one of the shutters, deflecting the light from their faces. His first thought, as he drew up another chair, was that the room was shabby and hopelessly cluttered. His

Persian rug, which he had always considered beautiful, was, he now saw, almost worn through; the leather arms of the chairs were white with use. Books had overflowed from the shelves onto the table and the desk, were even stacked on the floor. Among the ornaments on the piano, the photograph of his wife, Teresa, was warped and faded in its plush frame. The piano itself, which had scarcely been used since Teresa's death, was an antiquated upright of no distinction whatever, decorated with brass fittings for candles. He stared vaguely about as though he, rather than his visitor, were the prospective tenant.

His second thought, also accompanied by a sense of irritation, was that Mrs. Murray, as Giuseppina had suggested, was quite beautiful. Her face was almost a countenance—a pensive sunburned oval elaborated with brown eyes, a short nose, and a defenseless smile. Her fair hair, streaked by the sun, was coiled around her head and drawn to one side, in the style that was being worn in Italy that year—it was 1957. Her cotton dress was printed with blue flowers. About twenty-five or six, he supposed, looking at her almost with indignation, as though she had brought some disturbance into his house. She answered his look with her unsuspecting smile.

"My husband sends his apologies," she was saying. "He had to go to Florence for the day, on business."

"He is writing a guidebook?" asked Vittorio, wondering whether Francesco had got it right.

Apparently not, for Mrs. Murray hesitated, wrinkled her brow, and then said: "Well, a sort of guidebook. A description of the paintings, actually, in Siena. He went to Florence to see about reproductions. We expect to be here about two months, but it depends how long it all takes." She paused, and when he said nothing went on: "I believe you lived in England?"

"For nine years," he replied, thinking how remote his exile seemed to him. "I went there in 1937, after my wife's death, and came back in '46."

"I hope they were nice to you."

He smiled. "To be there at all, an Italian during the war, meant that I suffered. They realized that, and allowed me the stature of my condition. I have never known people so polite. And in my profession—I am a classicist—I could find immediately those who shared my interests."

"Well, I'm glad," she said, as though the responsibility had been her own.

"In England, life is a long process of composing oneself," he continued. "For us, the English are as strange as Orientals, with their formalities, their conventions, their silences. I should never have known, had I not lived there, how vulnerable they can be, and how sentimental."

On a tinkle of plates and silver, Giuseppina entered, bearing the tea tray. Vittorio, who took his tea each afternoon from a chipped ceramic mug, hastily cleared a space. The cake, ostentatiously intact, had been placed on a silver platter.

He began to spread the cups and saucers. "Or would you prefer a glass of something—*vin santo* . . . ?"

"No," she said, "this is lovely. Shall I cut the cake?"

When they were established across the cups and plates, he asked: "Your husband—is he an artist himself?"

"No. He's doing a series of these books—last year we went to Perugia. It's just that he's interested in it. As a matter of fact, at Oxford he read classics," she added, not urging this bond. A little wedge of cake, crumbling between her fingers, fell to the floor, and she bent to pick up the pieces. "Your lovely rug," she said.

"Do you work, too?" he asked.

"Not very much, I'm afraid. I keep card indexes, and that sort of thing, and I go round with Jonathan, though sometimes he prefers to be alone. We've hired a Seicento, and we usually drive somewhere in the mornings—the book is on Siena and the surroundings. Yesterday we went to Rosia; the church there has a painting by . . ." She paused.

"Matteo di Giovanni," he supplied, pleased by her ignorance. In England, he had taught Latin at a girls' school for a short time, and he sketched to himself her education—a little implausible history, some disproportionate geography, and a muddled, lasting familiarity with the poets. The Latin, he knew through his own defeat, he could discount completely. He saw again rows of pale, virtuous faces inclined over blotched books.

There was a short silence. Vittorio put down his cup. "I should tell you about the house," he said, "or, rather, show it to you. You would have the bedroom and the *salotto*. The bathroom is next to the bedroom. I would, you see, move in here, into this room, so you wouldn't be disturbed. No, really," he said as her look deepened to protest, "I'd be much happier. I often sleep in here, when my brother comes from Rome. Unfortunately, being immediately under the roof, the apartment is quite warm in summer, but my father—the whole house was once his own—kept the top floor because of the view. What else? Well, there is hot water, but in the mornings only, I'm afraid." He hesitated again, and then mentioned uncertainly the price he had proposed to ask.

"It seems so little," she said.

"I thought it was too much," he answered, matching her ineptitude.

Jonathan Murray was so tall that he stooped to enter Vittorio's apartment, and so thin that sinews and veins were plainly seen on his taut, bare arm, which was weighted with a suitcase. He was in his middle thirties, a handsome, deliberate man with somber eyes and straight brown hair. Depositing the suitcase in the entrance hall, he turned to shake hands with Vittorio. His look, as far as courtesy would allow, held all things in abeyance, and it was Isabel, coming in behind him with a rug and a portable typewriter, who spoke first.

"The hotel wanted our room before lunch—I hope we're not too early. . . ." She let Vittorio take the typewriter. "Thank you. This is Jonathan."

Vittorio, silent and shy, led them along the corridor to where Giuseppina was making final adjustments to the bedroom. It was a large, lofty room, with walls of a spent green. The domed ceiling was white, and in one or two places flaking. The furniture, so heavily rooted as to appear a natural outcropping of the floor, was of dark wood, and the bed was so wide it was almost square. The coverlet was the same faded gold as the central square of carpet, which lay on a floor of worn red tiles. On one wall, over a bookcase, were two framed photographs of Greek heads, and above the bed hung a worn reproduction on wood of a painting by Ambrogio Lorenzetti. The dark-green shutters were half closed against the morning sun; in the opening between them, at each of the two windows, was suspended a strip of Tuscan countryside.

The four of them stood in the middle of the room, like early guests at a party, trying to gauge affinities. Jonathan took the typewriter from Vittorio and put it on the floor by the bed.

"I hope you'll be comfortable," Vittorio said. "If you need anything, you will let me know?"

There was a murmur of thanks. Giuseppina, excused by the incomprehensible language, preceded him from the room.

Vittorio returned to his study and closed the door. He sat down at the desk, clasping his hands idly on the papers fanned out over the blotter, and waited for a feeling of imposition to overtake him. Apart from the occasional visits of his elder brother, Giacomo, who came from Rome on business connected with family property near Siena, he had not shared his house since Teresa's death. In England, the privacy of his lodgings in the house of a retired Indian Army major had been scrupulously respected; the major, indeed, had relaxed this principle on only one occasion, when he crossed Vittorio's threshold to press upon him a jar of hoarded chutney in celebration of the victory at El Alamein. Upon his return to Siena, Vittorio had entered the ordered seclusion of a celibate scholar. The greater part of each day was spent on his work—a third volume on aspects of classical Greek—and in the evenings he read. His social life was conducted almost exclusively in the café, where he could in the course of an hour or two meet everyone in the town whom he might wish to see. His friends were of his own condition—men of cultivated minds, distinguished manners, and diminished circumstances. The possibility of worldly success had never, by them, been entertained; they conjectured only as to the form their failure would take.

Three years earlier, Vittorio had bought a secondhand Topolino, and this extended his activities. From time to time, he drove into the hills to the south of Siena to inspect his family's villa, the house where he had spent his childhood and youth; closed and empty since the war, it was now the property of his brother Giacomo.

Vittorio was fifty-nine. He had considered and spoken of himself as an old man for so many years that his sixtieth birthday seemed long past, and he found it strange that he had yet to attain it. He dated his old age from the death of his wife twenty years before. Had it not been disloyal to Teresa, he would have admitted to himself that the date might be set even earlier; he could scarcely recall ever having felt sensations that might pass for youth. A childhood burden of family disturbances had, by his early marriage, been exchanged for the sorrow of Teresa's long illness, and subsequently for the lonely anxiety of his exile. His manner of living since his return to Siena represented the first true peace he had experienced; he could not willingly envisage any conclusion to it other than decrepitude and death.

Because he recognized these things in himself, it surprised him to find that the arrival of the Murrays caused him, as yet, no pain. Distantly, through the closed door, he could hear sounds of luggage pushed along tiled floors, and the raised voice of Giuseppina; and once, into a silence, flickered Mrs. Murray's laugh. He took up his pen and lowered his hand to the page, but still did not write, so greatly was he surprised by his own pleasure and by an agreeable echo of what he presumed must be excitement.

The spring that year was cool and wet, terminating in a week of blinding heat that announced the summer. Tourists wandered in the city's curving, shadowed streets and climbed its narrow towers, and ultimately slumped into chairs in the piazza, demanding iced drinks. Jonathan Murray complained that his work in the museum was interrupted by the monologues of German students and the reluctant tramp of busloads of visitors. Isabel smiled and, walking about the town, grew browner and seemed at ease.

In the mornings, as she had told Vittorio, she and Jonathan usually drove out of the city to visit some nearby church or museum. Giuseppina took coffee to their room at an early hour, and before long Isabel would return the tray and its emptied dishes to the kitchen. Sometimes Vittorio was there discussing the day's housekeeping when she came in, dressed in her white robe, and stately because of the burden of the tray, her hair hanging down her back in a heavy plait that was frayed and flat from sleep. Leaning with both hands on the kitchen table and laughing at her own halting Italian, she would chat with Giuseppina, and Vittorio, watching her, wondered why all women didn't wear long hair.

When they returned after lunch, Jonathan went to the museum and Isabel rested through the early afternoon. At four o'clock, she took tea with Vittorio, although the ceremony of the cake was never repeated. He had thought his long, solitary afternoon essential and immutable, and was almost shocked to discover that a new habit could be so quickly, faithlessly formed. He found himself preparing for her with little imagined conversations that never came to birth, and afterward he wondered what they had talked about. Her presence seemed an immoderate, contrasting luxury in his room. As on the first day, she sat across from him, the shuttered light striping her hair and her burnished arm and distorting the colored pattern of her dress.

If Jonathan returned from the museum in time, he walked with Isabel to the piazza in the evening, but more often she went alone and waited for him in the café. Like other tourists, they read foreign papers in the fading light, and watched the crowd, and lived vicariously the pleasant life of the town. Jonathan inclined his head to Isabel's talk with a detached, indulgent smile, and sometimes Isabel, too, fell silent. Every evening, they dined out in Siena, and when they left the piazza in search of a *trattoria* they walked away with slow, grave purpose, like members of a procession.

If they were still in the café when Vittorio arrived before dinner for his ritual Campari, he sat with them until it was dark, or when he was with friends stopped at their table to exchange greetings. He found Jonathan rather solemn for an Englishman, and almost defensively earnest about his work. His knowledge, which was considerable, seemed sheltered within reticence, as though it were too precious to be made a source of general pleasure. Vittorio wondered whether life were ever difficult for Isabel. He understood that they had been married for four years.

One evening, he did not find them when he arrived at the café, although a mild, beautiful day had brought him there earlier than usual. The café was on a slight elevation commanding the paved shell of the piazza, and he looked about with a tender, habitual pleasure at the ripe rose and gold of the buildings and the soaring rocket of the campanile. The open space fluttered with bright dresses and blue shirts and indolent pigeons. One or two passersby raised their hands to him in greeting, and the waiter, approaching the table with a tray under his arm, made him a little bow and wished him good evening.

"*Buona sera, Sergio,*" returned Vittorio. "*Come va?*"

"*Eh, Professore, si tira avanti; si tira avanti.*"

They contemplated the view for a moment together before Sergio disappeared to fetch Vittorio's Campari. Vittorio put on his reading glasses and took up his newspaper. As he did so, he thought he saw Isabel coming toward him across the square, and he paused, the folded paper in one hand. He could not be sure that it was she, and as she drew near he removed his glasses, crinkling his eyes into the late sunshine. When she was still some paces away, he stared at her and said, quite loudly: "You've cut your hair!"

She sat down beside him and laid her parcels on the table. Her hair, which exuded a singed, scented smell, framed her face in two Ionic curves just above her shoulders. She balanced one foot on the rod beneath the table.

Vittorio placed his paper and glasses on the cloth before him. "But why?"

She made a small, incompetent gesture. "Well, you know. It gets hot in summer, and when you wash it, it takes so long to dry. And then— Jonathan complained that there were long hairs over everything. . . ." She touched her head curiously. "I expect it will grow again."

"How long did it take to grow before?"

"Six years." She looked grave for a moment, and then began to laugh, partly at his agitation.

The waiter came up with Vittorio's Campari and looked at her mournfully. "*Si è tagliata i capelli, la signora.*"

Vittorio, glancing at her lowered, reddened face, gave Sergio a commiserating nod and, taking up his paper once more, ordered for her.

"I didn't think there would be such a fuss," she said.

He smiled. "The whole town will know by tomorrow."

"Hello," said Jonathan, making his way among the tables. He sat down on the other side of Isabel. "I got the *Observer*—I thought you might have bought the *Times* already. Have you ordered yet?" He looked around for Sergio. "You've had your hair cut."

"What do you think?" she asked, again raising her hand to her head.

"I suppose it's more practical." He leaned back in his chair, surveying the square.

Vittorio, absorbed in his own newspaper, avoided Sergio's eyes.

Jonathan spent the following morning at Asciano. Isabel stayed behind, promising to complete his card index, but she soon left the unsorted cards on the *salotto* table and went out shopping. She had lunch in the town, and Jonathan, returning earlier than expected, missed her and went to lunch alone. In the afternoon, he went back to the house on his way from the cathedral to the museum, and was told by Giuseppina that Isabel had come in some time ago and was having tea with Vittorio.

That evening, he left the museum before it closed and went straight home. He entered their room quietly, and closed the door behind him.

She was sitting at the mirror, painting her nails. She smiled into his reflection, but when he bent to kiss her she cried out: "Oh, be careful—my nails!"

He turned away impatiently and sat down on the bed, his hands on his knees.

She got up and came to him. He moved his feet apart to let her come between his knees, not lifting his hands. She rested her wrists on his shoulders, the fingers stiffly extended to dry.

"For God's sake, stop thinking about your nails. I've been looking for you all day." He looked up at her crossly. "Do you love me? An absurd question, as you're hardly likely to say no, even if you wanted to."

"It could be important that I went on *pretending*, couldn't it?" she asked. "That might be a kind of love." She frowned. "I don't much care for this conversation, though; couldn't we have a shot at something else?"

"The thing is," he went on, "that I need you. You know that, I suppose?"

"And you resent it."

"Yes," he said, "of course. But it could be worse, couldn't it? I mean, I don't shout at you or anything."

"You have no reason to."

"There wouldn't have to be a reason," he explained, reasonably. "What would you do if I did?"

"Cut my throat, perhaps?" she suggested.

He lowered his head against her arm. "That would ruin my whole life."

"And mine, too, presumably." She leaned against him. "Jonathan."

"Yes."

"Did anyone ever call you Jon?"

He thought. "In the Army they called me Jon. I rather liked that. It made the whole thing seem more unreal than ever."

"It's funny to think of you in the war. Being brave and everything."

"It helps," he responded dryly, "if you remember how much younger I was."

She half smiled. "You know what I mean. Explosions and death, and so on. It all seems too . . . immediate, for you."

"You should have married someone—immediate, as you say." He was silent for a moment. "I was thinking that yesterday, in the piazza. You know, when I showed up and everyone was dying for me to make a scene about your hair?"

"I understood about that," she said.

"Well, perhaps that's your trouble; you understand too readily. It makes it so easy for me. Anyway, I thought, Yes, that's what she needs. Someone who *would* make a scene. Someone who would make her his life's work. Someone like old Vittorio."

"What do you mean?" she said, not moving.

"What I mean, darling, is that the poor old chap's head over heels in love with you—in his quaint, Old World way, I hasten to add." He raised his head. "Did you realize that?"

"Well, yes, I did," she replied, "of course."

He shut his eyes. "That's what I can't bear about women. They always know everything first. They behave as though men were—Americans in Europe." He looked at her again. "Well, don't look like that. I'm not suggesting it's reciprocated. Hardly. It's just that he'd really be so much better for you, *mutatis mutandis*."

She drew away from him, clasping her hands vaguely against her breast, her nails forgotten. "What did you do today?" she asked.

"I went to Asciano, to see the museum at the church," he said. "And I saw a Sassetta in a private collection."

"Was it nice?" she inquired politely.

He smiled. "Well . . . it was a Sassetta."

She went back to her chair and took up the little bottle of lacquer. Jonathan watched in the mirror the uneven strokes of her hand and the sealed calm of her brow. He raised his head to speak again, but did not, although Isabel's hand paused at the abrupt intake of his breath. Presently he lay back across the bed and closed his eyes.

One hot afternoon at the end of July, Vittorio was returning from his brother's empty villa. He usually inspected the house every three or four weeks, sending Giacomo a note about anything that had to be done. The responsibility was something of a burden to him, for his visits left him dispirited, less by the nostalgia they evoked than by its insufficiency. He had always been resigned to the course of his life.

Driving into the city, he was obliged to circle the large piazza at the post office, and as he slowed at its central plot of garden he saw Isabel at a café table, reading in a patch of shade.

He drew the car up under a red and blue umbrella marked "Punt e Mes." "Mrs. Murray!" he called. "Mrs. Murray!" She did not hear him. He turned off the engine and, getting out of the car, went up to her table.

She was so startled that she splashed coffee into the saucer as she set down her cup. She looked up, shading her eyes and pointing with her other hand to the chair beside her.

He shook his head. "I've left the car over there, in the street. I've been to my brother's house. I wondered if you'd like a lift home."

"It would be nice," she said, as if she meant to refuse. But she rose and took up her handbag and book. Vittorio called the waiter.

Opening the car door, he cleared away a week-old copy of *La Stampa* and helped her in. They left the shadow provided by "Punt e Mes" and moved patiently into the main street, which was choked with its after-noon tide of cars and scooters and incautious pedestrians.

"Was it a long drive to your brother's house?" she asked.

"It only takes about twenty minutes by the Grosseto road," he told her. "When I was a boy, of course, we were much more isolated. It was considered a real journey to Siena. People didn't drop in—if they came at all, they stayed. And then, my father, as he got older, was more and more withdrawn from the world."

"What did he do?"

"He was a classical scholar—a good one." He smiled, not quite pain-lessly. "My name is the same as his, and I am always asked if I wrote his books. Giacomo—there were only the two of us—became an archae-ologist, but it was understood that I should be a classicist; just as some families put one son into the Church. Though, as it happened, it was what I would have chosen." How boring this must be, he thought, espe-cially to the English, who don't discuss themselves in this way. They had come to a standstill in the traffic, and, turning to confirm his dullness in her expression, he found her watching him, instead, with gentle concern. He smiled at her and added: "So you see, it didn't matter after all." He scarcely knew himself what he intended by the remark, except that all the obscure concessions of his life seemed with a deliberate, perverse extrav-agance to have brought him into her company.

They moved forward and were halted again, a little farther on, by a traffic light. "You will be leaving soon," he said, with the air of making an announcement.

"Early next month," she replied.

"That is sad."

After a moment, she said: "Perhaps we'll come to Italy again next year."

"I meant, for me." She doesn't know, he decided.

"Yes, I know," she said.

He thought, because at that moment he felt he could bear it, of how they would go away in a week or two; they would write him, together, one nice letter and perhaps a few post cards. The light changed to green, and he turned the corner into his own short street.

When he had parked the car, Isabel closed her window. Vittorio turned off the engine and, waiting for her to gather her things together, pulled his glasses out of his pocket and took up her book to examine its title. It was one of his own works.

He could not have been more embarrassed had he found her praying. "*Accidenti!*" he said. "How dull for you. But do you—?"

"Understand anything? Well, no, not much, naturally."

"Then why ever do you bother?"

Isabel took the book back and started to get out of the car. She looked oppressed and, he thought at first, offended. He opened his own door and went round to hers, astonishment still in his face.

And it was with astonishment, more than anything else, that he saw her eyes enlarge with tears before she turned from him toward the house—an unbearable astonishment that called upon all his capacities for comprehension. He followed her in silence. They entered the house together and began to climb the stairs. He was profoundly aware of her, moving slowly and sadly at his side, but it did not occur to him to speak. He felt that he must be alone to think about it, that there must be some rational, disappointing explanation. He could scarcely breathe, from the stairs and from astonishment. He had never been so astonished in his life.

IN ONE'S OWN HOUSE

I hope we didn't wake you, Miranda," Constance said.

Miranda had come downstairs in her dressing gown, forgetting that her mother-in-law always appeared at breakfast fully dressed. And there she was, Constance, in a linen dress and a green sweater, pouring out coffee. This early rising and dressing on Constance's part was rather uncharacteristic. She herself readily explained it to her guests as the necessity of setting a good example. "In one's own house," she would then add—it was an expression she was particularly fond of.

In other respects, Constance affected a charming disorder, which turned to downright vagueness in the face of other people's difficulties. Of independent mind and means ("a widow with a little money" was another of her favored phrases), she repudiated, shrewdly or selfishly, untidy elements in the lives of others. Within her own controlled variety of moods, coy or unfeeling, she maintained a handsome serenity—like a country that, suffering no extremes of climate, remains always green. Her affection was largely reserved for her younger son, James, now seated beside her at the breakfast table, holding his coffee cup in both his hands and resting his elbows on the edge of the table. With her other son, Miranda's husband Russell, she had never felt at ease. She saw him seldom—when he and Miranda visited her here in the country, or on her own rare trips to New York. She thought him sarcastic, intense, unknowable; his attitude toward her seemed to be one of continual reproach, and she could not help wondering what, in his mind, he accused her of. She was distressed, but not surprised, that he had managed to have a nervous breakdown.

Miranda said: "Oh no, not at all," and seated herself opposite James. At the other end of the table, a fourth place had been laid for Russell.

"Of course, time *is* getting on," Constance continued, "if you want to go to church."

"*Church*?" inquired James.

"Miranda does go to church," Constance rebuked him, the soul of open-mindedness.

"I went once," Miranda told him, "when we were here at Easter. I was the only woman without a hat. I felt like the Infidel."

"I'm sure, my dear, you get credit for good thoughts." Constance took Miranda's cup. "Like Abou ben Adhem," she added kindly.

"The sermon was very dull," Miranda said, placatingly.

"I don't doubt it." Having filled the cup, Constance passed it back. "I always think, don't you, that Catholic churches must be much more interesting than ours. So much more going *on*. Protestants are so docile—turning up in pairs on Sunday, like animals entering the Ark." After an insufficient pause, Constance went on: "Well, Miranda dear, you must go to church just as often as you like—if you really do mean to spend the summer here."

Miranda, unresisting, drank her coffee.

"Isn't Russell coming to breakfast?" James helped himself to the last piece of toast without waiting for the answer to this question.

"He's still sleeping," Miranda said. "I'll take a tray up to him when we've finished."

Constance felt—and not for the first time—that Miranda was indulging Russell. Which may well be the cause of his trouble, she added to herself. Aloud, she pointed out that there was still hot coffee in the pot. "If you want to call him now," she suggested.

Miranda almost sighed. "No," she said. "I think he should sleep. He has a long journey ahead of him tomorrow."

"My dear, he gets on a plane in New York and gets off it in Athens. That isn't so strenuous, after all."

Miranda thought it sounded utterly exhausting, but said nothing.

James said to Miranda: "Are you going to New York with him?"

"No. I'll drive him to New Haven and see him off on the train."

"Why don't you go to New York?"

Miranda said bravely: "Because he doesn't want me to," and began to collect the empty dishes within her reach.

Damn Russell, thought James; everything connected with him led to trouble and hurt someone's feelings. Rather, hurt Miranda's feelings—and that's all I care about, he said to himself—looking at her briefly, so that his mother wouldn't notice, but seeing everything: her meekly attentive face, still faintly smeared with night cream and dominated by her wide, now colorless mouth, the straight black hair she had already brushed into a careful line along her shoulders, and the rose-colored dressing gown that opened on the white curve of her breast. Damn Russell, thought James.

Oh Russell, my darling, why must you do this, Miranda wondered, grieving above the plates and cups. Is it really going to help you to be away, to be without me? Will you really come back? She pushed her chair out from the table and wrapped her dressing gown about her, resting her hand for a moment against her body. It's strange, she thought, that these trite expressions should have such meaning—"My heart bleeds"; "It cut me to the heart" . . . One *does* feel it here. Something to do, perhaps, with circulation or breathing.

"A very good color for you, Miranda, that pink," Constance declared. She had a proprietary way of admiring other people's possessions, as if all good taste were in some measure a tribute to herself. "Yes, an excellent color," she repeated, in this flat, confiscating manner of hers, as Miranda trailed out of the dining room toward the kitchen. Then she looked adoringly at James, who was still eating his breakfast.

Constance's husband had died in the war, shortly after James's birth. The fact that she had, unaided, raised this remarkable young man was a daily source of gratification to her. James's strong and subtle personality, his intelligence, his good looks would have more than met her own requirements. That he should, into the bargain, have turned out to be charming and kind was an unlooked-for bonus that, as far as Constance was concerned, simply vindicated his gifts in the eyes of a jealous society. He was so attractive, she sometimes thought, that he was really entitled to be a bit nasty; instead—magnanimously, she felt—he was very nice. He would go a long way—always in the right direction; they all said so, his professors, his college friends, even Russell. Russell himself had done well enough, until now, but James would do more. James was more singular, his talents less diffuse. If only, she prayed, if only he would get over these grotesque notions about Miranda. (Thank God Miranda herself hadn't noticed yet.) It really couldn't be worse, if the two of them were to be in the house all summer. "Poor little Miranda's looking rather drawn, I thought," she said.

"Seemed all right to me," James replied. "Perhaps she'll cheer up after Russell goes."

Someone will cheer up anyway, Constance thought grimly, watching him. "She'd be better advised to cheer up beforehand. It only makes Russell worse to see her subdued like this."

"Russell's not exactly clamorous himself," James pointed out. He wiped his hands on a paper napkin and left it in a ball on his plate. "And never has been."

"All the more reason for Miranda to provide a little contrast . . . Proust, if you recall, says that Swann was instinctively repelled by the very women whose depth of character and melancholy expression exactly reflected his own."

"I don't, no."

"Don't what?"

"Recall." But James was pleased to note that his mother had inadvertently credited Miranda with a depth of character she usually managed to deny her.

Constance got up from the table, picked up James's empty dishes, and followed Miranda to the kitchen. She found her daughter-in-law leaning one elbow on top of the refrigerator, waiting for the toast to be done. A set tray stood on the kitchen table.

"May I take the paper for Russell?" Miranda asked.

"Oh of course. I'll see it later."

"Oh, not if you're not finished with it."

"My dear, I'm sure there's nothing of interest in it. I can very well wait." Constance watched Miranda buttering the toast. "Though I must say, Miranda, I don't think you ought to pander to Russell quite so much."

Why must you say it, Miranda wondered. "Constance," she said, carefully putting butter at the corners of the slice, "Russell is very sick."

Sick, Constance repeated to herself, now thoroughly exasperated. *Sick*. People seem quite incapable of using straightforward words these days. My son questions, as well he might, the very nature of our existence, and they discuss him as though he had German measles. Sick—that's the word they use now when people become exercised over the human condition. Sick, indeed. "Do you have any idea, Miranda darling, how all this started?"

Miranda put the toast on the tray and took the coffee off the stove. "It's a long story," she said.

When one says that it's always something fundamental that could be explained in a single sentence, Constance remarked to herself. She pushed the door open for Miranda to pass through.

Turning back into the room, she saw that Miranda had left the newspaper on the table.

When Russell had finished his breakfast he lay in bed with his hands folded under his head and watched Miranda making up her face. He could see that this unnerved her, from the attention with which she handled the succession of little jars.

"Why do you need all of those?"

"Oh, they're all different, you see."

"They can't *all* be different. It's ridiculous. An obsession."

She thought with mild resentment of the equipment he carried on his own person. He was always looking for his lighter, running out of cigarettes, forgetting his glasses. She, who did not smoke or wear glasses, would not have dreamed of complaining of these things. But his irritation, she knew, was not concerned with the jars on her dressing table: directed at herself, it was the antithesis of love.

"Oh—perhaps you're right. It's probably silly."

"I hate the way you keep saying 'Oh.'" He saw, in the mirror, her eyes deflect. "And the way you keep agreeing."

"Agreeing?"

"Humoring me. Backed like a weasel. Very like a whale. How true, my lord."

She lowered her head, defeated, and began to put the contents of the dressing-table drawer in order. These onslaughts of his were like outcroppings of rock in the surface of her day. Sometimes, as now, her heart twisted and broke under his determination to wound her. At others, she was almost convinced that she felt nothing more for him, that he had overdrawn on her endurance: then she would stay silent for a while, almost at peace, beyond his reach, not knowing whether she had been utterly vanquished or become completely invincible. However, it required merely some slight attention on his part to restore all her apprehensions—for these extremes of feeling only existed within the compass of her love.

Russell, still watching her, experienced the sensation of being abandoned that always accompanied such victories, as if he had lost the one person who connected him to reality, whose very pain was a guiding thread in the endless labyrinth of his anguish. He thought with despair of her selfishness, all her anxiety for him originating in her own need for his love. She imagines, he thought bitterly, that I could simply be *nicer* to her; that I could easily be kind if I wanted to, treat her better if I would only try. She had completely failed to realize how far he had descended into this dark place from which no consoling speech could deliver him, no outstretched hand—even hers—bring him back. While *she*, at one word from him, could be fully restored to life and power and thought. What could she complain of, then, he demanded of her inclined head. Her misery was vicarious, almost parasitical; she knew its cause precisely. It might, in fact, be said of her that she stood continually at the brink of utter happiness. Why, she should count herself among the most fortunate of mortals—blessed art thou among women, Miranda Richmond.

But occasionally he did feel her suffering—as it were, through the screen of his own. The night before, they had lain down in silence, immensely remote from each other in this comfortable bed in his mother's best guest room. He had behaved so cruelly to Miranda all day that he knew he could not decently approach her (here he made a mental note to be more careful this evening), and they slept without touching. But that morning he had wakened very early and watched her sleeping—her grief showing even then, for her closed fist was pressed against her mouth as if she had fallen asleep stifling her sobs. For a moment he had wanted intensely to awaken and reassure her, to take her out of sleep back into his embrace before she could recollect what stood between them. For that moment he had lain wanting her to know that help was at hand. But the moment passed, and with it the impulse to rescue her. He could not face her surprise, her pleasure, her tears. He could not face his own inability to sustain this moment of sanity, and the absolute certainty of her disappointment.

"I must say these things, you know," he told her, in a fairly pleasant voice. "I don't care for them either, but they do come out, ugly as they are."

She turned round on the stool and looked at him. "Russell, tell me why."

He lowered his eyes from the ceiling and looked at her again, still with his hands behind his head. "I suppose they represent me at the moment—I mean, that I *am* ugly. Wouldn't you think? Something like that?"

"No."

"I tell you yes, Miranda. That's the way it is. Envy-and-calumny-and-hate-and-pain, darling—the bloody lot." He smiled at her. "Where's the paper?"

"I didn't bring it up. I think Constance wanted to see it."

"Oh, *she's* turned nasty again, has she? God, darling, I can't see you sticking out the summer here. Even the city in a heat wave is better than Constance."

"She's not so bad. You have to know how to handle her."

"Which, as it happens, neither of us does."

Miranda laughed. She took off her rose-colored gown and started to dress.

"Could you hand me those folders." He sat up and took a bundle of travel leaflets from her. She sat on the bed at a little distance from him, buttoning her dress. Between them, over the blanket, he spread a topographical map of the Greek peninsula and the islands. "You understand that I have to do this?" he asked her, for the twentieth time. "That I have to be away—be alone?"

For the twentieth time she responded: "Oh yes." She subdued the folds of the map with her fingers. She bent her head over the fantastic pattern of blue sea and green islands with an assiduous show of interest, like a child examining an invitation for a party to which she has not been asked.

"I may go to France later," Russell remarked unsparingly. The studied absorption of her attitude and his awareness of her unshed tears could not touch him. He felt again that she was obtruding her trivial, untimely demands onto a scene of disaster, and he felt justified in setting her down. Being away from all this, and from her, was now the only prospect that gave him pleasure; tomorrow could not come quickly enough. And yet— the idea of anyone else receiving this tender, faultless love of hers, or being subjected to its relentless self-denial, was unthinkable. Even if he never came back to her—though he supposed he would—he must be able to think that she wanted him, always. "Was James around this morning?" he asked, discarding one pamphlet after another.

"He was having breakfast," she said.

"Is he going to hang about here all summer? Really, Constance indulges him. I always had to work at least part of the vacation."

"She does spoil him, of course. It's the gap in your ages, don't you think?" Russell was fourteen years older than James. "Still, James is turning out rather well." Miranda cast about uneasily for a means of turning the conversation. She felt it would be the last straw if James's interest in her, ridiculous as it was, were to come to Russell's attention now.

Russell could only hope that James would get over it soon. It was better, he had decided, not to mention anything to Miranda. But she really was impossible—any other woman would have noticed such a thing immediately. She lives in a world of her own, he thought, as he looked at her innocently sorting the papers on the bed. "I suppose it's time I got up," he said.

"Where's Miranda?" James asked, when Russell appeared alone in the bright garden.

"She had letters to write." Russell walked on down the path, nodding to his mother, who sat, sewing buttons on a shirt, in a cane chair beside James. James's effrontery, the ineptitude of Miranda now ceased to interest him. He walked along the flagged path, onto which the flood tide of his mother's flowers had overflowed, fully engaged in maintaining his own equilibrium. This required an effort so intense that it became, at times, almost, physical and he walked like a person under a strong sedative, slightly stupefied, his body braced against the return of pain. In so far as he noticed at all, he saw only a threat in the brilliant delicacy of the flowers, the smooth sweep of grass, and the light shredded through trees and shrubs at the end of the path. These were things—unlike his relations with Miranda, or his inability to work, which were matters inextricably entangled with his life—offered gratuitously by fate to impede his struggle for sanity. He felt that if he did not soon reach a place of shelter and darkness he would have to turn and go back inside. He crossed the foot of the lawn and pushed his way into a small wood with the instinctive haste of someone who, at the point of suffocation, seeks fresh air.

"This seems to be one of Russell's bad days," remarked Constance, looking troubled.

"I can't make out what's wrong with him," James said.

"He's just dreadfully depressed, dear. He feels we're all doomed—which is, after all, no more than the truth, though one can't afford to give it undivided attention. These things happen to people—they say he will get over it. It's as though the Life Force has been temporarily cut off."

"You make it sound like part of the utilities. In the meantime, how awful for Miranda."

Constance's frown deepened. "Well, my dear, she must take the rough with the smooth, as the marriage service says." After this somewhat loose quotation, she paused to examine the rest of the buttons on the shirt, and attacked one with her needle. "Marriage is like democracy—it doesn't really work, but it's all we've been able to come up with. . . . Given the best of circumstances, it's exceedingly difficult. I suppose, if Dan had lived"—Dan was Constance's husband—"we would have had our difficulties too." Constance only said this to make her point: nothing would have made her believe, particularly in retrospect, that she and Daniel might ever have quarreled.

"What will Miranda do with herself while he's gone?"

"I've been wondering about that. Perhaps she might get out her things and do a little painting again. If we were nearer to a town, she might have taken a little job." All Miranda's accomplishments seemed to be diminutive ones. "If she had been more conclusively religious—and I must say she is just the type for it—it would have been a splendid opportunity to make a Retreat." She snipped a thread, and then added: "As though one ever makes anything else."

Miranda was writing to her mother. She had just put "Russell is very excited about his trip" (since this was another person whose abundant sorrows left no room for Miranda's), when the door opened. She looked up quickly, expecting her husband's haggard face to give her words the lie, but it was not Russell who came into the room. "Oh, James," she murmured, her elbow on the table, her pen in the air. He might have knocked, she thought.

"I thought you might like the paper." He laid it on the bed and then sat down beside it. He crossed one foot over his knee and leaned forward, grasping his ankle.

She went on writing and, after a pause, said dismissingly: "Thank you."

He continued to sit there on the edge of her bed. He saw Russell's two suitcases, half-packed by Miranda, on the floor near the door; Russell's jacket over a chair; Russell's black leather slippers near his own feet. He looked about the room, repelled by all these implications of Russell's presence, all these reminders that Russell was privileged to enter at any moment—without knocking and without incurring Miranda's frown. It pained him to think that Russell and Miranda were so much together, so much alone; he was appalled by the idea that they made love.

He got up and wandered first to the windows, and then to the dressing table. This at least seemed to be entirely Miranda's. He picked up a bottle or two, and set them down with an unpracticed hand. "Is this your scent? . . . How fascinating—all these little jars." Miranda glanced up briefly but did not speak, and he sat down again on the bed. "Dearest Miranda," he said. "I would do anything to comfort you."

This time she did not look up. "Stop that," she said. She signed her letter, and took out an envelope and addressed it.

"Anything," he repeated.

"I don't need comforting," she told him. Unconsciously giving a more gentle echo to Russell's savage denunciations, she said: "I have nothing to complain of. It's Russell who needs to be comforted."

"What's the matter with him anyway?" James asked this in a tone of anticipatory disbelief, but Miranda looked up from a fresh page to give him a serious answer.

"He is in despair," she said. "Not the sort of despair that you or I might have, for a day or two, to be shifted by circumstances or surmounted by an effort of the will, but something that seems to him, I imagine, almost— like a discovery of the truth."

"But why, Miranda? What could be wrong with him? He has a good life." James, indeed, felt that Russell had cause for perpetual rejoicing.

"Young as you are," Miranda began heartlessly, "you must already know that the ebb of meaning in life is unaccountable. I'm sure Russell is going to get over this. But I saw it approaching for a long time. . . . No, I can't tell you why. Some of it may be my fault." Because this was unbearable to her, she had to add: "Though they say not." She went back to her writing, and James allowed a decent interval before he reverted to what was for him the main topic.

"Do you know—you're more yourself with me than with anyone else. I mean, in talking, that kind of thing."

This was so irrefutably the case that after a moment she simply said "Yes."

"Why is that?"

"It must be," she said, "because you have nothing I want."

"That's cruel."

She thought that yes, she was being cruel. But it was the truth. She wanted Russell's love, Constance's approval, and her relations with each were pervaded with constraint and supplication. James's reactions were of practically no interest to her—or was it, she wondered, more complicated than that: that she knew he would, for the present at least, go on caring for her no matter what she said to him?

James continued: "I, on the other hand, am better with anyone else than with you."

"Goodness, why?"

"I suppose I can't think of anything good enough to say to you. Anything worthy of you. And then—you make me feel that I'm young."

Heavens, she thought, studying the paper before her. He thinks I am a woman of the world. She gave an inward smile of astonishment. "I'm ten years older than you," she said. "Ten important years."

He said suddenly: "Miranda, I love you so. . . . Now what's the matter? Can't I even say the word?"

"It seems rather like taking the name of the Lord thy God in vain."

"In vain? What do you think this is, then, if not love?"

"Oh—something to do with the spring," she said lightly. "The regenerative process."

He said sullenly: "I'm not thinking of the regenerative process."

She smiled. "But it may be thinking of you."

"But I do love you. You *must* feel something."

"Why?" she asked coldly, addressing another envelope. "Why must I? I have been your age and in love—we all have. And had nothing from it."

"Then—what happens?"

"What happens?" She looked up, again with large serious eyes. "Why . . . it just hurts and hurts until it wears out." They stared at each other in dismay for a moment, and then she went on: "James, don't you feel any loyalty to Russell?"

"You mean, in connection with you? He treats you so badly."

"That isn't for you to say. I meant—because he's fond of you."

"Well, it *is* all rather biblical, I must say."

"It might be, if it were serious."

"But it *is* serious. Miranda, it *is*."

She leaned back a little in her chair. "James, don't be absurd. What could you possibly hope for from me?"

"It's what I wonder myself, of course—I see there isn't anything . . . I suppose I hope that you would like me a little, and show it—would say something I could remember and be pleased about. . . . And then—these are my wildest imaginings—I think we might go away together for a while."

She kept calm. She said, with a faint smile: "Your mother would be displeased." (And with reason for once, she added to herself.)

"We could go away separately, and meet."

It would be frightful, she thought, imagining it all in the space of a second. Everyone in the hotels would see the difference in our ages. We would run into someone we know. I would have to pay—I would hate that. "That's enough. Now leave me alone," she said.

"Let me stay."

"No." She went on writing, annoyed at last.

"I shan't bother you. I promise."

Glancing at him, she saw that his face had altered and was full of pain. He unclasped his hand from his ankle and extended it a little toward her. "Let me stay," he said again. "You don't have to say anything to me. It's simply to see you. To know what you're doing. Be in the room with you." He stared at her, his hand opened in that artless appeal.

She stopped writing and, still holding the pen, rested her brow on her hand and shielded her eyes in what he took to be a gesture of exasperation. It was, instead, that she felt suddenly touched. To make oneself completely vulnerable, to offer one's love without reserve—even Miranda had long since lost that capacity, before she met and married Russell. You learned—it was all understood—that you must not forfeit any advantage, and that love itself was a subtle game of stoutly maintaining or judiciously yielding your position. . . . She was all at once ashamed of this seedy knowledge, and envied his ability to declare himself. From behind her arduously constructed defenses, she felt she had now no way even to pay tribute to his generosity, his innocence; to love itself. She sat still, with her hand over her eyes.

"James? I think he must be studying," Constance said.

Russell removed James's book from the chair, dropped it on the grass, and sat down. He looked sideways at his mother, and then shifted his position so that he could see the garden. Constance went on sewing, apparently unaware of his restlessness. Finally he lay back in the chair and looked at the sky. After a moment, however, he turned his head again, and said abruptly: "Be kind to Miranda this summer." He felt a little awkward, delegating to his mother the task he had been incapable of performing himself.

"Well of course," replied Constance, too readily. "It's why I suggested she come here. You know I'm devoted to her."

You're a hard, frivolous woman, Russell thought. "You're very kind," he said.

"Not at all. It was the least I could do."

And therefore you did it, he observed. "Miranda's unworldly," he said. "She has no idea of looking after herself."

If he's worried about James, Constance thought with justifiable edginess, he should stay here himself; how could I possibly interfere in that? "Don't you worry," she told him. "We'll take care of her."

How can I leave Miranda to this, Russell wondered. He said: "I'll write as soon as I get there."

"Russell." Constance laid down her sewing and looked at him. "Is there anything I can do for you? If you aren't going to work for all these months, you may need some money."

Oh Christ, Russell thought, she's not going to take it into her head to behave well. His antagonism to his mother was too deeply rooted to allow her any act of disinterested kindness. He said aloofly: "Thank you, Mother. No."

"If I can give you anything," she went on, "you would only have to ask."

But you *would* have to ask, Russell noted remorselessly. He would not meet Constance's earnest look. Of all her expressions, it was the one with which he was least familiar. He preferred to think of her more usual aspects—arch, superficial, peremptory: those moods of his mother's which he now found all the more infuriating because he had, as a boy, so greatly admired them.

No less defeated than Miranda, Constance took up her sewing. "I hope you'll get what you want from this trip."

Russell, relenting, gave her a wry, intimate smile he could never have given Miranda. "The main thing seems to be to get away . . . since all the things I should face up to are here. I feel like a fugitive from justice."

Constance was herself again. She sighed. "We are all that," she said.

"Do you think you'll be able to get out of here?" Russell asked, having parked the car, miraculously, in a short space outside the station. He turned off the engine.

Miranda nodded. Reversing the car and driving home belonged to afterward, when she would be alone. She would not think of that. How disproportionate, she marveled, were the varied limits of human endur-ance: she, who got sick if she sat in the sun, or fainted if she had to stand too long in a crowd, would survive this devastating morning without any appreciable loss of physical control and would, in fact, conclude it with a twenty-mile drive. She began to gather up Russell's papers from the floor of the car.

It will be better for her when I'm gone, Russell thought. He really meant, It will be better for me—because he could have no peace in the presence of Miranda's pain. Once out of sight, her suffering would quickly become bearable to him. He pictured her driving home, putting the car away, going up to their—her—room, and closing the door. His imagi-nation refused the next scene, where she lay down on the bed and wept.

Holding his books and magazines in her lap, she looked up at him and then away. He touched her white cheek with his hand. He said, with what was at that moment total irrelevance: "You're so beautiful, Miranda."

Without turning to him, she opened the door of the car and got out. He came round to the curb and unloaded his luggage from the back seat.

"Give me those," he said. He took two books from her and stuffed them in the pockets of his raincoat, which he laid on top of the suitcases. Then he stood still, between the car and the steel mesh fence of the parking lot, looking at her.

"Better watch the time," Miranda said. She had not lifted her eyes.

"I have plenty of time." Now, as he put his arms around her, her anguish communicated itself to him at last. He could feel it pressing onto his breast as she leaned against him, weightless, submissive. For an instant he wondered, with genuine mystification, What have I done to her? Will she ever get over this? He released her a little, and passed his fingers over her eyes and mouth in a curious, sightless gesture. "Don't come to the train," he said.

"Let me." She drew away from him. When he bent to pick up his luggage, she brought a handkerchief out of her pocket and wiped her eyes. They walked into the station side by side.

A train was coming in, at another platform, slowly obliterating the further wasteland of tracks, shunted locomotives, and spiritless grasses. As soon as it stopped, businessmen jumped off, holding newspapers and brief cases. Hands and handkerchiefs waved from windows and doors. Old people were helped down by the conductor, and young people sprang into each other's arms. The entire train was emptied in a matter of moments. One or two couples greeted each other silently, with an abrupt kiss, and walked away, scarcely speaking, not holding hands.

How will it be when he returns, Miranda wondered, watching them from the other platform; how will we greet each other? Will we be silent too? And if we speak, what will we have to say?

VILLA ADRIANA

They got down from the bus in the middle of a straight, flat stretch of the Via Tiburtina. It was the midday bus from Rome, loaded with visiting relatives and returning farmers, and at the windows heads turned to watch the two foreigners descend to the country road. First, the man got down, his camera strap over his shoulder, his jacket over his arm, a book in his hand. The bus waited, quivering. He extended his free hand to the woman, who, slightly gathering her dress, negotiated the deep steps.

"*Vanno alla villa*" was exchanged around the bus.

The conductor called to the driver, the door clanged, and they were left behind in a cloud of dust.

Because this was the higher part of the plain across which they had come, they could see it stretching back in the direction of Rome—a dry, untidy shrubbery posted with olive trees and cypresses and a litter of small houses, rammed by the sun. Behind them, where the bus was already climbing the steep slope to Tivoli, the mountains were white, almost featureless in the heat, and scrabbled with vineyards and umbrella pines.

VILLA ADRIANA, said the notice under which they turned off into a lane. Where it joined the main road, the lane was quite suburban. It was lined with raw, shuttered houses and with groups of oleanders that gave no shade and weighted the air with a sugary smell. But a little farther the countryside closed in, and the two of them wandered on in shadow, scarcely speaking, her hand through the crook of his free arm. In the middle of a wood, the trees gave way to a parking area. Crossing this open space between two empty tourist buses, they entered the gates of the villa.

"So you see," she said, as though they had been having a long conversation, "there wouldn't be much point." They rounded a corner and stopped in the avenue to look at the ruins of a small amphitheater.

"This is called the Greek Theater." He closed his book, and they walked on between two lines of magnificent cypresses.

"I'm sure you agree," she continued, with that offhandedness, he thought, so uncharacteristic of her, that she had developed in these last few days—like a parody of what she objected to in his own manner. As if to irritate him even further, she added, "on the whole," as they paused at the top of the avenue before one extremity of a colossal wall.

There was a restaurant to their right, among the trees. "Shall we have something now, or later?" he asked her.

"It's so hot," she said.

He put his book in his pocket, and they went into the café and stood at the bar. The boy took two wet glasses from the draining board and filled them with *aranciata*. In the garden at the back, a girl was clearing the deserted lunch tables. Her stiff, short skirt spread out around her and exposed the backs of her knees each time she bent over to collect another dish. She took, in her high-heeled sandals, such tiny, tapping steps that it seemed she would never complete the journey from one table to the next. Now and then she glanced at the boy in the bar, and whenever she looked up he was watching her.

"On the whole" indeed, the man thought angrily as they left the café and passed through a gap in the great wall into an open field of ruins. "I'm not quite sure what we're talking about," he told her, although nothing more had been said.

"Simply that it wouldn't work." She stood still to gaze at a sheet of water, a long, shallow pond in which a few lilies were trailing. "We would make one another unhappy—we do already—and it's as well that we found out in time. That's all. It's quite impossible."

"I don't understand," he said stubbornly.

"And that," she returned, "is precisely why."

I must have hurt her vanity, he decided, since she was not usually cruel. Opinionated, sulky sometimes—but even that she couldn't sustain; she would give in at the first appeal. (Preferring consistency, he could not value such concessions.) If he were to say now, for example, whatever it might be she wanted him to say—that nothing mattered to him but their love for each other, something along those lines—she would come round. Though why she should need that, why she minded so, he couldn't imagine. She herself, after all, had other things in her life, had, in fact, loved before this, more intensely; he didn't know who it was—and had not the least desire to know, he told himself, his mind ranging hastily over the circle of their friends.

"I don't really think you care deeply about anything," she was saying now, as though the observation might be of passing interest. "Except, of course, your work."

He reflected that she was probably the only person he knew who didn't attach importance to his work. And it *was* important; something would be changed in the field, however imperceptibly, when his book came out. She, who knew nothing, nothing at all, and was always exalting her miserable intuitions into the sphere of knowledge—how dare she speak of his interest in his work as though it were something pedestrian, discreditable? She had no feeling for the elements, the composition of things. Once, for instance, in Rome, they had seen an ancient inscription on a wall, and he had begun to translate it aloud when she, brushing aside the syntax, rendered the sense of it in half a dozen words and turned away, having temporarily deprived him of his reason for living.

"Perhaps it's true that I care most about my work," he said. "But then I do care—about other things. In any case, I can't be what I'm not."

They were walking now on a path of small stones.

She persisted, relentlessly: "You gave a different impression when we first knew each other."

He halted, opening his hands helplessly. "Well—that was human."

This, unexpectedly, seemed to be an acceptable answer, and they turned off the path into a vast shell of red Roman brick, and entered an inner courtyard. Water was seeping over the ruined paving and around the plinths of the broken columns that unevenly supported the sky. Releasing his arm, in which her own had remained, she made her way across the drier slabs of stone to a pillar and seated herself in its shadow.

He followed her, reopening his guidebook. "This must be Hadrian's retreat—the Maritime Theater," he said. He sat down on the base of the column, and they held the book between them.

> We love to indulge in the generally entertained tradition, and fancy the Emperor Hadrian in his moments of spleen and misanthropy slipping off by himself and recover his spirits from the grievous weight of the care of the empire. . . .

She took off one of her sandals and inspected a blister on her foot. Pulling the strap back over her heel, she glanced at the young man, who was reading carefully. To him, she thought, life was a series of details—a mosaic rather than, say, a painting. He had to have reasons for everything, even if it meant contorting human nature to make it fit into them; so concerned with cause, he ignored consequence. And sometimes, no doubt, it was the right thing. It was the way men's minds worked, she supposed; the process, in fact, by which the world was provided with machines and roads and bridges—and ruins. But they chose to forget that their whole system of logic could be overturned by the gesture of a woman or a child, or by a single line of poetry. This business of reasoning, she reflected, was all very well, within reason, but if one had nothing to be passionate about one might as well be dead.

". . . from the grievous weight of the care of the empire," she read again. They were, very slightly, leaning on each other.

"*Und hier, meine Damen und Herren, war die Zufluchtsstätte des Kaisers,*" said a voice behind them.

There were about a dozen in the group, all with reddened faces under their new straw hats, all with woolen socks under their new sandals, all, she noticed, with cameras and guidebooks. They assembled inside the arch, and made notes as the guide pointed and explained. "*Man nennt es das Wassertheater. . . .*"

The two by the column sat in silence until the group withdrew. Then she clasped her hands around her knees, turning to him. "It's just that you do seem to take yourself rather seriously," she said.

He considered this. "Well . . . in the end, I suppose, one must."

"Exactly. So why begin that way?" But this she said almost as an entreaty, adding: "Anyway, you know, you're so much better than I."

"In what way, for God's sake?"

"Oh, I don't know. Accurate, reliable—"

"It sounds," he remarked, "like an advertisement for a watch."

"*Et ici nous voyons le refuge de l'Empereur,*" a new voice announced from the entrance. "*On l'appelle le Théâtre Maritime.*"

"Shall we go?" he asked.

Outside, the heat was rising in waves from the plain. The withered countryside enclosing them again, the man and woman crossed a miniature railway that had been laid to carry masonry to and from the works of excavation and restoration. A workman with a paper cone on his head was crushing stones for a new path, using a roller improvised from the broken shaft of a column. They passed from the Large Baths into the Small Baths, and walked along the side of another pool, disturbing the sleep of two or three dusty swans. They found their way into a small museum, where she admired a Venus. ("Her sandals are the same as yours," he said.) Behind the museum, a grooved track took them, through a farm, onto a wooded incline.

It was cooler on the slope. Wild flowers were growing beneath the trees and across the path. Walking in silence, they could hear the birds. The sounds of the plain came to them more remotely, for they were approaching the foot of the mountain; as they reached the first ridge, the white houses and shops of Tivoli could be distinguished, grouped high above the lines of olive trees.

Pausing on the ridge, they kissed—for some unknown reason, as she told herself, still clasped in his arms. She could see over his shoulder the next slope rising, and the next, the black pines lost in thicker vegetation or swept away in areas of cultivation. Her interest in the scene at that moment struck her as ludicrous, and she wondered if he, in his turn, might be studying the countryside behind her head. She drew back, but he kept her hand tightly in his, although the path was too narrow for them both. They were standing quite still, side by side. They might almost, she thought, have been defending one another from two different people.

"We must go back," he said.

There was a washroom near the café, and she combed her hair in front of a scrap of mirror and attended to the sunburn on her face while he selected a table in the garden. An elderly woman in a floral apron brought her a can of cold water, and she washed her feet, sitting on a white wooden chair borrowed from the restaurant. When she took off her sandals, the woman carried them out and brushed them in the garden, and stood watching her while she put them on again.

"Your husband?" the woman asked, smiling and nodding toward the restaurant.

"Yes," she said, because it seemed simpler.

They had a table in the shade. The waitress, moving slowly across the garden, arrived at last beside them and set down their drinks on the cloth. There was a different boy in the bar.

"When I ordered," the man said, "she asked me if we were married."

"What did you tell her?"

He looked surprised. "Why—that we weren't, naturally."

Even under the trees, the heat was intense. She lifted her hands from the table and closed them around the cold glass.

"There's a bus in half an hour," he said. "We should just do it. We may even see it coming down from Tivoli." He thought she seemed tired, but then they had been walking all afternoon. And they hadn't decided anything—although at one point, he remembered, she had told him that it was impossible. She was looking at him, and for a moment he thought he would be able to tell her that nothing else mattered (or whatever it was). But they had walked too far; his head ached slightly from the sun. And now she had turned aside.

CLIFFS OF FALL

If you have to be unhappy," Cyril said, "you must admit that there couldn't be a better place for it."

He was speaking to Elizabeth Tchirikoff, who sat on his right at the breakfast table. His wife, Greta, was at his left. They were seated this way, in a row, because the table was on the terrace and commanded across the lake a fine view of the Alps. At their back, past the side of the house, the garden merged into fields and vineyards on the flat green plateau and appeared to stretch, with the interruption of scarcely a single house, to the range of the Jura. On the Jura, this magnificent September, there was no snow whatever. Even on the Alps the snow line was exceptionally high, revealing great jagged precipices of black rock that had seldom seen the sun. Along the lake, the bathing places were still crowded in the afternoons, the weekend traffic was still lethal on the Route Suisse, the tourists still sat outside in the cafés of Geneva. It was weather more majestic, less distracted than summer, and untouched by decay—the improbably fine weather, without evocation or presentiment, that is sometimes arrested in a colored photograph.

Greta looked up warningly at Cyril, but Elizabeth had smiled—as he meant her to—and even made an uncompleted gesture of touching his hand with hers. As if he had set off some small mechanism in her, she made a few more motions with her hands—brushing a wasp away from the strawberry jam and placing the melting butter in the shadow of a loaf of bread—before settling back again in the white wooden chair and closing her eyes against the sun. She had been staying with the Stricklands for three weeks and was very brown, browner than she had ever been in her life. The brown of her breast and back and shoulders fitted exactly to the cut of the blue-and-white striped sun dress she wore almost every day. Her feet were patterned with the lines of sandal straps, and the outline of sunglasses was palely imprinted over her cheekbones. "I feel quite well," she told herself as the sun made circles of yellow and mauve through her eyelids. "If I feel anything, it is that: quite well."

"But then I really don't feel anything," she had told Greta on the day of her arrival, driving back from the Geneva airport. "At the beginning there was the shock, but now I don't feel anything." And when Greta explained in a lowered voice to visitors—the women who came for tea in little pale-blue or gray cars, and the couples who came for dinner—that she was still suffering from the shock ("They had only just been married. He was killed in an accident"), Elizabeth had a sensation of receiving their concern under false pretenses—and of spoiling their visits, since no one could decently enjoy themselves in her presence. For I don't feel anything at all, she told herself. Before leaving New York, she had been given prescriptions for pills that would stimulate her, or calm her, or help her to sleep. In plastic containers, the pills (green and triangular, white and circular, red and cylindrical) lay in a pocket of her suitcase, along with tablets for airsickness and a bottle of cold-water soap. She had not needed any of them.

She opened her eyes a little and looked at the sky, which was now violet, cloudless. A hawk had risen from the pines bordering the road that ran toward the lake; it plunged and soared over the house, dispersing smaller birds, its flight sustained on still, spread wings. It looked, Elizabeth thought, like a child's kite on a string. Will I ever feel anything again, she wondered. Unfeeling, she felt strangely imperiled, as though she might now perpetrate any crime, commit any indiscriminate act, say any unspeakable thing, unless she consciously applied a restraint that had formerly been instinctive—as people who have lost the sense of heat and cold will touch fire and burn themselves, uninhibited by pain.

"There's the postman," said Greta, rising from her chair and wrapping her dressing gown of much-washed turquoise chenille about her. The postman was coming up the road—a young boy in a dark uniform and cap tenaciously weaving his bicycle over the slight incline. Elizabeth sat up and leaned her elbows on the table, watching him. She did not herself understand her interest in the mail, which was delivered twice a day. Nor did she understand why her interest should make the Stricklands so uneasy; after all, she thought, they can hardly imagine that I expect a letter from *him*. The letters addressed to her still expressed sympathy, enumerated the virtues of the dead, emphasized the importance of his brief life. Vaguely, she felt a resentment at being left to answer them all—just as, previously, she had been obliged to acknowledge the letters of good wishes and congratulation, and the receipt of wedding presents. Trying to find something different to say for every one of her short replies, she wondered that the event did not fully strike her now that it was commemorated in other people's words and her own. But she wrote, each time: "Your sympathy has meant so much to me," or, "I was very touched by your kind letter," not easily but without real pain. Once, she turned her writing pad over and wrote on the back: "He is dead," and watched the letters turn fuzzy on the gray cardboard, hoping to comprehend them. But she remained as numb as before, and after a moment stroked the words out heavily with her pen so that they were indistinguishable. If Greta saw it, she told herself, she would think I had gone out of my mind.

At times, she wondered whether it was simply too soon for her to miss him. He had been dead little more than a month. Six weeks ago, they had eaten their meals together, made love, driven about in a car. It was no time at all. During his lifetime, they had quite often been parted for several weeks because of his work, and once for almost three months when he had gone on business to the Far East. But she *had* missed him, then. Missed him unbearably, wept at the airport when he set out and again when he came home—thin and exhausted, having been ill and overworked in the Hôtel des Indes or the Raffles or whatever it happened to be. And how, she asked herself, could I have missed him then and not now? Testing herself a little at a time, she found that she could think with equanimity about any aspect of their life together, although she expected continually as she pursued these thoughts that at some point her stillness would be shattered, and grief and anguish would begin.

But the identical days broke, hung suspended, and were absorbed into the green plateau between the Alps and the Jura. Every weekday, and sometimes on Saturday, Cyril walked half a mile to a tiny station overgrown with roses and took the train to Geneva. He worked for an international organization and had a solid-looking office in the Palais des Nations with a view of the gardens. Greta would begin the day with some housework and, at eleven, tea in the kitchen with Elizabeth and the maid, Charlotte. The house had just been built; there were interminable difficulties with newly installed electrical appliances, and a procession of mechanics came to the back door in the mornings on their bicycles— young men with perfect manners and unbelievably high, clear coloring, who lay on the kitchen floor with their heads in the oven, or under the dishwasher, or otherwise obscured according to their particular compe- tence, and were made the object of untimely demonstrations of affection by Aurélien, the Stricklands' spaniel.

Greta and Elizabeth usually lunched on the terrace and sat there in the sun, watching the mechanics and the electricians depart. There was scarcely any traffic on the narrow road, which led only to this house. Occasionally, a farm laborer with that same high coloring, and wearing deep-blue overalls and cap, crossed the fields beyond the garden. Some plowing was going on, discreetly, at a distance. The newly laid lawn that sloped down from the outer edge of the terrace ended in a series of raw garden beds. After lunch, Greta and Elizabeth worked in the garden, bringing fresh black earth from boxes in the garage to cover the exposed clay. Greta worked bareheaded, her coarse black hair pinned up, but Eliz- abeth wore a straw hat she had found in the closet in her room. Even so, the sun burned through, and when she took the hat off, her brow always showed a red crease and small painful imprints from the rough straw.

At four o'clock, they stopped work and went inside to bathe and dress. Unless visitors were expected to tea, Greta got the car out and they drove to Geneva. In the town they did a little shopping and had *café crème* and pastel-colored cakes outside the Hôtel des Bergues. Tall, delicate women in pretty dresses came and went at the hotel, or walked their small dogs in and out of shops. The avenue along the lake was full of traffic on those beautiful afternoons. Foreign cars drew up at the hotel; elderly men rode slowly past on bicycles, holding limp brief cases over the handlebars. It could be seen from the way in which people drove, or rode, or walked, that everyone was conscious of the weather. Weather was the chief topic of conversation in the café—it was incredible, it wouldn't last, it was warm, it was too warm; the Mont Blanc had been visible every day for a week. No one could recall such a September.

When it was time to pick up Cyril, Greta and Elizabeth took their packages to the car and drove to the Palais. In the stream of people issuing from the main building, Cyril would be the only man without a brief case, the only person without sunglasses. He was not tall; he had blue eyes and receding yellow hair, and a curious rolling walk. ("You are the only human being I know who limps with both legs," Greta had once told him.) His greeting was always the same. "Move over," he would say, as he squashed them into the remainder of the front seat and kissed Greta abruptly on the side of the head. They would sit there, squeezed in the hot car, deciding how to spend the evening. Sometimes they crossed the lake and had dinner in the Old City. Occasionally, they crossed the border into France and dined at the inn of some village in the hills. More often, they had dinner at home, where they sat at the kitchen table, by the windows, and watched the sun dying in the fields and the Jura flickering with high and lonely lights. They talked all the time. Cyril entertained them with outrageous impressions of bureaucracy, his office having apparently been designed to provide him with a daily supply of absurdities; or he read aloud from the evening paper accounts of the local *crimes passionnels*—a remarkable number of which were apparently committed at the foot of Calvin's statue. Elizabeth got used to the sound of her own laugh, which she had at first found faintly improper. She discovered that she could speak about her life in New York without any awkwardness. If the occasion demanded it, she said "we" or "us" with no hesitation, and in a voice that sounded to her completely natural.

Now, leaning back in her chair at the breakfast table and considering the stability of her emotions as a doctor might survey the course of a fatal disease, she found that her behavior throughout these weeks had been quite normal. I'm a bit odd in the evenings, she conceded, but that's because of the dreams. Since she had come here, she had repeatedly dreamed a stifling, fearful dream of her own death. For that reason, she stayed up long after the Stricklands had gone to bed, reading, or playing the same records over and over again on the phonograph. When at last she went to bed, exhausted, she slept immediately. Each time that she had the dream, she cried out in her sleep and awoke to find the light on and Greta beside her, calling her name. Greta would sit on the bed and take her in her arms, and Elizabeth, unable to speak or weep, pressed her face into the strong, chenille-covered shoulder and trembled. (For months afterward, she could not see turquoise chenille without feeling vaguely reassured.) She did not tell her dream to Greta, from horror and from a kind of shame; she thought that the Stricklands attributed the dreams to grief—and how can it be that, she asked herself, when I never dream of him? When it is not his death I dream of, but my own?

She saw that the Stricklands had put their own concerns aside on her behalf. Their own pleasures, sorrows, quarrels had all been submerged in an effort to help her. She had never felt so protected and consoled. In spite of the calamity that brought her there, the time assumed a simple perfection, so that years later, when she and the Stricklands had become, nonsensically, estranged, that September remained in her memory as something like happiness. It was as if the world had become, briefly, a place where suffering could only occur in dreams, or by accident.

She sat up once more with her elbows on the table and shielded her eyes with her cupped hands. "What shall I put on?" she asked. "Will it be cold?"

It was Saturday, and they were going for a drive in the Alps. Elizabeth was surprised to find herself mildly excited by this prospect. Friends of the Stricklands, Georges and Eugénie Maillard—a short, round, ginger couple who lived in Geneva—were coming over in their car, with a visitor from Paris, at ten o'clock. They would drive together into the mountains and lunch at a restaurant the Maillards had discovered, high up in Savoy. Elizabeth had been in the Alps only once before, in a train. She remembered the long, black tunnels, and the gorges suddenly opening onto Italy. One sees nothing from a train, she thought.

"You'll need a jacket," Greta was saying. "And a sweater. And something for your head. We go so high, you see."

The Maillards led the way, in an ancient Austin. On the other side of the lake, the two cars crossed the border and began climbing into the French Alps. Etienne, the Maillards' friend, sat in the back of the Stricklands' car to keep Elizabeth company. He was a dark, attenuated man who looked like an anarchist (she thought, never having seen one). His hair rose into the air above a prominent forehead, his eyes were serious, even sorrowful. He was staying with the Maillards, on his way back to Paris from Italy, to recover from a road accident. A truck had overturned his car on a mountainside near Domodossola. The car, miraculously, had not tumbled into the ravine and he had tried to continue his journey by train. He had, however, been unable to go farther than Geneva.

"It is the shock, you see," he explained. "One doesn't realize. When I first got on the train in Italy, I read a magazine, had my dinner, and so on. But in a little while the tunnels bothered me, and then the sound of the train. By the time we got to Lausanne, I was shaking from head to foot— had a fever of thirty-nine degrees." For Elizabeth's benefit, he added in a solemn aside: "I am speaking in centigrades, of course."

"But that was the same day?" she asked. "The day of the accident?"

"The evening, yes." He looked beyond her, out of the car window. Although they were still far below the snow line, the mountains rose all round them, green and black and peaked with white. Elizabeth, sitting on the side of the car that overlooked the drop, could not see the edge of the road—just tufts of grass, a few inclined shrubs and poplars, and the slit of the valley below.

Etienne gave a short, apologetic laugh. "Hardly the moment to discuss my accident. But, after all, one could as easily be killed on the streets of Geneva—or in an airplane." There was an uneasy silence in the car; Elizabeth's husband had been killed in a plane accident.

Elizabeth stretched her neck to see the road winding ahead, up the mountainside. At an incredible distance, the white peak overhung them. "Can we really get up there?" she asked.

"We can, but we will not," he said. "There's a pass, at about a kilometer, and we take another direction. Does the height trouble you?"

"Not now. It used to, at one time." She spoke as if that were in the remote past rather than a few weeks earlier. "The mountains bother me more—I mean, the look of them."

"The drama," he said. "Yes. Because they have something analogous to our emotions. They look like a graph of one's experience. Isn't that it?"

"I suppose so," she agreed. "There's a poem—

> "*O the mind, mind has mountains; cliffs of fall*
> *Frightful, sheer, no-man-fathomed. Hold them cheap*
> *May who ne'er hung there.*"

Having said this, she gave him a sunny smile.

There was a small fox on a long chain in the garden of the restaurant where they stopped for lunch. The house was built on a spur of the mountain projecting into an immense valley and surrounded by shoulders of the Alps. They had lunch sitting on the veranda in the sun, at a long table made of weathered boards, and the fox moved about on the grass below them, just out of reach, clinking his chain and watching them out of bright, despising eyes. There were very few people there, and they were served by the owners of the house, a gentle elderly couple who recognized the Maillards and were pleased that they had returned.

Elizabeth took off her jacket, and then her cardigan, and hung them over the back of a chair. She opened the neck of her blue cotton blouse. She sat on a bench at the table, between Cyril and Etienne. Etienne looked sadder than before and spoke to her in a less natural way, and she assumed that he had, in the meantime, been warned to stay off the subject of accidents. They had pâté and omelets and salad and cheese, and three bottles of wine. The sun moved slowly along the mountains opposite.

"I've never seen the Alps in such weather," Etienne said. "I usually come here in winter." To Elizabeth he added: "You should stay for the skiing."

"Alas, I can't," she answered. "I have to be back at work early in October—I only have six weeks' compassionate leave." It seemed to her, as she said this, an odd excuse to offer for not going skiing.

After lunch, the Stricklands and the Maillards lay down in long green canvas chairs on the veranda and went to sleep, with their faces in the shade. Etienne and Elizabeth leaned on the veranda rail, looking at the mountains and scarcely speaking, and in a while they walked down the steps into the garden. Elizabeth carried her jacket on her arm, and Etienne hung a sweater over his shoulders, the sleeves crossed on his chest. In his open shirt and thick, battered corduroy trousers he looked more like an anarchist than ever.

They walked through the garden, the little fox tinkling after them on his chain until he could follow no farther. The same path wound for some distance down the mountain; they could see it grooved through the grass and wild flowers. There were no trees or shrubs on this part of the spur, only the bright-green grass and the tangled flowers. In the great valley, below the black belts of fir trees, a twisting road was lined with fields and farmhouses. Elizabeth kept her eyes lowered to the narrow track on which they walked, pausing now and then to look up at the mountains across the valley. The descent from the track was gradual. The ground sloped away so that the drop, though very steep, was not precipitous. One would probably roll quite a long way, she thought indifferently, before falling into the ravine. She stopped, and Etienne, who was walking behind her, drew level and presented her with a frond of white heather he had picked.

She had nothing to pin it with, but she took it and arranged it in the pocket of her blouse so that it could be seen. She understood that it was the sort of offering a child makes, of the first, valueless thing that comes to hand, to show sympathy. She thought without interest that he was kinder than most people. The sun was in her eyes, and she turned her back to the valley and looked into his face. If he wants to kiss me, he may, she decided. For a moment it seemed almost essential that he should—for surely that, she thought, would shock her into realization; surely *he* (and she could only picture him in a Sunday-school Heaven not much higher than the mountains around them, not much higher than he had been when the plane exploded in the air) would find the means of making his indignation known to her. In the next instant, she was conscious that her head had begun to ache.

Without moving, Etienne had slightly withdrawn. He was no longer looking at her. Perhaps he had not the least desire for her—or perhaps, she told herself with conscious formality, he is respecting my grief. She turned away from him and said: "I don't feel well. Can we go back?"

"It's the altitude," he replied, keeping pace with her and obliging her to take the inward side of the path.

In any case, she thought, I should not let him kiss me—it would be too disillusioning for him; knowing what has happened to me, he would think there was no loyalty left in the world.

That night she did not dream. She awoke before daylight, feverish and violently ill. Her head still ached. She took aspirin, and was immediately sick again. She lay down on her bed, moaning with pain and confusion, and waited for the night to pass. Her thoughts, although otherwise disconnected, were all concerned with the excursion into the Alps. She saw again, over and over, the thin leaning poplars blowing silently outside the car window, the steep turns of the road, the bright eyes of the fox. In detail, she repeated the descent from the mountain, which had seemed endless at the time, and recalled her own exhausted chatter in the car and the strangely anxious face of Etienne. (She considered his anxiety to be without foundation; knowing herself to be a little out of control, she had made a particular effort to behave naturally during the return journey.) More hazily, she remembered coming home and, for the first time, going to bed early. She also remembered that for the first time she had been struck by her solitude when she lay down.

Still, she reflected (as though feeling might attempt to take her unaware), these things have nothing to do with his death; it is all concern for myself. She raised herself on her elbows and hung her head, overwhelmed with nausea. She could hear her own quick breathing; her nightgown clung to her damply about the waist. I am sick, she thought self-pityingly, and closed her eyes. The pain in her head was almost intolerable.

When the wave passed, she lay down again on her side. She stayed this way, quite rigid, for a few moments, and then all at once pressed her face into the pillow, sliding her arm up to encircle her head. She thought suddenly and clearly of her husband, and was surprised to hear her own voice say his name aloud.

The doctor was speaking to Greta in Swiss-German—although, since he practiced in Geneva, he could doubtless speak French. It is so that I won't understand, Elizabeth thought without resentment, glad to have this detail explained. Dizziness overcame her again, and when her mind had steadied itself the low voices were speaking French. Greta asked what Elizabeth's temperature was, and the doctor told her. "Of course they are speaking in centigrades," Elizabeth quoted to herself, and smiled. Greta said something about food poisoning. Opening her eyes a little, Elizabeth could see that the doctor's national pride was involved; he was frowning—a slight, blond, youngish man with a rosy Swiss face.

"*En Suisse, Madame,*" he said incredulously, spreading his hands.

Perhaps it would help, Elizabeth thought, if he knew that we lunched in France yesterday. Was it yesterday? Then this was Sunday, unless she had slept through a whole day. She thought she had been given an injection, but perhaps it had only been spoken of—she couldn't be sure that she was not recollecting something in the future. Now they had gone out of the room, and she felt safe in opening her eyes again. The sun, through the gauze curtains, was immoderate, remorseless. Will it go on forever, this weather, she wondered irritably, with an effort putting her hand up to cover her eyes. Will it never rain, never be night, never be winter? If Greta would come, I could ask her to close the shutters. She felt helpless, victimized by the glare. Unwittingly, she had let herself in for all this. She had only meant to marry, settle down, have children—be safe, or a little bored; it came to the same thing. And here, instead, was all this derangement (she felt it, positively, to be his fault)—expense, journeys, illness, and now the sun glaring in at her. All this punishment simply because (she clasped her hand more tightly over her eyelids to shut out the sun) she had loved him. That was it. Because she had loved him.

She sighed. Her arm ached from being raised to her eyes.

"What is it, dear?" said Greta.

"The sun," she explained. "Could you close the shutters?"

"But darling, it's quite dark now."

Elizabeth opened her eyes and found the room in darkness, except for a small lamp on the dressing table. Her hands were folded on the sheet. Greta was holding a tray.

"I can't eat anything," Elizabeth said immediately. The pain had gone from her head. "I feel better, but I can't eat."

"A piece of dry toast."

"No."

"Just tea, then."

"*Please*," she said, almost passionately. Why can't anyone understand, she wondered. She didn't quite know what they should understand—not merely that she should be let alone; rather, a sense of impending catastrophe that rendered absurdly insignificant all this taking of temperatures and bringing of tea. She had no way to describe to them the calamity that was about to befall, no way that would sufficiently prepare them for it. In that respect, it was like her dream.

When she next awoke, the light had returned, but dimly. She thought it must be dawn, but presently she heard Cyril leave for work. When Greta came in, Elizabeth was sitting up in bed. "It's still so dark," she said. "It *is* morning, isn't it?"

"It's been raining," Greta told her. She sat down on the bed. "Do lie down. How do you feel?"

"Better," she said. She knew she was no longer sick.

"You look terrible," Greta said, and smiled, and kissed her. "You poor thing. I'll get you some toast and tea."

When she had eaten, she lay down again and began to be aware of the room. There were bookcases facing her bed, all the way up to the ceiling. She decided that there was nothing worse than to be sick in bed with a room full of books; the titles marched back and forth before her eyes. Her attention was repeatedly arrested by the same combinations of color and lettering, or by a design on a book's spine. Hazlitt, Mallarmé, and twenty volumes of Balzac; Dryden and Robert Graves; Cicero and Darwin, and, between them, a brand-new copy of *By Love Possessed*. She closed her eyes, but the cryptic messages, vertical and horizontal, went on transmitting themselves under her eyelids.

She could hear, outside, the faint sound of the plow in the nearby fields. Charlotte was moving the furniture in the living room; one of the accredited mechanics called out from the kitchen. In a little while, there was the ring of the postman's bicycle bell, and the sound of the front door being opened and closed. (Elizabeth was too tired to be interested.) Everything goes on and on, she thought, and did not know whether this reassured or isolated her. It was not, of course, to say that only she had been excluded from the current of life; perhaps others merely conducted themselves better in their exclusion—Charlotte, the mechanics, Greta. Besides, she reminded herself, it's not even as though I were actually suffering; it is only this apprehension that troubles me—the uneasiness I brought down from the mountain.

In the afternoon, she got up and took a bath. The sun had come out, and she lay in a chair on the terrace, wrapped up in a woolen dressing gown of Cyril's and covered with a blanket, because the breeze blowing from the mountains was unexpectedly cool. The sun, too, was not quite so strong, and on the farther shore of the lake—less luxuriantly green today—the neat, opulent villas were slightly veiled. The dog, Aurélien, chased the smaller birds up and down the new lawn, and fled from the larger ones. From time to time, Greta came out of the house to see how Elizabeth was, and once she brought her sewing and sat beside her for a while. They said very little. Greta sat peacefully sewing, occasionally calling the dog away from the birds, or glancing up to smile at Elizabeth. Elizabeth felt bored with her own self-centeredness; she did not know how to stop studying her moods, or even to divert attention from them.

"I must go soon," she said.

"Yes, it's getting colder," Greta said. "I'll just finish this and we'll go in."

"I mean to America."

Greta looked up. "Elizabeth darling, it's only the end of September.

Don't think about it for a week or two. You aren't able to go yet. I don't mean because you're sick—I mean because you're . . . not yourself."

She said: "I make no progress."

"Toward what?"

"Toward him," she said.

Elizabeth was allowed to stay up for dinner, which they were to have early on her account. When Cyril came home, he kissed her and, having ascertained that she felt better, declared she had never looked worse. She thought she looked odder than she otherwise might because of her deep tan, which made a curious glaze over her pallor. Her hair hung lankly down on her shoulders in separate dark tails. "I'll wash it tomorrow," she said, pushing it back behind her ears. "If I feel up to it."

They were in the kitchen, Greta standing by the stove and Cyril taking down glasses from a shelf. Elizabeth was sitting, still in Cyril's woolen dressing gown, at the kitchen table, with her back to the window. It was almost fully light, although behind her the sky was reddening and the Jura darkening. Leaning her cheek on her hand, she felt more peaceful than she had all day. With her left hand she made a space for Cyril to put the glasses down among the places laid on the table.

"What would you like to drink?" Cyril asked Greta.

"No," she said absently, stirring the soup. "I mean, not a real drink. Just Perrier—something like that. Put some syrup in it, if there is any."

"Disgusting," he said. He found a bottle of raspberry syrup and made a pink, foaming concoction for her with mineral water. "What an infantile taste," he remarked, setting it down at her elbow. Greta smiled without looking at him, took a long drink, and put the glass down again. She went on placidly stirring.

"What would you like?" Cyril asked Elizabeth, coming back to the table.

"The same," she said. It occurred to her that she had been thirsty all day. She could hardly take her eyes off the red glass on the stove.

"God," he observed, putting an inch of syrup in a glass and reopening the bottle of Perrier.

"I'm so thirsty," she said. She reached out her hand to take the drink from him.

Greta looked round abruptly. "But, Cyril, what are you doing? She can't have that—she's been sick. Have some sense." She put the spoon down on the stove and looked at him reproachfully. Cyril made a face of comic apology to Elizabeth and turned away with the full glass in his hand.

Elizabeth kept her hand outstretched for a moment longer. Then she withdrew it and propped up her cheek again. The room, the white table-top, the forks and knives, glasses and plates swam in her tears. The only motion of concealment she made was to turn her face a little into her palm, half covering her mouth. Otherwise, she wept resistlessly and almost silently, without attempting to find her handkerchief or even take her napkin from the table to wipe her eyes. She went on crying—for a long time, or so it seemed—while the Stricklands stood still in the middle of the kitchen, watching her, and not looking in the least astonished that a grown woman should cry because she was refused a glass of raspberry soda.

The sign, high up in the main hall of the airport, was decorated with an enormous cardboard watch and said in English

WELCOME TO GENEVA

PATEK PHILIPPE

"Anyone would think they were expecting some foreign dignitary," said Cyril.

Elizabeth smiled, and put her hand in Greta's. They were sitting on a sofa covered with hard red plastic. Unnerved by the climate of departure, they spoke disjointedly and were rigidly silent when a flight was announced. Elizabeth had buttoned up her black coat and put a scarf around her neck. Like most of the people in the airport, she looked inordinately sunburned for the raw gray day.

"At least, there's no fog," Greta said. "Though the *bise* is still blowing." The drear, chilly wind had gone on for days. "Do you have your pills?"

Elizabeth touched her handbag. "I took one just before we set out. There are only three left, but I'll be able to get more tomorrow."

"I hate the idea of your going back to work."

"It's the best thing, isn't it?"

An elegant woman walked past with a poodle on a leash.

"We should have brought Aurélien," said Greta. "He would have enjoyed it."

Elizabeth felt reconciled to the journey; like someone facing an operation, she only hoped she would behave well. She could not envisage her arrival or make plans for the resumption of her ordinary life. For over a week now, she had been managing to contend with each separate circumstance as it arose, and could look no further. The flight to New York at that time took sixteen hours, and she was ready to be overwhelmed by the prospect. Having taken the pill to stave off the worst of grief, she could not expect to sleep and must spend hours staring, upright, at the sky that was now to be associated with him always.

"*Attention*," the voice said. They got to their feet, and Cyril picked up her overnight bag. They walked past glass cases filled with clocks and watches, and metal stands stacked with chocolate boxes.

"Would you like something?" Cyril asked her.

"Nothing. Thank you. Really."

"Let me get you some chocolate."

"But they feed you all the time on these planes."

"You never know." When he came back with the package in his hand, she was reminded of Etienne handing her the rough, useless flowers on the mountainside.

At the gate, they embraced her. A young man in uniform examined her passport and her ticket and gave them back to her. She held them in her right hand, with the packet of chocolate. Every action now seemed to her to involve an important and costly effort, as though she were being presented with obstacles which she must continually surmount. Irrationally, she believed that her departure itself represented such an undertaking, and that it would have been possible for her to stay, protected, in the flat green garden between the two lines of mountains without ever fully acknowledging what had brought her there. It was almost like consenting to his death, she thought, walking into the railed enclosure with the other passengers.

WEEKEND

Lilian, on waking, reached up her arm to pull back the curtain from the window above her bed. The cretonne roses, so recently hung that their folds were still awkward and raw-smelling, tinkled back on brass rings, and sunlight fell around the walls in honey-colored warpings. It was like being under water, she thought, bathed in that delicate light; she had forgotten these contradictions of spring in England—chill, dreary evenings like yesterday's, and bright mornings full of early flowers. She pushed the blankets away and knelt up on the bed to look out the small, paned window. The outer air, the garden glittered; the meadows—for they could hardly be called anything less—unfolded beyond, crowned by a glimpse of the village and the fifteenth-century church. All as suitable, as immaculate as the white window sill on which her elbows rested.

But the room was, of course, cold, and she sank back into the bed-clothes. During the night, she had wakened several times to hear the wind rattling the windowpanes and had pushed herself further down the bed, trying to warm her shoulders. (The little electric radiator had been taken away during the day to dry the baby's washing and had not been returned.) Going to bed last night, she had actually consoled herself with the prospect of departure—that it would be her last night in the house.

And tonight, no doubt, back in London, she would wonder about the weekend, and comfort herself by telephoning Julie and by thinking out the long, loving letter she would write when she got back to New York. The letter, in her mind, was already some paragraphs advanced.

Like some desolating childhood disappointment, she thought, this anxiety to get away when she had so longed to come here—so longed to see them, and to see Julie most of all. Because, even though Ben was her own brother, it was to Julie she felt closer; Julie she had missed more in these two years away. Given only this weekend, Lilian felt the need to precipitate confidences—"Are you happy, is this really what you want?" she had almost asked Julie last night, coming upstairs. Which was nonsense, impertinence; one couldn't ask it, and in any case Julie would have laughed and told Ben afterward ("Whatever do you think Lilian said to me?"). Married couples always betrayed their friends that way—probably for something to say, being so much together. And Ben, indifferent, would say: "How perfectly extraordinary," or "I'm not in the least surprised," or "Poor old Lilian."

Lilian's room was in the old part of the house—seventeenth-century, Julie had said. Lilian allowed a century either way, for Julie's imprecision and the exaggeration of the estate agent. She lay approving the uneven walls, the heavy beams of the roof, the sturdy irregularities of the window and door. The only furniture other than her bed was a new chest of drawers, a cane chair, and a small, unsteady table. On this table stood a china lamp and *Poets of the Present*, a frayed volume in which Thomas Hardy was heavily represented. The room—in fact, the whole house—looked bare. They needed so many things, Julie had said—practically everything—but for a while nothing more could be done; buying the house had taken every penny. On Friday, when Lilian arrived, Julie had shown her around, walking through the rooms with her hand in the crook of Lilian's arm, separating apologetically at doorways. (All the rooms were at slightly different levels, and there was a step or two at each entrance—sometimes dropping, dangerously, beyond a closed door.) Julie's shy, artless face, lowered so that strands of silky hair drooped on Lilian's shoulder, had seemed tired, frail. Her sweater and skirt were aged, unheeded. Too much for her, Lilian thought, this house, and the baby, though I'm sure it's lovely. "Lovely," she had repeated later, in the nursery, over a mound of blue blanket. In the hallway, it was Lilian who linked their arms again.

She pushed the bedclothes back once more, and lowered her feet to the cold, glossy floor. And Ben, she thought, shivering and resting her elbow on her knee and her chin on her hand. She found it hard to believe in Ben as Julie's husband, Simon's father, a member (as she supposed he must be) of the community, traveling up to London every morning of the week, and at home seeming settled and domestic, reading the evening paper with the air of one who must not be disturbed. She supposed that in his way he must love Julie, but she couldn't really imagine him intimate with anyone. She thought of him as a source of knowledge rather than experience; a good, though not contemporary mind, a person rather than a man.

"I adore you," Ben said, without opening his eyes, "but why are you up so early?"

Julie, at the mirror, uttered a strangled sound. She took a bobby pin from between her teeth and fastened up the last, escaping lock of hair. "I have to take care of Simon until the girl arrives. And think about lunch. . . . And then, there's Lilian."

"What about her?" Ben stretched out into the depression left by Julie's body in the other half of the bed. His eyes, now open, were surprisingly alert. "Come and talk to me."

She came and sat beside him, reaching her arm across his body to rest her hand on the bed. "I just mean I have to think of her—make sure she's not cold or anything."

"Difficult to see how she can be anything else, when we've got both the radiators."

"Oh, Lord! I forgot. . . . *Don't,* darling, after all the trouble I took combing it."

"Why is it done differently?" He loosened another strand.

"I don't know—I suppose because Lilian eyes me as though I should Do Something with myself. She makes me feel that I look . . . *married.*"

"Scarcely astonishing, in the circumstances." He drew her elbow back so that, losing the support of her arm, she collapsed against his breast. She remained there, and he put his arm around her. "'Old, married, and in despair'—is that the idea?"

"Something like that."

"Too soon for that," he observed, encouragingly. "But I know what you mean. Since she's been here I can hardly read the paper without feeling that I've sold my immortal soul."

Julie giggled. "Don't be awful." She drew away from him and put her hands up to her hair, assessing the damage. "Do you think she's happy? I get the feeling she doesn't *want* anything—you know, doesn't know what she should do with her life. . . ." She opened another bobby pin with her teeth and replaced it at the back of her head. "We, at least, know where we are."

"'I am between water and stone fruit in India,'" declared Ben, looking up at Lilian over the *Times*. "In eleven letters."

"Any clues?"

"None."

"Pondicherry," Lilian said, after a moment's silence.

Ben wrote. Pleased with herself, Lilian curled her legs up on the sofa and wondered if she should be in the kitchen, helping Julie. There were to be guests for lunch.

"'A secret'—blank—'in the stream.' Tennyson. Nine letters."

"No clues?"

"Begins and ends with 's.'"

"Sweetness," said Julie unexpectedly from the dining room. She appeared for a moment in the doorway and added: "*In Memoriam*," polishing a glass with a dish towel.

"Twenty across," Ben resumed, but Lilian got up and followed Julie.

The kitchen smelled of roasting lamb, and of floor polish and mint sauce. What an appalling stove, Lilian thought; surely they'll replace it.

"Do sit down," Julie told her, pulling out a chair by the table. "We'll be five for lunch—some neighbors called Marchant and the three of us. No, darling, thank you, there's nothing; everything's done. Unless perhaps you'd like to shell the peas." She turned her attention to the meat. "It's quite efficient, really, this kitchen—though, as you see, we had to put in a new stove."

Lilian began to break pods over a colander. "What are they like, your neighbors?"

"The Marchants? We scarcely know them. They drove over one day, in a Volkswagen, to call—we'd been introduced by the previous owners of the house. And they asked us to dinner last week, but we couldn't leave the baby. Seem all right—a bit dull." Having basted the lamb, Julie slid it back into the oven and straightened up. She plunged the basting spoon into suds in the sink. "Nothing against them, really, apart from the car."

Arriving late in their Volkswagen, the Marchants brought with them a big, restless Dalmatian called Spot. Mr. Marchant was stocky and bald, with heavy glasses and a suit of limp tweed. Mrs. Marchant was slight and ginger-haired, and wore a green pullover and a gray flannel skirt. They stood for some minutes in the hall, commenting on improvements in high, authoritative voices, before they could be induced to enter the living room. Mrs. Marchant did not sit down at once, but moved across the room to stare at a picture before veering sharply away to the window. Rather, Lilian could not help thinking, like a small colored fish in an aquarium. Spot, after a brisk canter around the furniture, flopped down to pant in a corner, where Ben was preparing drinks.

Mrs. Marchant gave Lilian her divided attention. "You've just been— thank you, with a little water—to America?"

"She lives there," Ben said, stepping over the dog. "Out of the way, Fido."

"Spot," corrected Mrs. Marchant, scenting disparagement.

Mr. Marchant, who was a lawyer, produced some formidably documented views on the conduct of government in the United States. Congressional legislation appeared to him as a series of venal disasters— catalogued, Lilian felt, with a certain satisfaction.

Julie was quietly interrogating the dog, now sitting at her feet. "Are you a good doggie?" Spot smiled, but kept his counsel.

Unable to refute Mr. Marchant, and badly situated for conversation with Spot, Lilian kept silent. Perhaps it's a system, something one gets used to again, she told herself—like doing the *Times* crossword puzzle.

Mrs. Marchant was inclined to be tolerant. "The Americans who come over here seem pleasant enough, don't you think?"

"Oh, absolutely," Ben agreed. He put out his cigarette, and added: "A trifle assiduous, perhaps," before lighting another.

Mrs. Marchant persisted. "But I've always got on well with them. We had four in our house—remember, Hugh?—during the war. Well-behaved boys. They read aloud in the evenings." She nodded to reinforce this surprising memory.

"Did they really?" Julie, who had risen, paused at the door of the dining room. "What?"

Mrs. Marchant's approval diminished. "Well, I *was* hoping for Wordsworth, which Daddy would have so loved—my father was living with us then. But instead they read an interminable thing about a whale—a *whale*, I assure you. I thought we'd never see the back of that whale. But mercifully, when the good weather came, they opened the Second Front."

Lilian, glancing up in dismay, was astonished to find Julie's face disarrayed with amusement.

They sat down to lunch, and Ben carved the meat. Spot, having found his way under the table, squeezed back and forth among their legs, his firm, bristly sides heaving with cheerful interest, his tail slapping wildly. Julie looked pained, and once laid down her knife and fork as though she were about to speak—but didn't. At last Mr. Marchant got up from the table, apologizing, and called the dog to the door.

"Out, damned Spot," he said, pointing. Everyone laughed except Mrs. Marchant, who had heard the joke a hundred times. The dog pattered out as if he had intended this all along.

Julie washed the dishes, and Lilian dried them. The Marchants, waving, had disappeared with Spot in their car, shortly after lunch. Ben had gone out to work in the garden ("Before the rain comes," Julie said, although there was no sign of rain). In the sun outside the kitchen window, Simon slept in his pram.

"Is he warm enough there?" Lilian asked.

Julie looked up, her hands in the sink. "Oh, don't you think so?" she asked anxiously, alarming Lilian, who had expected a confident reassurance.

"It's beginning to get chilly," she said. Together, they looked uncertainly at the strip of sunshine on the grass. Their shoulders touched.

"Oh, God!" shouted Ben from the garden. He crossed rapidly in front of the kitchen window and came in at the back door, a bundle of drooping plants in his hands. "Julia," he said, using her full name to emphasize his displeasure. (How infantile men are, Lilian thought.) "Julia, the lupines are all dug up. Will you please tell those people for Christ's sake not to bring their filthy dog here again?"

"Yes, dear," Julie replied seriously, apparently memorizing the message in order to convey it with complete accuracy. "Can't they be replanted?"

He shook his head. "The blighter's chewed them."

Lilian wiped the draining board and hung the wet dish towel on a rod to dry. "I'll bring Simon in, shall I?" she said smoothly, and made her way past Ben into the garden.

"Leave the pram," Julie called. "Ben will bring it."

Outside the kitchen door, the grass was sparse and trampled, and flaked with wood shavings from the recent passage and unpacking of furniture. Beyond, however, it became lavishly green, in need of cutting and scattered with spring flowers. The garden, more delicate than ever in the already dying light, was surrounded by ancient trees and, on one side, by a thick, trim hedge of box. A memory even as one stands here, Lilian thought, saddened by anticipation of her own nostalgia—and yet pleased all at once to have come out at this moment, to find the scene imposing some sort of misty symmetry on the untidy events of the day. I may cry, she told herself with surprise, as she lifted the sleeping Simon.

Ben, still grasping the ravished lupines, looked at her with interest as he came out of the house.

Lilian gathered up the trailing blanket with her free hand and walked slowly away. He will say: "Poor old Lilian," after I've left, she reminded herself. In the kitchen, she handed Simon over to his mother. "Now I must really go and pack," she said.

Lilian leaned from the window of the train. "I'll telephone you from London," she told Julie.

It will come right again, on the telephone, they assured each other silently.

Julie, suddenly pale and tired, brushed away tears. "It's cold. I should have brought a coat."

"What?"

"It's cold."

"Next time I'll come in the summer."

Crying, Julie laughed. "It'll still be cold. But come back soon."

"Do you have everything you need?" Ben asked, too late for ambiguity, glancing at the magazine stall.

"Yes, thanks. Oh, goodbye." The train drew away. "Goodbye!"

"Goodbye! Lilian . . . goodbye."

They waved, close at last for a moment, before the train ran into the darkness.

The two on the platform stood still for a few seconds, convalescent, before they walked away to their little car. In the clear, black, country air outside the station, Julie shivered again. The wind had risen, as it had the night before. They got into the car without speaking. Only when the engine started, on the third try, did Julie move up against Ben. He put his arm briefly around her, and then withdrew it. The car moved off.

"Poor old Lilian," Julie said.

HAROLD

Every evening of the summer, lanterns were hung from the oleanders and they had dinner in the garden. The table was a long and
rickety affair on trestles, and there were always insects because
of the lights, but on balance it was worth it. The evenings were cool even
after the August days, which recorded heat, long after dark, in the villa's
outer walls. The wall facing onto this terrace-garden was still warm to the
touch, although it was past nine o'clock and Signora Ricciardi and her
guests were sitting down to dinner.

The scene, too, was worth the discomfort: the white table, three flasks
of wine, pale dishes of bread, red dishes of meat, green bowls of salad; the
summer-colored dresses of the women, and a crimson shawl hung on a
chair; everything scented by flower beds, in eclipse beyond the lanterns,
and by lemon trees, which stood about in great stone urns. Above the line
of hills facing across a valley, the sky glowed from the lights of Siena, but
the house at night rode its hilltop in rolling, dark countryside with the
purposeful isolation of a ship at sea, and people around the table, too,
assumed something of the serene animation of voyagers.

Bernard Tourner was as lean and astringent as his wife, Monique,
was plump and soft—a dove in her gray dress. For many years they had

come from Paris to spend their summers at this *pensione*, and each morning they would disappear in their little ancient car for an excursion to Arezzo or Volterra, or simply into the Chianti hills, returning as children return from a trip to the seaside, refreshed and exhausted and painfully sunburned.

Bernard's appearance was an index of his personality, sensitive and slightly waspish. A quick understanding and a rich, ready memory made him an excellent companion at the table, but because of his occasional moodiness it was felt that Monique was not to be envied. However, they were deeply dependent upon each other, and Monique seemed always sweetly and unheroically content.

They were sitting, this evening, on either side of Charles Holmes, who was an Englishman, and who, from shyness, talked and listened with a habitual vagueness, glancing at Dora, his wife, sitting opposite. Dora passed the wine to him across the table; Dora was dark and beautiful and not shy at all.

"*O pittore*," called Signora Ricciardi, from the head of the table. Charles turned to her, always charmed that she should address him in this way, since he was an amateur and not very gifted painter, on holiday from a business concerned with lead and zinc. "*O pittore*, have you seen our three boys at all? Have they come back yet?"

Charles gestured toward the house, as if to conjure up the three young men, who at that moment came hurriedly into the garden and seated themselves at the table, murmuring apologies. Englishly alike in grave manners and incisive speech, in an almost womanish refinement of feature and fair skin reddened but not tanned by the sun, they had the names of antique Romans: Julian, Adrian, Antony. With quiet fortitude they had received, that summer, telegrams confirming success in their examinations at Cambridge. At twenty, they already offered a certain distinction and the promise of charm. The only criticism that might have been made of them was that their background and prospects had been provided so amply as to encroach a little on the scope of the present; nothing had been left to chance—perhaps on the assumption that chance is a detrimental element. "*Tutto a posto*," the Signora said of them.

In her way, the Signora herself was as much "in place" as these boys;

she would never have been mistaken for a voyager. Sitting at the end of the table, a slender, ageless woman with a disproportionate share of accomplishments, she chatted and rejoiced and sympathized with her guests, sharing their confidences and fulfilling their expectations, giving them a sense of infinite leisure, as though these symmetrical days of summer were to last forever. Their recollections of the villa would be almost indistinguishable from memories of her.

A little withdrawn from the talk that evening, she was listening for the arrival of a pair of unknown guests, a mother and son who were the friends of a friend. All day they had been expected—a not unwelcome intrusion into the intimacy of the present guests, who had been in one another's company all summer. Though, indeed, it had all gone very well this year: no one had been ill or quarreled or fallen in love. They were all on the best of terms, even with Miss Nicholson.

Miss Nicholson was a diminutive middle-aged Englishwoman who played—surprisingly—the cello and was attending the summer courses at the music academy in Siena. She did not attempt even the simplest of Italian phrases, and she spoke of England with a longing as constant as though she had been condemned to exile. Most surprising of all, she wore a hat to the lunch table, a navy-blue sailor hat with a group of white flowers at one side of it, and in this hat she would take the bus to Siena every afternoon to attend her lesson. The small, prim figure burdened with the cello had become familiar in the spiraling main street that led to the academy, and the instrument was recognized as a token of sympathy and permanence, the antithesis of the camera usually carried by foreigners.

The boys were at their best with Miss Nicholson, who represented a type familiar to their own family circles. They were kind and deferential, invariably willing to help with the inevitable cello or to find out where she could buy an English newspaper. In return, she regarded them with real affection and an almost personal pride.

Now, as the meal began, the arrival of the new guests was announced by one of the maids, the smiling, circular Assunta. "*O Signora,*" she said, the formal vocative "*O*" of Tuscany coming oddly from that genial face, "*son appena arrivati da Firenze.*" Arriving at Siena by the late train, the new guests had come out to the villa in a taxi and were seeing to the unloading of their luggage. The Signora, taking up her red shawl, went into the house to greet them, and around the table there was a short, expectant silence.

"*Una vecchia signora*," whispered Assunta, handing around the *pasta*, "*e un giovane grande.*" Two chairs were added to the table and two more places set. Conversation resumed, but now they were all detached, awaiting this diversion.

Presently a voice could be heard, raised as a voice sometimes is in a strange house, and the Signora brought the new guests through the doors that led from the living room into the garden; the two women were followed by the "*giovane grande,*" a tall young man who remained in shadow behind them while introductions were made. The men rose from the table, scraping their chairs over pebbles.

The mother, large and handsome, was of that vigorous type of Englishwoman generally caricatured for its addiction to outdoor life. Gray hair, squarely cut, contributed to the strength of a face almost grimly straightforward, a directness scarcely modified by an impression of unhappiness. She was wearing a dress of brown linen much creased across the lap from the train journey and, around her neck, a heavy pendant of Mexican design. On her arm was a silver bracelet of incongruous delicacy, and Florence had contributed the sandals in which her feet were firmly planted apart.

Names were pronounced and mispronounced to her by the Signora, and she smiled politely, repeating them like a lesson. She was led to the place laid for her next to Bernard and settled into it.

Her son's name was Harold. He stepped forward into the circle of light to be introduced and stood silent while chairs were shuffled along the table to accommodate him. The three boys, now reseated, looked him over with courteous reserve, exercising that perception for affinities and failings with which public-school life had endowed them.

This boy had none of their diffident grace. Long-limbed and excruciatingly awkward, he was still, at their age, almost grotesquely adolescent. He was very brown, and dressed in khaki trousers and a blue shirt with rolled sleeves, and scratches on his arms were blotched with that purple antiseptic upon which British mothers place such reliance. His blond hair and eyebrows, sun-bleached to a startling fairness, contributed to a look of vacancy that really began at wide-spaced, wide-staring eyes. On his behalf, certainly, there would be no telegraphed confirmation of outstanding performance in examinations; rather, one imagined an education interspersed with letters from school principals, sympathetic and unyielding: "Harold's gifts are not suited to the discipline of the school curriculum."

Stumbling to his chair with an embarrassed acknowledgment of greetings, he sat down next to Dora. His mother was already embarked on an easy tide of conversation concerned with her journey. "So hot in Florence . . . a little tired, yes, but what a beautiful journey . . . light most of the way . . . Lovely country . . ."

Bernard was helping her to *pasta*. "Yes, it's a journey one never tires of, that trip from Florence to Siena."

"So much to see," she went on. "That scenery, sometimes vast and sometimes almost in miniature, like a fairy tale . . . A great fortress quite near here, what would that be?"

"That was probably Monteriggioni," replied Bernard. "It's from the thirteenth century. But Tuscany is crowded with these hilltop fortresses and walled towns."

"Tomorrow you will see another, just below the house," the Signora told her. "Montacuto. It was ruined by Barbarossa."

"So hard to associate violence with this countryside," the new guest said, and sighed, comforted by antiquity.

"It isn't all as remote as that," the Signora said. "In the last war the front passed through here. The Germans were in this house."

"You see how it is," said Bernard, with a faint smile. "In this country everything has been *done*, as it were—even this landscape has been done to the point where one becomes a detail in a canvas. And they all know too much. In Italy one is almost too much at ease, too well understood; all summer here I feel that nothing new can happen, nothing can surprise or call our capacities into question; that none of us can *add* anything."

"Does this mean we shan't see you here next year?" asked Dora, laughing because Bernard had come there for so many years.

Bernard laughed, too. "Well, you English, you find a sort of prodigality here, too—an easy acceptance which you enjoy but which, after all, you don't wish to emulate."

"You mean that we have scruples about giving but none about receiving?" Charles asked.

"Not even that," Bernard said. "I simply mean that in our countries one must still be prepared for a few surprises, but here all experience is repetition, and that gives one an outrageous sense of proportion. That's why we feel so comfortable—why we find it so attractive to come here. After all, France is certainly as beautiful as this"—Bernard included the Italian peninsula in a brief gesture.

"And England," said Miss Nicholson, misunderstanding.

"Well, it isn't a competition, after all," replied Charles, filling her wineglass. "Do you know France, Miss Nicholson?"

Miss Nicholson replied that she did not, adding that she had been there several times.

The new guest remarked that she knew France well but that this was her first visit to Italy, and took the opportunity to resume her account of it. Yes, Florence was lovely, lovely, but a week was nothing, one must go back. "There is too much, far too much," she added accusingly. With a forkful of salad she indicated infinite riches.

"And you." Dora turned to the boy beside her. "What did you think of Florence?"

He stared at her uneasily, shifting his feet on the pebbles beneath the table. His mother's face clouded with a recognizable intensification of the discontent already seen there. "He scarcely saw anything of Florence," she said. "He wouldn't even have seen the cathedral if I hadn't insisted on it."

"I had to do some work," he murmured.

His mother appealed to the table. "Such an opportunity at his age. One would think he'd make the most of it." She gave the three boys a covetous, comparing look. Disconcerted, they vaguely protested their own inertia, not wishing to appear to advantage.

"I'm determined that he shall see Siena properly," she persisted.

Something in this prospect seemed to dishearten the boy even further, and he went on with his meal. He did not look at his mother. While she chatted on again about Florence—the heat, the della Robbias, the bargains in tooled leather—she directed toward him a current of censure and disappointment, evoking from him a slow, painful awareness.

But for the wondering eyes, the boy's expression would have been intense. It was a look that concentrated hard but could not quite find its object. Once or twice he entered the conversation, to express agreement with an enthusiasm suggesting that he seldom found his views shared, or to disagree with an emphasis which confirmed that impression. Between times, he maintained a state of subdued apology for his outbursts; in fact, apology appeared to be for him an involuntary means of self-expression. "I'm sorry," he said, passing dishes or reaching his daubed arm for the salt; "I'm sorry," as his wineglass was refilled. His self-effacement was, in its way, demanding; his youth, his gaucheness called up a collective effort of reassurance and encouragement, but he, in a sense, was proving the stronger character. As the evening drew on, his ineptitude pervaded them all.

Signora Ricciardi always left the table early, to negotiate with the cook the meals for the following day. At this interruption, Harold's mother rose, too, tired from her long day, and nodded around the table. "Don't stay up late," she told Harold, who stood to wish her good night. "You know how tired you are."

This knowledge passively acquired, Harold prepared to hurry with his fruit. Dispelling a momentary, hopeful silence, the other guests encouraged him to stay, describing to him the house and its surroundings, proposing excursions into the town. They listed for him the attractions of Siena, from *pinacoteca* to post office, and he listened diligently, leaning forward and twisting his napkin about his fingers. He was taking them and their attentions very seriously, almost as seriously as he took himself. A burden of compulsory activities could be seen mounting in his imagination, although he might easily have guessed that those hot days would dwindle into a catalogue of churches unvisited and pictures unsurveyed. At last, with an effort, he mentioned anxiously that he intended to keep part of the day free for his work.

"You must be studying?" asked Dora.

"No, no, I'm not studying anything now."

"What is your work then?"

"I mean my writing."

"Writing?"

More vulnerable than ever, he glanced around the table. He was repeating a familiar experience.

"I mean poetry. Well . . . yes, poems."

Into the silence Miss Nicholson said gently: "Well, I hope you will read them to us."

He raised his eyes toward her with his concentrating, round-eyed look, not doubting her word. "I have them here, upstairs," he said.

The evening seemed to have lost its balance. They allowed him to fetch his poems, feeling the extent of their indulgence and a sense of imposition. They were already inventing to themselves noncommittal expressions of interest and wondering how soon they might stop him. Their manners preventing an exchange of glances, the three boys smiled down at their plates, comfortably appalled; they were all at once drawn together, dissociated from so flagrant a breach of regulations. It was entirely possible that they also wrote poetry, but only within the bounds of a fastidious reticence. Charles Holmes pushed back his chair a little to stretch his legs and muttered: "Let him read one, then—just one. I'm ready for bed."

The boy came out of the house again, clutching a bundle of papers. When he placed them on the table, they slid outward—single, scribbled pages of all sizes. Seated, he examined them, rustling through an apprehensive silence. He read to himself for a moment, and his audience suddenly saw that he was no longer intensely aware of them, or, indeed, of himself, and that his face was unrecognizably calm. Even his arm, resting on the table's edge, was curved toward the papers in a controlled and easy gesture. They were slowly troubled by an idea that formed among them. Without looking about, each knew, too, that it had occurred to the others: an idea almost to be repudiated, requiring, as it did, so much accommodation.

When he had read aloud for a few minutes, the boy looked up, not for commendation but simply to rest his eyes. Charles said quickly: "Go on." The inclined young face had grown, in the most literal sense, self-possessed. Their approval, so greatly required in another context, had now no importance for him. He spoke as though for himself, distinctly but without emotion, hesitating in order to decipher corrections, scattering his crumpled papers on the table as he discarded them. It seemed that no one moved, although the three boys no longer held identical positions; they had separated into solitary, reflective attitudes that conceded this unlikely triumph.

Assunta came to remove the last dishes, but left, after a moment, without disturbing them. A moth thudded against one of the colored lanterns. The evening was at its best, cool and clear. From time to time, his voice tiring, the boy paused to shuffle his papers, or he made some brief explanatory comment on the subject of a poem before reading it. When someone asked whether this was all recent work—as though it could possibly have been otherwise—he replied that it had all been written in the last year or two. "There are more all the time," he said, and laid his hand on the shaggy papers as if they had taken him by surprise.

The wall overlooking them suddenly broke open at a square of light, shutters clattering back against stone, and Harold's mother leaned from the window. Framed in ivy tendrils, she presented, in metal curlers and a dark dressing gown, an altered version of that type of post card in which ringleted maidens used to lean toward one over window sills. The boy stared up at her blankly, his eyes emptied of all impression. Without looking at the others, she reminded him that he had traveled all day and that it was almost one o'clock. The wall was abruptly resealed.

Harold continued to look up for a moment, and it could be seen rather than heard that he muttered: "I'm sorry." He began to put his papers together, at first slowly, and then quickly and nervously, picking up pages that fluttered to the ground. His authority relinquished without a struggle, he rose from the table holding the bundle insecurely against him. "Good night . . . thanks awfully . . . good night," he said, and disappeared into the house with his ungainly steps.

Presently they heard a sound like a splash, a sound that could only be his papers falling across the tiled floor of the living room. They gave him time to gather them up, convinced that alone there in the half darkness he was saying: "I'm sorry."

THE PICNIC

It was like Nettie, Clem thought, to wear a dress like that to a picnic and to spill something on it. His wife, May, was wearing shorts and a plaid shirt, and here was Nettie in a dress that showed her white arms and shoulders—and, as she bent over the wine stain, her bosom; a dress with a green design of grapes and vine leaves. He could tell, too, that she had been to the hairdresser yesterday, or even this morning before setting out to visit them. She hadn't changed at all. Unrealistic, that was the word for Nettie. . . . But the word, suggesting laughter and extravagance, unexpectedly gave him pleasure. Feeling as though Nettie herself had cheated him of his judgment, he turned away from her and glanced down the hillside to where May was playing catch with Ivor, their youngest boy.

If May had left them alone deliberately, as he assumed she had—and he honored that generosity in her—she was mistaken in thinking they had anything to say to one another. They had been sitting for some minutes in complete silence, Nettie repacking the remains of the lunch into the picnic basket or, since the accident with the wine, fiddling with her dress. But what could two people talk about after ten years (for it must be getting on to that)? Nettie, though quite chatty throughout lunch, certainly hadn't said much since. Perhaps she expected him to mention all that business; it would fit in with her sentimental ideas. Naturally, he had no intention of doing anything of the kind—why bring up something that happened at least ten years ago and made all three of them miserable enough, God knows, at the time? Yes, that would be Nettie all over, wanting to be told that he had often thought about her, had never forgotten her, never would—although whole months passed sometimes when Nettie never entered his head, and he was sure it must be the same way for her; at least, he presumed so. Even then, he would remember her only because someone else—May, perhaps—spoke of her.

In fact, it was because someone else brought her to his attention that the thing had come about in the first place. He had not, in the beginning, thought her attractive—a young cousin of May's who came to the house for weekends in the summer. He had scarcely noticed her until a casual visitor, the wife of one of his partners, spoke about her. A beautiful woman, she had called her—the phrase struck him all the more because he or May would have said, at most, a pretty girl. And Nettie, that day, had been dressed in a crumpled yellow cotton, he remembered—not at her best at all. Later, he had reflected that his whole life had been jeopardized because someone thoughtlessly said: "She is beautiful."

Now Nettie looked up at him, drawing her hair away from her face with the back of her hand. Still they did not speak, and to make the silence more natural by seeming at his ease Clem stretched on his elbow among the ferns. Nettie released the loop of hair and poured a little water from a thermos onto the mark on her dress. Her earrings swung; her dress shifted along one shoulder. Her head lowered intently—he supposed that she had become shortsighted and refused to wear glasses.

He could hardly recall how it had developed, what had first been said between them, whether either of them resisted the idea. His memories of Nettie were like a pile of snapshots never arranged according to date. He could see her quite clearly, though, sitting in a garden chair, and in a car, and, of all things, riding a bicycle; and facing him across a table—in a restaurant, he thought—looking profoundly sad and enjoying herself hugely.

If, he told himself, I were to say now that I've thought of her (just because it would please her—and they would probably never meet again), she might simply get emotional. Not having thought of it for years, she might seize the opportunity to have a good cry. Or perhaps she doesn't really want to discuss the past; perhaps she's as uncomfortable as I. . . . All the same, she looked quite composed. He might almost have said a little satirical, as though she found his life quite dull and could rejoice that, after all, she had not shared it. (He saw himself, for an instant, with what he imagined to be her eyes. What a pity she had come just now—he had worked hard last winter, and he thought it had told on him.)

It was true, of course, that he had responsibilities, couldn't be rushing about the world pleasing himself, as she could. But no man, he assured himself irritably, could be entirely satisfied with what had happened to him. There must always be the things one had chosen not to do. One couldn't explore every possibility—one didn't have a thousand years. In the end, what was important? One's experience, one's ideas, what one read; some taste, understanding. He had his three sons, his work, his friends, this house. There was Matt, his eldest boy, who was so promising. (Then he recalled that during lunch today he had spoken sharply to Matt over something or other, and Nettie had laughed. She had made a flippant remark about impatience; that he hadn't changed at all, was that it? Some such silly, proprietary thing—which he had answered, briefly, with dignity. He knew himself to be extremely patient.)

Yes, Nettie could be quite tiresome, he remembered—almost with relief, having feared, for a moment, his own sentimentality. She made excessive demands on people; her talk was full of exaggerations. She had no sense of proportion, none whatever—and wasn't that exactly the thing one looked for in a woman? And she took a positive pride in condoning certain kinds of conduct, because they demonstrated weaknesses similar to her own. She was not fastidious, as May was.

That was it, of course. He had in his marriage the thing they would never have managed together, Nettie and he—a sort of perseverance, a persistent understanding. Where would Nettie have found strength for the unremitting concessions of daily life? She was precipitated from delight to lamentation without logical sequence, as though life were too short; she must cram everything in and perhaps sort it out later. (He rather imagined, from the look of things, that the sorting process had been postponed indefinitely.) For her, all experience was dramatic, every love eternal. Whereas he could only look on a love affair, now, as a displacement, not just of his habits—though that, too—but of his intelligence. Of the mind itself. Being in love was, like pain, an indignity, a reducing thing. So nearly did it seem in retrospect a form of insanity, the odd thing to him was that it should be considered normal.

Not that it wasn't exciting in its own way, Nettie's ardor, her very irresponsibility. It was what had fascinated him at the time, no doubt. And she was easily amused—though that was one of her drawbacks; she laughed at men, and naturally they felt it. Even when she had been, so to speak, in love with him, he had sometimes felt she had laughed at him, too.

In all events, his marriage had survived Nettie's attractions, whatever they were. It was not easy, of course. In contrast to Nettie, May assumed too many burdens. Where Nettie was impetuous and inconsiderate, May was scrupulous and methodical. He was often concerned about May. She worried, almost with passion (he surprised himself with the word), over human untidiness, civic affairs, the international situation. He was willing to bet that the international situation never crossed Nettie's mind. May had a horror of disorder—"Let's get organized," she would say, faced with a picnic, a dinner party; faced with life itself. If his marriage lacked romance, which would scarcely be astonishing after twenty years, it was more securely established on respect and affection. There were times, he knew, when May still needed him intensely, but their relations were so carefully balanced that he was finding it more and more difficult to detect the moment of appeal.

He felt a sudden hatred for Nettie, and for this silence of hers that prejudiced one's affections and one's principles. She tried—he could feel it; it was to salve her own pride—to make him consider himself fettered, diminished, a shore from which the wave of life receded. And what had *she* achieved, after all, that she should question the purpose of his existence? He didn't know much about her life these past few years— which alone showed there couldn't be much to learn. A brief, impossible marriage, a lot of trips, and some flighty jobs. What did she have to show for all this time—without children, no longer young, sitting there preoccupied with a stain on her dress? She couldn't suggest that he was to blame for the turn her life had taken—she wasn't all *that* unjust. She had suffered at the time, no doubt, but it was so long ago. They couldn't begin now to accuse or vindicate one another. That was why it was much better not to open the subject at all, actually. He glanced severely at her, restraining her recriminations. But she had lost her mocking, judicial air. She was still looking down, though less attentively. Her hands were folded over her knee.

Well, she *was* beautiful; he would have noticed it even if it had never been pointed out to him. . . . All at once he wanted to say "I have often thought of you" (for it was true, he realized now; he thought of her every day). Abruptly, he looked away. At the foot of the hill, May had stopped playing with the children and was sitting on a rock. It is my own decision, he reminded himself, that Nettie isn't mine, that I haven't seen her in all these years. And the knowledge, though not completely gratifying, gave him a sense of integrity and self-denial, so that when he looked at her again it was without desire, and he told himself, I have grown.

He has aged, Nettie thought. Just now, looking into his face—which was, curiously, more familiar to her than anyone else's—she had found nothing to stir her. One might say that he was faded, as one would say it of a woman. He would soon be fifty. He had a fretful, touchy air about him. During lunch, when she had laughed at his impatience, he had replied primly (here in her mind she pulled a long, solemn, comic face): "I have my faults, I suppose, like everyone else." And like everyone else, she noted, he was willing to admit the general probability so long as no specific instance was brought to his attention. He made little announcements about himself, too, protesting his tolerance, his sincerity. "I am a sensitive person," he had declared, absolutely out of the blue (something, anyway, that no truly sensitive person would say). He was so cautious—anyone would think he had a thousand years to live and didn't need to invite experience. And while, of course, any marriage must involve compromise (and who, indeed, would know that better than she?), that was no reason for Clem and May to behave toward one another like a couple of . . . civil servants.

She could acknowledge his intelligence. And he had always been a very competent person. Wrecked on a desert island, for instance (one of her favorite criteria), he would have known what to do. But life demanded more, after all, than the ability to build a fire without matches, or recognize the breadfruit tree on sight. And one could hardly choose to be wrecked simply in order to have an opportunity for demonstrating such accomplishments.

Strange that he should have aged like this in so short a time—it would be precisely eight years in June since they parted. It was still a thing she couldn't bring herself to think of, the sort of thing people had in mind when they said, not quite laughing, that they wouldn't want their youth over again. Oddly enough, it was the beginning, not the end, that didn't bear thinking about. One weekend, they had stopped at a bar, in the country, on the way to this house. It was summer, and their drinks came with long plastic sticks in them. Clem had picked up one of the sticks and traced the outline of her fingers, lying flat on the Formica tabletop. They had not said anything at all, then, but she had known simply because he did that. Even now, the thought of his drawing that ridiculous plastic stick around her fingers was inexpressibly touching.

Naturally, she didn't imagine poor old Clem had planned an affair in advance, but even at the time she had felt he was ready for something of the kind—that she was the first person he happened to notice. For the fact was that they were not really suited to one another, which he would have discovered if he had ever tried to understand her properly. He had no idea of what she was like, none whatever. To this day, she was sure, he thought her trivial, almost frivolous. (And she was actually an acutely sensitive person.) No wonder they found nothing to say to one another now.

It *was* a strain, however, their being alone like this. And how like May to have arranged it this way, how ostentatiously forbearing. Magnanimous, Clem would have called it (solemn again), but May had a way, Nettie felt, of being magnanimous, as it were, at one's expense. Still, what did it matter? Since they had invited her, after she had run into May in a shop one afternoon, she could hardly have refused to come. In an hour or two it would be over; she need never come again.

It did matter. It wouldn't be over, really. Her life was associated with Clem's, however little he might mean to her now, and she must always be different because she had known him. She wasn't saying that he was responsible for the pattern of her life—she wasn't that unjust. It was, rather, that he cropped up, uninvited, in her thoughts almost every day. She found herself wondering over and over again what he would think of things that happened to her, or wanting to tell him a story that would amuse him. And surely that is the sense, she thought, in which one might say that love is eternal. She was pleased when people spoke well of him in her hearing—and yet resentful, because she had no part, now, in his good qualities. And when she heard small accusations against him, she wondered whether she should contest them. But, for all she knew, they might be justified. That was the trouble with experience; it taught you that most people were capable of anything, so that loyalty was never quite on firm ground—or, rather, became a matter of pardoning offenses instead of denying their existence.

She sympathized with his attitude. It was tempting to confine oneself to what one could cope with. And one couldn't cope with love. (In her experience, at any rate, it had always got out of hand.) But, after all, it was the only state in which one could consider oneself normal; which engaged all one's capacities, rather than just those developed by necessity—or ship-wreck. One never realized how much was lacking until one fell in love again, because love—like pain, actually—couldn't be properly remembered or conveyed.

How sad it was. Looking into his face just now, finding nothing of interest, she had been so pierced by sadness that tears filled her eyes and she had to bend over the stain on her dress to hide her face. It was absurd that they should face each other this way—antagonistically, in silence—simply because they had once been so close. She would have done anything for him. Even though she no longer cared for him, saw his weakness quite clearly, still she would do anything for him. She cared for him, now, less than for any man she knew, and yet she would have done anything. . . . It *was* a pity about her dress, though—wine was absolutely the worst thing; it would never come out.

Upright on her rock, May gave a short, exhausted sigh. She closed her eyes for a moment, to clear them, and Ivor called out to her that she must watch him, watch the game. She looked back at him without smiling. On either side, her palms were pressed hard against the stone.

THE WORST MOMENT OF THE DAY

This is the worst moment of the day," said Daniele.

The table—with the emptied wine flasks, the grapes and figs left in large bowls, the clusters of stained napkins—was like a beach from which the tide had ebbed. Conversation had dwindled until slow afternoon sounds could be heard through shutters striped with heat.

The long room had windows at each end, and on one side opened through double doors into the drawing room. The opposite wall, slate blue, was bare except for two paintings hung together like illuminations on a blank page. They were landscapes painted by Marina some years ago, before she and her brother turned the villa into a *pensione* and her time ceased to be her own. She sat at the head of the table, straight and slender in a faded green dress, red-gold hair falling on her shoulders. Her hands were loosely clasped in her lap, and in her face poetry and reason met without the customary signs of struggle. She turned toward her brother's remark with a faint smile.

As though at a signal, the diners drew themselves together to surmount this worst of moments. Chairs scraped, a glass was knocked over; some inconclusive suggestion was made for a drive down to Florence in the evening.

It was late in the season, and the four guests—an elderly English couple and a young one—stood around the table as singly as the surviving fruits lay in the china dishes. Old Mr. Fenwick, who had been at the villa just a week, pushed his chair back into place and crossed to the windows. Unlatching one of the shutters, he peered into the garden, and only his wife's going over to join him suppressed his daily utterance concerning a brisk walk. There was something of fearful symmetry about the Fenwicks, he slim and inflexible, she plump and stately. It was their first journey to Italy, and they had been gratified to find so many forebodings justified.

Through the slit that now parted the shutters, the old man stared despondently at the day. The scene, it was true, was of dimensions comparable to those of his own land—in fact, he had made the comparison all too frequently, as though Tuscany were remarkable only for this similarity—but then there was that sky. He had never experienced such a sky. In England, where heaven is a low-hung, personal affair, thoroughly identified with the King James Version, a sky such as this would not have been tolerated for a moment. It was a high, pagan explosion of a sky, promising indulgence for all kinds of offenses to which he had not the slightest inclination. He felt, beneath it, exposed and ridiculed. And the light, too—a light that not only illuminated but was an element in itself, as distinct as rain . . . He would go and read in his room, after all, for he realized that the brisk walk, if taken, would be somehow impeded by that dazzling light.

The younger couple, the Stapletons, lingered at the table, folding their napkins. The Stapletons had spent other summers at the villa, but this year, for the first time, they had brought with them some unconfided anxiety of their London life. Francis, a fair man with a sensitive and orderly manner, contrived to conceal his present unhappiness—or at least to give it a reasonable, disciplined air that made it socially presentable. But his wife, Harriet, carried her part of their suffering publicly, and in return received, unfairly, a greater deference.

Marina had begun to stack the dishes for the maids, who had their lunch at this hour. "*Vai riposarti, cara,*" she told Harriet, drawing the napkin out of her hand.

After a moment, Harriet did go—but not, immediately, to rest. She disappeared into the drawing room, and they heard the opening creak of the side door and the thud of its closing. Francis was helping Marina to clear the table, walking around it to bring her the littered fruit plates. It was a relief to him to be here, in this cool room, doing automatic tasks, but he knew that in a moment he must go and look for his wife. He took a tray from the sideboard and arranged on it the glasses gathered together by Marina. Marina, who seemed to know everything—and he found it rather shocking that with her secluded life she should know so much—stood silent, pushing the grape seeds onto one large dish with a knife and making a pile of the stained plates beside her, but he felt soothed and understood, as if she had said something to console him. He dropped the napkins into their basket and, with a murmured excuse, left the room.

In the drawing room, he recovered his book and reading glasses—placed on the table when the lunch bell rang—and opened one of the shuttered doors into the garden. The door was weighted with the heat that met him as he stepped outside; it fell heavily back into place behind him. It annoyed him that Harriet should go out at a time when all other people—all of Italy—rested; annoyed him that he was unable to turn his annoyance into anything but concern, for real anger might have alleviated his misery. He made his way around to the front of the house, his mind presenting his predicament to him in words so simple that they might, but for the context, have been uttered by a child: "She does not love me any more."

Then: "She loves someone else." But if that was so, why were they here, together, trying to make things work again? He brushed with his shoulder the dying fronds of wisteria at the corner of the house, and stood in the wall's shadow, looking for Harriet.

In front of the house was a formal garden, and from this a crescent of graded steps descended to an avenue of ilex. The short avenue was never used now, the house having been connected with the road by a separate, graveled drive that led to the kitchen door. The trees, which needed trimming, met overhead and stood deep in weeds and wild flowers. Throughout the day, hens wandered into the avenue and picked among the straggling grass and made their way haltingly up the steps to stare into the ordered garden. From time to time, on the road below, a car passed, going toward Florence, and country sounds reached the house from the surrounding slopes.

Harriet sat now on the lowest of the arc of steps, her back curved in the sun, her face pressed into her arms, which were folded on her drawn-up knees. The sleeves of her pink blouse had been rolled up, and her skin was moist with heat. Her cotton skirt was carelessly bunched under her. She was motionless, not even roused by the hens rustling near her feet.

Her attitude was so abject, so forlorn, that Francis, at the top of the steps, stood quite still before he called her name. "Harriet."

The face she raised to him, however, was smooth and preoccupied, only creased above the eyes by the pressure of a bracelet. He came slowly down, dropping from step to step, and sat just above her, his knee touching her shoulder. She put no weight on him. After a moment, she resumed her former position without speaking.

He opened his book at the beginning and shaded the print with his hand. He had had a shock, coming upon her like that. And her calm uplifted face had not reassured him—because what was shocking, he thought as he turned the first page, was that it had seemed perfectly plausible that she, who had been chattering pleasantly enough at the lunch table a few minutes before, might have come out here and thrown herself down in this abandoned attitude in real anguish. It would have been terrible to find her so, but not surprising; people in general, and he and she in particular, were so separate that anything was possible. That knowledge moved him to press his knee once more against her bent shoulder. Feeling, perhaps, that some response was required of her, she turned her cheek toward him, her eyes closed.

"Hens are ghastly," she observed. And then: "Read me something."

He read aloud the lines he had just reached:

> ". . . *Ferme les portes*
> *Il est plus facile de mourir que d'aimer.*"

"Heavens," she said, and turned her face back into her arms.

He closed the book and put it on the stone step beside him. He looked down at her huddled body and dark, shaggy head, her brown arms and exposed knees, the tail of her blouse, which had come out of her skirt. He parted the hair on her neck and laid his hand there. "Come inside," he said. "We can't stay out in this heat."

She tilted her head once more. "In a moment," she replied.

"No," he insisted. "Really. It's the worst part of the day."

"In a moment," she repeated, wishing he would take his hand, which had become quite damp, off her neck. One can't ask to be left alone, she thought, or not to be touched, even once in a great while, without creating a scene—without changing everything. Do we have anything in common at all, she wondered—almost idly, because the sun had drained her. Will we manage it? Sometimes it is all right. But not today.

She sat up straight, thrusting her hair back from her forehead. He rose and helped her to her feet. She brushed at her skirt and made a perfunctory effort to push her blouse back in at the waist. They went up the steps together.

The hallway was cool and darkened and smelled strongly of the carnations that stood, white and red, in a big ceramic jar on the marble table. The stairs, which were of white stone, projected from a wall of colossal depth, so that, climbing them, one imagined oneself scaling a cliff. The house had been intended for pleasure, and perhaps that was why it was built like a fortress.

The Stapletons' room also was in darkness, for the maids had closed the shutters throughout the house. When Harriet opened them, it seemed that heat, no less than light, filled the room, igniting the red stone tiles, the pale walls, the two narrow white beds and their ornaments of brass. Below the window, as she looked down, a garden enclosed by a tall hedge of ilex was brilliant, too, a square of oleander, phlox, and petunias. Descending softly from the house, the country rose again into a freshly plowed hillside and a skyline black-penciled with cypresses.

She lay down on her bed. Francis came and sat beside her on the edge of the bed, filling her vision. She moved her head toward him on the pillow without rising, like a sick person. She had spoiled his tranquil, costly summer. Too much was wrong between them for these fine days to be enjoyed, or this idyllic place. They did not blame each other, having been educated since the days when faults could be attributed; nevertheless, it seemed that the sense of grievance was very strong. It was the worst moment of the day—an inarticulate exchange of pain. She could not speak yet, or make promises, and in any case the reassurances she could give were too meager to offer. Detached, she pitied him, too, and saw that she had never been more dear than now, when she lay there excluding him with her indifference and her look of displeasure. On her knee, his fingers became points of heat through the light cotton skirt.

"All right?" he asked, helplessly.

"I thought I might sleep."

"Shall we go down to town before dinner?"

"See how we feel. After I've rested, I may take a walk." And, to forestall him: "I'll be back in time to go into town."

He rose and pulled one of the shutters, so that her face was shielded from sunlight. With indignation and longing, he felt disqualified from kissing her as he turned to leave. It was almost as if he did not dare to.

"If I were you," she said, elaborating their estrangement, "If I were you, I should have a look at the car before we go."

Pondering the discomfort of having hurt her husband and the relief afforded by his departure, Harriet folded her hands across her breast. Somewhere, one of the maids was ironing, her soft singing accompanied by the thump and clash of the iron. Down at the road, a dog and a scooter barked together through the roar of a truck climbing the hill; a woman called; a child cried out.

Harriet stared at the ceiling, the physical displacement of her sorrow expanding within her—difficulty of respiration, and an aching in ears and eyes. She wondered if this were, after all, the worst moment of the day, and thought of the scene in the kitchen every morning when the letters came. (It was the butcher who brought the mail from Florence once a day; his small gray delivery car trundled up the drive about eleven o'clock. Occasionally he was late. There was talk with the maids before the bundle was laid down, with the day's meat, on the kitchen table, and there were papers, circulars, letters to be turned over before Harriet could be sure that there was nothing for her. Sometimes there was an envelope with an English stamp, and for a moment anxiety would be replaced by apprehension—for what could now be written that she might want to read?)

She knew she must not weep, and she watched the ceiling with the same impassive face and dry eyes she had turned to her husband in the garden. It seemed to her that the tears were flowing inside her head.

The wheel of her mind turned laboriously on a familiar route, as though a required number of revolutions might set it in easy motion. The ray of sunlight lay flat on the farthest wall, patterned by the vines about the window frame. The house at this hour became a well of greenish light filtered through the color of its shutters. From time to time, a cicada droned from the garden, pressing upon the silence a weight that seemed to seal it completely. The afternoon swung Harriet, immobilized, between sleeping and waking, and slowly closed on the distraction of pain.

When Francis came downstairs, he found Marina preparing to go into the garden.

"It's all right," she told him, lifting her hand a little to check his protest. "I'm going to tie up one or two plants and come straight back." There had been a storm the night before.

He followed her into the garden, feeling rather like a child with whom other children will not play, and who is allowed, for that reason, to trail about after the grown-ups.

Marina put her implements down by a bed of dahlias and drew on a pair of blackened gardening gloves. She knelt to examine the fallen plants, and after a moment looked up at Francis, shielding her eyes from the sun with her gloved hand. "The sticks," she said. "Would you mind? In the shed at the back of the house. But not the short ones," she called as he turned away. "The long ones, in the corner near the door."

Francis walked down the path, the sun pressing on his head and shoulders. The dim shed, smelling of earth and fertilizers, was cool after the garden. In the corner near the door were a hoe, a rake, a stack of pots, and an encrusted trowel. The only sticks he could find, on a shelf, were too short for Marina's purpose, but after a hasty search in the half darkness he took them back into the garden.

Marina did not hear him return, and he stood looking at her as she bent over the plants. All her actions were complete and reassuring, all her attitudes graceful and yielding. As she worked, she watched her own hands with a reflective smile, and her hair fell forward across her cheek and swung with the movements of her arms. It occurred to Francis that he had never been so close to beauty. His need for deliverance, for human comfort, was so great that for a moment he thought he had actually taken Marina in his arms, and could feel under his fingers the worn material of her dress and the delicate bones of her shoulders.

"Oh, Marina." He fell on his knees beside her, his hands still full of the sticks from the shed. "Marina."

She looked up abruptly. Kneeling, they stared at each other.

His eyes dazzled. He lifted his closed hands. "I could only find the small sticks."

She was very pale. For an instant, he could imagine how she might look if she were ever to lose her composure.

She sat back on her heels. "They must be there," she said. "I'll go and look." She got up and left him on his knees on the grass, his hands extended and full of short, blunt sticks.

Mr. Fenwick, at his window, was relieved to see the young man get up and come inside; the sun was downright dangerous. Surely the summer should be over by now, even here, he expostulated to himself. He would have expostulated to Mrs. Fenwick, but a deep, regular breathing from the bed promised him little response. She had taken off her shoes and lain down to sleep, with a scented handkerchief on her forehead, as soon as they came upstairs from lunch. But Mr. Fenwick maintained, at the window, something approaching a vigil, holding his book (Trollope: *Phineas Finn*) firmly on his knee. Someone must, after all, keep their wits about them.

When he saw Francis leave the garden, Daniele closed and latched his shutters and sat down in an armchair. He propped his feet on the end of the bed and laid his open book (Ausonius: *Mosella*) upside down in his lap.

Marina asks for this, he told himself—invites confidences, implies sympathy, and then isn't prepared to go through with it. She is as incapable of living, of truly living, as I, he conceded—with a suggestion of high praise. She likes to preside serenely over the emotions of others, but she doesn't care to participate. And those who do participate seem shrill or untidy by comparison.

This wave of resentment, subsiding, was replaced by an image, as true as if he had risen to confirm it from the window, of Marina alone in the garden in the heat, patiently restoring the dahlias.

Still, he continued to himself (effortlessly, because he considered these things almost every afternoon), we *are* unreal. We shall never do anything now except go on here, feeling the extent of our losses. We've been obsolete since . . . (Here he left in his mind the row of dots that stood for Fascism, the war, debts, the last illness of his father, the death of Marina's husband, who had had a heart attack in 1949 while hanging a painting in his house in Milan—matters now too familiar to cause pain or merit reiteration.)

On the other hand, he concluded, Harriet and Francis—exasperating as they may be at the moment—are *real*. He pictured Harriet intrepidly hailing a London bus or standing in a crowded room with a glass in her hand. (He himself never entered a shop or made a new acquaintance without reluctance and apprehension.) And there was something admirable about being close enough to love to be able to quarrel over it. The thought of Harriet, now, lying tormented on her bed—crying, possibly—because of love, filled him with wonder and envy.

He turned his book over and switched on the lamp at his side.

Lying on her back with her eyes closed, Harriet reached out her arm for the little traveling clock, lifted it onto her chest, and held it there, too sleepy to look at it. It rose and fell on her breastbone for a few moments, and then tumbled forward with a glassy slap.

Raising the clock before her face, she opened her eyes. "Five past four," she announced. She put the clock back on the table and looked about the room. On the wall, the sunlight seemed less certain now, the design of leaves a little blurred. "Yes?" she called, in answer to a knock on her door.

Marina came into the room and leaned on the high brass rail at the end of the bed. Harriet once again had the sensation of being treated as an invalid, and sat up, cross-legged, smoothing her skirt over her knees. "You've changed your dress," she said.

"I got muddy from gardening," Marina explained.

"You shouldn't have gone out in the sun," Harriet said, with satisfaction.

"It did me no harm. Did you sleep? I came to ask if you would come down for tea." Tea, unexpectedly, was always precisely that—thin, hot tea in chipped cups, uncompromised by cakes or biscuits.

"Is it really time for tea?" Harriet glanced again at the clock. "I thought the afternoon would never end. Didn't you?"

Marina straightened her back and smiled. "Every afternoon of the summer, I have serious doubts of the evening," she said. "No amount of repetition reassures me." She released the brass bar of the bed. "I must go and see if Daniele wants tea."

Harriet lowered a foot to the floor, feeling for her sandals, and promised to come downstairs. But as the door closed, she crossed the room and, resting her hands on the window sill, looked again into the garden. The light was the easier light of late afternoon. Farther along the wall, between the columns of the loggia, geraniums were fluttered by a faint breeze. On a nearby hill, a bell was rung—an unmelodious, useful country bell. Two little barefoot girls in faded pink dresses and straw hats were carrying to the kitchen a basket of zucchini for the evening meal. Each held a handle, and the tilting basket was covered by the golden flowers of the plant; these would be fried tomorrow for the lunch table.

Harriet turned to the mirror, where a face glimmered in the glass, shadowed by tousled hair. She would go and look for Francis, with some atoning suggestion for a walk together. Oppressed by obligation, she leaned her elbows on the bureau and heard him calling her somewhere in the house. Inaudibly and mechanically, she answered him. "Yes, dear."

The endearment was disconcertingly sharp, but she looked again into the glass and, as his steps drew near, slowly began to comb her hair.

Mrs. Fenwick stirred, lifted the handkerchief from her brow, and wondered where she was. At the window, the pages of *Phineas Finn* slipping under his fingers, Mr. Fenwick closed his eyes and slept.

PEOPLE IN GLASS HOUSES

NOTHING IN EXCESS

T he aim of the Organization," Mr. Bekkus dictated, leaning back in his chair and casting up his eyes to the perforations of the sound-proof ceiling; "The *aim* of the Organization," he repeated with emphasis, as though he were directing a firing-squad—and then, "the *long-range* aim," narrowing his eyes to this more distant target, "is to fully utilize the resources of the staff and hopefully by the end of the fiscal year to have laid stress—"

Mr. Bekkus frequently misused the word "hopefully." He also made a point of saying "locate" instead of "find," "utilize" instead of "use," and never lost an opportunity to indicate or communicate; and would slip in a "basically" when he felt unsure of his ground.

"—to have laid greater stress upon the capacities of certain members of the staff at present in junior positions. Since this bears heavily"—Mr. Bekkus now leaned forward and rested his elbows firmly on his frayed blue blotter—"on the nature of our future work force, attention is drawn to the Director-General's directive set out in (give the document symbol here, Germaine), asking that Personnel Officers communicate the names of staff members having—what was the wording there?" He reached for a mimeographed paper in his tray.

"Imagination," Germaine supplied.

"—imagination and abilities which could be utilized in more responsible posts." Mr. Bekkus stopped again. "Where's Swoboda?"

"He went to deposit your paycheck, Mr. Bekkus."

"Well, when he comes in tell him I need the figures he's been preparing. Better leave a space at the end, then, for numbers of vacant posts. New paragraph. Candidates should be recommended solely on the basis of outstanding personal attributes, bearing in mind the basic qualifications of an international civil servant as set forth in Part II (that's roman, Germaine) of the Staff Regulations with due regard to education, years of service, age, and administrative ability. Read that back. . . . All right. We'll set up the breakdown when Swoboda comes across with the figures. Just bang that out, then—copies all round." Mr. Bekkus was always saying "Bang this out" or "Dash that off" in a way that somehow minimized Germaine's role and suggested that her job was not only unexacting but even jolly.

"Yes, Mr. Bekkus." Germaine had closed her book and was searching for her extra pencil among the papers on the desk.

"You see how it is, Germaine," said Mr. Bekkus, again leaning back in the tiny office as if he owned it all. "The Director-General is loosening things up, wants people who have ideas, individuality, not the run-of-the-mill civil servants we've been getting round here." His gesture was apparently directed toward the outer office, which Germaine shared with Swoboda, the clerk. "Not just people who fit in with the requirements. And he's prepared to *relax* the requirements in order to get them."

Germaine wrinkled her forehead. "But you did say." She turned up her notes again.

"What did I say?" asked Mr. Bekkus, turning faintly hostile.

"Here. Where it says about due regard."

"Ah—the necessary qualifications. My dear girl, we have to talk in terms of suitable candidates. You can't take on just anybody. You wouldn't suggest that we promote people merely to be kind to them?" Since Germaine looked for a moment as if she might conceivably make such a suggestion, he added belligerently, "Would you?"

"Oh—no." And, having found her pencil under the Daily List of Official Documents, she added, "Here it is."

"Why, these are the elementary qualifications in any organization today." Holding up one hand, he enumerated them on his outstretched fingers. "University education"—Mr. Bekkus would have been the last to minimize the importance of this in view of the years it had taken him to wrest his own degree in business administration from a reluctant provincial college. "Administrative ability. Output. Responsibility. And leadership potential." Having come to the end of his fingers, he appeared to dismiss the possibility of additional requirements; he had in some way contrived to make them all sound like the same thing.

"I'll leave a blank then," said Germaine. "At the end of the page." She tucked her pencil in the flap of her book and left the room.

Stupid little thing, Mr. Bekkus thought indulgently—even, perhaps, companionably. Germaine at any rate need not disturb herself about the new directive: she was lucky to be in the Organization at all. This was the way Mr. Bekkus felt about any number of his colleagues.

"Yes, come in, Swoboda. Good. Sit down, will you, and we'll go over these. I've drafted a memo for the Section Chief to sign."

Swoboda pulled up a chair to the corner of the desk. Swoboda was in his late thirties, slender, Slavic, with a nervous manner but quiet eyes and still hands. Having emerged from Europe after the war as a displaced person, Swoboda had no national standing and had been hired as a clerk by the Organization in its earliest days. As a local recruit he had a lower salary, fewer privileges, and a less interesting occupation than the internationally recruited members of the staff, but in 1947 he had counted himself fortunate to get a job at all. This sense of good fortune had sustained him for some time; it is possible, however, that after more than twenty years at approximately the same rank it was at last beginning to desert him.

Bekkus wanted to be fair. Swoboda made him uneasy, but Bekkus would have admitted that Swoboda could turn in good work under proper supervision. Mr. Bekkus flattered himself (as he correctly expressed it) that he had supervised Swoboda pretty thoroughly during the time he had had him in his office—had organized him, in fact, for the maximum potential. Still, Swoboda made him uneasy, for there was something withdrawn about him, something that could not be brought out under proper supervision or even at the Christmas party. Bekkus would have said that Swoboda did not fully communicate.

But Bekkus wanted to be fair. Swoboda was a conscientious staff member, and the calculations he now laid on the corner of the desk represented a great deal of disagreeable work—work which Bekkus freely, though silently, admitted he would not have cared to do himself.

Bekkus lifted the first page. "All right. And did you break down the turnover?"

"Here, sir. The number of posts vacated each year in various grades."

Bekkus glanced down a list headed Resignations and Retirement. "Good God, is that all? Is this the total? How can we fit new people in if hardly anyone leaves?"

"You're looking at the sub-total. If you'll allow me." Swoboda turned the page to another heading: Deaths and Dismissals.

"That's more like it," said Bekkus with relief. "This means that we can move about fifty people up each year from the Subsidiary into the Specialized grades." (The staff was divided into these two categories, and there had been little advancement from the Subsidiary to the Specialized. Those few who had in fact managed to get promoted from the lower category were viewed by their new colleagues much as an emancipated slave must have been regarded in ancient Rome by those born free.)

"The trouble, of course," went on Bekkus, "is to find capable people on the existing staff. You know what the plan is, Swoboda. The D.-G. wants us to comb the Organization, to comb it thoroughly"—Bekkus made a gesture of grooming some immense shaggy animal—"for staff members of real ability in both categories who've been passed over, keep an eye open for initiative, that kind of thing. These people—these staff members, that is—have resources which have not been fully utilized, and which *can* be utilized, Swoboda . . ." Mr. Bekkus paused, for Swoboda was looking at him with more interest and feeling than usual, then pulled himself together and added, "within the existing framework." The feeling and interest passed from Swoboda's expression and left no trace.

Bekkus handed back the tables. "If you'll get Germaine to stick this in at the foot of the memo, I think we're all set. And then bring me the file on Wyatt, will you? That's A. Wyatt, in the Translation Section. I have to take it to the Board. It's a case for compulsory retirement."

"Got one." Algie Wyatt underlined a phrase on the page before him.

"What?" asked Lidia Korabetski, looking up from the passage she was translating.

"Contradiction in terms." Algie was collecting contradictions in terms: to a nucleus of "military intelligence" and "competent authorities" he had added such discoveries as the soul of efficiency, easy virtue, enlightened self-interest, Bankers Trust, and Christian Scientist.

"What?" Lidia asked again.

"*Cultural mission*," replied Algie, turning the page and looking encouraged, as if he studied the document solely for such rewards as this.

Lidia and Algie were translators at the Organization. That is to say that they sat all day—with an hour off for lunch and breaks for tea—at their desks translating Organization documents out of one of the five official languages and into another. Lidia, who had been brought up in France of Russian and English parentage, translated into French from English and Russian; Algie, who was British and had lived much abroad, translated into English from French and Spanish. They made written translations only, the greater drama of the oral interpretation of debates being reserved for the Organization's simultaneous interpreters. The documents Algie and Lidia translated contained the records of meetings, the recommendations of councils, the reports of committees, the minutes of working groups, and were not at all noted for economy or felicity of phrase. However, both Algie and Lidia were resourceful with words and sought to convey the purport of these documents in a faithful and unpretentious manner.

In the several years during which Lidia and Algie had shared an office at the Organization, it had often been remarked that they made an odd pair. This is frequently said of two people whose personalities are ideally complementary, as was the case in this instance. It was also commonly agreed that there was no romance between them—as is often said where there is nothing but romance, pure romance, romance only, with no distracting facts of any kind.

When Lidia first came to share his office, Algie was about fifty-five years old. He was an immense man, of great height and bulky body, whose scarlet face and slightly bloodshot blue eyes proclaimed him something of a drinker. His health having suffered in the exercise of a great capacity for life, he shifted himself about with a heaving, shambling walk and was breathless after the least exertion. When he entered the office in the morning he would stand for some seconds over his desk, apparently exhausted by the efforts, physical and mental, involved in his having arrived there. He would then let himself down, first bulging outward like a gutted building, then folding in the middle before collapsing into his gray Organization chair. For a while he would sit there, speechless and crimson-faced and heaving like a gong-tormented sea.

Although education and upbringing had prepared him for everything except the necessity of earning his own living, this was by no means Algie's first job. During the thirties he had worked for the Foreign Office in the Balkans, but resigned in order to go to Spain as a correspondent during the Civil War. He spent most of the Second World War as an intelligence officer with the British Army in North Africa and during this time produced a creditable study on Roman remains in Libya and a highly useful Arabic phrase-book for British soldiers. After the war, his private income having dwindled to almost nothing, he entered the Organization in a dramatic escape from a possible career in the world of commerce.

It was not known how Algie came to apply to the Organization; still less how the Organization came to admit him. (It was said that his dossier had become confused with that of an eligible Malayan named Wai-lat, whose application had been unaccountably rejected.) Once in, Algie did the work required of him, overcoming a natural indolence that would have crushed other men. But he and the Organization were incompatible, and should never have been mated.

The Organization had bred, out of a staff recruited from its hundred member nations, a peculiarly anonymous variety of public official, of recognizable aspect and manner. It is a type to be seen to this very day, anxiously carrying a full brief case or fumbling for a *laissez-passer* in airports throughout the world. In tribute to the leveling powers of Organization life, it may be said that a staff member wearing a sari or *kente* was as recognizable as one in a dark suit, and that the face below the fez was as nervously, as conscientiously Organizational as that beneath the Borsalino. The nature—what Mr. Bekkus would have called the "aim"—of the Organization was such as to attract people of character; having attracted them, it found it could not afford them, that there was no room for personalities, and that its hope for survival lay, like that of all organizations, in the subordination of individual gifts to general procedures. No new country, no new language or way of life, no marriage or involvement in war could have so effectively altered and unified the way in which these people presented themselves to the world. It was this process of subordination that was to be seen going on beneath the homburg or turban. And it was Algie's inability to submit to this process that had delivered his dossier into the hands of Mr. Bekkus at the Terminations Board.

To Algie it seemed that he was constantly being asked to take leave of those senses of humor, proportion, and the ridiculous that he had carefully nurtured and refined throughout his life. He could not get used to giving, with a straight face, a continual account of himself; nor could he regard as valid a system of judging a person's usefulness by the extent of his passion for detail. He found himself in a world that required laborious explanation of matters whose very meaning, in his view, depended on their being tacitly understood. His idiosyncrasy, his unpunctuality, his persistence in crediting his superiors with precisely that intuition they lacked and envied, were almost as unwelcome at the Organization as they would have been in the commercial world. He was, in short, an exception: that very thing for which organizations make so little allowance.

Sometimes as Algie sat there in the mornings getting back his breath, Lidia would tell him where she had been the previous evening, what she had been reading or listening to, some detail that would fill the gap since they had left the office the night before. When she did not provide these clues, it usually meant that she had been seeing a lover. She would never have mentioned such a thing to Algie, because of the romance between them.

Like many of the women who worked at the Organization, Lidia was

unmarried. Unlike them, she remained so by her own choice. Years before, she had been married to an official of the Organization who had died
on his way to a regional meeting of the Global Health Commission in
La Paz. (His car had overturned on a mountain road, and it was thought
that he, like many of the delegates to the Commission, had been affected
by the altitude.) Lidia had loved this husband. For some time after his
death she kept to herself, and, even when this ceased to be the case,
showed no inclination to remarry. She was admired by her male colleagues and much in demand as a companion, being fair-haired, slender,
and not given to discussing her work out of office hours.

"Mustn't forget," Algie now said. "Got an appointment at two-thirty.
Chap called Bekkus in Personnel."

Lidia gave an absent-minded groan. "Bekkus. Dreary man."

"A bit boring." This was the strongest criticism Algie had ever been
known to make of any of his colleagues.

"Boring isn't the word," said Lidia, although it was. She became more
attentive. "Isn't he on the Appointments and Terminations Board?"

"What's that?"

"Committee for improving our caliber."

Algie quoted:

> *"Improvement too, the idol of the age,*
> *Is fed with many a victim."*

There was nothing Algie enjoyed more than the apt quotation,
whether delivered by himself or another. It gave him a momentary sensation that the world had come right; that some instant of perfect harmony
had been achieved by two minds meeting, possibly across centuries. His
own sources, fed by fifty years of wide and joyous reading, were in this
respect inexhaustible. He had an unfashionable affection, too, for those
poets whom he regarded as his contemporaries—Belloc, Chesterton, de
la Mare—and would occasionally look up from his work (the reader will
have gathered that looking up from his work was one of Algie's most pronounced mannerisms) to announce that "Don John of Austria is gone by
Alcalar," or to ask "Do you remember an Inn, Miranda?"

From all of which it will readily be seen why Algie's file was in the hands of Mr. Bekkus and why Algie was not considered suitable for continued employment at the Organization. It may also be seen, however, that Algie's resources were of the kind never yet fully utilized by organization or mankind.

"Yes, here it is." Lidia had unearthed a printed list from a yellowing stack of papers on the heating equipment beside her. "R. Bekkus. Appointments and Terminations Board."

"Well, I've *been* appointed," Algie remarked, pushing his work away completely and preparing to rise to his feet, "so perhaps it's the other thing." He pressed his hands on the desk, heaved himself up, and presently shambled off into the corridor.

Lidia went on with her work, and for fifteen minutes there was silence in the office she shared with Algie. It was a room typical of offices throughout the Organization—gray-walled, like that of Mr. Bekkus, and floored with rubber tiles of a darker gray. Panels of fluorescent lighting were let into the white soundproofing that covered the ceiling. A wide low window sill was formed by the metal covers of the radiators, and along this ledge at various intervals were stacked small sheaves of papers—the lower ones yellowing, the upper ones filmed with the grit that found its way through the aluminum window frames. (In each office the heating could be adjusted to some extent, so that in all the rooms of the Organization its international character was manifest in temperatures that ranged from nostalgic approximations of the North Sea to torrid renderings of conditions along the Zambesi.) Algie's and Lidia's desks were pushed together, facing one another, and each had a gray chair upholstered in dark blue. Blue blotters were centered on the desks and surrounded by trays of papers, black desk-sets, stapling machines, and dishes of paper clips—and, in Lidia's case, a philodendron in a cracked ceramic *cache-pot*. On each desk there was also a telephone and a small engagement pad on a metal fixture. There was a typewriter in one corner of the room, and a bookcase—into whose upper shelves dictionaries and bound documents had been crammed—stood with its back to the wall. On the lowest shelf of this bookcase were a pair of galoshes, a watering can, an unwashed glass vase, a Wedgwood cup and saucer, three cafeteria spoons, and a single black glove.

On one wall, a calendar—the gift of a Japanese travel concern—was turned to the appropriate month (this was not always the case in Organization offices), displaying a colorful plate which bore, to Algie's delight, the legend "Gorgeous bunch of blooming peonies."

From the windows, which were vast and clean, one looked on to a wide river and to its industrial banks beyond. The presence of the river was refreshing, although it carried almost continuously the water traffic—coal and railway barges, tugs, tankers, and cargo vessels—of the great city in which the Organization was laid. Oceans and rivers with their simple and traditional associations of purification and continuity are excellent things to have outside office windows, and in this case helped in some measure to express that much misrepresented, highly commendable, and largely unachieved thing—the aim of the Organization.

"Some bad news, I'm afraid." Tong put his head round Lidia Korabetski's door—this was literally true, since Tong's small neat head and long neck were all of him that showed. Tong was beaming. "Some bad news, yes." Not naturally malicious, he had developed rapidly since entering bureaucracy.

Lidia, lifting her head, could not help asking, "What is it?"

"Wyatt at lunch?" Tong nodded toward Algie's empty desk.

"He's been back from lunch for ages," said Lidia defensively. Lunch at the Organization was officially one hour, and Algie was often overdue.

"They're not renewing his contract."

"What contract?"

"His Permanent Contract, of course." Permanence, at the Organization, was viewed in blocks of five years, and a Permanent Contract was subject to quinquennial review. "The Terminations Board decided against renewing. They're going to let him retire early instead."

"But he doesn't want to retire early. How unfair."

"Another sort of place would have fired him."

"And *another* sort of place would have promoted him."

"Look—I like him too—everyone likes him—but there's a limit." Limits were often proudly cited at the Organization.

Lidia took up her pencil again. "He's a good translator."

"Well—that's an opinion I never went along with. We worked together once, you know—on the Preliminary Survey of Intolerance. I had to correct him repeatedly."

Lidia raised her eyebrows, but merely asked, "Do you get full pension if you're retired before time?"

"Wouldn't be a bit surprised if he ends up better off than we do."

"Oh, come."

"Well, at least they're not firing him. They're being decent. That's one thing you can say for the Organization. They're decent about this sort of thing. They wouldn't fire him."

"He'd get more money if they did." (Certain indemnities were involved in the rupture of Permanence.) Lidia put her head back down to her work. "I've got to get on with this."

Tong, passing Algie coming from the elevators, raised his hand in cordial greeting. "All O.K. with you, I hope, Wyatt?" (Tong was a man who could reverse himself in this way.)

"Splendid," grunted Algie. (Algie was a man who could grunt such a word.) He went slowly along the corridor to the office he shared with Lidia.

An odd pair, Tong thought. He still had not told the news about Algie to his friend Pike in Inland Waterways on the floor below. Rather than wait for the elevator, he opened a dangerously heavy door marked "Sortie de Secours" and ran down the emergency stairs.

"Tong was here," Lidia said.

"Saw him in the corridor." Algie let himself into his chair. "Tong," he mused. "The very word is like a bell."

Lidia had no way of telling whether Algie had been informed that he was to be retired early. She would have liked to make him some show of solidarity but could only offer him a peppermint, which he refused.

"You free for lunch tomorrow?" she asked—Algie's telegraphic manner of communication having rubbed off on her to some extent.

"Tomorrow—what's tomorrow?" Algie turned several pages of his desk calendar. "Sorry, no. Lunching with Jaspersen. Could change it, perhaps?"

"No, no," said Lidia hastily, for Jaspersen was the one friend of Algie's who held an influential position in the Organization. "Some other day."

"Better make it soon," remarked Algie—from which Lidia realized that he knew his fate.

They went on with their work in silence for some moments. Then Algie let out a snort of laughter. "Listen to this. Chap here got it in a nutshell: *'In the year under review, assistance was rendered to sixty differing countries.'*"

Olaf Jaspersen was a year younger than Algie Wyatt and had been at Cambridge with him. People found this hard to believe, for Jaspersen was lean and fleet, his eye was clear, his features youthful. He wore dark, well-cut clothes during the week, and tweeds on Saturday mornings—which he invariably spent at the office. He had joined the Organization shortly after Algie. From the first he had been given important responsibilities, which he handled with efficiency and charm. He now held one of the most senior posts in the Organization and had established a reputation for common sense, justice, and rather more style than was usual. Things seemed to go right with Jaspersen. His career was prospering, his wife was beautiful, his children intelligent; he had even come into a small inheritance lately.

But something had happened to Olaf Jaspersen in recent years. He had fallen in love.

He had fallen in love with the Organization. Like someone who for a long time enjoys the friendship of a beautiful woman but boasts that he would not dream of having an affair with her, he had been conquered all the more completely in the end. During his early years on the staff, he had maintained his outside interests, his social pleasures—the books he read for nothing but enjoyment, the conversations he had that bore no apparent relation to his Organization duties. This state of affairs had flagged, diminished, then altogether ceased to be the case. He was still an able man, but his concept of ability had been colored by Organization requirements; he found it harder to believe in the existence of abilities that did not directly contribute to the aim of the Organization. He was still, on occasion, gay—but his wit now sprang exclusively from Organization sources and could only be enjoyed by those in the Organizational know (of whom, fortunately for this purpose, his acquaintance had come to be principally composed). He had joined the staff because he believed sincerely, even passionately, in the importance of the Organization; that importance had latterly become indistinguishable from his own. He held, no doubt correctly, that the dissolution of the Organization would be calamitous for the human race; but one felt that the survival of the human race, should the Organization fail, would be regarded by him as a piece of downright impertinence.

Algie liked Olaf Jaspersen. He admired his many good qualities, including those gifts of energy and application which had not been bestowed upon himself. Algie's youthful memories of a lighter, livelier Jaspersen contributed to the place of the present Jaspersen in his affections. Jaspersen, in turn, had recollections of an Algie full of fun and promise, and regretted that the fun had increased in inverse ratio to the promise.

If his loyalty to Algie was in part due to Algie's never having rivaled him professionally, this was a common human weakness and need not be held against him. Jaspersen was genuinely grieved when he learned that Algie was to be retired before time, and genuinely wished to assist him. He therefore came to their lunch appointment prepared to give good advice.

The staff of the Organization took their meals in either of two places: a large and noisy cafeteria where they stood in line, or a large and noisy dining room where they could—at additional cost—be served. The food, which was plain and good, was substantially the same in both places, although it may be said that in the dining room the plates were slightly lighter and the forks slightly heavier. It was to the dining room that Olaf Jaspersen took Algie for lunch this day.

Jaspersen, a man of too much taste to adopt the line of "Well now, what's this I hear?," found it difficult to raise with Algie the delicate question of enforced resignation. In Jaspersen's view, expulsion from the Organization was a very serious matter—more serious, one might even have said, than it was to Algie himself. When Algie and he were settled with their Scotches and had ordered their respective portions of codfish cakes and chicken à la king, he bent toward Algie. "A bad development," he said. "Can't tell you how sorry."

"Ah well," said Algie, "not to worry." He gave Jaspersen an appreciative nod, and went on with his drink, which he had already gone on with quite a bit.

"Rolls?" asked the waitress, wheeling up a portable oven.

"Er—one of those," Jaspersen said.

Putting it on his plate, she identified it with the words, "Corn muffin."

"Mistake," said Algie. "Nothing but crumbs."

"Look here, Algie, I know these fellows—on the Board, I mean. Not bad chaps—not villainous, nothing like that—but slow. Not overloaded with ideas. Only understand what's put in front of 'em. Got to be played their way or they can't grasp, you know."

"Ah well," said Algie again, briskly setting down his glass as if to herald a change of subject.

"Let me get you another one of those. My point is—in order to handle these chaps, you've got to get inside their minds. Talk their language." He fished a pamphlet out of his pocket. "I brought this for you. It's the Procedure of Appeal." He began to hand it across the table, but at that moment the waitress came up with their lunch.

"Codfish cakes?"

"Here," said Algie, making room. He took the pamphlet from Jaspersen and laid it on the table beside his plate. His second drink arrived, and Jaspersen ordered half a bottle of white wine.

"The Board," Jaspersen went on, spearing a cube of chicken, "is not the ultimate authority. That Bekkus is just a glorified clerk."

"Point is," Algie observed, "he *has* been glorified."

"I've been thinking about your case," said Jaspersen, "and I don't see how you could lose an appeal. I honestly don't. But get moving on it immediately—you don't have a moment to waste."

"What year is this?" inquired Algie, turning the bottle round. "Not at all bad." When he had demolished the first codfish cake, he said, "It's good of you, Olaf. But I'm not going to appeal."

Jaspersen looked less surprised than might have been expected. "Think it over" was all he said.

"No," Algie said. "Really. Better this way."

After a pause, Jaspersen went on kindly. "You have, of course, exactly the sort of qualities the Organization can't cope with. With the Organization it has to be—moderation in all things. I sometimes think we should put up in the main lobby that inscription the Greeks used in their temple: 'Nothing in Excess.'" Jaspersen was pleased to have hit on this reconciliation of Algie's virtues with those of the Organization, for Algie was generally a pushover for the Greeks.

Algie finished another codfish cake and drank his wine, but when he replied Jaspersen was startled by the energy in his voice.

"Nothing in excess," Algie repeated. "But one has to understand the meaning of excess. Why should it be taken, as it seems to be these days, to refer simply to self-indulgence, or violence—or enjoyment? Wasn't it intended, don't you think, to refer to all excesses—excess of pettiness, of timorousness, of officiousness, of sententiousness, of censoriousness? Excess of stinginess or rancor? Excess of bores?" Algie went back to his vegetables for a while, and Jaspersen was again surprised when he continued. "At the other end of that temple, there was a second inscription—'Know Thyself.' Didn't mean—d'you think—that we should be mesmerized by every pettifogging detail of our composition. Meant we should understand ourselves in order to be free." Algie laid down his knife and fork and pushed away his plate. He handed back to Jaspersen the Procedure of Appeal. "No thanks old boy, really. Fact is, I'm not suited to it here, and from that point of view these chaps are right. You tell me to get inside their minds—but if I did that I might never find my way out again."

"But Algie, what about your pension? Think of the risk, at your age."

"I do get something, you know—a reduced pension, or a lump sum. And then—for someone like me, the real risk is to stay."

After that, they talked of other things. But Jaspersen felt disturbed and sad, and his sadness was greater than he could reasonably account for.

Lidia was coming down in the elevator when Millicent Bass got in. Lidia, on her way to the cafeteria, was pressed between a saintly Indian from Political Settlements (a department high on Algie's list of contradictions in terms) and Swoboda from Personnel, who greeted her in Russian. Behind her were two young Africans, speaking French and dressed in Italian suits, a genial roly-poly Iranian, and a Paraguayan called Martinez-MacIntosh with a ginger moustache. In front of her was a young girl from the Filing Room, who stood in silence with her head bowed. Her pale hair, inefficiently swept upward, was secured by a plastic clip, so that Lidia had a close view of her slender, somewhat pathetic neck and the topmost ridges of her spinal column. The zipper of her orange wool-jersey dress had been incompletely closed, and the single hook above it was undone. Lidia was toying with the idea of drawing this to the girl's attention when the elevator doors opened at the sixteenth floor to admit Millicent Bass.

Miss Bass was a large lady with a certain presence. One felt that she was about to say "This way please"—an impression that was fortified, when the elevator doors disclosed her, by the fact that she was standing, upright and expectant, with a document in her hand. She got in, raking the car as she did so with a hostile stare. Her mouth was firmly set, as if to keep back warmer words than those she habitually spoke, and her protuberant eyes were slightly belligerent, as if repressing tears.

Lidia knew her well, having once worked on a report for which Miss Bass was responsible. This was a Report on the Horizontal Coordination of Community Programs, for Miss Bass was a member of the Department of Social and Anthropological Questions.

"Hello Millicent."

"Haven't seen you for a while, Lidia." Miss Bass squeezed in next to the girl in orange and, as far as she was able to do so, looked Lidia up and down. "You're far too thin," she announced. (She had the unreflective drawl of her profession, a voice loud yet exhausted.)

When the elevator disgorged them at the cafeteria, Miss Bass completed her scrutiny of Lidia. "You spend too much money on clothes."

Lidia was pondering the interesting fact that these two remarks, when reversed ("You are far too fat" and "You should spend more money on clothes"), are socially impermissible, when Millicent took her off guard by suggesting they lunch together. Rather than betray herself by that fractional hesitation which bespeaks dismay, she accepted heartily. Oh God how ghastly, she said to herself, dropping a selection of forks, knives, and spoons loudly onto a tray.

As they pushed their trays along, Millicent Bass inquired, "How much does a dress like that cost?" When Lidia was silent, she went on handsomely, "You don't have to tell me if you don't want to."

I know that, thought Lidia. It's being *asked* that annoys me.

"This all right for you?" Millicent asked her as they seated themselves near the windows. Lidia nodded, looking around and seeing Bekkus deep in conversation with a colleague at the adjacent table. They transferred their dishes from the tray and placed their handbags on a spare chair. Millicent also had her document, much annotated about the margins, which she pushed to the vacant side of the table. "I was going to run through that," she said regretfully. She unfolded a paper napkin in her lap and passed Lidia the salt. "Those codfish cakes look good."

Lidia began her lunch, and they exchanged casual remarks in high voices across the cafeteria din. (While talking with Miss Bass of things one did not particularly care about, one had the sensation of constantly attempting to allay her suspicions of one's true ideas and quite different interests.) Miss Bass then spoke in some detail of a new report she was working on, a survey of drainage in Polynesia. Conditions were distressing. There was much to be done. She gave examples.

"Poor things," Lidia murmured, stoically finishing her meal.

"It's no use saying 'poor things,' Lidia." Miss Bass often took it on herself to dictate the responses of others. "Sentiment doesn't help. What's needed is know-how."

Lidia was silent, believing that even drains cannot supplant human feeling.

"The trouble with you, Lidia, is that you respond emotionally, not pragmatically. It's a device to retain the sense of patronage. Unconscious, of course. You don't think of people like these as your *brothers*." Miss Bass was one of those who find it easy and even gratifying to direct fraternal feelings toward large numbers of people living at great distances. Her own brother—who was shiftless and sometimes tried to borrow money from her—she had not seen for over a year. "You don't relate to them as individuals." In Miss Bass's mouth the very word "individuals" denoted legions.

Lidia, casting about for a diversion, was softened to see that Mr. Bekkus had brought out photographs of what appeared to be a small child and was showing them to his companion.

"Who *is* that man?" Millicent asked. "I've seen him around for years."

"Bekkus, from Personnel." Lidia lowered her voice. "He's on the Appointments and Terminations Board."

"My baby verbalizes," Bekkus was saying to his colleague. "Just learning to verbalize."

"Speaking of which," Millicent went on, "I hear you're losing your friend."

Lidia hesitated, then dug her spoon into her *crème caramel*. "You mean Algie."

"Well, there's a limit after all," Miss Bass said, sensing resistance.

"I'll miss him."

Miss Bass was not to be repulsed. "He is impossible."

Lidia laughed. "When people say that about Algie, it always reminds me of Bakunin."

"One of the new translators?" asked Miss Bass, running through the names of the Russian Section in her mind.

"No, no. I mean the Russian revolutionary."

"He a friend of Algie's?" Millicent inquired—sharply, for politics were forbidden to the Organization staff, and a direct affiliation with them was one of the few infallible means of obtaining summary dismissal.

"He died a century ago."

"What's he got to do with Algie?" Miss Bass was still suspicious.

"Oh—he was a big untidy man, and he once said—when someone told him he was impossible—'I shall continue to be impossible so long as those who are now possible remain possible.'"

Millicent was not amused. "The Organization cannot afford Algie Wyatt."

"He's a luxury," Lidia admitted.

"Pleasure-loving," said Miss Bass, as if this were something unnatural.

"Yes," Lidia agreed.

"And always trying to be clever."

"That's right," said Lidia.

"I'd prefer a more serious attitude," said Miss Bass. And it was true; she actually would.

Lidia held her spoon poised for a moment and said seriously, "Millicent, please don't go on about Algie. I don't like it."

Millicent's only idea of dignity was standing on it, and she did this for some minutes. Soon, however, she forgot what had been said and inquired about the terms of Algie's retirement.

"I really don't know anything about it." Lidia dropped her crumpled napkin on her plate.

"He has a choice, I believe—a reduced pension or a lump sum. That's the arrangement for enforced resignation."

"I don't *know*," said Lidia. "Shall we go?"

When they left the cafeteria, they walked along together to the elevators.

"Now I hope you won't think me hard," Miss Bass was beginning, when the elevator arrived—fortunately, perhaps, for her aspiration.

Algie was sitting at his desk when Lidia entered the office. They smiled at each other, and when she was seated at her desk, Lidia asked, "Did you have a nice time with Jaspersen?"

"Splendid," grunted Algie, going on with his work. He added, for once without looking up, "Wanted me to appeal my case. Shan't do it, though."

"Perhaps you ought to think about it?"

Algie shook his head, still writing. A little later he murmured aloud, "Never more, Miranda. Never more."

"Algie," Lidia said, putting down her pencil. "What do you think you'll do, then? Take a reduced pension?"

Now Algie did look up, but kept his pencil in his hand. "No. No. Take my lump sum and look for a small house somewhere along the Mediterranean. In the south of Spain, perhaps. Málaga, or Torremolinos. Good climate, some things still fairly cheap."

"Do you know anyone there?"

"Someone sure to turn up." He went on with his work for a moment. "Only thing is—it's very dangerous to die in Spain."

"How do you mean?"

"Law insists you be buried within twenty-four hours. Doctors not allowed to open your veins. If you should happen still to be alive, you wake up and find yourself in your coffin. When my time comes, I'm going down to Gibraltar and die in safety. Very dangerous to die in Spain."

"But what if one's really dead?"

Algie looked solemn. "That's a risk you have to take."

Algie died the following year at Torremolinos. He died very suddenly, of a stroke, and had no time to reach safety in Gibraltar. An obituary paragraph of some length appeared in the London *Times*, and a brief notice in the Organization's staff gazette, which misspelled his name. For so large a man, he left few material traces in the world. The slim remnants of his lump sum went to a sixteen-year-old nephew. His book on Roman remains in Libya is being reissued by an English publisher with private means.

Just about the time of Algie's death, Lidia became engaged to a handsome Scotsman in the Political Settlements Department. Although they have since been married, Lidia has kept her job and now shares her office with a Luxembourgeois who seldom looks up from his work and confesses to having no memory for verse. No one mourned the death of Algie more than Olaf Jaspersen, who remarked that he felt as if he had lost a part of himself. Jaspersen has recently attended important conferences abroad, and has taken to coming into the office on Sundays. Millicent Bass is being sent to Africa, and regards this as a challenge; her arrival there is being accepted in the same spirit.

Swoboda has been put forward for a promotion, but has been warned that there may be some delay. Mr. Bekkus has received *his* promotion, though over some objections. He is still combing the Organization, with little success, for unutilized sources of ability and imagination. He continues to dictate letters in his characteristic style, and his baby is now verbalizing fluently along much the same lines.

Algie's last letter to Lidia was written only a few days before he died, but reached her some weeks later, as he had neglected to mark it "*Correo Aéreo.*" In this letter he reported the discovery of several new contradictions in terms and mentioned, among other things, that Piero della Francesca died on the same day that Columbus discovered America, and that there is in Mexico a rat poison called The Last Supper. Such information is hard to come by these days; now that Algie was gone, Lidia could not readily think of another source.

THE FLOWERS OF SORROW

I n my country," the great man said, looking out over hundreds of up-lifted faces, "we have a song that asks, 'Will the flowers of joy ever equal the flowers of sorrow?'"

The speech, up to then, had been the customary exhortation—to uphold the Organization, to apply oneself unsparingly to one's work—and this made for an interesting change. Words like "joy" and, more especially, "sorrow" did not often find their way into that auditorium, and were particularly unlooked-for on Staff Day, when the Organization was at its most impersonal. The lifted faces—faces of a certain fatigued assiduity whose contours, dinted with the pressure of administrative detail, suggested habitual submergence beneath a flow of speeches such as this—responded with a faint, corporate quiver. Members of the staff who had been half sleeping when the words reached them were startled into little delayed actions of surprise, and blew their noses or put on their glasses—to show they had been listening. In the galleries, throats were cleared and legs recrossed. The interpreters' voices hesitated in the earphones, then accelerated to take in this departure from the Director-General's prepared text. "*Les fleurs du chagrin,*" said the pretty girl in Booth No. 2; "*Las flores del dolor,*" said the Spanish interpreter, with a shrug toward his assistant.

The man on the rostrum now repeated the words from the song, in his own language—and apparently for his own satisfaction, since throughout the hall only a few very blond heads nodded comprehendingly. He went on in English. "Perhaps," he said, "perhaps the answer to that question is No." Now there was a long pause. "But we should remember that sorrow does produce flowers of its own. It is a misunderstanding always to look for joy. One's aim, rather, should be to conduct oneself so that one need never compromise one's secret integrity; so that even our sufferings may enrich us—enrich us, perhaps, most of all." He had laid his hand across his mimeographed text, which was open at the last page, and for a moment it seemed that he meant to end the speech there. The précis-writers were still scribbling "our sufferings may enrich us." However, he looked down, shifted his hand, and went on. He thanked them all for continued devotion to their duties in the past year, and for the productivity illustrated by an increased flow of documentation in the five official languages. There would be no salary raise this year for the Subsidiary Category. The Pension Plan was under review by a newly appointed working group, and the proposed life-insurance scheme would be studied by an impartial committee. It was hoped to extend recreational facilities along the lines recommended by the staff representatives. . . . He greatly looked forward to another such meeting with the staff before long.

The speaker stood a few moments with his speech in his hand, inclined his head politely to applause, and withdrew. In the eyes of the world he was a personality—fearless, virtuous, remote—and the ovation continued a little longer without reference to the content of the speech, although some staff members were already filing out and others had begun their complaints while still applauding.

"Scarcely a mention of the proposed change in retirement age." A burly Belgian youth from Forms Control gave a last angry clap as he moved into the aisle. "And not a word about longevity increments." This he said quite fiercely to a Canadian woman, Clelia Kingslake, who had a modest but unique reputation for submitting reports in advance of deadlines.

"That might come under the pension review," she suggested.

"He would have said so. It's just a move to hold the whole thing over for another year." He held the heavy glass exit door for her. The vast hallway into which they passed was brightly lit, and thickly carpeted in a golf-links green. "And what in God's name was all that about flowers?"

They were joined by Mr. Matta from Economic Cooperation. "Yes, what was that?" Mr. Matta, from the Punjab, had a high lilting voice like a Welshman's and often omitted the article. "Has D.-G. gone off his head, I wonder?"

A group passed them heading for the elevators. Someone said violently, ". . . not even on the agenda!"

When they arrived at the escalator leading to the cafeteria, Miss Kingslake asked the two men, "Are you coming up for tea?"

"Maybe later," said the Belgian boy. "Must go back to the office and see what's come in with the afternoon distribution."

"Back to the shop, I'm afraid," said Mr. Matta from Economic Cooperation. "Our workload has reached the point of boiling."

Clelia Kingslake, who had graying hair and a light-gray dress, got on the moving stair alone and went up to the cafeteria.

The cafeteria was full. It usually was—and invariably after a staff meeting. Miss Kingslake joined the queue and when her turn came took a tray from the rack and a fork and spoon from the row of metal boxes. First there was a delay (someone ahead was buying containers of coffee for an entire office—a breach of good faith), and then the line moved along so quickly that she found herself at the cake before she had decided what to have. She would have preferred a single piece of bread with jam, but she had passed the butter and it would have been unthinkable to go back for it. So she took down from the glass shelf what seemed to be the largest piece of cake there. A sweet-faced Spanish woman at the tea counter fixed her up with a cup of boiling water and a tea-bag, and she paid.

She wandered out into the center of the room looking for an empty table. There did not seem to be one, and certainly not one by the windows on the river side. She moved along beside the tables with the unfocused, purposeful step of a sleep-walker. Hot water spilled over into the saucer of her cup.

"Miss Kingslake. Miss Kingslake."

"Oh, Mr. Willoughby."

"I've got a table at the window, if someone hasn't taken it."

"I thought you'd gone to the Field. I heard your assignment to mission went through."

"I leave tomorrow night. But not for Santiago after all. That was changed. Let me have your tray. They're sending me to Kuala Lumpur."

"Thanks, but I'd better not let go. I hadn't heard."

They made their way through to the windows. She balanced her tray on a corner of his table while he cleared it of the cups, plates, and tea-bags discarded by the previous occupants. When he had stacked these on the heating equipment, they sat down.

Claude Willoughby was a spare, fair-haired Anglo-Saxon who resembled nothing so much as a spar of bleached wood washed up on a beach. He was, for so industrious a man, remarkably able. He and Clelia Kingslake had been thrown together in Interim Reports, before her upgrading to Annual Reports and his lateral transfer to the World Commodity Index.

"I might—" he began.

She said at the same moment, "I'm so glad—"

They both said, "I'm sorry."

"You might?" she inquired, squeezing her tea-bag and putting it in the ashtray.

"I was going to say that I might have inquired whether you really wanted to join me. You seemed to be in a trance."

"I was afraid of seeing someone I didn't want to sit with. Instead, what a nice surprise." She took two paper napkins from the metal dispenser on the table, and gave him one.

"You were going to say?" he asked. "Something about being glad?"

"How glad I am, that's all, to see you before you go. I thought you must have left without saying goodbye."

"I've been terribly busy. Forms, clearances, briefing—and of course my replacement hasn't even been appointed. They're holding the post for an African candidate—or so I'm told. And then, at home—you can imagine—all the packing and storing, added to which we've already taken the children out of school." Mr. Willoughby, having four children of school age, was a substantial beneficiary of the Staff Education Grant. "But don't let's get into that. And of course I wouldn't have gone without saying goodbye."

When he had said this, she stared out the window and he turned his head toward the next table, where two officials of the Department of Personnel were getting up from their coffee.

"Shouldn't have said that about the flowers," one of them remarked—a ginger-haired Dutchman in charge of Clerical Deployment. "Unnecessary."

"I should think," agreed his friend, Mr. Andrada from Legal Aspects. "If I may say so, not good for morale."

"Particularly that part about the answer being No."

"Isn't it curious," Mr. Willoughby said to Miss Kingslake, "how uneasy people are made by any show of feeling in official quarters?" He placed his paper napkin under his cup to absorb spilt tea. "I suppose they find it inconsistent. What did you think of those remarks today—I mean, about the flowers?"

Miss Kingslake was still looking out at the broad river and the wasteland of factories on its opposite bank. She held the teacup in both hands, her elbows on the table. "I don't quite know. I think I felt heartened to hear something said merely because it was felt. Something that—wasn't even on the agenda. Still, I did find all that stuff about one's integrity a bit Nordic. After all, it would hardly be possible for most people to get through a working day without compromising their idea of themselves."

"I think he said '*secret* integrity.'" Mr. Willoughby drank his tea. "We can check it tomorrow in the Provisional Verbatim Record."

"I suppose," she conceded, "it would depend on how secret one was prepared to let it become."

The noise in the cafeteria, like that of a great storm, was beyond all possibility of complaint or remedy. It was a noise in some ways restful to staff members from quiet offices, and Clelia Kingslake was one of these. Eating her cake with a fork, resting her cheek on her left hand, she looked quite at ease—more at ease, in fact, than was appropriate to her type.

"You busy at present?" Mr. Willoughby asked her.

"Oh yes," she said. (It was a question which had never in the Organization's history been known to meet with a negative reply.) "We're finishing up the report on Methods of Enforcement."

"How is it this year?"

"A much stronger preamble than the last issue. And some pretty tough recommendations in Appendix III."

Someone leaned over their table. "You using this chair?"

A group of the interpreters had come in. The interpreters were always objects of interest, their work implying an immediacy denied to the rest of the staff. They stacked their manila folders on the heaters and pushed up extra chairs to the table vacated by the officers of Personnel. Two of them went to fetch tea for the entire table. The rest sat down and began to talk loudly, like children let out of the examination room.

"One could see something was coming when he looked up like that."

"*Les fleurs du chagrin* . . . I suppose one could hardly have said *Les fleurs du mal*. . . ."

A Russian came back with a loaded tray. "What are you laughing at?"

One of the English interpreters said, "It would be better not to give us a prepared text at all than to make all these departures from it."

"What did you think of the speech?" Mr. Willoughby asked a white-haired Frenchman who paused to greet him.

"Most interesting." Mr. Raymond-Guiton bowed to Miss Kingslake over his tray. "And particularly well calculated—that interpolation about the flowers."

Miss Kingslake said, "I rather thought that seemed extempore."

Mr. Raymond-Guiton smiled. "Most interesting." The repetition of the remark had the effect of diminishing its significance. He passed on with his tray and disappeared behind a screen of latticed plants.

"Now wasn't it he," Miss Kingslake asked, wrinkling up her brow, "who refused to go to the Bastille Day party because of his aristocratic connections?"

"You're thinking of that fat chap in the Development Section. This one's too well-bred to do a thing like that. Miss Kingslake, shall we go?"

No sooner had they risen from their chairs than two pale girls in short skirts came up with their trays of tea and cake and started to push the empty dishes aside. Miss Kingslake and Mr. Willoughby lost one another briefly in the maze of tables and met again outside the glass doors, in the relative shelter of a magazine stand.

"May I see you to your elevator bank, Miss Kingslake?"

"That would be lovely," she said.

They went down a short flight of steps and walked slowly along a gray-tiled, gray-walled corridor lined with blue doors.

"I wonder," she said, "if we will ever meet again."

"I have been wondering that too," he answered without surprise. "In a place like this there are so many partings and reunions—yet one does find one's way back to the same people again. Rather like those folk dances they organize at Christmas in the Social and Anthropological Department. I feel we shall meet."

They reached a row of elevator doors. Mr. Willoughby pushed the Up button.

She said, as if they were on a railway platform, "Don't wait."

"I really should get back to the office," he said, "and see if my Travel Authorization's come in yet."

"Of course."

"Shall we say goodbye, then?"

"Why yes," she said, but did not say goodbye.

A Down elevator stopped but no one got off. A messenger boy went slowly past wheeling a trolley of stiff brown envelopes.

"Miss Kingslake," Mr. Willoughby said. "Miss Kingslake. Once, in this corridor, I wanted very much to kiss you."

She stood with her back to the gray wall as if she took from it her protective coloring.

He smiled. "We were on our way to the Advisory Commission on Administrative and Budgetary Questions."

Now she smiled too, but sadly, clasping her fingers together over the handle of her bag. This prevented him from taking her hand, and he merely nodded his farewell. She had not spoken at all—he had gone quite a way down the corridor before that occurred to her. He was out of sight by the time the elevator arrived.

"Thirty-seven," she announced, getting in.

Someone touched her shoulder. "So good to see you, Miss Kingslake." It was Mr. Quashie from Archives.

"Oh, Mr. Quashie."

Mr. Quashie, wearing a long, light-colored robe and scrolling a document lightly between his palms, moved up to stand beside her. "I suppose you were at the meeting?"

"I was, yes."

"I thought the D.-G. looked tired." Mr. Quashie stepped aside to let someone get out. "But then—I hadn't seen him since he addressed the staff last Human Dignity Day."

"Nor had I."

"What a job he has. One wonders how anyone stands it. No private life at all. What did you think of the speech, by the way?"

"Quite good. And you?"

"Oh—here's my floor." Mr. Quashie glanced up at the row of lighted numbers. "I didn't hear much of it. We were busy in the office, and I stayed to answer the phones. Getting off, please. Getting off. And then I took the wrong staircase in the conference building. So I only came in at the very end. I was just in time to hear about the flowers, you know. About how we need more flowers of joy."

THE MEETING

J ust before the meeting, which was fixed for three-thirty, Flinders took a walk in the Organization's rose garden. This garden was set in a protected angle of the buildings and looked toward the river. Seagulls—for the river was in reality part of an estuary—swooped over Flinders's head as he crunched up and down the pebbled paths between beds of wintry spikes tagged "Queen Frederika" or "Perfect Peace" or "British Grenadier." About him, plane trees scored the sky and frozen lawns rolled down to the cold river. With the exception of two uniformed guards and a statue ferociously engaged in beating swords into plough-shares, Flinders was the only human figure in sight. The grounds were closed to the public at this season, and the staff were sealed in their narrow cells, intent on the Organization's business.

Enclosed on three sides by the congested streets of a great city, the Organization was nevertheless well laid out in the ample grounds of its foundation-granted land, and stood along the banks of the river with something of the authority that characterizes Wren's buildings on the Thames at Greenwich. Here as at Greenwich the river's edge was faced with a high embankment and bordered, where the lawn ended, by a narrow walk. From this walk one looked across the river to the low-lying labyrinth of docks and factories, surmounted by an immense Frosti-Cola sign. Behind the Organization's back, the skyscrapers of the city rose as abruptly as the Alps, an ascending graph of successful commerce. The setting impressed all newcomers, and still had an effect on even those members of the staff who had been with the Organization since the signing of its Founding Constitution. Flinders, who had spent the past two years in the North African countryside, was all but overwhelmed by it.

A forester and agricultural conservationist, Flinders had been recruited by the Organization two years before to serve as an expert in its Project for the Reforestation of the Temperate Zone. With a single stop here at Headquarters for briefing, he had flown from his home town in Oregon to a still smaller town some hundred miles to the south of the Mediterranean. Now, on his way home with his mission at an end, he was at Headquarters once more in order to report on his work and to be— although the word was yet unknown to him—debriefed.

He had no idea of what he should say at the meeting. He had never attended meetings at all until he got involved with the Organization. His profession had kept him out of offices. His two years in North Africa could not be contained within reportable dimensions in his mind. Throughout his assignment he had, as instructed, sent in quarterly technical reports to his opposite number at Headquarters, a certain Mr. Addison. These Reports on Performance in the Field (an expression which allowed Flinders to fancy himself capering in a meadow) had given a faithful account of his initial surveys, the extent and causes of erosion in the area, the sampling of soils, availability of water, and ultimately the selection and procurement of young trees and the process of their planting.

In addition, he had reported in person, as he was required to do every few weeks, to the Organization's regional office at Tangier. Apart from these trips to the coast, he had lived a solitary life. At El Attara, where the Organization had provided him with a comfortable house, he dealt with the local farmers and landowners, who were cheerful and polite, and with the local officials—who, though less cheerful, treated him well. He kept two servants and a gardener for the overgrown terraces that surrounded his little house. In the evenings he strolled in the medina and drank mint tea in the café, or he stayed at home studying Arabic by an oil lamp. He wore the djellabah—in summer a white one, in winter one of rough brown wool. He learned to walk as the Arabs do, with a long stride designed to cover many miles, and to ride sideways on a donkey when necessary. He drove his jeep to his work in the hills, and sometimes camped at the planting sites for days at a time. At the beginning he was appallingly lonely, and for the first two months crossed off the single days on a Pan American calendar he had tacked up on his bedroom wall. But he was accustomed to an independent, outdoor existence and gradually became absorbed in his work and in the simple life of the town. The silence in the hills, the peace and variety of the countryside pleased him immensely. During his obligatory trips to Tangier, he swam in the ocean, ate French food, bought books and toothpaste, and took out an enigmatic girl named Ivy Vance who worked at the Australian Consulate. When Ivy Vance's tour of duty presently came to an end and she was posted to Manila, Flinders began to postpone even these short trips away from his work.

By the time his mission was over, he had completed not only his own assignment but also that of two other experts, once promised him as assistants, who had never materialized. No mention of this appeared in the communications he received from Mr. Addison; nor did Flinders expect or wish for any. Flinders had no complaint. His salary checks, having been afflicted by some early confusion, were arriving regularly by the second year of his stay: there was nothing to spend money on at El Attara and he saved a useful sum. Also toward the end of his mission he received full instructions for his return journey, and a large envelope containing a Briefing Kit that outlined the work for which he had been engaged and that had been omitted at the outset. Otherwise, all had gone smoothly. Mr. Addison had replied to his letters with reasonable punctuality—five weeks having been the maximum delay—and had run up a creditable score of answers to questions asked. Flinders had no complaint.

Flinders had no complaint. This fact alone, had it been known, would have made him an object of curiosity in the Organization.

Two days before, on his return to Headquarters, he had met Mr. Addison—a singularly small person to have been selected as opposite number to a man as tall as Flinders. Mr. Addison greeted him pleasantly and introduced him to his secretary, to whom Flinders gave, for typing, a sheaf of handwritten pages containing his suggestions for conserving and extending the plantations at El Attara. The tentative inquiries he made of Mr. Addison mostly seemed to fall within the competence of some other authority. Mr. Addison had replied anxiously, "Mr. Rodriguez-O'Hearn will tell you about that," or "That belongs in the province of Mr. Fong," or "You'd better ask Miss Singh in Official Records." And, "Sorry your final check isn't ready. Our accountant is on leave without pay." Otherwise, all had gone smoothly.

Mr. Addison explained to Flinders that he was himself under great pressure of work, at the same time producing a ticket for a guided tour of the building. The secretary to whom Flinders had handed his manuscript then showed him where to take the Down elevator and gave him a yellow slip on which was written the time and place of this afternoon's meeting.

Flinders looked at his watch, and turned back toward the main building. The gravel paths were narrow and at each of his impractical long strides his coat was clawed by Gay Flirtation or Pale Memory. His Rush Temporary Pass had not yet been issued and he was obliged to explain his business to the guard at the door, and once again at the cloakroom where he collected his brief case and papers. It was exactly three-thirty when he took the elevator to the meeting.

Patricio Rodriguez-O'Hearn, short, bald, blue-eyed, and in his fifties, came from Chile. His reserve was unusual in a man of Latin and Irish blood, but would not otherwise have been noticeable. He was calm and courteous and, since he made a policy of being accessible to his staff, often looked exhausted in the afternoons. Within DALTO—the Department of Aid to the Less Technically Oriented—he was responsible for the overseas assignments of experts. It was to Mr. Rodriguez that Mr. Addison and his colleagues in the Opposite Numbers Unit reported, and Mr. Rodriguez reported in his turn to the Chief Coordinator of DALTO. Rodriguez had been married twice, had a number of young children, and was known to play the piano rather well. When he sat at his desk or, as at this moment, at the head of a conference table, he would occasionally follow imaginary notes with his fingers while waiting for discussion to begin.

Flinders was quite far from Rodriguez, having been placed midway down the table. A large lady sat on Flinders's right, and Addison had naturally been seated opposite. There were some fifteen other members of the meeting, and Flinders found that he was not the only expert reporting that afternoon. On his left, a shock-headed young man named Edrich, back from a three-year assignment as a Civic Coordination expert in the Eastern Mediterranean, was leafing confidently through an envelope of documents. Senior members of DALTO were taking their seats, and there were, in addition, representatives from political departments of the Organization—a thin gentleman with a tremor from the Section on Forceful Implementation of Peace Treaties, and a young woman in a sari from Peaceful Uses of Atomic Weapons. A secretary was distributing pads of white paper and stunted yellow pencils. The room was low-ceilinged, without windows, and carpeted in yellowish-green. At one end of it stood a small movie-screen and at the other a projector. At Flinders's back, a bookcase contained a 1952 *Who's Who*, and a great number of Organization documents.

Flinders, having turned to look at the bookcase, soon turned back to the table. By assuming an alert expression he tried to include himself in various conversations taking place around him, but no one paid him any attention. A young man next to Addison said, "These problems are substantive, of course, not operational," and Addison replied, "Obviously." "Essential elements," declared a Japanese, and "Local infrastructure," responded a Yugoslav. The Forceful Implementation man looked very angry, and the girl from Peaceful Uses put her hand on his arm and murmured, "Under great pressure." Someone else said soothingly, "We'll put a Rush on it."

When all the places were taken, Rodriguez-O'Hearn coughed for silence, welcomed the two experts to Headquarters, and introduced them to the meeting. The large lady leaned across Flinders to ask Edrich a question, but Edrich was nodding around the table and did not see her. Edrich, Flinders noted enviously, seemed to know everybody and had greeted several people by first name. Apart from Addison, who had gone into temporary eclipse behind the leaning lady, Flinders knew no one at all.

Mr. Rodriguez-O'Hearn called on Edrich to describe his work to the meeting; he then leaned back in his chair and took off his glasses.

Edrich bent forward and put his glasses on. He placed on the table a list of points he had drawn up. "I have," he said, "recently submitted, in six copies, my final report and this will shortly be available"—he turned up another paper—"under the document symbol E dash DALTO 604"—he glanced again at the paper in his hand—"slash two." He therefore proposed, he said, to give only a brief summary of his work to the present meeting, and with this in mind had prepared a list of points on which emphasis might effectively be laid. (Flinders, looking over his shoulder, saw that there were fourteen of these, on which emphasis had already been effectively laid by underlinings.) Moreover, in accordance with instructions, Edrich had brought with him a short film showing various stages of his performance in the field.

Rodriguez-O'Hearn here suggested that the film be shown first, in order to give even greater reality to Edrich's list of points. A young man was sent for who, under Edrich's supervision, set up the reel in the projector. Rodriguez shifted his chair, and Flinders, who had his elbows on the table, was asked to move back so that the lady on his right might see the screen. Edrich borrowed a ruler from the outer office, the lights were put out, and the film was set, hissing and crackling, in motion.

Flinders was immediately struck by the similarity of the opening scene to the countryside he had just left. The eroded hills, though steeper, were garlanded with terraces of vines and fruit trees and glittered white in the meridional sunshine. The village, though even smaller than El Attara, was composed of the same whitewashed houses, the same worn steps and pitted doors. At the well, the women stood talking with their jars at their feet or their children in their arms, and outside the single tavern the old men played cards. The camera wavered over flat roofs and small peeling domes and squinted at stony hills. And upon the whole, as though marking a target, Edrich's ruler now described a great circle.

"This was the deplorable condition of the area when I arrived. Low level of overall production, cottage industries static for centuries, poor communications with neighboring towns, no telegraph or telephone system, partial electrification, dissemination of information by shepherd's rumor, little or no interest in national or international events. In short, minimal adjustment to contemporary requirements, and incomplete utilization of resources."

Screaming with laughter, a child raced into the camera's path in pursuit of a crowd of chickens.

"As you know," Edrich continued, "the object of the Civic Coordination Program is to tap the dynamics of social change in terms of local aspirations for progress. These aspirations may be difficult to establish in a society where there has been no evolution of attitudes or change in value orientation for generations and where there are no new mechanisms for action within the community structure. In order to create a dynamic growth situation resulting in effective exploitation of community potential, aspirations must be identified in relation to felt needs. The individual thus feels himself able to function as a person, at the same time participating in implementation of community goals."

"What are the group relationships?" The lady next to Flinders sat forward tensely for the reply.

"I'm glad you ask that, Miss Bass. Owing to traditional integration of the family as a unit, the individual seems reluctant to function in a group or sub-group situation. These social patterns may take some time to break down. And this is natural."

"Yes. This is predictable." Miss Bass relaxed in her chair.

"Immediately after my arrival, meetings were set up with local officials to alert them to Civic Coordination projects in the vicinity and to inform them of the terms of my assignment as agreed between their own government and the Organization." Edrich returned to the film, where a herd of shaggy goats had appeared in the main street, followed by a donkey. "A committee was appointed to evaluate needs and resources and to establish work priorities." The scene changed to a row of sunburned men in dungarees and open shirts. One was leaning self-consciously on a tall staff; another was waving at the camera. "After a certain initial language confusion—owing to a particularly corrupt dialect spoken in this region—my project was accepted enthusiastically, although a slower time-table was eventually agreed upon."

Here the film came to a splicing, and a series of horizontal black lines twitched frantically up the screen.

"I believe the pictures will speak for themselves from here on."

There followed, when the film resumed, a succession of scenes involving prodigious bodily labor of all kinds. One by one the men and women of the town passed across the screen—carrying great baskets of earth, digging deep and narrow ditches, or with muscles braced and heads bowed, pushing against a boulder. Once Edrich himself was glimpsed sitting on a rock and mopping his brow. And once, to the horror of Flinders, a tree was chopped down. A bridge was built, across a stream whose course was subsequently diverted. A little blockhouse of raw brick was laboriously constructed among the whitewashed domes and in no time at all bore the legend "Administration Building" in three languages. In the final episode, every able-bodied member of the community was shown on hands and knees, breaking stones for a road that would connect the area to the nearest industrial center.

The film came to its end in a shower of black and white flecks, and the lights were turned on. Members of the meeting got up to stretch their legs and to question Edrich about his fourteen points. A concealed fan was switched on and vibrated with a slow hum. The technician was running the film back onto its spool. Watching him, Flinders regretted that the course of events could not be similarly rewound. What of the women at the well, he wondered? What of the laughing child that somewhere on the machine spun back to his former deplorable condition—and the flock of chickens now laying their eggs in electrified coops all through the night? What improvements were being inflicted on those static industries that had for centuries repeated themselves in the graceful jars about the well?

"Coordination," the voices were insisting, and "basic procedures." Edrich was pulling out his chair and saying "issue-oriented." Flinders resisted claustrophobia: the room was like an upholstered bomb-shelter.

"You have your films with you, Mr. Flinders?"

Rodriguez-O'Hearn was looking at him. Flinders brought up his brief case from beside his chair and produced an envelope of colored slides. "Only a few stills, sir."

The meeting was settling down again. He was being listened to. He knew that he cut a poor figure with his nine or ten slides, after Edrich's film. The Arabs had rather disliked being photographed, and in any case he had often forgotten to take a camera on field trips. He handed the envelope over to the technician with a sinking heart. "They're not too clear," he said.

Flinders had never made a speech before. He had been intimidated, too, by the eloquence of Edrich. His hands were shaking, and he placed them flat on the table before him. All the faces were turned, waiting for him to begin.

"In classical times," he said, "the lands bordering the Mediterranean were much more thickly vegetated. We know this, for example, from Euripides' description of the area around Thebes, or Homer's account. . . ."

Here he paused to draw breath, and the Chief of Official Records asked if he had submitted his final report.

Mr. Addison confirmed that a short account of Flinders's performance in the field was at that moment with his own typist.

"But your final report, Mr. Flinders," the Records Chief persisted with thinly veiled patience. "Your evaluation of the success of your assignment, in six copies, your recommendations for future concrete measures."

"Given the fluidity of the situation," Edrich put in, with a sympathetic nod to Flinders.

Flinders said slowly that the success of a mission such as his must depend on the survival of trees which had only just been planted.

The Records Chief declared that such a condition could not be regarded as an obstacle to the submission of a final report.

"One must give them a chance," Flinders said. "The growth of a hybrid poplar or even a eucalyptus may be very little in the first seasons."

"A long-term project, in other words," said Edrich.

"In other words," Flinders agreed.

Rodriguez-O'Hearn addressed him down the table. "Why, Mr. Flinders, have we been subjected to so much erosion since classical times?"

Flinders looked at him. "In the main, sir, it is due to overgrazing."

Edrich said, "Correct."

How does *he* know it's correct? Flinders wondered irritably. He went on to speak of the movement of soil at certain elevations and in certain winds, the presence of useful or destructive insects, the receptivity of the land—all the circumstances, in fact, which had led to the selection of the trees at El Attara. "In conditions such as these," he said, looking along the row of fatigued faces, "the drought-resistant species has the only hope for survival."

"And it is this type you are concerned with?" asked Rodriguez-O'Hearn.

Flinders nodded. "Very often these don't give dramatic results. You see—some of the most valuable types in the world are unspectacular. But they hold their own by . . . perseverance."

The slides had been set up, and the technician asked for permission to turn out the lights. Flinders got up and stood by the screen. In the dark he could not find Edrich's ruler, and at first, being a rather awkward man, he got in the way of the picture. The slides were in color and, although Flinders had no skill whatever as a photographer, they did derive a certain clarity from the sharp air and splendid light of the countryside.

The first slide had been taken from a hilltop; it was a panorama of the area to the south of El Attara. The contours of this country were European rather than African, and Flinders had often found it possible there to imagine how France or Italy might have looked before spaciousness was diminished by overpopulation. The hills were sometimes covered by green grasses so short that after heavy rain the soil showed through in violet streaks. This picture, however, had been taken in summer, and the pebbled course of a dry stream wound through a valley of orange groves and cypress trees. The next pictures were of a depleted slope, furrowed by weather, on whose receding earth a number of sheep were pessimistically feeding.

Flinders said, "This is the site we chose for the first plantation."

The pictures that followed were so repetitious that he could not help wondering why he had taken them. The same hillside, and a large area nearby, were shown in various stages of preparation—but these preparations were so gradual and so little obvious to the layman that there seemed to have been no purpose in recording them.

"The work near El Attara," Flinders said, "serves as an experiment. The country has a conservation program now, and the local authorities have their own plans for the future."

Someone said uneasily, "And this is good."

Flinders said, "Naturally."

Edrich called out, "Correct."

Rodriguez-O'Hearn's voice inquired whether Flinders spoke Arabic.

"Not very well, sir, I'm afraid." Flinders hesitated. "I've been studying for three years. Semitic languages are difficult for Westerners."

"You made yourself understood, however?"

Flinders smiled. "As to that, sir," he said, "how does one know?"

The last slide came onto the screen. It was a shot taken by Flinders on the morning of the first planting. Halfway up a slope, a parked truck leaned inward on a narrow, unsurfaced road. The angle of the truck was made more precarious by the ditch into which it was partly sunk and the way in which the photograph had been taken. That the truck had just stopped was evident from the cloud of white dust still rising about its wheels. Nevertheless, the gate of the truck's open back was down, and two young men in djellabahs had scrambled aboard. One was already handing down to a forest of upstretched hands the first of the small trees with which the truck was loaded. The waiting peasants—the men in brown robes, the women mostly unveiled and wrapped in the bright colors of the country folk—reached up excitedly, but the youth on the truck held the plant with extreme care. Behind him in the truck, young trees were stacked up in even rows, their roots wrapped in burlap; on the hillside above the road, dozens of small craters had already been turned in the fresh earth.

Flinders had forgotten taking the picture, although now he remembered it with a pang of nostalgic pleasure—the brilliant January morning, the shouts of delight which greeted the arrival of the loaded truck, the many serious shakings of the hand, the good omens invoked, and the long day's work that followed. He recognized all the faces in the picture— most were from the vicinity of El Attara, and a few from villages close to the planting site. Everyone in the photograph seemed to be smiling, even two children who were rolling up stones for the wheels of the truck.

A voice in the dark said, "*They* look happy, at any rate."

The technician said, "I guess that's all."

The lights went on, and the slide, remaining a moment longer on the screen, grew pale. Flat and dreamlike, the hillside stood at one end of the conference room, and the reaching figures threw up their arms on an empty wall.

With a click, the picture vanished. Addison lit a cigarette. The members of the meeting were looking at their watches and speaking of appointments, perhaps thinking of their afternoon tea. A girl with flat black hair had come in and was handing a message to Rodriguez-O'Hearn. The one or two questions asked of Flinders had, he felt, little to do with what he had said, and he thought this must be his fault. Addison made an appointment to lunch with him next day, and the girl from Peaceful Uses said shyly that she looked forward to discussing with him the effects of nuclear testing in the Sahara. In the meantime, Rodriguez-O'Hearn, whom Flinders had wanted to meet, had disappeared. A secretary came in to empty the ashtrays and align the empty chairs. It occurred to Flinders that another meeting was about to take place here: the very idea was exhausting.

He left the room and walked down a gray corridor. He wished he had gone to the trouble of taking a proper film, like Edrich, or had at least prepared the right kind of final report. At El Attara he had thought these things peripheral, but here they seemed to matter most of all. He should have been able to address the meeting in its own language—that language of ends and trends, of agenda and addenda, of concrete measures in fluid situations, which he had never set himself to master. At El Attara they had needed help and he had done what he could, but he found himself unable to speak with confidence about this work. He knew the problem of erosion to be immense; and the trees, being handed down that way, had looked so few and so small.

At the elevator he met Edrich. Edrich seemed older and shorter than he had in the conference room. Flinders would have told him what was in his heart, but he somehow felt that Edrich was not the right recipient for the information. They took the Down elevator together, and Edrich got off at the Clinic. Flinders continued to the main floor and, leaving the building by a side entrance, went out through the rose garden.

Rodriguez-O'Hearn put down the telephone. Hearing him ring off, his secretary brought him his afternoon coffee in a cardboard container.

"Thank you, Miss Shamsee."

"Regular with sugar." She pulled up a metal blind. In the early outside darkness, red and yellow lights were being turned on. The river icily reflected the crimson Frosti-Cola sign.

"Any other messages?"

She put a slip of paper in his calendar. "Tomorrow afternoon, meeting at three-thirty. Two experts reporting: Suzuki in public accounting, and Raman, malaria control."

"Better get up their files."

"I've already sent for them."

Rodriguez-O'Hearn drank his coffee, and made a space for the container among the papers on his blotter. He tipped back his chair. "To think," he said, "Miss Shamsee, that when I was a young man I wanted to be the conductor of an orchestra."

She took the empty container off the desk and dropped it in the wastebasket. "That's what you are," she said, "in a manner of speaking."

"No, no," he said, but tipped his chair down again. "Such mistakes we make," he said.

When the girl went out he looked through his In-tray. He then wrote a note asking Addison to bring Flinders to see him the following day, signed several recommendations for new experts, and began to read a report, making notes in the margin. When his secretary next came in, however, with an armful of files, she found him looking out of the window.

"Miss Shamsee," he said gravely, "I'm afraid we have suffered much erosion since classical times."

She was used to him, and merely put the files in his In-tray. She saw, as she did so, that on the edge of his blotter he had drawn a small tree.

SWOBODA'S TRAGEDY

It was the documents that finally got Swoboda down. His colleagues supposed that the further postponement of his promotion had been the last straw, but in fact it was the documents that did it. In the past he had been ready to carry out the often tedious duties imposed on him by the Organization—he was by nature almost too ready in this respect—but the documents finally did it. It was too much.

Like most great turning-points in life, the matter presented itself gradually. Mr. Bekkus had stopped one day at Swoboda's desk and casually asked, "Oh Swoboda, would you," and Swoboda had said, as he had always said, "Certainly Mr. Bekkus," and that was how it began. The arrangement was that he would send out these documents each morning, just for a few days until someone else was found to do it. The documents, which came in various related series all beginning with the symbol "SAGG" (Services of Administration and General Guidance), then started to arrive daily, in stacks of one hundred apiece, on Swoboda's desk. He had been instructed to send them out in separate large brown envelopes to their eighty-five designated recipients throughout the Organization, in his spare time. But several factors operated against this plan. In the first place, Swoboda had no spare time. In the second place, it was impossible for him to attend to any of his normal clerical work until he had cleared the stacks of documents off his desk each morning; by then much of the day was gone and he was faced with the necessity of staying after hours. And thirdly, no attempt was ever made to find another person to cope with the documents and they were thus laid, almost literally, at Swoboda's door forever.

Swoboda was not a brilliant man. He was a man of what used to be known as average and is now known as above-average intelligence. The years during which he might have been formally educated had been spent by him in a camp for displaced persons, but he had educated himself by observation and reflection, and had exploited to the full a natural comprehension in human affairs. He was not audacious; he lacked aptitude for self-advancement. As a member of the Social and Anthropological Department once put it, Swoboda was over-adjusted to his problem. However, if he had lost his opportunities, he had kept his self-respect. Now he felt this to be threatened. Mr. Bekkus had let him down—if this expression may be used where there has been no bolstering-up. The work was not fit for Swoboda to do. It was work one might have given a deficient person in order to employ him.

At intervals in the course of his years with the Organization, commendatory remarks had been entered on Swoboda's personal file. From time to time, one of his superiors had told him that he deserved promotion—that it was a pity, even a disgrace, that nothing had been done for him by those responsible. At first, on these occasions, Swoboda had felt encouraged and had related them at home to his wife as a guarantee of advancement in the near future. Eventually, however, it became clear to him that responsibility for his promotion lay with the very officials who deplored his condition, and that they had no intention whatever of exerting themselves to the necessary extent on his behalf—having, as they imagined, dealt with the matter by proclaiming it a disgrace. Their exertions, if any, were reserved for those more insistent, less self-effacing than Swoboda. Finally grasping this situation, Swoboda declined to make life hideous for himself and those about him by constant complaint, as was the habit of so many of his colleagues. He kept his trouble to himself and sought consolation in his natural philosophy.

All the same, it hurt him. It was demoralizing. It amounted simply to this: that no one was willing to take a chance on him.

For several months Swoboda uncomplainingly sent out the SAGG documents. For several months he arrived home in the dark to find his dinner in the oven, his wife in distress, his child already in bed. If he were absent for a day, for illness or holiday, he was haunted by the certainty that a double load of documents would await him on return. During his annual vacation, an empty office on another floor had to be appropriated to house the accumulation. At last a day came when he was visited by a sensation that had been familiar to him years before, but which, even in his worst moments at the Organization, he had not re-experienced until now. And this sensation overcame his diffidence. He acted.

It was a sensation associated with his first job, in a time before he came to the Organization. Released from his DP camp, equipped with a coveted visa, sped on his way by relief committees, the young Swoboda had obtained employment in a fruit factory. Here he was to earn his first wages and his first right to call himself an independent person. This factory was to provide the slipway from which his sane new life would be launched. Here the world would make amends for his deprivation. Willing, even jubilant, Swoboda had reported for duty and punched his clock for the first time.

The section of the factory for which Swoboda had been engaged was concerned with the treatment of cherries. By the time the cherries, in vast metal trays, came to Swoboda's attention they had already been divested of stalks, stones, and color—in short, of everything that had hitherto contributed to their character as cherries. Gouged and blanched, they had then been immersed in a crimson dye so that their color might emerge uniform. It was Swoboda's task to attach to these multitudinous, incarnadined cherries the red plastic stalks—also uniform—that would subsequently enable them to be pulled from cocktails and, as the case might be, eaten or discarded. And it was to such ends that he diligently applied himself for one long year.

The job at the fruit factory, as has been noted, was important to Swoboda. He was untrained. He had no other means of making his living in a new country—a country of whose ways he was ignorant and whose language he did not, at that time, speak with confidence. Moreover, he wished to acquit himself in the eyes of those who had assisted him. Above all, he wanted to do well in this first paid occupation.

The day he gave his notice was the happiest day of his life.

And now, amid the sheaves of documents, it all came back to him. Shaken by the same repugnance, he arrived at the same conclusion—that such work was not for the adult and civilized, not for mature and feeling persons. Swoboda did what he had never done: he took an extra half hour at lunchtime. During this half hour he made his way to the Bureau of Lateral Substitutions and requested transfer to another department.

Nominees for promotion at all levels were considered twice a year by a Promotions and Probations Board, and a printed list of the successful candidates was subsequently circulated throughout the Organization. Since those directly concerned were told in advance of the verdict in their case, the main interest of the list lay in keeping abreast of the fortunes of one's fellows. It is a rare heart that truly rejoices in a friend's prosperity, and it must be confessed that the offices and corridors of the Organization were swept, every six months, by gasps of indignation, of disgust and incredulity, at the revelation of the latest promotions—and by correspondingly magnified sighs of solicitude on behalf of those rejected.

Just such gusts as these were sweeping the small gray office of Mr. Bekkus when Swoboda entered it on the morning of the half-yearly list. Mr. Bekkus—as a member of a similar group, the Appointments and Terminations Board—was practically bound to hold his colleagues on this parallel body in low esteem. And his ill-humor was increased, that day, by the fact that he was once more faced with the task of explaining the absence of Swoboda's name from the Promotions roster.

As Swoboda came into the room, Mr. Bekkus was standing by the window and holding the list to the light as if to verify the evidence of his eyes.

"Claude *Willoughby*! Claude *Willoughby*!" he repeated, as if of all Claudes this was the most unsuitable. "Cedric Sandaranayke! After this, anything's possible. Sit down, Swoboda." Still standing in the light, Mr. Bekkus turned the page and read on. "Kenneth Eliufoo—that's geographical of course, though it won't satisfy the Africans, you can be sure of that. Paquita Vargas—well, we all know how *she* got here. . . . And I see old Marcel made it at last." Reluctantly turning from self-punishment, he placed the list on his desk and sat down. "Er—Swoboda," he said, looking about his papers as if trying to recall what Swoboda was doing there.

Swoboda looked at Mr. Bekkus with something more than his usual composure. It was part of Swoboda's misfortune that he pitied Mr. Bekkus; that in his resistance to Mr. Bekkus he was inhibited by the knowledge that Mr. Bekkus was pathetic. Not that this insight was in itself supernatural—for others would have quickly arrived at the same conclusion—but what made Swoboda unusual was that he persisted in the belief even though he had spent some years in the power of Mr. Bekkus and had suffered from the silliness and insensibility that constituted Mr. Bekkus's pathos. By now, surely, the sense of pathos might have given way to indignation at being subordinate to such a figure. But no. Swoboda had never said to anyone, "I'm sorry for him" (although, in the Organization, this was a recognized means of expressing contempt for an unsympathetic superior—"I'm sorry for him, I truly am; he's pathetic" being uttered frequently and fiercely through clenched teeth). He had not even said it to himself. But in his heart he knew that Bekkus was a foolish man, a small, ignorant, and pretentious man, and that he, Swoboda, was his superior in all but official rank. Swoboda was aware that Mr. Bekkus had treated him ungenerously, had often been petty and unjust. He sometimes dwelt on this, almost hopefully, in his mind. But it was no use. He continued to find Mr. Bekkus pathetic. And therein lay Swoboda's misfortune—one might even have said, Swoboda's tragedy.

"I suppose," Mr. Bekkus began, as if Swoboda had requested the interview, "you will want to discuss certain factors of your situation." Personal matters, for Bekkus, came in situations, elements, and factors. When Swoboda said nothing, he went on. "As you know, I myself have done everything possible to expedite the processing of your upgrading." After a pause he added, "That goes without saying." Swoboda evidently concurred in this, for another silence fell. "There are some very slow-thinking individuals on the Promotions Board, Swoboda. And then, when you see who *is* accepted . . ." He lightly dashed the promotion list with the back of his hand as if Swoboda would hardly wish to make one of such a disreputable company. "Well, we all know the delays that—ah—mitigate against rapid advancement in the junior grades. But I think I can assure you, Swoboda, that your upgrading will be followed through in the foreseeable future—that is, at the next meeting of the Board." Mr. Bekkus lowered his voice. "This is confidential of course."

Swoboda merely said, "I see, sir."

Bekkus began to be irritated with Swoboda. "I trust, Swoboda," he said with some severity, "that you are not too dissatisfied?"

After a moment, Swoboda replied, "Yes, Mr. Bekkus."

Mr. Bekkus, who had been scoring his blotter with a pencil, hesitated. Before he could make up his mind whether the ambiguity of Swoboda's reply bore investigation, Swoboda himself elucidated.

"I mean, Yes, I am too dissatisfied, Mr. Bekkus."

Mr. Bekkus covered his surprise with a veneer of forbearance. He even smiled—a patient smile, an administrative smile, a smile that bespoke experience and concern. "It's natural that you should feel disappointed," he began.

"Yes, sir."

"But, as I've just explained to you," continued Mr. Bekkus, smiling less, "if you take the overall view, you need *not* feel dissatisfied on a long-term basis."

Swoboda looked steadily at Mr. Bekkus. "It is with the overall view and on the long-term basis that I feel dissatisfied," he said.

Now it was the turn of Mr. Bekkus to be silent, though he cast about with one hand in a circular gesture, as if attempting to turn the procedural wheels that had in this moment so unaccountably ground to a halt.

Swoboda went on calmly, "And I have applied for a transfer."

Mr. Bekkus stared. Regaining the power of speech, he said, "Words fail me." (A poor workman will tend to blame his tools.) He emphasized the extreme gravity of the situation by putting the pencil down and folding his hands before him on the blotter. "Swoboda," he said very quietly, as if Swoboda were a dangerous lunatic, "why did you do that?"

"Because," replied Swoboda, "of the long-term basis."

"What do you complain of? Your relationships here have been good."
Mr. Bekkus took up the pencil again and began a series of ticks on his
blotter. "Your working conditions are not unpleasant." He made a second
tick. "You got your within-grade increment." (His tone so clearly implied
"What more do you want?" that Swoboda almost smiled.) "Your func-
tions have been meaningful."

"No Mr. Bekkus."

"Do you have some specific problem?"

"The documents."

"The documentation?" Bekkus was baffled. "*The documentation?*"

"The SAGG documents. They have become a burden. You may have
noticed that."

Bekkus shrugged. "I have been dimly aware," he said. It was the best
description he had ever given of his general state of mind. He took up a
more aggressive approach. "This transfer, when did you request it?"

"About six weeks ago."

"Your application—was it made verbally or just orally?" Mr. Bekkus
was fond of this imaginary distinction.

"I requested an interview with a Mr. Yu in Lateral Substitutions."

"But did you actually see him—visually, that is?"

Swoboda nodded. "The matter was to be confidential until a vacancy
came up. However, I prefer to tell you now."

"I should have been consulted at the outset." Bekkus was getting angry.
"Is this the normal procedure?"

"Yu said so."

"What? Ah—yes. Well, I can tell you, Swoboda, that I consider this a
breach of good faith on your part." He leaned forward, his eyes belligerently bright. "Yes. After our years together—our relationship, that is—I
would have liked to see some show of good faith." He rightly implied that
this spectacle would have to be provided by others: Bekkus was a victim
of the ancient delusion that loyalty is to be had for nothing. "I must tell
you that I resent your behavior in having directly approached the Bureau
of Substitutions." His voice rose. "It was—it was—"

He's actually going to say it was an outrage, thought Swoboda, amused.
But here Swoboda misjudged Mr. Bekkus, for such a simple,

expressive word was not at his command. Bekkus hunted through his vocabulary—no lengthy task—for appropriate expression. At last it came. "It was," he cried passionately, "a—*unilateral action*."

When Swoboda moved to the section headed by Mr. Patricio Rodriguez-O'Hearn, he carried his belongings in an Out-tray. It was as radical a change as can exist within the Organization, the new section being not only in a different department but even on a different elevator bank. Mr. Rodriguez-O'Hearn was Chief of Missions in DALTO, the Department of Aid to the Less Technically Oriented. The work of this department—to induce backward nations to come forward—stemmed from a humane conceit and apparently enjoyed some success, for since its inception a number of hitherto reticent countries had become very forward indeed. The department in general, and Mr. Rodriguez in particular, had a relatively good reputation within the Organization, and this favorable impression had been confirmed to Swoboda in a preliminary interview.

Swoboda was scheduled to arrive C.O.D. (Commencing Official Duties) on a Monday in the middle of June, and on the morning of this day he appeared in the doorway of Mr. Rodriguez's suite of offices, carrying his tray. He was received kindly by Mr. Rodriguez's secretary, Miss Shamsee, who showed him into the neighboring room he was to share with two other clerks. His possessions—a paperback Roget, a leather-framed photograph of his wife and child, an Orlon sweater, a bottle of aspirin, and an unusually efficient stapling machine—were quickly transferred to his new desk, a blotter was found for him, and his Out-tray was relabeled "In." One or two minor tasks were set him, but before he was able to begin these or take stock of the square, wide-windowed room that constituted his future premises, his new colleagues arrived.

These two men were much of Swoboda's age, and, although the yellow-haired one smiled and the dark-haired one was offhand, Swoboda formed no immediate impression of them, his mind being so full of new and nervous sensations this momentous morning. As is the way of people who are to spend many months in close company, the three of them bided their time at the outset, and the first hours passed in comparative silence.

Swoboda gathered that his two new associates had already shared the office for some time, and was reassured by the fact that they were evidently on good terms.

Swoboda having been given various files to study in preparation for his new duties, it was not until the late morning of this day that he felt himself free to size up his surroundings. As he raised his head to do this, the smiling man looked up from a form on the blotter before him and, with pencil poised, inquired Swoboda's first name.

Assuming that this was required for some official purpose, Swoboda tonelessly responded, "Stanislas." The young man then sprang up from his chair by the window and in a moment was before Swoboda with his hand outstretched, saying "Mordecai." On the far side of the room the dark man also rose up from his desk, uttering, "Merv." They all shook hands and exchanged greetings. Mordecai then took his jacket off a stand near the door and said, "How about some lunch?"

Thus began, for Swoboda, at the age of thirty-nine, his first taste of ordinary companionship. The relations of the three men were less demanding than would have been the case with women similarly thrown together. Their work was connected only indirectly, so that most of their conversation was personal; and their personalities offered sufficient contrast to keep them interested in one another.

On Mordie's head the yellow hair stood out in a spiky halo suggesting a sun-god rather than a saint. The word "sunny" would have come to mind in any attempt to describe Mordie, for everything about him—hair, skin, and disposition—seemed to have been touched by light and warmth. The turmoil of history and of his own circumstances had swirled about and across him—for Mordie was a grandchild of those Russian Zionists who formed the first *kibbutzim* in Palestine in the early years of this century—without taking toll of his serenity, and even seemed to have attached him the more strongly to it. Such tranquility often includes a measure of detachment, and Mordie was somewhat like a ship that stands offshore from a beleaguered city, ready to receive survivors, to evacuate the wounded and retreating—to do, in effect, everything but participate in the conflict. This attitude of a friendly neutral did not originate in aloofness or timorousness but from Mordie's instinct for the way in which he could best be of service to his friends. Moreover, though he would not impair his usefulness by exposing it to pointless damage, it was conceivable that Mordie might yet one day suffer himself to be annihilated in some single glorious intervention.

Mervyn was in all things unlike Mordie. He was an Australian of the short and saturnine variety. His last name was Lomax and he had been born in Narrabeen, an outlying suburb of Sydney, the only son of humble but contentious parents. He had shown interest in acquiring knowledge, even while still at school, in preparation for some wider, more accomplished world which he felt sure awaited him. Since his formal instruction was limited and he had, as a youth, few like-minded companions, his self-education ranged wide, altering course almost from day to day; many subjects were touched upon, though none exhausted, and surprising gaps were left. (These arbitrary gaps subsequently contributed to an impression that Mervyn had educated himself on a desert island, by means of an *Encyclopaedia Britannica* of which one volume—say, that from LORD to MUMPS—happened to be missing.)

A schoolmate, returning one day to Narrabeen from an envied trip to Europe, had informed Mervyn that the Parthenon was highly disappointing. From the vehemence with which the statement was made, Mervyn perceived that the disappointment of this youth lay with his own reaction, and that the blame had been laid upon the Parthenon as being, of the two, the more able to bear it. There followed the realization that, if beauty were not precisely in the eye of the beholder, it was at least essential for that eye to be open and favorably disposed. Mervyn's eye became in consequence so fervently well disposed that a measure of disappointment unavoidably awaited him when at last he made his appearance in the Western Hemisphere. Because of this slight disillusionment, certain of the rewards—rewards rendered for the most part in aesthetic currency—with which Mervyn's struggle for enlightenment was eventually crowned were greeted by him with defensive skepticism. He continued to court knowledge, but, like a lover once deceived, now qualified his suit with all manner of reservations and deprecation and even, from time to time, with a touch of that very hostility which had so detracted from the littoral beauties of Narrabeen.

Another anticlimax awaited him in the form of the Organization, which he joined some years later. By then Mervyn was getting ready to settle, and he stayed with the Organization, though many were the misgivings he both felt and voiced. His scholastic attainments lacking academic endorsement, they had no validity whatever in the eyes of the Organization, and he was, at the time of this story, attending a third year of evening classes which were intended to culminate in a degree in Commercial Science and the right to represent himself as an educated man—a right which his time-consuming pursuit of culture had hitherto obliged him to forgo.

Swoboda, with his aptitude for such things, quickly saw that Mervyn, finding no whole and perfect world, felt himself betrayed by the ubiquitous human lapse. This was exactly the opposite of Swoboda, whose overdose of fatalism led him to value above all things the kinship of human error. The discrepancy led them into innumerable, inconclusive exchanges.

"Stan," Mervyn would say, as they sat gingerly holding their hot containers of morning coffee, "who are your heroes?"

"Pardon?"

"Great minds. Who?"

"Oh—" Such renderings of account were unfamiliar though not unpleasant to Swoboda. "Kant, perhaps."

"Kant hadn't a particle of poetry in his entire nature."

"Newton, then?"

"Newton went wrong on Time."

Swoboda tried another tack. "Who are *your* great minds, Mervyn?"

"Ah." Mervyn began to rub his left hand absent-mindedly up and down his lapel, caressing his heart like an old wound. "There are no great minds, Stan," he said sadly. To be great, in Mervyn's opinion, was to be infallible.

Both Mordie and Mervyn were somewhat senior in grade to Swoboda, and both had encountered Mr. Bekkus during their careers at the Organization.

"I bet Bekkus blighted your life," Mervyn remarked one day.

Swoboda's reserve would have produced some noncommittal reply, had Mordie not seconded this view. "Ah—Bekkus. I too recall him as a Life-blighter. How long were you in his office?"

"Nearly four years. Ever since Specific Cases Unit was merged with Overall Policy."

"Christ, Stan, why did you stick it?"

There was no answer to this—unless Swoboda were to allude to the nature of his tragedy. Slowly, however, his life with Mr. Bekkus was unfolded to his new friends. Mordie and Mervyn were able to size up the situation in their respective ways and to savor the triumph of Swoboda's final interview with Mr. Bekkus.

"Stanislas, you did right."

"Good on you, Stan."

"Not," went on Swoboda, "that we parted on bad terms. That, indeed, would have introduced a new sincerity into our relations. Far from it. Not knowing my new telephone extension, Mr. Bekkus pointed out that I should have to call him in order for us to, as he put it, get together."

"And will you?"

Swoboda paused. "On my last day, Mr. Bekkus walked with me to the elevator. He put his hand on my back and said 'Remember, Swoboda, it will be your fault if we don't get together soon.'"

"What did you say?"

Swoboda smiled modestly. "I said—'That's right.'"

Mordie's smile shot up to his ears.

Mervyn slapped his hand on the desk. "Stan the Man! The *Original* Man!"

Mordie said, "Stanislas, I confess to a pleasant surprise."

"You would have expected me to weaken?"

"Not exactly. But I thought perhaps you are one of those who gives in for the good old times' sake."

"That expression, Mordie," said Mervyn, "is '*for old times' sake.*' Nobody ever said it was *good* old times' sake."

Swoboda was also kindly treated by Miss Shamsee and, though he saw less of her than of Mordie and Merv, not a day passed without his exchanging some friendly words with her or consulting her about his work.

Miss Shamsee had been ten years with the Organization and was now a little over thirty. Her face had the gloss of a ripe olive. Her black hair was flat, parted in the middle, and drawn back in an immaculate knot. She invariably wore a sari—sometimes a beautifully bright one, sometimes a drab and flimsy one—and this graceful garment contributed a stateliness, though she was not tall. She had a remarkable walk—it was the curving, sinuous walk of Hazlitt's Sally Walker—which, combined with the semi-circular folds of her dress, gave her an effect of coiling and uncoiling as she passed through offices and down corridors, as she glided between filing cabinets or along cafeteria queues.

In addition to these physical advantages, Miss Shamsee possessed a good mind and pleasant manner. She should, by any fair standard, have been an attractive woman; yet it cannot be said that she was. All the elements were there, but Miss Shamsee was like a resort town in bad weather: some spark, some animation, some synthesizing glow was missing. She had been too long with the Organization.

Girls like Miss Shamsee pursued, year in, year out, their stenographic or clerical duties at the Organization, and were to be seen each day lunching in the cafeteria with two or three of their kind. Their salaries were low, but every year they earned a little more money, and every ten years or so they went up a notch in the clerical scale. No professional advancement was offered them, except over such a length of time as to invalidate it. Marriages were rare, resignations even rarer (for, somewhere about the age of twenty-seven, they started to be concerned over the drawing of their eventual pension). If fortunate, they might be assigned to one or two Organizational meetings abroad; if desperate, they might apply for long-term service in the less technically oriented lands.

The previous year, Miss Shamsee had been sent to the Organization's branch office in Geneva to assist at a summit conference of the less technically oriented. There she had met and fallen in love with an official of the World Geophysical Union, an international agency affiliated with the Organization. The man was married, and Miss Shamsee's assignment was for six weeks only, but the affair was poignant and sincere. Toward the end of the conference they arranged, by intricate deceptions, to go away together for a brief time. (In this they were aided by the Organization holiday of Self-Determination Day which, falling on a Monday, provided a long weekend.) Other cities in Switzerland being rendered perilous to them by the various headquarters of agencies of the Organization (the Global Health Commission at Lausanne, the Bureau of Legal Standards at Berne, and so on), and the Riviera being out of the question owing to a large Organization-sponsored Poverty Congress then in progress at Cannes, they decided on Milan as the neighboring city least fraught with international aspirations. There they duly arrived by train and stayed at a large old-fashioned hotel near the station.

These days were to be the most inspiring of Miss Shamsee's life. She and the geophysicist walked about the city in a kind of trance, with arms linked. Although it was May, the weather was cold and Miss Shamsee wore a cardigan over her sari, and a gray woolen coat she had bought on sale in the *Grand Passage* in Geneva; ankle socks kept her feet warm in her sandals. Even thus modified, her rippling walk attracted much favorable attention. The air was filled by the spring seeding of the great poplar forests of the Lombardy Plain, with the result that tufts of soft white down fell throughout the city like a gentle, continuous snow. This, and the unexpectedness of sudden love, made the situation seem fantastic and spiritual.

Their respective shares of the hotel bill having been carefully calculated by the geophysicist, they returned to Geneva by separate trains, and met only once more, for the following day was Miss Shamsee's last on full *per diem*; she was due to fly back to Organization Headquarters that evening. They said goodbye in the Contemplation Room, where they could be sure of not meeting anyone they knew. The geophysicist asked her not to write to him. In her heart she knew this to be abject, but she gave him a look of understanding so as not to spoil things. They parted without touching. Thus ended Miss Shamsee's meeting at the summit.

Back at Headquarters, she did not repine. She was deeply moved, but triumphant. This at least had happened to her. Though she said nothing, it gradually became known that something of the kind had occurred, and it gave her prestige among her sad companions. Once in a while, when Mr. Rodriguez-O'Hearn dictated a letter to the World Geophysical Union, she could allow herself to think that her lowercase initials in the corner of the page might act as a message to her lover—that somehow, eventually, they might come to his attention as he thumbed through the relevant file. And one day at the beginning of winter, when for the first time she hung up her gray coat in the office, she found a scrap of white poplar-down in the sleeve. She pressed it that day in the Organization Yearbook.

Swoboda discovered, through his companions, the varying degrees of esteem in which the rest of the DALTO staff were held—who was to be relied upon, who to be supported, who avoided. He also learned of the existence of one or two natural enemies.

"Take a dekko at this," Mervyn would say, holding up a sheaf of memoranda, each marked with a red HASTE sticker. "Bloody Battle of Hastings."

"Sadie Graine, I suppose?" inquired Mordie. Miss Sadie Graine was the secretary of DALTO's Chief Coordinator, Mr. Achilles Pylos.

Swoboda, who as yet knew the lady only by sight, dwelt on her name. "Sadie. I didn't think women were called Sadie any more."

"Short for 'Sadist,'" Mervyn explained, sorting out the papers. "Affectionate diminutive."

(This is not the moment to relate in full the story of Miss Sadie Graine. In the history of the Organization, as in the annals of all organizations, that narrative has a place—for Miss Graine's is a figure known in all large institutions, and even in some smaller ones. Her presence in any substantial office is as inevitable as that of filing cabinets and paper clips; no departmental scene is complete without her. Her own position is subordinate, yet she commands, fearfully, inexplicably, the ear of authority. She accepts no criticism, she possesses no humor; her tyranny is self-righteous, her vengeance inexorable. The sole—and unwitting—contribution made by her presence is to join together those who would otherwise find no common ground. For concerning Miss Graine there can be no divergence of opinion. Before her, all stand united in adversity.

The story of Miss Sadie Graine may yet be told.)

In the new comradeship enjoyed by Swoboda, there was one element more remarkable, more sympathetic than all the others. And that was the bond that developed between Swoboda and Mr. Rodriguez-O'Hearn.

Mr. Rodriguez-O'Hearn was, at the age of fifty-three, one of the most senior officials in DALTO. He was not the Chief Coordinator of the department—that office being filled by Mr. Pylos—and his secondary position was shared with two or three others. Still, he was a person of authority by Organization standards—and more ample standards might only have augmented his prestige.

The accidents of politics and geography which sometimes united to provide the Organization with its higher officials had seldom combined so happily as in the case of Mr. Rodriguez-O'Hearn. His was a mind of uncommon scope and flexibility. He was humorous, compassionate, and incorruptible—these invaluable qualities being here listed by order of importance. His sensibilities revealed themselves, as sensibilities will, continually; and not least in his mannerism of fingering a piece of music from time to time on an imaginary piano. And he was, to a degree unusual in the Organization, a cultivated man. There was, one felt, almost nothing he might not have done.

Yet Mr. Rodriguez-O'Hearn had colleagues of less ability who had gone further; of less energy who had done more.

In all Swoboda's years with the Organization he had not encountered any official of this caliber. His natural kinship with Rodriguez-O'Hearn went beyond that which he enjoyed with Mervyn, Mordie, and Miss Shamsee. Admiring as Swoboda was of Rodriguez's gifts, he was also drawn to him by the inconsistencies he began to detect under Rodriguez's thoughtful exterior.

Confronted, for example, with some Daltonian dilemma, Rodriguez could instantly see what should be done. He would perhaps ask Swoboda to prepare such-and-such a draft memorandum to that effect. Swoboda would do so but, by the time the draft had reached the In-tray, a dozen fanciful doubts had been raised in Rodriguez's mind and a dozen specters of possible misfire sat about Rodriguez at his desk. The strength of the doubts appeared to be in direct ratio to the significance of the issue and the clarity of the proposed solution. "Thinking it over, Swoboda," Rodriguez would say, "I feel we should add . . ." Swoboda began to dread these final paragraphs, these postscripts or parenthetical observations that so often merely served to draw attention to potential errors that would never otherwise have been committed. "Perhaps it should be pointed out" or "I need hardly warn the members of the committee" or, worst of all, "In order to avoid confusion" frequently preceded a knockout blow to the argument so lucidly adduced in the body of the letter.

Caution, concluded Swoboda, is a very dangerous thing.

There were, in addition, issues that Rodriguez would perpetually and ignominiously evade rather than oppose—a multiplicity of useless regulations, an inundation of documents whose pages were more commonly committed to the wastepaper basket than to memory, the infringements of troublesome subordinates, the harassments of Miss Sadie Graine. (It would not have been accurate to say that Mr. Rodriguez-O'Hearn was afraid of Miss Sadie Graine, but it would have been so nearly accurate that it did not quite bear thinking about.)

Rodriguez had a peculiarity, too, of gratifying—almost of acting out—another's misunderstanding of him. With those who thought him unyielding, he would be at his most taciturn; with those who thought him irresolute, at his most discursive. Swoboda saw these things and, feeling he understood the matter, regretted them. Yet it cannot be said that they lowered Rodriguez-O'Hearn in Swoboda's regard. They were authentic human aberrations, and Swoboda's tolerance of them only increased the friendship which, for all its restraint, gradually grew up between him and his new chief.

Swoboda had come to Rodriguez-O'Hearn as a virtually unknown quantity. It is true that his personal file had been sent to Rodriguez in advance, and that these dossiers were compiled in conformity with the latest administrative techniques. A form in the file had accordingly notified Mr. Rodriguez that Swoboda was punctual and in good health, that he upheld the aims of the Organization, and that his output was high. The form was composed as a questionnaire, and against each question a series of boxes invited the appropriate tick—such methods as these having been painstakingly devised in order to avoid anything resembling a personal opinion. Since, in this modern world of incomparables, a tick in anything less than the topmost box for each item would have been highly damaging to a staff member, Rodriguez-O'Hearn also learned—and expected to learn—from the file that Swoboda was of ineffable good humor, that his initiative was unremitting, his imagination inexhaustible, and his

judgment invariably sound. Had the file contained a more reasonable estimate of Swoboda's capabilities or suggested the slightest singularity, the
implication would have been such that neither Rodriguez-O'Hearn nor
any other Organization official would have felt justified in accepting him.

It was therefore without prompting of any kind that Rodriguez discovered Swoboda's true nature. Rodriguez was a man of insight, and the
significant outlines of Swoboda's past gradually became as apparent to
him as if he had been informed of them in detail. He valued Swoboda's
industry; he respected Swoboda's discretion; he even came, little by little,
to apprehend Swoboda's tragedy.

And so it came about that Swoboda thrived. With all his new colleagues he
worked in the utmost goodwill. There was much to do, but no injustice cor-
responding to the SAGG documents darkened Swoboda's days or length-
ened his nights. His tendencies, though orderly, were ingenious, and he
developed an uncomplicated system of shading in the progress of DALTO
operations on the graphs entrusted to his care (so many experts sent to
instruct needy nations, so many grants awarded to the less technical for
orientation abroad—their shadow, on Swoboda's charts, never grew less).
Together with Mervyn and Mordie he drafted letters, added up columns,
and filed cards. There was nothing novel or intriguing in this, other than
the sense of being appreciated. All the same, Swoboda felt his life was moving forward again and, in his modest way, he was hopeful about the future.

Toward the end of the year, when Swoboda had been some months
with DALTO, the question of his promotion was once more raised in his
mind. The Board was soon due to hand down its six-monthly decisions.
He mentioned this to Merv and Mordie.

"You'll be all right," Mervyn assured him. "He likes you."

"Who?"

"Old Rodrigo. Can't think why, but he does."

"What has he to do with it?"

"He'll have to endorse you. That's what happens when you move to
another department. You have to get put up again for promotion by your
new chief."

"It's a formality," Mordie said. "They'll bring it to his attention. Don't worry."

A week or two later, Miss Shamsee whispered to Swoboda that Rodriguez had dictated to her the recommendation for promotion. Smiling, she showed Swoboda a page of cryptograms. "One of the best recommendations he's ever given," she said. "It's marvelous."

Swoboda thanked her, warmly but calmly, and walked away. Nevertheless, in that moment, he was as close as he had ever been to exultation. He went down to the cafeteria and had a cup of coffee. There, leaning on the Formica tabletop, absently stirring the sugar round in his thick cup and crumbling his Danish, Swoboda reflected on the goodness and ultimate meaning of things. How right he had been to stand up to Mr. Bekkus. There was much in life that one must let pass, much that did not merit the taking of positions or the agitating of one's breast; much, in fact, that it would be demeaning to take issue with. On the other hand, certain matters were not to be ignored unless one were to cast oneself away entirely, and here Swoboda had vindicated himself. He had repudiated Mr. Bekkus's treatment of him; he had demanded a more suitable standing in the world, and he had got it. He had, through his own fortitude, come forth into a new life of comradeship and esteem. He would receive a little more money, he would stand a little higher in the lowly lists of the Subsidiary Category. Swoboda was content. (It may be felt that he was easily content, but he is not the less to be envied for that reason.)

In a sense, too—or so it seemed to him—the Organization itself stood to profit from this development. Having dedicated itself to the rights of man, the Organization was, in some subtly heartening manner, only as good as the way it treated Swoboda. One could not completely believe in any enterprise that required one's own diminution.

Thus Swoboda, as he lingered over his coffee in the cafeteria. Not since the departure from the cherry factory had his heart been so light.

The days passed quickly at the end of the year. There was great activity in DALTO at that time. The deadline for submission of the DALTO annual report was drawing near, and Swoboda with his charts was deeply involved. As this vast report required some months in the preparation, it was always begun in the middle of the year it purported to cover. Necessarily incorporating an element of conjecture, it was an earnest effort for all that. It was Swoboda's first experience of the reporting strategy and he was quick to grasp its tactics of defense: a program, for example, was "particularly" efficient; a situation had been "carefully" examined; a success was "outstandingly" successful—these adverbial badges of insecurity being designed to take the opponent by surprise.

Swoboda's normal work was disrupted by the report, but he was assured that this was a temporary inconvenience and he did not mind. Cheerfully he pieced together the scissored paragraphs ("Two experts in metallurgy served in Tanzania during the year under review. . . ." "Four awards were made for the study of sanitary engineering abroad. . . ." "A fruit factory was erected in Kashmir. . . ."). Swoboda was surprised to see how the very items that had been the subject of so much anxiety and dispute throughout the year appeared, when reported, to be part of some grand and faultless design to which no disharmony could ever conceivably have attached. He tried to reflect that this was perhaps, in some final and overwhelming sense, no more than the truth.

In the days before Christmas, the long corridors of the Organization were gay with plastic wreaths, and in the main lobby the Organization Singers chanted carols interspersed with the Founding Constitution set to music. It was on the afternoon of the DALTO Christmas party that Mr. Rodriguez-O'Hearn asked Swoboda to come into his office. Swoboda was, of course, in and out of Rodriguez's office all through the working day; but there is an atmosphere, a closing of doors, a lowering of voices, a pushing away of papers, that unmistakably announces an interview of more personal character. (I am sorry to say that, although such interviews do occasionally bring good tidings, their general climate is one of foreboding.) Swoboda assumed of course, and rightly, that the discussion would have to do with the matter of his promotion, which he had been expecting Rodriguez to mention. It was known that the Board would soon meet—perhaps it had even met already, and Rodriguez was now authorized to give Swoboda the good news.

"Swoboda, sit down," said Mr. Rodriguez-O'Hearn. He performed a scale or two with the fingers of his right hand and said nothing more for some moments. Swoboda was oddly reminded of Mr. Bekkus. But he put this out of his mind with a dismissing mental smile.

"Swoboda," Mr. Rodriguez said again, "I'm sure you know that I have the highest opinion of your work." He was looking not at Swoboda but at his own right hand, which was now executing more complicated fingering. "And, I may say, of your character." He then interpolated, "The two cannot, in any case, be separated."

Swoboda did not speak. He observed Rodriguez carefully. He was interested in human nature and his intuition told him that he was getting an important demonstration of it.

"You must be aware," Rodriguez went on, now looking briefly at Swoboda out of his fine blue eyes, "that the question of your promotion was due to come before the present meeting of the Promotions and Probations Board. And that my endorsement was required."

"Yes, sir."

"Quite so. Well, Swoboda—" Here Rodriguez stopped. Swoboda, watching him, wondered what word should be used to describe his expression. He decided that the most fitting word was "desperate." Rodriguez then continued. "I did in fact write the recommendation on your case. And I may say that it was unequivocal. It was, indeed, wholehearted. However—"

"However?" Swoboda inquired gently, since silence seemed likely to descend.

"However—some questions were subsequently raised. I mean, after I had drafted the report on you. It was felt that, since you had joined this department so recently, others here might feel—ah—supplanted in the matter of your promotion. I do not say that I agree with this view, but it was presented to me as a possible source of grievance. . . . Miss—er— Graine did in fact raise the matter with Mr. Pylos, or so I understand, and he felt . . . Then, too, an official of Personnel—Mr. Bekkus, in whose office you formerly worked—seems to have said . . ." Rodriguez-O'Hearn's voice trailed away. He summoned it back and added more firmly, even defiantly, "And so, taking all these things into account, I did not send my recommendation."

"I see, sir."

"Swoboda," said Mr. Rodriguez-O'Hearn—and Swoboda now concluded that the word for his expression was "hopeless"—"this doesn't mean anything more than postponement. You realize that, of course."

"I see, sir," Swoboda repeated. He was still looking at Rodriguez-O'Hearn—at his expression, his rapidly heaving chest, his intricately moving fingers. A sensation was welling up within Swoboda as he looked, and this sensation, though he struggled against it, held him fast and threatened to overcome him.

"In fact I think I can safely say that at the next meeting of the Board— that is, the one after the present one—the one that meets in June—this is confidential, of course . . ."

Mr. Rodriguez's voice halted, wandered on. Swoboda sat still. Soon he would rise and go. Was there not the Christmas party to attend, and had he not promised Abdul Karim of Fellowships to help him serve the drinks? There was nothing to stay for here, nothing more to be said, even though Mr. Rodriguez was still talking, for Swoboda had now surrendered to the familiar feelings that had assailed him in the past few moments. He had fought against them, but to no avail. Try as he would, Swoboda could not change; he could not help himself. There was nothing to be done about it. The fact was that he pitied Mr. Patricio Rodriguez-O'Hearn. He pitied him with all his heart.

It was nothing short of tragic.

THE STORY OF MISS SADIE GRAINE

The moment his new secretary was introduced to him, Pylos knew it would not do. He looked at Miss Sadie Graine and, even as he smiled and shook her hand, he knew that it would not do. It was his first day at the Organization and, although his appointment was a lofty one, he did not wish to begin with a complaint. But the next day, or the following one at latest, he would ask for a different secretary.

Miss Sadie Graine was a tiny woman. She was barely five feet tall. Her features and bones were birdlike, her head tightly feathered in gray. She was an angular little creature, sharp of nose, eye, and tongue; but her lips were her most singular characteristic, being in repose (though that is not the word) no more than a small straight line. People meeting Miss Graine for the first time were apt to exclaim afterward, "But the mouth. My God, the *mouth*."

It had not always been so. There existed, in fact, a childhood photograph from which a tiny Sadie gazed forth with eyes large and luminous. These eyes—from taking in less and less, from peering ever harder into ever narrowing interstices—had contracted to their present dimensions. It is not the purpose here to study the causes for shrinkage. (Causes there were, for Sadie Graine's story was, like everybody's, a tale of truth and consequences.) Miss Graine's tale will rather be told in the form—the outmoded and discredited form—of her effect on others.

Achilles Pylos was a Greek, and it gave him a pang to see what had become of this woman of the Western world. Had the faces of certain male colleagues been pointed out to him as correspondingly ravaged, he would have replied that, in the case of a woman, a more aesthetically pleasing article had been despoiled. For Mr. Pylos was well disposed toward women. His own wife was beautiful. He was prepared to discover beauty in almost any woman, and it depressed him when, as in the case of Sadie Graine, he was utterly thwarted. It must not be thought, however, that Pylos recoiled from Miss Graine merely for her lack of looks: he was not a profound man but he was not entirely superficial and his glance penetrated at least as far as the upper substrata of Miss Graine's configuration. His own nature, beneath its outward pretensions, was an easygoing one, and he knew that he could not keep Miss Sadie Graine.

Miss Graine returned his smile with one of her own so pointedly summoned just for him that it seemed to seal her off from the others in the room—his new administrative chief, a flannel-suited man called Choudhury, and his fiscal officer, a Mr. Chai. Miss Graine was wearing a coat and skirt, and a blouse so unfrivolous that it at once suggested the absence of a tie. Mr. Pylos fleetingly took in these details as he walked across his new office to the windows (of which, since the room was a rather grand one by Organization standards, there were three). His token gesture toward pulling up the venetian blinds brought the others quickly to his side, and in a moment he was looking down some thirty stories to the Organization gardens below. He was unused to great heights, and steeled himself to a vertiginous future.

"This will be the west, I suppose?"

"The east," corrected Chai. "Or so I believe."

"Ah—the east. Of course." Pylos bravely kept his eyes on the scene below. "And these are the gardens," he went on, not risking further conjecture.

"The gardens," Choudhury agreed. "Yes."

"Is that something being built down there? Or demolished, perhaps?"

"Where, sir?" They all leaned forward to see.

"There. Near that clump of trees."

"I don't quite— Ah yes. Yes of course. No, that's a sculpture, sir. The gift of Denmark, I think. Or is it the Netherlands? I can easily find out if—"

"No, no, just curiosity. Yes, I see now. Very modern, of course. Very— er—" Pylos waved a well-kept hand.

"Very *free*," Choudhury supplied.

"Free, yes," Pylos echoed, taking the opportunity to liberate himself from the window. "Now where does this lead?" He strode across the bright blue carpet and got a shock when he laid his hand on the metal knob of a door.

"The carpet, you see, sir. That's what does it," Miss Graine pointed out. "It's the electricity in the carpet."

Chai hurriedly explained about the door. "That's your conference room, sir. There are three doors, as you see—the one to your outer office, this to the conference room, and the other leads to—er—Miss Graine."

But not for long, Pylos added reassuringly to himself. "Well, gentlemen," he said, going behind his desk and standing there with his fingertips resting on the blotter, "this all seems very satisfactory. It will take me a while, naturally, to . . ."

"Naturally," and "Of course" came readily from the lips of his two subordinates. "If in any way," they said, and "Anything at all." Miss Graine all the while stood by, and Pylos had the impression that she was waiting for the others to leave. He therefore said, "And now, since I understand I have a busy afternoon of meetings, I'd like to get on with these"—he laid his hand on a pile of documents with which he had been provided (the Founding Constitution of the Organization, the Basic Legislation Governing Extension of Aid, the Standard Conditions of Application)— "interesting papers." He smiled as if his thoughts were already elsewhere, and kept smiling like that until he had the room to himself.

Pylos sat down at his desk and really looked at everything for the first time. There were more gadgets than in his previous office, in a ministry in Athens—two telephones, each with a battery of numbered buttons, a small transmitter for the relaying of debates from Organization auditoriums (an arrow on the dial of this device could be turned to any of the several languages into which discussions were interpreted), and an intercom freshly marked "Miss Graine." Otherwise, the room did bear a certain bureaucratic resemblance to his former premises, and he really had to remind himself that beyond these walls lay no prospect of the Acropolis or Mount Lycabettus but a dizzy panorama of the peaks and ledges of immense office buildings.

As he sat with his hands folded on the immaculate blue blotter, he could not help wondering again how he came to be there. The new department that Pylos had been asked to head—a body to aid impoverished areas of the world—had been formed as a result of recent Organizational deliberations. Barely two months had passed since Pylos had received in Athens the cable offering him the post of Chief Coordinator in this new department. The conditions seemed not unfavorable, the salary—when translated into drachmae and calculated together with allowances—not ungenerous. His Athenian post in foreign affairs was soon relinquished (with satisfactory arrangements made to perpetuate his pension rights); his furniture was soon crated, his bags soon packed, his colleagues envious, his wife overjoyed. On the ship he carefully studied the Organization papers that had been sent to him, and he and his wife read aloud to one another from the *Reader's Digest* in order to improve their English. To no one, however, did Pylos express the surprise he felt: he was too much a Greek for that. He assumed it would eventually become clear to him how he, Achilles Pylos, a civil servant with no Organizational connections, with the merest smattering of knowledge in economics, should have been chosen for this post. He did not worry unduly about his suitability: he had been a bureaucrat too long for that. But he determined to go quietly until he got the lay of the Organizational terrain.

The matter was in fact a simple one. When the Organization's Governing Body created a department to aid retarded nations, the question of a chief for that department instantly arose. He must be a national of a certain kind of country—a country not too contrastingly prosperous, yet not conspicuously delinquent; a country with an acceptable past, a decently uncomfortable present, and a reasonably predictable future. The man, likewise, must walk the middle path—a man of middle years and middle brow was wanted, a man not burdened with significant characteristics.

Certain governments were asked to suggest candidates. Some sent the names of those they wished to be rid of, some proposed the ancient or the controversial. There were candidates who spoke no English, candidates who were chronically ill. One or two were overqualified and would have made trouble by taking up positions. A committee deliberated. The field was narrowed. At last the word went round. "They're trying to dig up a Greek."

Some weeks of archaeological jokes and official indecision were followed by the announcement of Pylos's appointment. The staff of the new department—who had all been drawn from other areas of the Organization—at first rejoiced, without knowing why. In Organization circles, the devil you don't know is always preferable, and it was readily believed that Pylos was a man of outstanding talents. Rumors circulated that he had been a hero of the Greek Resistance, that he possessed a famous collection of antiquities, that his wife owned a shipping line, that he had come to prominence from poverty-stricken origins, that his family was a princely and immensely rich one. At last, as his arrival drew near, the staff reconciled themselves to reality. Their reception of the real Pylos had nothing to do with the legends that preceded him, for in their hearts they had known all along how closely he would resemble his peers. So close, indeed, was this resemblance that the official sent by the Organization to meet Pylos at the dock picked him out at once from a throng of fellow-passengers.

And now, alone in his new room, still wondering what particular quality of his had struck the Organizational hierarchy, Pylos could not know that it was precisely his lack of striking qualities that had brought him there.

He got up and went over a second time to the closed door that led to his conference room. Taking out his handkerchief, he turned the metal handle cautiously. At this moment a single knock was instantly followed by the opening of another door, and Miss Sadie Graine came into the room.

Pylos smiled again at Sadie Graine. The sooner she goes the better, he thought, putting away his handkerchief. But he came—as it were, obediently—back to his desk where she stood, and sat down.

"I've prepared a list of your meetings this afternoon," said Miss Graine, placing this on the corner of the desk.

Pylos drew the paper toward him and saw that it was, in fact, a useful description not only of the meetings he was to attend and the officials who were to be at them, but even of the issues that might be raised and what the background of those issues was. He said, "Thank you, most helpful," in a minimizing way, but it was clear to him that the paper was invaluable, and he felt that this was also clear to Miss Graine. He laid it casually to one side.

She now indicated the pile of documents which had been left for study, and which he had not touched. "Shall I go through these for you?"

Pylos looked up. "But shouldn't I—" he began, and then began again, "It was felt by Mr. Choudhury and Mr. Chai . . ."

Miss Graine dismissed Choudhury and Chai with a slight grimace which, while improper, contrasted flatteringly with her deferential attitude to Pylos. "They mustn't bother you with trivialities." She took away the Organization's Founding Constitution. "I can mark passages for your attention, if you wish." She paused. "Of course, if you prefer . . ."

"No, that will be quite all right." Pylos could not help being pleased to find his time was precious. "Most helpful," he said again, this time with irrepressible sincerity.

Miss Graine gave him one of her brief, pin-pointing smiles. "I'll do it immediately." She took the pile of documents and left the room.

When the weighted door had given its ultimate sealing click, Pylos placed the list of meetings before him. The fact that Sadie Graine had proved efficient in no way lightened his spirits—on the contrary, it oppressed him with disproportionate foreboding. He felt that her derogatory reference to Choudhury and Chai should not have been allowed to pass. But then, she really had not made any remark about them—and were they not, in truth, a rather Rosencrantz-and-Guildenstern pair? In any case, Pylos thought, pulling himself together, it's all absurd. She won't be here more than a few days. Appeased by this thought, he took up Miss Graine's useful list, leaned back in his Organization chair, and began to study it.

Recounting the day to his wife that evening he mentioned Sadie

Graine. "What a secretary they've given me," he said. "A real battle-axe. But I'm going to ask for a change tomorrow."

There followed some weeks of what Pylos was later to think of as the Phony War. As he made his first steps across the Organizational scene, Miss Graine was ever at his side and, although he could not relish the proximity, Pylos admitted to himself that she was worth her weight in gold. He now told himself that he would retain her merely for these weeks of settling-in. Disturbingly, he felt that Miss Graine herself sensed this callous intention—but perhaps this was imagination. Considering how much he had to cope with at this time, it was odd the way Sadie Graine preyed on his mind.

Pylos's first official act was to name his new department. The interim titles that had been used—"Economic Relief of Under-Privileged Territories" and "Mission for Under-Developed Lands"—were well enough in their way, but they combined a note of condescension with initials which, when contracted, proved somewhat unfortunate. Pylos consulted with senior members of the Designation and Terminology Branch, seeking some descriptive but trenchant phrase, some phrase that would neither patronize nor minimize. No agreement was reached until Miss Graine, clearing his tray one afternoon, offered her suggestion. So it was that DALTO came into being—the Department of Aid to the Less Technically Oriented.

Nevertheless, Pylos intended to rid himself of Miss Sadie Graine. It was the case of Ashmole-Brown that brought matters to a head.

In creating the staff of this new department, heads of existing departments had been asked to nominate those staff members in their ranks most fitted to initiate a program of aid to the world's less-privileged. Many departments having naturally recommended those they could no longer tolerate themselves, a strangely assorted (and not wholly unsympathetic) crew was gradually assembled on a hitherto-unused floor of the building, and as DALTO reached its full complement of personnel, the remainder of the Organization's staff were able to close their expurgated ranks with a sigh of relief.

It was from this background that there advanced upon Achilles Pylos, a few weeks after his arrival at the Organization, the case of Ashmole-Brown.

Until he was assigned to the new department, Ashmole-Brown had been working away at his cluttered desk in the Department of Social and Anthropological Questions. Within a matter not of weeks but of days after the formation of DALTO, the contents of that small office, including Ashmole-Brown, had been completely transferred to the freshly partitioned premises three floors below. His papers were rushed through by hand, an unusual circumstance which in itself would have denoted emergency. To Ashmole-Brown it made not the slightest difference whether he was on the thirty-first or the twenty-eighth floor: his work was everything to him, and he pushed on with it, oblivious of change, his head bent to his swelling manuscript, his hand moving evenly from line to line. He was to be seen on his way to the Organization library, a closely written list in his hand; or returning, his head already lowered as if in anticipation of the next page, each arm bowed with a load of the heavy books so soon to be exchanged for others. His desk, his window-ledge, his bookshelves, even his gray-tiled floor, were piled with flagged volumes and curling documents. Whatever else Ashmole-Brown might be, he was no slacker: there could be no doubt that he was hard at it.

Hard at what? This was the question that had so perplexed the Social and Anthropological officials and, the answer eluding them, had finally resulted in the frenzied transfer of Ashmole-Brown to DALTO. Ashmole-Brown had been hired, long ago, to undertake a study—that much was certain. But why? And by whom? He had a contract in which the nature of the study was defined at length, and its terms of reference by no means precluded the incorporation of Ashmole-Brown in DALTO: they would scarcely have prevented his inclusion in any public institution, so liberally studded were they with the many-faceted gems of the sociological lexicon. Even to the most experienced decodifiers, the central message of this contract seemed indecipherable. Ashmole-Brown alone was certain of his task.

And did Ashmole-Brown then refuse to divulge the theme of his labors? Far from it. He liked nothing better. Jovially, he would seat the inquirer (and at first there had been a succession of these, some of them officially propelled) on his single extra chair—depositing the displaced pile of books onto the floor—and explain by the hour. He would show references to illustrate points, or drag out, from under a teetering stack, some document or article he had found invaluable. It all seemed to hang together at the time—the visitor would find himself murmuring, "Most interesting" and even "Fascinating"—but no one had yet emerged from such an interview with a coherent tale to tell. Ashmole-Brown's presence became a public confession of failure—a living expression of what his colleagues in Social and Anthropological Questions called the inability to communicate. Was he not using up official time and space? Was his rounded back in its antiquated tweeds not turned to two potentially useful windows? Might not the fluorescent light that shone down on him have shone more profitably on another? The Social and Anthropological Department, as a group, had experienced a meaningful, rewarding, and fully integrated sense of release when Ashmole-Brown was shunted off to DALTO.

One thing, however, had been overlooked. Ashmole-Brown's contract—his famous contract—contained a renewal clause. The contract in its present form had but short time to run, and the question of its renewal was presently brought to Mr. Pylos's attention by Miss Sadie Graine.

Pylos was busy with affairs of the less technically oriented when Miss Graine came in with Ashmole-Brown's file. He waited for her to lay the papers on his In-tray and depart, but when she stood expectantly by the desk he knew that it was some matter to which she attached importance. Raising his head—not without some intrepid show of irritation—he invited, and received, the history of Ashmole-Brown. Miss Graine was at this time becoming more vocal, and she left no doubt as to the correct course to be followed. She would not, she explained, have bothered Pylos with the case had it not been for the rank of Ashmole-Brown. This—as Pylos saw from the cover of the file—though temporary, was substantial.

Alone again, Pylos laid aside the less technical and examined the dossier.

The Organization kept two sets of files on its personnel. One of these recorded the halting progress of the staff member on his Organizational journey and, as has been noted, was uncompromisingly official in character:

this was known as the Personal File. The other, known as the Confidential File, contained only personal details and was available to an authorized few. (Nothing can describe the repugnance felt by the staff for the existence of these Confidential dossiers. They believed, not unreasonably, that secret files could only contain facts, or fictions, that exposed or defamed them, and the knowledge that an extensive system was devoted to the accumulation of such records caused distress of a natural and well-founded kind.)

Pylos found that he had been given both files on Ashmole-Brown, bound together with a rubber band. Neither was large, and few minutes were required to read them. Ashmole-Brown had come in with the century, had been educated at a college in the north of England, where he had written a thesis on the legend of Perceforest, and had since been employed at universities and in the government. During the war he had spent some time in the Royal Navy until invalided out for allergies. He had served on government committees. His hobby seemed to be linguistics, and his single publication was a pamphlet entitled "The Abuse of the Superlative in North America." The only damaging item was a letter, in the Confidential file, in which a department store asked the Organization's assistance in obtaining payment of a small account one year overdue.

Ashmole-Brown was respectable. But was he respectable enough to stand up for?—to stand up for (though Pylos did not say it, even to himself) against Miss Sadie Graine? What if Ashmole-Brown should be around for years, a perpetual testimony to Pylos's administrative naïveté? If the name of Oxford or Cambridge had appeared in the file, Pylos would have taken heart on behalf of Ashmole-Brown. But Ashmole-Brown was not endorsed by either of these infallible bodies: his background was unmistakably red-brick in texture, and Pylos wavered.

It was not usual in the Organization for a department head to visit the offices of his staff. On taking up his appointment, Pylos had made an inaugural progress through his little domain, attended by Chai and Choudhury, and by his Chief of Missions, Rodriguez-O'Hearn. He had genially shaken hands and asked unexacting questions. He had stopped to chat with a filing clerk here, a secretary there; had spoken Greek with a Greek, and French with a Congolese. The staff had stood around their hastily tidied desks, and all but the most disillusioned had smiled. Pylos had peered into a Chinese typewriter and worked a Fotofax machine. He had admired the magnificent views from windows and refrained from commenting on the gloom of the windowless areas, which were more extensive. Within half an hour he had been safely back in his own room, his duty done. Since then, he had attended a departmental party, and made a token appearance in the staff cafeteria. What more could possibly have been asked?

The Chief Coordinator's decision to call on Ashmole-Brown was therefore a departure. Even Miss Graine looked startled, although she at once picked up her telephone and confirmed that Ashmole-Brown was in his cubicle at the far end of the corridor. Scattering a trio of gossiping girls, bringing alarmed heads up from drinking fountains as their owners prepared for flight, Pylos strode forth. Ultimately entering a labyrinth of partitions, he was shown into a narrow room by a wide-eyed secretary.

The only person who did not seem surprised was Ashmole-Brown.

Ashmole-Brown went through his usual chair-clearing process and, when Pylos was seated, settled himself back behind his desk. He was a broad, awkwardly jointed man. His sagging tweeds and forward-flopping hair were of the same pepper-and-salt combination; even the round eyes shining out through the round lenses were densely speckled. The cheeks had retained their hectic schoolboy flush. The mouth was large, even generous, and presently said as if it meant it, "Great pleasure to see you here, sir. Great pleasure."

Pylos commented civilly on the evidence of Ashmole-Brown's industry, waving his hand toward the voluminous stacks—and in this way bringing one or two loose papers to the floor, where they were allowed to lie. He then said, with a serious leveling of voice, "Mr. Ashmole-Brown, I should like you to tell me something about your work."

Ashmole-Brown beamed. "Mr. Pylos," he said, "I have worked—labored, I may say—at this opus of mine for nearly four years, and I marvel, sir, I marvel, that today of all days you should choose to make this inquiry. I marvel." He paused to do so. "For today—this very morning—I reached a significant point in my journey. There is light, Mr. Pylos—light at the end of the tunnel. The end of my pilgrimage is in sight."

Pylos expanded with relief. "I am delighted to hear it," he said. "That is, we all, I am sure—"

"Quite, quite." Ashmole-Brown was radiant. He tilted back his chair. He took off his glasses and, holding them by the stems, twirled them round and round, allowing his eyes to sparkle unconfined.

"And how would you estimate the—ah—usefulness of your work?" Pylos inquired. "At this stage."

Ashmole-Brown pursed his lips reflectively. His glasses rotated more slowly between his fingers. "It is sound," he said judicially. "Yes, I would say—it is sound."

"Sound?" Pylos frowned. "Not more than sound?"

"No more—yet no less. Sound, sir. Sound is the word I should choose." There was silence while Ashmole-Brown politely declined to add another adjective. He broke into smiles again. "The completed work, however, has become—if not a reality—no longer a myth. In another three years, I should say—yes, another three—"

"Three years *more*?"

"Give or take a few months, naturally. My path lies plain before me. There is, as I say, light: light at the—"

Here Ashmole-Brown gave an exultant twirl to his glasses and they spun out of his hands, hit the desk, and fell to the floor. After a moment's surprise he dropped forward in his chair and fumbled shortsightedly on the floor around him. His speckled back heaved above the desk like the dorsal mound of some half-submerged sea monster. Pylos could hear him breathing in short grunts. "Now, where the devil . . . Ah, yes, yes, here we are." Ashmole-Brown hove into sight once more, pinker in the face, holding the glasses in his hand. Pylos saw that one of the lenses was completely shattered.

Ashmole-Brown stared at the glasses for some moments. He then laid them on the desk before him. He seemed to have forgotten that Pylos was there. He shook his head heavily. "This," he said, apparently to himself, "will slow me down considerably."

Pylos stirred in his chair, and Ashmole-Brown gave him a nod of recognition. He took up his glasses again and prodded the shattered side despondently with his forefinger. "O piteous spectacle," he declaimed. He then held the unbroken side vertically to his eye like a lorgnette and, after squinting through it at Pylos, lifted a half-completed page from the desk and attempted to read. His lips slowly formed the words as he identified them. He put the glasses down, seeming relieved. "Daresay I can go on like that for a while," he said.

"But surely," Pylos exclaimed, aghast, "they can be repaired in a matter of a day or two."

Ashmole-Brown stared. "My dear chap, no sense in that. No sense at all. I'm going on home leave in a few weeks. In England I can get a brand-new pair for nothing."

After the dismissal of Ashmole-Brown, Pylos felt himself to be full-fledged. It was as if he had passed through some ceremony of Organizational initiation, forged some invisible bond with his fellow administrators. He now settled in to his coordinational duties in earnest. With Miss Graine's assistance, a pattern was formed—one he was to follow for years, a routine of discussions, decisions, and correspondence which his position invested with parochial grandeur.

During the process of establishment, Miss Graine proved indispensable—so much so that Pylos eventually relinquished all intention of dispensing with her, and even forgot that he had wished to. A man like Pylos, between whose abilities and whose position there lie certain gaps, needs a woman like Miss Sadie Graine. For Miss Graine made it her business to plug those gaps—with flattery of Pylos, with disparagement of his equals, with inequities to his underlings, with whatever unsightly wadding came to hand. It was her daily task to fortify the dikes of Pylos's self-esteem. The excessive credence he put in her high opinion of himself soon naturally extended to her other views. He came to accept her judgments, and these judgments gradually took on a note of instruction.

For Miss Graine, too, the incident of Ashmole-Brown had been significant. After that she became steadily more vocal, more peremptory. Silence lends stature, and Miss Graine, growing talkative, revealed herself to her colleagues as petty and acrimonious. She condemned unthinkingly, and was open to no rational explanation. (She had a curious habit of saying "I'll admit that," "I grant that," "I'll say that much," as if acknowledging that any reasonable admission must be forced out of her.) She quickly made her new power felt, letting it be known that she had instigated the fatal investigation of Ashmole-Brown, and becoming feared as a result. A few tried, with fleeting success, to ingratiate themselves with her; most merely sought to keep out of her way, saying they would not go against The Graine. Keeping out of her way was not easy. She set up in her office an intricate system of files covering the activities of the department, so that Pylos might have immediate access to them. These files were methodically kept: though it were method, however, there was madness in it—or at least obsession, for they duplicated, from various angles, other records kept elsewhere. No one dared to point this out. She also miraculously retained in her head, keeping it otherwise vacant for the purpose, all manner of statistics referring to the less technically oriented as well as to the DALTO personnel.

In assessing Miss Graine's character, her single status was taken into account—inevitably, but perhaps excessively. For had Miss Graine ever been seriously contemplated as a life partner, had she even been asked—let alone taken—in marriage, her demands on the world might have been different.

Senior members of Pylos's staff would compliment him on her efficiency, saying "What would you do without her?" As time wore on, a note of wistful speculation crept into this rhetorical inquiry, and it developed the ring of a real question. There was, indeed, no way of knowing what his stature at the Organization might have been, had he fallen under some other influence than that of Sadie Graine. As it was, he came to feel pleasantly important as he trod the Organization's lobbies or rode its elevators. His dark, portly good looks were recognizable, and he was greeted wherever he went. He gradually formed a circle of acquaintances: not precisely intimates, these were more in the nature of cronies—their talk did not extend beyond shop, but this shop was sometimes talked in their living rooms as well as their offices. Although exalted in Organizational rank, they were not remarkable men. First-class minds, being interested in the truth, tend to select other first-class minds as companions. Second-class minds, on the other hand, being interested in themselves, will select third-class comrades in order to maintain an illusion of superiority; and it was this way with Pylos.

A lingering adroitness saved him from utter mediocrity, and it was this adroitness, together with the promptings of Miss Sadie Graine, that helped him sense the temper of the Organization and dictated the tone of his dealings with his staff.

There was, for example, his masterly handling of Choudhury's request for promotion. Although this came soon after the Ashmole-Brown episode, Pylos was already acting with more assurance. When Miss Graine, with lips meaningly tightened, admitted Choudhury to his office, Pylos was prepared. And when Choudhury, with unprecedented eloquence, pleaded his case, Pylos made no outward resistance. As it happened, he had just come from a top-level meeting at which the Director-General of the Organization had enjoined his departmental chiefs to administrative stringency, due to a crisis in Organization funds. Pylos could conceivably have given Choudhury this straightforward and authentic reason for refusal; the fact that he did not shows the velocity with which Pylos was learning the Organizational ropes. He did tell Choudhury that he had discussed the matter of promotions with the Director-General that very morning. The Director-General, he went on, put a certain emphasis on seniority. Years of service, years of experience—age, in short—mattered to him, perhaps more than they did to . . . (here Pylos gave a rueful, self-indicating smile) . . . others. Choudhury, for all his outstanding ability, was a comparatively young man. Could he not be patient? At his age, a matter of two or three years—what were they? Could he not take them in his youthful stride? So Pylos appealed, and Choudhury submitted.

Yes, Mr. Pylos had an appealing manner, and he used it for that purpose. He aimed to please, and his aim was directed to the highest circles. After a while he developed a posture that had always been latent with him—an excessively upright posture verging on a strut. He walked as if he were bending over backward.

Miss Graine's responsibilities having increased, she was provided with the help of a typist, who was accommodated in an inside office that had

been—and continued to be—used for hats and coats. The makeshift setting was well-suited—and perhaps contributed—to the constant turnover
of the girls engaged. One of these girls, it is true, made an attempt to relate
the story of Miss Sadie Graine to the Department of Personnel during
the third year of Mr. Pylos's administration. The tale, told with earnest
lucidity, moved her hearer—a personnel officer of mature years and large
bun—to send subsequently for the Confidential file on Miss Graine. But
on finding this to be a veritable treasure-house of testimonials lavishly
endorsed by the upper echelons of DALTO, she returned it unmarked
to the registry and requested in its place the file on the typist—in which
she entered a brief account of the typist's appeal, adding a notation with
respect to paranoid tendencies. Shortly afterward the girl was sent to assist
the less technical in rugged country northwest of Kabul.

The environs of Kabul were not the only locality to benefit in this way.
Those who served the Organization in DALTO projects throughout the
world soon began to give an impression of being divided into two groups:
those who had volunteered for such service, and those who had displeased
Miss Sadie Graine. The senior officers of Pylos's staff were dedicated men;
in order to conserve their efforts the more completely for the far-flung
needy of the world, they took the precaution of doing nothing for those
close to them. One or two who fell below this lofty standard and intervened
on behalf of their subordinates were quickly eliminated by Miss Graine.

Of the more junior staff, some—and particularly those who foresaw a
sojourn in Kabul—condemned Pylos. Others, of larger nature, contended
that he was a weak man but a man of goodwill. Whatever their view, not
a day passed without their taking some stock of the situation. Over their
typewriters, over their desks, over their morning coffee, over a period of
five years, the staff of Pylos recounted to one another, week in, week out,
successive chapters in the tale of Sadie Graine.

With regard to the less technically oriented, all the efforts of Miss Graine
were required to shield Pylos from troublesome ambiguities. He sincerely
wished to assist the laggard lands commended to his care. Yet he looked
about him at the fully oriented, and in his heart he wondered. Was this

the state of mind one sought to purvey to the less privileged? It was true that the grievous condition of many of the countries assisted by DALTO seemed to justify almost anything that was done to them—providing, as it were, a mandate for any change, the bad along with the good.

About the development process, there appeared to be no half measures: once a country had confessed to backwardness, it could hope for no quarter in the matter of improvement. It could not accept a box of pills without accepting, in principle, an atomic reactor. Progress was a draught that must be drained to the last bitter drop.

Once, after a day-long conference on Civic Coordination projects, it occurred to Pylos that progress might have taken different, unimagined forms; but he soon dismissed this idea for what it was, the result of mental strain. Occasionally he wondered if more thought might not have been given to the ultimate consequences of such drastic technical change— change about which, indeed, the word "impact" was frequently used. More thought—but by whom? Not by Pylos. Pylos was intent on staying on top of things, not getting to the bottom of them. If there was one thing Pylos didn't go for it was being asked to consider complexities at any length and for their own sake. He could turn quite nasty if pressed to do so.

Achilles Pylos could only hope that the backward nations, once technically oriented, would make some happier use of this condition than their mentors had.

He found himself obliged to participate in what were called farreaching decisions concerning countries of whose language he was ignorant, whose customs he had never studied, whose religion was a puzzle to him, whose politics a labyrinth, whose history a mystery. For this purpose he was provided with advisers whose qualifications did not in every instance exceed his own capacities—and with documents whose abundance invariably did. And at intervals he made headlong journeys to inspect the work of DALTO around the world.

When in this way he visited DALTO projects in the field—to gain, as the saying goes, firsthand knowledge—he was generally received in spacious offices and whisked about, to institutes and farms, to factories and dam-sites, in large cars. He stayed in air-conditioned hotels and was entertained in important houses. He could not quite convince himself that this led to firsthand knowledge. But since he did not believe in useless suffering he was also displeased when he came upon a DALTO mission existing without such amenities, and would depart promising to rectify the situation.

These contradictions caused him dismay, but Pylos suppressed his misgivings, with the help of Sadie Graine—who urged upon him matters of more immediate importance, such as jurisdictional disputes with fellow aid-agencies over specific rights to assist the needy. Any important deviation from established Organization practices would have necessitated a character very different from his. Faintly he trusted to the larger hope—that something less than ill would be the final goal of good. Sometimes he consoled himself with the simple fact that he, one of DALTO's own officers, was aware of such inconsistencies. This seemed to help somewhat.

On the fifth anniversary of Pylos's arrival at the Organization, a new leaf, turned by an unexpected hand, was opened in the story of Miss Sadie Graine.

That evening, for the first time, Sadie Graine came to dinner at the Pylos apartment. Mrs. Pylos had often spoken with Miss Graine on the telephone, and had glimpsed her occasionally in her husband's office. Once in a while she had said to Pylos, "Shouldn't we ask your secretary to dinner?" Pylos, from some instinct which he could not then explain but which was later vindicated, had repeatedly turned the suggestion aside. At last the anniversary celebration presented itself, and Mrs. Pylos, saying "Achilles, don't be ridiculous," had telephoned Miss Graine and invited her to dinner.

The evening seemed to go well enough. There were several other guests, and along the table Pylos saw his wife talking in her usual charming way with Miss Sadie Graine. He even heard her say, "Do call me Ismene." It was unnecessary, even indecent, to contrast his wife, with her elegant golden head and great gray eyes, with Sadie Graine, with her tight little lips and tight little dark-blue dress; but Pylos was touched to observe that Sadie Graine had a new permanent wave for the occasion.

When the guests had gone—and, being official guests, they left early—Mrs. Pylos put her feet up on the sofa while her husband went around opening windows and replacing a chair or two. They remarked how So-and-So had put on weight, how his wife had been wearing a wig; how someone else had been allergic to the mousse. And at last the conversation reached Miss Sadie Graine.

"Really darling," said Mrs. Pylos, taking off her bracelet and laying it on the coffee table beside her. "What an ἀπολειφάδι."

Pylos was startled. His wife was a kind woman—in fact, as beautiful women go, a very kind woman. It was not her habit to take strong dislikes or to use strong language. He opened a window he had just closed. "How is that, my dear?"

"I should have thought," his wife went on, "that you might just as well have kept the first one."

Pylos now came and sat down. "Ismene, I don't understand you at all. What first one?"

"Why Achilles, don't you remember? When you first joined the Organization, they gave you an impossible secretary—some nasty old thing, you told me—and you sent her away and asked for a different one. Now, don't tell me you've forgotten. All I'm saying is—she couldn't have been much worse than this one."

Pylos lit a cigarette. He looked so concerned that his wife concluded he must be thinking of something else. Eventually he said, however, "I suppose it does come to much the same thing."

The following morning, Choudhury had an early appointment to see Pylos. The two men sat down together, freshly shaven and smelling faintly of cologne, in Pylos's office. The morning light was particularly brilliant, and Pylos was taken aback to notice a change in Choudhury. Choudhury was looking seedy. His eyes were circled, his cheeks sunken, his black hair coarsely threaded with white. Pylos realized that, although he saw Choudhury almost daily, he had not really looked at him for some time. Ah well, he told himself, we're all getting on, I suppose, and there's nothing we can do about it. "How are you getting on, Yussuf?" he inquired pleasantly. "And what can I do for you?"

"Mr. Pylos," said Choudhury, leaning forward in his chair and putting his hand earnestly on the edge of the desk, "you may remember that I once spoke to you about my promotion."

Pylos responded, "Of course"—not because he remembered at all, but because it really *was* a matter of course: it seemed to Pylos that scarcely a day passed without some member of his staff raising the question of their promotion, and there was no reason why Choudhury should have been an exception. Like most department heads at the Organization he had come to regard these petitioners as neurotic nuisances—and in fact by the time they reached Pylos they were often acting pretty queerly. In each case he received the applicant with a sense of long-suffering, even of martyrdom.

"I know you have a lot on your mind," Choudhury went on, "and I haven't bothered you again until now. I kept hoping that something would develop. But I wonder—it's been so long—can you tell me how my case stands?"

Pylos saw that he would have to deal more or less frankly with Choudhury. The Director-General was at that moment discouraging promotions—due to a severe financial crisis—and the prospects of advancement for someone like Choudhury were distant indeed. Pylos leaned his elbows on the desk and brought the tips of his fingers together. He looked hard at Choudhury, and it struck him again how worn Choudhury was looking. Taking his cue from Choudhury's appearance, he spoke.

"Yussuf," he said, "as you know, we now have a new Director-General— a younger man, a man of great energy and—I say it in no pejorative sense—ambition. He has made it known that he will want the upper positions of the Organization to be filled increasingly by men and women of youth and vigor like himself. Naturally, he respects the abilities—I may say, the devotion—of" (here Pylos gave a rueful smile) "old-stagers like ourselves. But I would be less than honest with you if I did not mention that this new emphasis on a younger staff may hamper your prospects for the immediate future."

As Pylos uttered these words and leaned back in his chair, not displeased with himself, Choudhury's hands convulsively grasped the edge of the desk, and Choudhury himself turned gray. He got to his feet and, still gripping the edge of the desk as if he would tip it over, uttered a stream of agitated words in his own language. Pylos, greatly shocked, remained seated with an effort, looking up into Choudhury's wild eyes. Such a thing had never happened to him before, and fortunately it did not last long. In a moment or two Choudhury subsided, and sank down trembling into his chair. His breath came and went sobbingly; his forehead was wet, his hands quivered. He murmured a distraught apology.

Maintaining a certain reserve, Pylos reassured him. "You must have been overworking," he said. "Letting things get you down."

But Choudhury, doubtless not wishing to compound the impression of decrepitude, denied this. Limply he asked leave to go. Pylos saw him to the door. He put his hand on Choudhury's arm. "We'll have to see what can be done about your future," he said—his thoughts already turning toward Kabul.

When Choudhury had gone, Pylos sat down again. He wanted to forget what had just taken place, but he could not face the contents of his In-tray so he simply sat there for a while, feeling uneasy. It wasn't so much Choudhury's going to pieces that bothered him: it was what Choudhury had said. Not that Pylos understood a word of Urdu, of course. But he knew well enough when he heard the name of Sadie Graine.

Once in a great while, it happens that a scholarly book, a large, difficult, and demanding book, a book not devoid of footnotes and statistics, will by its very erudition engage the public interest. It was so with Gibbon's first volume; it has happened more recently with the respective works of Professor Myrdal and Doctor Kinsey. And thus it was with the work of Ashmole-Brown.

The Organization had forgotten Ashmole-Brown. Five years earlier, Ashmole-Brown had been handed his final paycheck, an envelope containing his travel authorization and steamer-tickets, and a receipt for his relinquished *laissez-passer*. He had got into the Down elevator and gone out through the Organization's revolving doors, and there had been no reason to think of Ashmole-Brown ever again. Ashmole-Brown had been terminated. What, then, was Ashmole-Brown doing on the inside page of the morning newspaper, grinning broadly as he stepped ashore on the very pier from which he had been summarily dispatched? According to the legend beneath the photograph, he was arriving for the publication of his book *Candle of Understanding*, which had recently created a sensation in England.

The photograph was indistinct, the legend brief. But it was Ashmole-Brown all right. The same eyes beamed through (intact) spectacles, the same shaggy tweeds were furled around ungainly limbs. Those at the Organization who saw the photograph were subtly troubled by this breakdown in the natural order of things. It was as if an old film had been run through the projector in reverse, and Ashmole-Brown were seen descending instead of mounting the gangway of his outbound vessel. It gave them a sense of witnessing some act of prodigious insubordination.

A few days later, glancing through a picture-magazine at the Organization barber-shop, Pylos came upon the same photograph of Ashmole-Brown—this time, large, sharp, and glossy and followed by several others. "Great to be back," Ashmole-Brown was quoted—somewhat improbably—as having said. The caption proceeded to explain that he had been to these shores before and that he had at one time worked for the Organization. In a brief interview on the facing page, Ashmole-Brown was reported as having, among other things, modestly brushed aside the assumption that he had resigned from the Organization in order to devote himself exclusively to the completion of his great work. "Resigned? Not a bit of it," he exclaimed (with, so it was recounted, a genial guffaw). "Dismissed, more like it. Turfed out. Jolly well turfed out." No particular importance was attached to this revelation, and the sequence of photographs went on to depict a series of genial guffaws.

During the weeks that followed, Pylos saw much of Ashmole-Brown. His guffaw, along with innumerable copies of his immense and expensive book, was to be seen in bookshop windows, in railway carriages, and on coffee tables. *Candle of Understanding* was advertised, lyrically and at length, in newspapers which also reviewed it with no less lyricism and no greater brevity. It was praised by specialists and laymen alike. One learned that Ashmole-Brown was lecturing to various august assemblies, and that he would discuss his book late at night on a television program called "Last Gasp." Finally Pylos came home one evening to find the book in his own living room. The next day he took it with him to the office.

There he placed the book before him on his desk and examined its black and white jacket. "A Study in Technology and Humanism" was printed below the title. From the front flap Pylos learned that Ashmole-Brown had spent eight years compiling this examination of what was called "the diverse traditions, merging present and common destiny of men." Ashmole-Brown, so the paragraph said, had concerned himself with the historical and current effects of technical change on indigenous cultures; had based himself on the ingenious premise that there was something to be learned from the chronicle of human experience. There followed a brief summary of the author's background, with a mention of his four years at the Organization. Ashmole-Brown was married, had a grown daughter, and cultivated his garden near Colchester. Pylos turned the preliminary pages and began Chapter I.

Half an hour later he closed the book and laid his hand upon it. Between his fingers the jacket interjected "Literate" and "Illuminating." He could not deny it. Ashmole-Brown had obviously written an extraordinary book. Here were the contradictions which Pylos had failed to confront during his years with the less technically oriented. Here—but presented with what sympathy, what grace, what goodwill, and yet with what authority—were just such insights as Pylos would have wished to have; just such solutions as he would have wished to propose. It was undeniable: the book was masterly.

There was something grotesque, even terrifying, about the idea that Ashmole-Brown's great work had all this while been accreting, like an iceberg, for the good ship Pylos to founder upon. Pylos groaned, and opened the back flap of the jacket.

From this he learned that Ashmole-Brown had taken his title from the Apocrypha. Well, why not? Was not Ashmole-Brown himself out of the Apocrypha, in a manner of speaking? But why the devil had the man not said his work was this important? "Sound," he had said; Pylos could just see him saying it: "I should call it sound." Did he not realize that no one talked like that these days? One did not minimize one's achievements—in fact, such diffidence was open to damaging psychological interpretations. It wasn't done. And yet—Ashmole-Brown was exactly the type who would do it, and Pylos felt he should have known. Damn the man, had he not even written some pamphlet—now it all came back to Pylos—yes, a pamphlet on the abuse of the superlative? (This work appeared in paperback shortly afterward and, advertised as "Early Ashmole-Brown," sold extensively.) Pylos groaned again, and he turned the book over on its face. From the back cover, Ashmole-Brown's round face looked up at him, creased for a mild guffaw.

Pylos was a man who could recognize his own defects. He could not, however, dwell on them. Tracing the Ashmole-Brown débâcle back to its origins, he swiftly recalled that he had been new to the Organization at the time, and that Ashmole-Brown had been virtually unknown to him. Soon he was reproaching himself for nothing more than having relied too heavily on the judgment of others. And these others were quickly fused into a single figure.

Miss Graine, seeing Ashmole-Brown's book on Pylos's desk, had experienced a feeling of dread. It was not simply the existence of the book; it was the fact of Pylos's having left it there, in flagrant violation of their mutual security pact. The sensation that her power was passing communicated itself, mysteriously, from Miss Graine to her colleagues. Exhibiting a new sense of impunity, several people drew her attention to articles on Ashmole-Brown, ingenuously asking if she remembered him. One morning she found a magazine on her desk, opened to a large heading: "Are You an Ashmole-Brown Enthusiast?"

The Ashmole-Brown development was in fact causing unrest throughout DALTO. The sooner his candle of understanding guttered out, the better it would be all round, and especially for Pylos. But Ashmole-Brown's success gave no sign of flagging. The fact that no official recognition had been forthcoming for this exceptional case was encouraging a sense of injustice in all—where a juster system would have imposed proportionate expectations. The staff, though naturally enjoying the discomfiture of authority, felt that the joke was somehow on them. Some token acknowledgment of their dissatisfaction was called for.

It happened that Miss Graine, passing by the Organization bar one day on her way back from lunch, glimpsed Mr. Pylos in earnest conversation with one of his friends—another Greek, named Apostolides, who had recently become head of the section dealing with staff assignments abroad. Now there were a hundred official matters that Pylos might have earnestly discussed with Apostolides, and there was no reason why Miss Graine should have been alarmed by the sight of the two together. Nevertheless it is true that all the way back to her office she was haunted by a quotation that she could neither place nor complete: "When Greek meets Greek," she repeated to herself, and wondered what came next. If she had ever known, she could not remember. But she felt sure it was nothing good.

When Sadie Graine was assigned to Central America, she appealed the decision. She contested it on the grounds that she did not speak the language—a not unreasonable objection but one which had not operated on behalf of those still laboring in localities like Kabul. Her objection was overridden and her assignment confirmed for a period of two years, with possibility of extension.

It will be thought that Miss Sadie Graine got what she asked for. But who, surveying the course of his own life, can honestly say that he has not asked for something he yet hoped not to get?

It only remained to choose a farewell present for Miss Graine and give her a departmental party. Pylos, when asked for his advice regarding the gift, suggested a suitcase. The idea was proposed to the subscribing staff members, and met with such enthusiastic response that a set of Spanish language records was bought with the money left over.

There had been many farewell parties in DALTO since its inception, but none so well attended as the one given for Miss Graine. It was held at the end of the day, in a private room adjoining the Disarmament Council lounge. Drinks were served, with nuts and potato chips, and the merriment seemed at times almost saturnalian. When gaiety began to verge on rowdiness, Choudhury—who was looking particularly fit—called for silence, and Pylos made a short speech. It was a speech similar to many he had given before, expressing fervent appreciation for Miss Graine's services, profound regret at her departure, and great pride that she had been selected for this difficult mission. He dwelt, with some office pleasantries, upon his own self-sacrifice, depicting himself as a man willing to renounce his own well-being for the greater good: Mr. Pylos, in effect, had loved not Caesar less, but Rome more. The response to his jokes was overwhelming, the ultimate applause deafening. The suitcase, and a box of records labeled "Never Too Late to Learn," were brought forward. So was Miss Sadie Graine. Pylos made the presentation, calling her Sadie for the first time.

He had intended to kiss her on both cheeks, but could only rise to one when the moment came.

OFFICIAL LIFE

Tuesdays are the worst," Luba said. She was sitting on a chair in Ismet's office taking off her waterproof boots. A succession of people had used the chair for the same purpose in the last fifteen minutes because the office coat-rack was just outside Ismet's door. This annoyed Ismet in general, and he minded particularly when it was Luba.

Luba, a beauty, was looking terrible—her auburn hair newly released from a plastic headdress but soaking all the same, her open coat revealing a succession of sweaters, her sleep-flattened face not made up. "Tuesday mornings are worse than Mondays, I tell you why. Mondays you're still fresh from the weekend. Wednesday you already look forward to Friday. But Tuesdays—Ismet, I tell you, Tuesdays are No Man's Land." Now she had her boots off but still sat on the edge of the chair, holding each boot up by its top. Her accent thickened when she got emotional, which was a good deal of the time. "What a morning. An hour to get here. What a country." She rolled her eyes toward the gray window. "Did you see the television last night? Not one thing worth seeing. I watched till midnight. I told my husband, What decadence."

Go away, Ismet was saying, in his mind and his own language. Go away.

"What would I give to go away. Now the pension can be drawn at fifty-five, I count to myself, how many years. Still so many." Luba put her hand to her lank hair and repeated quickly, "So very many."

"Jaspersen's going to the Committee this morning." Ismet drew attention to the work on his desk. "I have to prepare—"

"Jaspersen's going down? What's being discussed?"

"Item Six. The Question of Unification." Ismet again pointed to the papers on his blotter. The Question of Unification came up annually. Countries had been divided, subdivided. Some pleaded to be put back, others demanded guarantees that it would never happen.

Ismet's phone rang. He snatched it up without looking to see if his secretary had arrived at her desk by the coat-rack. "Contingency Section, Ismet." Before anyone spoke, he gave Luba an apologetic nod over the mouthpiece, denoting a long conversation. "Ah—Mr. Nagashima, yes, I called you yesterday evening but you'd already gone. . . . No, no, of course, it was well after hours, I was working late and didn't keep track of the . . . Yes, the Question of Unification. I think you have a false docket from the main file."

Luba stood up, still holding a boot in each hand. "That Nagashima loses things," she said. "Once, a whole set of working-papers."

Ismet said into the phone, "When you find it, then, perhaps you'd call me."

Luba nodded. "Another time, a folder of MOVs." These were Miscellaneous Obligating Vouchers.

"Let us lunch some time," said Ismet, prolonging the telephone conversation in the hope that Luba would leave. "Yes. Thursday would be fine." He turned the pages of his desk calendar with his left hand and found the day blank. However, since Luba now did leave, he said into the phone, "Sorry, I do have something—another day perhaps. Let's be in touch when you find the file then." He replaced the receiver quietly and lifted the uppermost folder from his tray.

A shadow on the frosted-glass partition alongside his open door informed him that Leslie, his secretary, had arrived. Not wishing to advertise her lateness, she alone of all the section did not use his chair to take off her boots.

"Leslie," he called.

There was a scuffle and a suppressed metallic scraping as she hung up her coat, then Leslie appeared. Leslie had long brown hair and darkly outlined eyes. Her stockings, yesterday of black wool, were of white lattice today. She said truculently, "I'm sorry." She was new to the section and had not quite established her right to address Ismet by his first name, although she invariably used it behind his back. Since he was only Step Two in the Specialized Category, she disdained to address him formally. "This rain," she said. "Pee-*ew*!"

Ismet could not get up the nerve to admonish her after all. He said, "I'm preparing a paper. I don't want to be disturbed unless it's urgent. Do you have something to go on with?"

"I'm collating."

"How long will that take you?"

Leslie made an estimate, doubled it. "Half an hour."

Ismet added to his many defeats by letting her go. At her desk outside he heard her take up the phone and dial her friend in the typing pool. Her husky voice was at its most pervasive when lowered. "I went to this dance," she said, "the one on the bulletin board. Pee-*ew*!"

Ismet drew a typed sheet toward him. A memorandum—to, through, and from higher authorities, with copies to those higher still—had been sent to him for a draft reply. "Pending accrual," it began. Ismet bowed his head over his work.

Nagashima was standing by his window, watching the rain. These winter downpours were, to be sure, no worse than the spring rains of his own country, yet how he disliked them, what nostalgia he felt, leaning from this window of another world, looking on a scene that contained scarcely one familiar item. An immense building was being demolished nearby, the walls smashed by repeated blows of a swinging metal ball. An almost identical building would certainly rise from these smashes. In Japan, too, temples had been erected and re-erected on the same sites over centuries. Obviously a similar sense of continuity was involved, but he had not been able to link the two traditions.

He looked down at his window sill—a broad inner ledge formed by the covers of the heating apparatus and, in Nagashima's case, completely stacked with dossiers, with folders, with innumerable, unmemorable documents. (Just yesterday he had been informed once more that it was forbidden to cover the heating vents in this way, but where then could these papers possibly go?) The false docket—such a strange name, like some treacherous Dutchman—that Ismet wanted was there, he knew, must be there, but he would never find it. He would lift them all, examine each title, his fingers would become frantic, his palms moist, but he would not find it. This had happened so often now that he sometimes did not look at all. The papers had ceased to be—had perhaps never been—quite real to him. If he actually believed in the existence of the file, then he might find it.

Once he had almost believed in these files and their dockets; had come, indeed, to the Organization as full of assiduity and goodwill as the refinements of his upbringing would allow. But his goodwill had glanced off the Organization like calf-love off a courtesan—the Organization did not require or even notice it. Unrequited, it had become a somewhat humiliating burden, furtively borne. Nagashima sighed, shifting but not unsettling this weight.

He began to turn over the first pile of folders. Ismet's file wouldn't be there—but here was the set of vouchers someone had wanted last month, that woman, also of Ismet's section, the one with the face like a cliff. Nagashima put the vouchers in an old interoffice envelope and sent them to Luba, having heavily scratched out his name on the envelope as former addressee.

"If I had high cheekbones like yours," said a chubby little girl named Gabrielle, "I'd do my hair like Greta Garbo." She came to stand next to Luba at the mirror where she was making up her face. Through an oversight, the ladies' room had an inordinate share of windows, but the fluorescent tube over its mirrored counter gave a light so ghastly that it was rumored to have been systematically chosen as the result of a time-and-motion study.

Luba, whose ability to admire her own image, however poorly illuminated, was a match for any time-and-motion study, went on applying rouge. She looked pleased. "It is the planes," she said.

Gabrielle looked toward the window. "Planes?"

"The planes of the face." Luba was growing rosier with every twirl of her fingers. "Garbo has planes. I see her in the street. No makeup, old clothes, nothing fashionable. Only planes. She is the friend of a very close friend."

"I can't use that." Gabrielle was examining Luba's powder-box. "I have it specially made. My skin is too sens—"

"Who's looking after the phones?" asked Luba abruptly. "The phones must be covered. Time after time I say it. Time after time, every girl leaves his desk."

Gabrielle said sulkily, "Leslie's there." At that moment Leslie came into the room, and Gabrielle went out without a word.

Leslie came to the mirror and whitened her lips a little with a lipstick taken from her pocket. (She carried a small assortment of cosmetics in her pocket in order not to be seen leaving the office with her handbag.) Over her ashen face she flicked a chalky puff. "What do you use?" she asked, taking up Luba's powder-box.

Luba finished with her hair and took the powder-box back. "I'm just using that up," she said. "It's not really right for me. My skin's too sensitive." Seeing Leslie's skeptical look in the mirror, she added, "Would you like it?"

Leslie said coolly, "Jaspersen was looking for you."

"What? Just now?" Luba began ramming objects into her handbag. "Why didn't you tell me?" She met her own wild eyes in the glass. "No time. Never any time." She transferred her glance again to Leslie. "No wonder we look as we do."

"It's O.K." Leslie brought out a bottle of iridescent nail lacquer from her pocket and began to shake it, her first vigorous action of the day. "He's gone to the Committee now."

Jaspersen took up his resolution—his draft resolution, that is to say, with its folder of proposed amendments—bent over his In-tray to read a note on the topmost file there, and walked across to the windows. Jaspersen's office was carpeted, an obvious indication of senior rank; the carpet was gray and somewhat worn—a more subtle suggestion, perhaps, of modifications within seniority. On Jaspersen's desk the density of paper was as great as on Nagashima's window sill, but these papers of Jaspersen's—these files and false dockets, these drafts for approval and final versions for signature—gave an impression of having just alighted, or of forming the course of an ever-flowing stream, whereas Nagashima's were as still and stagnant as lake water.

Jaspersen was a man whose Out-tray was fuller than his In-tray; whose head was above water, whose feet were on the ground. Who administered a section, and would one day direct a branch. Jaspersen had everything to live for—in short, every reason to get up in the morning and come to his office. For years he had tranquilly pursued his work as head of the Contingency and Unresolved Disputes Section, and would eventually go on to even more gratifying tasks in areas yet more contentious.

Nevertheless, on this morning when the Question of Unification was coming up for debate, Jaspersen was in a melancholy mood. Although this was unusual for him, it had happened before, and he understood that the mood would pass away. Jaspersen had been heard to say that the Organization was his religion, and it is well known that moments of unaccountable doubt are the earmarks of the devout. Jaspersen had even gone so far as to make this analogy to himself. At such times he had learned to immerse himself more deeply than ever in his work, and with this in mind he now lifted two documents—the Provisional Report of the Working Group on Unforeseeable Contingencies, and a Study on the Harnessing of Cartographic Skills—from his window sill and set them aside for reading at home that evening.

This mood of Jaspersen's would not even have been discernible beyond the Organization's walls. Had it been suggested, for instance, by some uninformed outsider, that the Organization had ever seriously erred in some particular, that it had ever acted with less than its potential effectuality, Jaspersen would have been as ready as always to correct this misconception with precise legal and statistical information; to cite chapter and verse—or, rather, resolution and amendment (while acknowledging, with wry witticisms, the larger but more bearable truth of universal human fallibility).

Jaspersen looked at his watch. It was now long past the hour set for the opening of the Committee meeting, and even a little past the time at which it might actually have begun. Jaspersen left his office, inquired for Luba of one of the secretaries, and, not finding her in, put his head around the door of his deputy, an Italian named Pastore.

Girolamo Pastore had been standing by the window. In fact, his window was directly below Nagashima's and, had the human eye been capable of distinguishing forms thirty stories up, the two would have been on view in identical attitudes, one a few inches above the other and quite unaware of the proximity. Pastore's gaze traveled over buildings of glass, buildings of aluminum, a building with a sharp pinnacle that looked like a hypodermic needle stood on end. Why was it, Pastore was wondering, that at the very moment when architecture began to use the limitless upward resource of the sky the ceilings had become so very low? More than commercialism: something to do with man's ceasing to demand noble rooms for himself, taking less pride in being a man. A man by himself—what was that these days? One counted merely as—a member of the staff.

In the Mediterranean town from which Pastore came, the streets were lined with small palaces whose every balcony invited the delivery of an oration (not that those balconies and their orators had proved entirely free from disadvantages); whose great doorways and windows offered glimpses of supreme moments in artistic creation; whose interiors gave onto courtyards adorned with fountains, with flowers, with curving stairs—

"You look as if you're delivering an oration."

Pastore turned round. "I was wondering whatever became of the *cortile*."

Jaspersen frowned. "The courtyard? I suppose it interfered with clean lines."

Pastore looked gloomy. "This clean-up campaign." He put his hand to his breast. "Western Man—"

How tiresome sometimes, thought Jaspersen, was Western Man with all his myths of Western Man. He interrupted. "I'm going down to the Committee. Will you keep an eye on things here? Luba's disappeared."

"I fear she can be traced." Pastore waved his hand. "Yes, yes, I'll be here."

Jaspersen was thin and straight with long legs, and he walked quickly even when going only as far as the elevators. Besides, he preferred to make his way as rapidly as possible through his section's depressing inner corridor—airless, windowless, and painted gray—where a dozen typists leaned woolen elbows on stained desks. Had there been some solution for these unfortunate conditions, Jaspersen, a humane man, would have proposed it. But he knew that nothing could be done—the designers of the building having judged such functional disadvantages to be small concessions made to outward harmony.

(The Organization had been founded at the end of a colossal world war—a moment when the spirit of international cooperation was naturally at its height. Scarcely had the Founding Constitution been signed by the participating nations when a commission of the world's foremost architects was formed to draw up plans for a building that would house this noble expression of human solidarity. The commission, in turn, had hardly sat to its task before certain fissures began to appear in the fabric of its deliberations: Dutchman contended with Swede, and Swede with Turk; Burmese fended off Brazilian, and Spaniard [through an interpreter] disparaged Swiss. The first to resign, a Frenchman who described his colleagues as being at loggers-heads, subsequently became a recluse. The second, an elderly Belgian, was taken on a world cruise by his spinster niece and ultimately regained his health. The eventual design, endorsed by a group of three, was remarkable for its extensive use of conflicting primary forms, and was fittingly hailed throughout the world as a true example of international cooperation.)

This being the case, Jaspersen hastened down the corridor to the elevators and pushed the Down button.

In the elevator he found Nagashima, a Step Three in the Mediation Unit of Jaspersen's section. Bowing courteously, Nagashima returned Jas-

persen's greeting; his perseverance with each syllable of Jaspersen's name
made it sound like a phonetic exercise.

Striking a personal note, Jaspersen inquired, "Your daughter at college now?"

"He's at the university, yes."

"I thought—"

"Yes, yes. Just the one son."

"What's he studying?"

"Humanities." Nagashima nodded, smiling.

"Only the one play?" asked Jaspersen, who thought he had said
"Eumenides."

Nagashima beamed. "Yes. Yes." The elevator stopped at the Organization Clinic and, with a polite farewell, Nagashima got out. The doors
were closing when a peremptory voice cried "Going down!" and the head
of Jaspersen's department stepped in, breathing heavily.

"Going to the meeting, Olaf? I'm on my way there myself." The Chief
made a gesture of fanning himself with his own folder of Committee
papers. "My word, they keep this place hot. Wasn't that Nagashima who
just got off? I thought so. Hadn't seen him for a while—was beginning to
think he'd got lost." The Chief laughed benevolently.

"He was telling me about his daughter—turning into quite a classical
scholar it seems." They arrived at the ground floor and Jaspersen stood
back to let the Chief precede him.

The Chief looked reflective as they walked along. "That sort of thing,
you know, Olaf, is the real work we do. Shaping the personal lives of our
own people, right here in this building. Merging their cultures through
their personal relationships; children adjusting to other environments,
colleagues becoming personal friends." They arrived at the top of an escalator leading to the basement. "We hear a lot about the Two Cultures, but
I say it's the Hundred Cultures we have to deal with. Bind them together,
forge the common links—" The Chief paused at the top of the escalator
to take in his vision of humanity manacled and trussed. "Never did like
these things. Fell on one as a child."

Warmly—with a ray of hope, one might have thought—Jaspersen
said, "I'm sorry."

"Oh—my own fault, of course. Didn't understand the principle. Step on and stay on." The Chief did this, gripping the rail tightly.

"Understandable, though," said Jaspersen, following.

"Hmm. Got to adapt oneself to the mechanism, Olaf, not fight it." He was making it sound as if Jaspersen were the child who had stumbled. "He who hesitates is lost."

"It lacks," said Jaspersen, who as a student had read the German poets, "the lovelier hesitation of the hand of man."

"What does?"

"The machine."

"Oh I quite agree." The Chief took on a look of liking nothing better than the larger view. He added obscurely, "The individual comes first." He gave his full attention to stepping off the escalator before he continued. "I want a word with you some time about next year's manning-table. We're getting overloaded in certain grades. Not enough slots to go round."

Now they were walking along a wide corridor that sloped downward, as it reached the Committee Room, like an undersea tunnel. Officials carrying papers came toward them and passed on purposefully, like salmon headed upstream. There was a multiplicity of doors, and a notice board that listed meetings. Another board displayed glossy photographs for the use of the press—the Spanish delegate enjoying a joke with the Custodian of Refugees, the Soviet representative opening the Children's Art Exhibit. When he reached a pair of handsome doors, Jaspersen grasped one of the inlaid handles that had been the gift of Finland and stood aside to let the Chief enter the chamber.

The ceiling of the Committee Room was earth-colored, the carpet blue: it was as if the skies had fallen. The room was formed like a theater, with a high public gallery. The action, so to speak, took place in the pit, where a more or less circular arrangement was created by an arc of tables—at which sat the representatives of various nations, all labeled, like plants in a public garden, with the exotic names of their countries. A certain bloc of seats was reserved for senior officials from the Organization itself, and it was in this section, in a leather chair, that Jaspersen seated himself, directly behind his Chief. The discussion had already begun, and Jaspersen, laying the folder of papers carefully on his knees, clipped over his ear the small electric interpreting device attached to the chair, his face assuming as he did so the grave and attentive expression of everyone else in the room.

Ismet concluded his draft memorandum with the word "implementation" and gave it to Leslie for typing. He then got up from his desk and stood at the window. Resting his fingertips on the inner sill, he closed his eyes. When he opened them, a face was looking back at him from the glass.

This reflection gestured, mouthed, nodded, and, pushing up the window, climbed into the room. "Gave me a turn, standing there like that," it said reproachfully, helping Ismet to pick up the papers circulated by the rush of air. "Wasn't expecting it."

"Why should they clean the windows on a day like this?" Ismet asked.

The man clapped the last memorandum down on the desk with an irreverent hand. He shrugged his shoulder before readjusting the harness over it. "Orders from above." He jerked his head skyward. "The way I see it—there's more chiefs than Indians round here."

Ismet said reasonably, "But that *is* the way you see it, isn't it? I mean, you only see the offices that have windows. The offices of the chiefs, so to speak."

"Plenty of Indians in the dungeons, eh?" The window-cleaner laughed uproariously, making Ismet regret his rational explanation. "I'm better off on the outside, if you ask me. Watch out for the bucket." Ismet had almost knocked this over in pulling out his chair. His visitor swung the bucket up over one arm and made for the door.

Ismet said, "I'm sorry I startled you."

"Should be used to it by now. Plenty of you looking out when I come along."

Setting his papers in order, Ismet heard the bucket loudly put down in Pastore's room next door. A moment later, Pastore was in the doorway.

"Nothing but interruptions all morning."

"Exactly," said Ismet.

"I need Leslie to take a message to Jaspersen in the Committee Room."

"She's doing a memorandum for me."

"This is urgent."

"So is mine."

"I've already asked her to go."

Nothing, Ismet thought, makes a more fanatical official than a Latin. Organization is alien to their natures, but once they get the taste for it they take to it like drink. They claim to be impulsive, but they're the most bureaucratic of all, whatever they may say. "Whatever you say," he told Pastore.

"The combination and interplay of such components," the speaker was saying, *"within deeply rooted conflicts—"*

Try as he would, Jaspersen could not take it in this morning. He pressed his hand to the device over his ear. He even glanced surreptitiously at the interpretation dial beside his chair, to make sure it was turned to the proper language.

"—obstruct the evaluation process . . ."

"Personal life," the Chief had said; "personal friend." One's life, one's friends presumably could not be other than personal, yet the distinction had developed. I suppose this is my official life, Jaspersen said to himself, looking about the chamber. "Official life" sounded like a posthumous document, some tedious work of commissioned biography with all the interesting incidents suppressed.

"My government takes the view . . ."

Everyone else was scribbling now, on scraps of paper, on the margins of documents, on pads provided for the purpose.

"My government thinks, my government feels . . ."

It gave him a sense of isolation, being the only one having personal thoughts in such an official chamber.

"Bearing in mind my government's long devotion—"

One said "relationship" nowadays about those one loved, and put one's friends in slots: words like "devotion" were reserved for official purposes.

A young man in gray had come to where Jaspersen sat, at the end of the row of seats, and was handing out copies of an amendment. Jaspersen, passing them along, thought how like church it all was. The deferential hush, the single voice intoning. O Organization, wherever two or three are gathered together in thy name . . . Jaspersen gave an unholy laugh.

Someone sitting beside the Chairman looked round repressively. One or two acolytes—the man in gray, a woman in black—silently carried papers back and forth across the room. The man had the stubby, earnest walk of a schoolboy; the woman appeared to glide over the blue carpet. In a man, Jaspersen thought, one could always see the child; whereas in a little girl one could always foresee the woman. The child Jaspersen who long ago had laughed in church, laughed in the schoolroom, had no place here, not even in memory. The idea that these guarded Committee faces had ever been childlike, or that they were sometimes even now transfigured by secular passions, was totally irrelevant.

"—to the preservation of freedom. For if freedom is to be effectively preserved, a solution must be found—"

One would have thought freedom was a museum piece—some extinct creature being pickled in a jar of spirits. The voice went on, on. Jaspersen's father, a gaunt old man who loved Schiller and had no knowledge of world affairs, would have quoted "No incantation can compel the gods" (might even, for he was getting quite eccentric, have quoted it out loud), but Jaspersen knew better; had more than once thrown in his lot with incantations in this very room and seen the gods compelled. Was it not worthwhile, this compelling of the gods in a good cause? And if so, why could Jaspersen not rejoice as he sat there this morning? The trouble was, official life had grown so remote from life itself.

"—together with adequate safeguards . . ."

Jaspersen was not a man to succumb to despair: in fact, with his quick walk, he had quite outdistanced it. He would never ask himself "What will become of me?"—much less the more terrible question "What has become of me?" Here, however, twenty feet underground, in filtered air and fluorescent light, amid the aspirations ratified by one hundred member nations, a certain depression had managed—God knew how—to penetrate. There is no armor, there are no adequate safeguards. Deeply rooted conflicts are within us and obstruct the evaluation process.

Leslie sauntered down the corridor, her head uncharacteristically lowered as she studied the effect of her new shoes, which buttoned across the instep. When the elevator came, she got in jauntily. She liked to have errands away from the section, and often combined them with a leisurely coffee in the cafeteria or a visit to her friends in the filing room. Her sense of responsibility took her first to the main floor, where she got out. Descending to the basement, she stood on her toes to avoid wedging her vinyl heels in the grooves of the escalator. At the end of a corridor, a guard admitted her to the Committee Room, and she discovered Jaspersen sitting in a row of seats near the door.

A speech was being made, and Jaspersen was listening so intently that she could not attract his attention. Someone motioned her to sit down behind him and wait, and she did this, feeling important as she sank into the leather seat and watched her skirt draw back above her white knitted knees. The room was brightly, hotly lit, and was decorated—somewhat datedly, Leslie thought—in blond wood and blue furnishings. Absently folding the message for Jaspersen over and over until it began to part at the creases, Leslie looked curiously up at the half-empty public gallery and the glass booths of the interpreters. This was more like the real thing: more, in fact, like television. It was the setting in which Leslie had imagined herself when she applied to the Organization, and of which she had not, until now, caught a single glimpse. Her duties consisted in the main of interleaving pages with carbon paper and typing on them at someone else's dictation: yet Leslie had repeatedly been told by her superiors that what was wanted was someone who would take an interest in this work. What was wanted, Leslie concluded, was some kind of a nut.

Leslie did not care to know what was going on here in the Committee; since everyone else obviously did know, involvement on her part seemed unnecessary. She felt agreeably secure in the presence of all these diligent faces. And Jaspersen, she noticed, was the most engrossed of all, his elbow bent on his knee, his hand supporting his intent brow.

"Recognizing the basic fluidity of the situation"—the speaker paused, poured water into a glass—*"and in the firm conviction"*—he drank—*"that the pooling of resources . . ."*

When Jaspersen raised his head, a hand appeared at his elbow. It was a curious little hand, plump and pink with astonishing silver nails. Some of these nails were of Oriental attenuation, others were bluntly broken off. Jaspersen, staring at the hand, was tempted to take it in his own. However, he merely accepted a pleated paper from its irregular talons.

He opened the paper, turned it round, and read. "Unification is postponed."

Jaspersen sat still for a moment or two, with the paper in his hand. He then put it in his folder and dismissed Leslie with a backward nod. He leaned forward and touched his own hand to the elbow in front of him.

The Chief's head veered to a familiar attitude—not detached from the proceedings of the meeting, yet inclined, receptive, authoritative. It was an attitude of head and shoulders that had been perfected within the Organization and was best demonstrated on the floor of a large conference room.

Jaspersen whispered into the leaning ear. "Unification is postponed."

The ear appeared to frown. "Not coming up?"

"Not today."

"—and fervently believing in the vital importance—"

"Nothing to stay for then," the Chief murmured, turning farther round.

"—and crucial significance—"

"Nothing at all."

They slid out of their seats furtively, like patrons leaving a bad film. Outside, Jaspersen said, "Now we'll never know who did it."

The Chief had a way of permitting a joke to register while denying it official recognition. "I'm anxious," he said gravely, "to have our item come up."

The postponement of Unification had gone to Jaspersen's head. "You realize," he said, "that they may not approve of what we've done?"

The Chief smiled tolerantly. "We must know how to accept criticism, Olaf." He spoke as if it were some useless gift to be stowed in a closet as soon as the guests had gone. "A most helpful discussion of Item Five, I thought, by the way."

"Didn't quite get it," Jaspersen said.

"Not get it?" The Chief had not known Jaspersen in this mood before. For a moment it seemed that he was going to stop in his tracks, halfway up the sloping corridor, on the rug donated by the Republic of Panama. "Not get what?"

Jaspersen took hold of himself: he did not want to go too far. (To go too far, in the Organization, was to travel no great distance.) "Oh— just an unfortunate phrase or two, perhaps—" They had reached the Up escalator, and the Chief had paused and was frowning. Pulling himself together at last, looking more like himself than he had done all morning, Jaspersen went on hurriedly, "In an otherwise excellent speech."

The Chief looked pleased, even relieved. Gripping the escalator rail, he stepped on and stayed on. So did Jaspersen, and they surfaced together at the high rise of the elevators, each tightly clasping his resolution.

Arriving back in his office, Jaspersen found his In-tray fuller than ever, his blotter studded with messages. The office was quiet. It was time for lunch—time for Subsidiary and Specialized to converge on cafeteria and dining room; for cronies from Public Relations, from Logistics, from Finance or Personnel to take up their positions on the warm ingle-benches about the Disarmament Bar; time for Jaspersen to send out for his plain yogurt and ripe banana. He sat down at his desk and began to go through the messages. Can you address the Assembly of Non-Accredited Groups next Monday? Human Dignity Section will call back. Please call Mr. Kauer in Forceful Implementation of Peace Treaties. Long-Range Planning has been trying to reach you. This last slip was marked RUSH.

"You all right, Olaf?" Pastore inquired from the doorway.

Jaspersen lifted his head in a manner intended to keep Pastore from entering. "Everything go smoothly up here this morning?"

"Everything was as usual," Pastore said ambiguously. "Unification is now set for tomorrow."

"I guessed as much."

"You all right?" Pastore asked again, hesitantly setting foot on the carpet.

"Well—I was feeling a bit low this morning, as a matter of fact. Feel better now. It was probably the weather."

"You know what it is." Pastore nodded. "I've been talking to Luba. She has an idea that Tuesdays are some sort of psychological low-point. It's an interesting theory—you talk to her about it. She thinks Tuesdays are the worst."

A SENSE OF MISSION

C arry your bags, Miss?"
It was the first remark addressed to her by those she had come to serve.

"A taxi?"

She nodded, reluctant to begin by speaking English, startled to find her language apparent. She spoke to the porter slowly in Italian, the *lingua franca* of this island. Someone was to have met her; they hadn't come. Yes, she would go to the hotel. Which hotel? Well—what hotels were there? A Bristol, a Cecil? A Majestic, perhaps?

The porter smiled. What she wanted was the Hotel of the Roses.

Only hours since she had stepped into the plane from the winter night of a northern city, Miss Clelia Kingslake was breathing mild morning air by the Aegean. The sun streamed down on valley, rock, and green hill, and the driver leaned against his taxi in his shirtsleeves. Miss Kingslake's pang of ecstasy was not a bit the less for her having recently entered her fortieth year—quite the reverse, in fact. All the same, when her baggage was aboard and they drove off, she became distracted from her new surroundings, wondering if she could possibly have missed her as yet unknown colleagues. She was to have been met at the airport; so she had been assured before leaving Organization Headquarters the night before. There had been no one the least colleague-like in the waiting room, and in any case they would have approached her. It didn't matter—she could manage for herself and they had more important things to do. For the time being, the entire region was dependent on their vigilance. After all, wasn't this an emergency mission?

The taxi rattled through a fertile valley toward the sea. When they reached the corniche, the driver slowed down, pointed out a row of Turkish houses, asked her why she had come to Rhodes.

She explained, on an assignment for the Organization.

"*Ah sì. La NATO.*"

Oh no, no. NATO was a military organization. Hers was a peace-keeping one.

The driver shrugged at this subtlety. He could not be bothered splitting hairs, and lost interest. Did she see those mountains across the sea? That was the coast of Turkey. And here, as they swung around a curve, was the city of Rhodes.

Clelia Kingslake had a glimpse of golden walls, of white shipping, of a tower, a fortress. She was revisited by ecstasy. A moment later she found herself in a driveway.

The hotel was formlessly vast, and brown—a dated wartime brown suggestive of inverted camouflage, as if it had been willfully disguised as a military installation. Upstairs, however, unlatching the shutters of a charming, old-fashioned room, she looked down over terraces and a pebbled beach to the sea and, once more, out to the blue Turkish coast. The open French windows formed, with their outside railing, a narrow balcony. She pulled up a chair and, leaning her arm on the rail and her chin on her arm, sat there in the winter sunshine, happy.

Clelia Kingslake was happy because, first of all, she was a Canadian. Fished out of the Annual Reports Pool at Headquarters, where she held a superior clerical post, flown to Rhodes at one day's notice, arriving there to sunlight and sea, to trees in leaf, flowers in bloom, to the luxury of finding herself beside the Mediterranean—all this by itself might not have been thoroughly enjoyable to her strict northern soul had she not come to assist in a noble undertaking. She had been sent to serve the peoples of the Eastern Mediterranean in their hour of need, and it was this that sanctioned her almost sensual pleasure in her surroundings as she sat gazing out from the Hotel of the Roses.

She was, in however modest a degree, the instrument of a great cause: in this setting redolent of antiquity she even risked to herself the word "handmaiden." A dozen years earlier, in Toronto, she had diligently studied Italian in order to take her elderly mother to Rome. In the end, that summer, they had settled for Lake Louise, but she had kept up a little with the language. And this dormant ability had posted her now, miraculously, to an emergency mission newly established in the Mediterranean as an antidote to an international crisis.

An employee from the hotel was opening colored umbrellas on the stony beach below. One or two hardy guests were bathing, although the sea looked neither calm nor warm. Apart from occasional shouts of "*Herr-lich!*" from the swimmers, the only sound was the rhythmic crunching of waves up the pebbled shore. "Sophocles long ago heard it on the Aegean," quoted Miss Kingslake to herself, and the consummation of the familiar line in an actual experience, combined with fatigue from an overnight plane journey, brought a rush of tears to her eyes.

The telephone rang and she jumped up to answer. It was the concierge. Yes, he had put the call through to her office. No, no one wished to speak with her. However, there was a message: a Signor Grilli (the concierge permitted his voice a faint smile, for the name meant "crickets") would come to see her at eight this evening.

She put the phone down. She had expected to be called to work at once and was disappointed. It was considerate of this Grilli, who was in charge of the new mission, to give her a day's grace, but she was anxious to take up her duties. She thought she would rest before unpacking and walking out to look at the town.

"Grilli. Downstairs."

"I'll be right down." She sat up, replaced the receiver, tried to think where she was. It was after eight. She sprang off the bed, pulled on her dress, combed her hair, alarming herself by muttering "My God" as she fumbled with buttons and looked for her shoes.

When she came out of the elevator there was no one to be seen. The concierge directed her to one of the lounges. It was a large room beside the bar, decorated with graceful murals of the seasons, and the one person in it was paring his nails beneath the harvest. Miss Kingslake realized that, because of the name, she had been expecting a slight brittle figure, whereas the man who glanced in her direction, put away his nail file, and made a minimal effort to rise was a big man, a fat man, too young a man to be completely bald. His Sicilian ancestry—from which he had inherited the knowledge of the Italian language that had brought him, too, on this mission—was not apparent.

She shook hands and sat down with an apology for keeping him waiting. "It must be the journey." She smiled. "I was in a deep sleep."

He glanced at her a second time, looked away. His hands quivered with the suppressed need to fidget. He said, "You haven't come here to sleep." When Miss Kingslake said nothing he went on, "I've been here three weeks. The first week I didn't sleep at all. No time. Kept going on coffee and cigarettes. Just as well you weren't here then, if you need so much sleep."

"I was assigned here only yesterday."

"And if you don't work out, you're going back just as fast."

The waiter came up. Grilli ordered fruit juice, Miss Kingslake a sherry. The drinks were put down, with a big dish of peanuts, and Miss Kingslake asked, "When may I come to the office?"

"Tomorrow, Sunday. A car will pick you up here at seven a.m. I'll be in it." The flat of his hand smashed down among the peanuts, a massive displacement that scattered them as far as Miss Kingslake's lap. He brought his fist back to his mouth and eventually continued. "Give Noreen a day off. If nothing else. Noreen's been here from the beginning. Work! You ought to see that girl work. A truck horse. You know Noreen at Headquarters?"

"Perhaps by sight."

"She's in our department there—Logistics. Not one of your fancy do-nothing departments. She's been in most of these emergencies—Suez, Lebanon, Cyprus, now here. If I had to go on another mission like this, I'd say Give me Noreen." Another peanut spun into Clelia Kingslake's lap. "Rather than any six others."

"Can you give me an idea of what I'm to do?"

"We all pull our weight here. I don't know what you do at Headquarters and I don't care. Here you'll do anything that comes to hand. Cables, letters, typing, accounts—"

"I can do any of those things."

"You'll do all of them. You'll be in with the Cap."

"The Cap."

"Captain Moyers. He's been seconded from Near East Peace Preservation. Assigned to us as Military Observer, but he's turned his hand to everything during the crisis. A Canadian like yourself. But a great guy." The eyes were wandering again, contentiously raking the walls, lingering suspiciously on Primavera. "A rough diamond, but a great guy. He'll be here any minute. He went out to the airfield to meet Mr. Rees."

Miss Kingslake pondered. Rees was head of the Logistics Department at Headquarters. "He's here?"

"Three-day tour of inspection. Oh, all the big brass have been through here this month—the Director-General himself came through, you know, on his way to the trouble spots. Mr. Rees was too busy to come before."

He pronounced it as if it were all one word, Mysteries. Miss Kingslake, her own gaze wandering, noted that the murals were by Afro. "I don't want to keep you." She allowed herself to add, "I'm sure you need your sleep."

Grilli was leaning forward, his hands splayed over the chair arms. All at once he changed color. He hoisted himself up, vast and padded—it was as if the armchair had come to its feet—and shot out between the glass doors into the lobby.

Mysteries, surmised Clelia Kingslake, signing the bill. She followed. Grilli was bowed over a little cricket of a man, while a military figure strode about the lobby roaring orders in English. When Miss Kingslake came up, Grilli introduced her.

"Mysteries, this is Miss Kingslake, the newest member of the mission."

Rees shook hands. He looked Miss Kingslake in the eyes and held her gaze. "Miss Kingsley," he said quietly, "I want you to know that people like you are continually in our minds at Headquarters. Sometimes staff members in the field tend to feel forgotten. Believe me, they couldn't be more mistaken. I want you to know that it's fully appreciated, the wonderful work you are doing here."

"Thank you."

"Believe me."

The three men were to dine together. Miss Kingslake was grateful that no suggestion was made that she should join them. While Grilli accompanied Rees up to his room, the Captain came over to Miss Kingslake, cap in hand, and introduced himself.

The Captain was also a fleshy man, though short. His face was red and puffy. He wore heavy dark glasses with square dark frames. The regularity of his black moustache suggested an inept disguise—another case of bad camouflage.

"We're sharing an office, I think?" said Clelia Kingslake, when they had exchanged names.

"So that's his idea, is it?" The Captain shot her a necessarily dark look. "More room in his office than in mine. What-have-you and so on. Could have requisitioned another office from the locals."

Miss Kingslake said, with a helpful air of making light of things that was one of her more difficult characteristics, "Oh well—it's an emergency mission."

The Captain slapped his cap against his leg with annoyance. "Emergency, bah. I've been in the Eastern Mediterranean five years. Seen nothing but a lot of so-called emergencies. Let them kill one another—best thing that could happen, what-have-you and so on. Or drop an atomic bomb on the lot of them."

Miss Kingslake stared. "The Organization—"

"Organization!" The red face inflated with facile rage. "A lot of clots, that's what they are, this Organization of yours. A lot of clots."

Miss Kingslake turned away. The Captain followed her to the elevator. "And the Arabs. Don't talk to me about the Arabs."

She made no attempt to. The elevator arrived.

"Vehicle at O seven hundred hours sharp. What-have-you and so on."

Just before seven Clelia Kingslake came down to the hotel lobby. A second sleep, a bath, and a new day had made a difference to her spirits. Waking in the dark that morning she had thought the situation over. Was it not true, after all, that she—through no fault of her own—had come belatedly to a mission where others had been under strain? That she had encountered them, yesterday evening, at the end of a fatiguing day spent in the faithful performance of their duties? Miss Kingslake's heart brimmed with understanding as she climbed into her claw-footed bathtub.

How much she had to be thankful for, she exclaimed to herself as she climbed out. In all her time with the Organization, she had longed to go on such a mission. Not that she discounted for a moment her two years spent in the field with the Survey of West African Trust Territories, a rewarding experience in useful work and heartening *esprit de corps*: but SWATT, an economic mission, could hardly compare with a dynamic political mission such as this one. It was the immediacy that took Miss Kingslake's breath away.

Twice before she had been assigned to a peace-keeping mission, only to be forestalled at the moment of departure—once by a bloody revolution in the country of her destination, another time because of a slipped disc. Now it had all come to pass. Even a lag in the Reports workload had helped to facilitate her sudden departure: only two days before, she had completed proofreading on appendices for the World Commodity Index.

Environment would always have been secondary to Miss Kingslake's wish to serve—adverse conditions, in fact, would merely have challenged her to make light of them in her helpful way. Almost guiltily, then, having fastened her skirt, did she cross to the windows and look out on the Anatolian sunrise as she buttoned her blouse. She had no right to expect that the fulfillment of her desires would take place in so much comfort.

She dwelt again, indulgently, on the encounter with her new colleagues. Grilli, a young man, evidently insecure, had been abruptly elevated to a position of unnerving responsibility. When Miss Kingslake's industry, her goodwill, made themselves apparent to him, his manner would change. And had he not himself described the Captain as a rough diamond? A display of diamantine qualities would soon put the Captain's opening remarks in perspective. *Pazienza*, thought Clelia Kingslake to herself, smiling in the glass as she put on the jacket of her best blue suit.

A black Chrysler was waiting in the hotel driveway, and Grilli was in it. Miss Kingslake greeted the Rhodian driver who handed her in, and asked his name.

"Mihalis," he told her. "Michele, Michel, Mike."

Grilli said, "The others are late too."

"You aren't at this hotel?"

"Managed to find a modern place." He jerked his head inland. "Brand-new. Air-conditioned. Music piped in." They sat in silence. He looked steadily at the folds of her skirt, then reached out and took her sleeve between thumb and finger. "Buy this out of your *per diem* advance?"

Pazienza, Miss Kingslake said to herself. She thought, This man is afraid of women. But she harbored the knowledge unwillingly and had not the faintest idea of what to do with it. The mere realization in itself suggested something unsporting, an abuse of power.

The driver opened the door. Rees appeared, carrying a camera and a brief case. Grilli made an attempt to stand up inside the car.

"Sorry to keep you busy people waiting." Rees settled himself on the other side of Clelia Kingslake. "I overslept, I'm afraid. The plane journey, change of hours—it's quite an adjustment."

"Certainly takes it out of you," Grilli agreed sympathetically.

"I hardly remember where I was, this time yesterday. Malta, was it, or Herakleion?" Rees smiled benevolently at Miss Kingslake. "How do you do."

"Cecilia Kingslake," Grilli said. "She's the latest arrival. I think you—"

Rees shook hands, turning to her full face. "Miss Kingsland," he said gravely, "I know from experience that staff members in the field tend to feel forgotten. It's natural, being so far from Headquarters—natural, but mistaken. Believe me. You people, and the wonderful work you're doing, are in our thoughts at Headquarters every day. I want you to know how much you're appreciated and remembered."

"I do know. Thank you."

Grilli moved uneasily. His hands shifted back and forth over his knees. "Here's the Cap."

The Captain strode from the hotel, got into the front seat, turned, and nodded curtly. Something had happened to him in the night. He was redder and flabbier, out of sorts and breath. The driver jumped in beside him, closed the door, reached for the starter.

"Well, get going, man!" cried the Captain impatiently.

The car rolled out of the hotel driveway. To their left, through a screen of eucalyptus leaves, they glimpsed an enclosure of long, leaning markers.

"A Turkish cemetery," exclaimed Miss Kingslake, leaning forward.

The driver slowed down. "It is the cemetery for civil servants."

They passed through an agglomeration of Mussolini's architecture, and came within sight of the harbor and the ancient city. At this hour the walls of the Crusaders were tangerine, their splendid order pierced here and there by a gleaming tower or a minaret. Clelia Kingslake sensed, again unwillingly, that an expression of interest would not be welcome. Nevertheless she said, "How marvelous."

"A façade," Grilli said, "that's all this is, a façade. This place is poor as hell. Without the big powers to back them up, they'd be nothing."

On the far side of Miss Kingslake, Rees beamed. "I'd like a picture of this."

"All right, man, you can stop here. *Momento*, what-have-you and so on. Not here, you fool, have a bit of sense, pull over to the wall."

"If we pulled out of here, all this would fold up tomorrow."

"The walls," said Miss Kingslake, "are in some places seven centuries old."

"Not getting out, Miss Kingsford?"

Having left the car, Grilli turned back, hung his fingers over the open window. "Take my advice, girlie. Don't try to be a wise guy."

Alone with the driver, Miss Kingslake asked, "Where do you live, Mihalis?"

He pointed, "Over there, on the façade."

They followed the road Miss Kingslake had traveled the day before. Rees was to pay a courtesy call on the commandant of the airfield, whose name he read out several times from a slip of paper. Grilli would leave him there and return for him. (Later Miss Kingslake was to discover that Grilli, self-conscious about his inherited Palermitan accent, preferred not to deal with purer-spoken officials—a complication that had not been foreseen at Headquarters.) Grilli and Moyers spoke of invoices, of supplies and equipment; and Miss Kingslake, considerately leaning back to facilitate their discussion, was reassured by this talk of tonnage and manpower. Was it not all this, ultimately, that mattered on an emergency mission?

When the car drew up, Grilli escorted Rees into the airport. The Captain also got out, and scrambled into the back seat, where he heavily and patriotically exhaled Canadian Club.

"That's it. What-have-you and so on."

"What?"

"The office. The mission. HQ Rhodes. For what it's worth."

Following the direction of his jabbing finger, Miss Kingslake discovered a large stuccoed cube alone in a rocky field.

"You mean, right here? At the airfield?"

"Converted military post. Lent to us by the locals. Supposed to be gratis, but they'll want their pound of flesh, just wait, what-have-you and so on."

Some minutes had passed in silence before Miss Kingslake inquired conversationally, "How far is it from here to Lindos?"

The door opened. "You didn't come here for sightseeing." Grilli climbed inside.

Having followed her companions up a short flight of steps, Miss Kingslake presently lost them in a maze of connecting rooms. The offices were high and wide, and floored with huge black and white tiles—hot weather rooms that were fringed with cold at this season. In the center of each stood a new electric stove attached by its cord to some far-off outlet. These cords went rippling and wiggling beneath desks, under double doors, out into corridors; those that had not lasted the distance had been extended with others. The whole establishment was swarming, a nest of vipers.

Clelia Kingslake made herself known to the mission accountant, a Dane, and to the radio operator, a Pakistani. With a new, urgent perception, she saw that both were of crushable substance, and her heart sank though she said some cheerful words. A room containing the local recruits, boisterous with laughter when she opened the door, at once fell silent. Half a dozen messengers and drivers sat on the edges of tables speaking Greek, and on the single chair a little old man was fitting a roll of paper into an adding machine. She inquired for the Captain's office and they showed it to her, pointing out its particular black cord writhing down the hallway.

Following this, Miss Kingslake went to meet her Minotaur.

She found herself alone in the room, and sat down at what was apparently her desk, at the lightless end of the room. She uncovered the typewriter, unlocked the drawers. A sheet of instructions had been left on the blotter and was signed Noreen. Miss Kingslake switched on her desk lamp and began to read. "Two pink flimsies Beirut, one white flimsy Addis—"

Mihalis came in with something in his hand.

"It's a light meter." She took it from him and put it on the desk. "I suppose it belongs to Rees."

Mihalis lingered.

"Thanks. I'll see he gets it." She picked up the list again. "Headquarters all yellow flimsies."

Mihalis leaned forward. Miss Kingslake looked up.

"It takes one hour to Lindos."

She smiled. "Thank you, Mihalis." With the best will in the world, she could not help feeling as if a code word had been slipped to her in prison.

The Captain's boots, having metal on them, were very loud on the tiled floor. "What was the driver doing here?"

"He left this."

"I'll take charge of that. Slack, that driver. Needs bracing up."

"Really?"

"Like the rest of them. Go into that room of theirs down the corridor, they're acting up all day long. Good mind to report the lot of them, what-have-you and so on. Not the Europeans, of course, just the local staff."

"The local staff *are* the Europeans."

"Paid far too much of course." The Captain was at that moment draw-ing an allowance from the Organization in addition to his Army pay. "The way this outfit of yours throws money around. Not theirs, of course, so they feel free."

Miss Kingslake lifted out the contents of her In-tray.

"Don't talk to me about drivers. Had a series of drivers in Kashmir, biggest lot of clots, what-have-you and so on. Rented a villa there, awk-ward driveway, narrow entrance between two concrete posts. Just room for the car, inch or two to spare. Made it a condition of keeping the drivers—they had to go through without slowing down. One scratch and they were washed up, through, no reference." The Captain laughed and crashed his mailed feet delightedly on the tiles below his desk. "They sniveled at first, of course, but they needed their jobs and they made it their business to learn." He tipped his chair back, rummaged in the desk drawer for cigarettes. "Don't talk to me about drivers."

Clelia Kingslake was setting out the incoming cables, like cards for solitaire. She could see the concrete blocks looming, feel the sweat on her brow and on her hands gripping the wheel. And to think that only yesterday she had wept over Matthew Arnold.

The Captain spoke out on a variety of subjects, always exhorting her not to talk to him of these matters. He was unused, he divulged, to women in his office. He liked his own office, with at most a corporal in attendance. He was a man who lived among men. (Four years earlier, although he did not say this, he had abandoned a wife and child in Battleford, Saskatchewan.) He was accustomed to working with men throughout the day; to returning in the evening to B.O.Q.

This, though Miss Kingslake could not know it, was Bachelor Offi-cers' Quarters.

"B.O.Q., that's the place for me."

"I'm sure."

When Rees looked in to retrieve his light meter, the Captain brushed away his thanks. "Delighted to be of service, sir."

"Sorry to disturb you busy people."

The sun came round to the front of the building, and the Captain went out and stood in it. He could be seen by Miss Kingslake from where she sat, planted with his back to the window and his feet wide apart. He had taken off his dark glasses for the first time.

Miss Kingslake got up from her desk and brought a mirror out from her handbag. Walking over to the light, she touched the discreet contours of her hair with an accustomed hand and took the opportunity to put on face powder. When this was done, she held the mirror up and made a face into it. In a high voice, as if mimicking a child, she said "*Pazienza.*" After a moment she added, also out loud, "What-have-you and so on." Standing there in a square of sunlight, she rocked back and forth on her sensible heels.

She put the mirror away and came back to her desk. She made up a large number of cardboard files, feeling ashamed of herself.

Miss Kingslake sat in a chair by Grilli's desk, a notebook in her lap, while he spoke on the telephone. Grilli talked loudly in order not to be afraid, like a person in the dark. If he does a good job, she reasoned, why should I be concerned about his personality? She wished she were less exacting. She wished she were more—

"Outgoing." Grilli dictated a cable, turning loose sheets on his blotter all the while. He drafted a short letter to his section at Headquarters. "Date that today," he said.

"Yes of course."

"I mean Sunday. Not '20th'—but '*Sunday* 20th,' get it?"

He slapped down a handwritten list on the desk by Miss Kingslake's arm. "Mr. Rees is throwing a party for the government officials here. Invitations to go out today, champagne party at the hotel, Wednesday, six o'clock."

Miss Kingslake placed the list on her knee, under her notebook. "Any special wording?"

"Yeah." Grilli read from the reverse of the paper on which Rees had written the commandant's name. "To express heartfelt gratitude, profound appreciation for cooperation, etc., you fix it."

"Shall I put 'R.S.V.P.'?"

"R.S.V.P.? Christ no. If they don't want to come and drink champagne they can go to hell." His quivering hand passed unimpeded over the top of his head. "What a day."

"You've been busy?"

"Nothing to what it was before, of course."

"Of course not."

"The first couple of weeks. Just me, Noreen, and the Cap. Kept going on coffee and cigarettes. The Cap's a great guy, don't you think? A rough diamond."

"They don't make them like that any more."

"Knows this region like the back of his hand. You should hear him. Not much of a talker, but when he gets going."

Miss Kingslake said, "He has a singular verbal tic."

She could not tell whether she had said something unspeakable or merely incomprehensible. Grilli stared at her. "I'm trying to get him recruited into the Organization. A senior post, of course. He's wasted in the Army. I've spoken to Mr. Rees about it. The Organization, that's the place for him."

Miss Kingslake said, "He seems so at home in B.O.Q."

Grilli returned to his papers. "A lot to do. Been a big strain, this job. Not the work, even, but the responsibility."

As long as he does his job. Miss Kingslake's pencil was at the ready.

"Being on your own, that's what gets you. Anything goes wrong, you're responsible."

"That's what I imagine." She lowered her pencil again.

"Dealing direct with the big brass. They want something—they want it now, like this." He snapped his thumb and forefinger twice.

"Frightening, sometimes."

"I can handle it."

"Naturally."

"Can't talk all day. I've got a job to do." He tipped his chair back and locked his hands behind his head. He looked expansive—not only in the physical sense, for his face assumed a contented anticipatory smile. "A letter. For today's pouch."

Miss Kingslake poised her pencil.

"One flimsy."

"Just one." She made a note.

"White." Grilli gazed upward, his eyes—half-closed in the act of composition—rotating over the motionless ceiling fan. His lips moved once or twice before he actually spoke.

"Dearest Mom," he began.

THE SEPARATION OF DINAH DELBANCO

Cornelia Fromme said, "The thing is, Dinah's got money now. Try one of these."

"As if the Organization could care less." Millicent Bass rolled her chair up closer to her desk. "No thanks, I like the soft centers. Does anyone know how much it is?"

"Hard to formulate a valid idea. It can't be much, since her uncle lived to be ninety-four. And then, Dinah's ambivalent, you know. Says she'd like to go on working for the Organization, but that she's got to have this upgrading."

"Think of Dinah making demands. I remember when she first came to Social and Anthropological. I remember when she could scarcely function within a given situation."

"And now she wants a Step Two."

"In the Specialized Category." Millicent Bass went on, "Of course, Dinah's a good person—"

"Oh, humanly speaking, Dinah's a good person."

"—but very competitive." Millicent opened the top drawer of her desk, handed one paper napkin to her friend, and wiped her own fingers on another. "There are tensions there. Plenty of staff members at the

Subsidiary level are holding down Specialized jobs—there's no discrimination in her case. She's being highly subjective." Miss Bass, a Step Four in the Specialized Category, appealed in the voice of reason. "After all, are *we* properly graded, Cornelia, you and I, in terms of performance? We could all make demands if we chose to. Just one more, then."

Millicent Bass, a large woman, belongs to a recognizable era in her profession. Her younger colleagues do not attire themselves, as Miss Bass does, in outmoded suits and golfing shoes. They no longer boast, as Miss Bass does, of caring for their complexions exclusively with soap and water. Their stockings are seamless, they have been known to dye their hair. They are, to use their own expression, changing their image. This metamorphosis not having as yet extended to their vocabulary, a conversation with one of them gives an impression less of change than of something having gone underground.

Cornelia Fromme had been Miss Bass's closest friend and colleague for eleven years, and should logically have been a slighter person. Instead, she too was a big woman with a penetrating voice. Nevertheless, she was the weaker of the two, and in that way the balance was preserved. Had she been of smaller stature, friction between the two ladies might have been less violent, Miss Bass being encouraged by her friend's stalwart appearance to treat her as a sparring partner of equal weight. Miss Bass made the most of a slender intellectual advantage over Miss Fromme; on the other hand, there had been a fiancé in Cornelia Fromme's past, and when driven to the wall she would appear with a small star-sapphire on her left hand. Their quarrels were famous and acrimonious, and always resolved in the same way: one or the other—but more often Cornelia—would come to the office even earlier than usual and leave a tastefully wrapped present on the blotter of the other. The presents were thoughtful—a chain with fastenings by which spectacles could be hung around the neck when not in use, a clear plastic rainhat disguised with clusters of white daisies, a rubber clothesline, complete with pegs, that could be fixed above a bathtub. The latest disagreement, a minor one, had resulted in the box of chocolates they were at that moment sharing.

During their temporary rifts, Miss Bass and Miss Fromme would circle the Section independently, each recounting the shortcomings of her friend. Newcomers to the office were sometimes misled into agreeing on these occasions, and even into adding their own parallel observations on the matter. All criticisms garnered by this means were subsequently exchanged by the two friends as part of their ritual of reconciliation.

"It's hard to understand Dinah's motivations. Obviously she won't resign, and she'll get herself marked as a troublemaker with Personnel. It's all so negative."

"Of course she won't resign. Nobody resigns. Even supposing this inheritance paid her rent, she couldn't live off her separation pay. And what would she do with herself? She needs a group relationship, like the rest of us. She needs work she can identify with. Say what you like about the Organization, Cornelia, it's meaningful."

"This is true."

"It spoils us for work elsewhere, our involvement here with a realistic system of values."

"And Dinah does work hard, of course."

"That's just overcompensating. Compulsive." Miss Bass shook her head. "All right, I can't resist, but this is the last."

"She says herself that she wants to go on with her work here."

"That proves that this inheritance can't be much. No, Dinah's simply trying it out. When she adjusts to her new situation, we won't hear any more about it. All she'll have done is to defer her chances of a Subsidiary D. It's self-destructive." Miss Bass lit a cigarette.

The two friends sat quietly for a moment. Then Miss Bass said, "But Dinah's a good person."

Miss Fromme nodded. "A warm human being."

"Yes, come in, Lidia."

Lidia Korabetski shut the door and, since Gregory was still writing, sat down in the chair opposite his desk. Gregory was her chief. His desk was heaped with the spoils of chieftainship—a stack of memoranda for signature, each with file attached, a pile of flagged reports in manuscript, another pile of freshly mimeographed ones. These trophies at no place overlapped: Gregory was an orderly man.

"Sorry, had to get this out." Gregory was a polite man. He pushed the routing slip he had written under a paper clip on the front of a file and tossed the file into the Out-tray. "Now look, I wanted to tell you—your friend did ask to see me, and I've just had a talk with her."

Lidia put her hand on the gray curve of the desk edge. "Thanks so much, I know how busy you are with the Governing Body. I wouldn't have suggested it if she weren't someone special."

"Well of course, you're absolutely right—she's preposterously under-graded, and she could be doing better things in any case. Since she's worked on reports practically her whole twelve years in Social, she could be very useful to us here."

"Exactly what I thought."

"In fact, I'm going to raise it with the Director—no use my taking it up with Personnel at this point. She herself has an appointment to see some-one in Personnel, but you can imagine how far that'll get her. Precisely nowhere. No, the thing would be for us to keep an eye on the manning-table. We'd have to have a slot for her—which we don't have at this moment—and *then* request transfer. But a good case could be made, and the main thing would be timing."

"I'm so glad."

Gregory lifted his hand. "Just a moment. Not so simple. She doesn't see it this way. She says she'll only come here if she gets the grade of the job—in other words, a Specialized Two—as part of the transfer. Which is nonsense, of course."

"Couldn't be done?"

Gregory clicked his tongue. "Now Lidia, you know better than that. How's she going to get from a Subsidiary C to a Specialized Two in one jump? What we *can* do is to stick her in the post, then put her up for pro-motion at the next half-yearly Board, and so on."

"What does it mean, 'and so on'?"

"Well—first of all, she won't get through on the first round, so we'd put her up a second time, for the subsequent Board. That would be for a Subsidiary D. *Then* she'd be in a strong position to ask for the Specialized Two."

"Several years, then?"

"Two or three." Gregory shook his head. He was a just man. "Not right of course, but what can you do? If you work here, you have to go by the rules. Or you can always leave, naturally."

"She's spoken of leaving."

"She won't, you know."

"What makes you think so?"

"One never does. Apart from anything else, what about pension? I'm not suggesting that your friend live an unsatisfactory life in order to collect a satisfactory pension—"

"An *un*satisfactory pension."

"—but at her age one begins to think about the future."

"That's what she's doing."

"Oh Lidia, come on now, be realistic. What would her separation pay be, after only twelve years here? And in our society there just aren't that many jobs for women around—well, how old would she be?"

"She's thirty-six."

"Say around forty, then. Not jobs interesting enough, that is, to make it worthwhile giving up one's security. You know that."

Lidia said, "I feel depressed."

"Well don't be. I believe there's a way out that would satisfy everybody, and I've suggested it to her."

"What's that, then?"

"Something that's been done before. I know of at least one other case, and I think an arrangement was made there about continuity of pension rights, if I'm not mistaken. It's this. She can resign from the Organization, and be re-recruited at the proper level. What counts against her, don't you see, is her twelve years in the Subsidiary Category. The Organization will know all about that, of course, but with qualifications like hers—and with our department asking for her—they'd probably close their eyes and pretend they'd never seen her before. They can be decent about things like that, you know. Much simpler to come in afresh as a Specialized staff member than to try to make the leap from a Subsidiary C."

"You mean—her experience here doesn't help her?"

"I'm trying to tell you, Lidia, it counts *against* her—the fact of her having accepted the Subsidiary Category in the first place." Gregory's eyes were wandering over his In-tray. "Well, there's no guarantee, and she should look into it carefully before taking the plunge. But that's my advice, for what it's worth."

"What did she say to this?"

"Oh, I think she may very well try it. She had me go over it all a second time, to make sure she'd got it straight. She said it was certainly something to think about. So let's see what she decides."

Lidia got up. "I won't take up more of your time. But thank you for seeing Dinah."

"Not a bit. I'll be glad to help her when the time comes. If you knew the trouble we have getting competent people for this kind of work—really, it's to our advantage to grab her if we can."

"Thanks anyway."

"Oh there's no generosity involved. Leave the door open, if you would."

Mr. Clifford Glendenning was staring at a telegram when his colleague Mr. Bekkus knocked and entered. It had been a busy morning for Glendenning, who was concerned with recruiting technicians from the corners of the earth to serve on short-term contracts in the Organization's aid programs. Only yesterday, in consulting the roster of those who had already completed such assignments, he had hit on the perfect chap to work with chemicals in the Congo. A cable had gone out to Paris, and here was the reply. Clifford Glendenning was standing up, leaning on the desk with both palms and staring at it:

PAS ENCORE PAYÉ POUR LA MISSION PRÉCÉDENTE.

That was not all. There had been, in addition, in a single morning, a statistician who wanted to take his dog with him to Katmandu, an expert in basic hygiene who had sent his laundry home from Baghdad in the diplomatic pouch, and the discovery of an impostor in the port facilities team on the Persian Gulf. (This last was the worst, since the recipient government had recently commended him as the best expert ever assigned there.)

Bekkus made his appearance with a paper in his hand. He came in and stood across the desk from Glendenning. "You once straightened me out on this Moslem nomenclature, Clifford, but I've lost track again. Too much on my mind. What name does an individual like this get filed under?"

Glendenning took the form held out by Bekkus, sat down, and studied it. "An easy one," he said, and smiled. Glendenning had a smile that turned up tightly at the corners and in this way matched his heavy eyebrows, which he had also trained into upward flourishes. The combination gave him a look of being between inverted commas. "Proper name, Mohammad; Ali's his father's name; and Abdulkader was his grandfather."

"What about this Hadji part?"

"That just means he's been to Mecca."

"And what's Scek?"

"That means his father was a religious leader. I wouldn't worry about that."

"Then what's this 'Néant'? That's what I originally had him filed under." Bekkus, seated now, leaned across and pointed.

Glendenning looked hard. After a moment he said, "Forget that. That's French for 'nil.' It's supposed to be in the box below, where it says *Marital Status*."

Bekkus sighed. "This Moslem nomenclature certainly presents administrative problems."

"If you think so, Rudie, it's just as well you weren't with me at Quetta." Glendenning had spent some part of his youth as an official in what is now Pakistan. "Ten thousand people in my bailiwick there, and every last one of them had a name, I assure you." Glendenning often spoke of these greater responsibilities of his past, oddly emphasizing his reduced authority. "Ministers of human fate, we were, Rudie. Ministers of human fate." When Bekkus looked blank, he added with a four-cornered smile, "Thomas Gray. 'Ode on a Distant Prospect of Eton College.'"

Bekkus objected. "But yours was a multipurpose, paternalistic administration."

"It was."

"You had built-in flexibility. You were operating within a broader framework."

"We were."

"It left room for scope." Bekkus crossed one knee over the other. "There was area for dialogue. Here at the Organization, on the other hand, we're functioning within unformulated personal situations, even at the decision-making level. Your post at least relates to staff members in the field, and involves less interfacing. Whereas in my outfit we're continually evaluating the individual problems of Headquarters staff. And there's no more time-consuming subject matter, I can tell you." Bekkus shook his head. "*Per se.*"

"Oh don't I know." Glendenning nodded. "*Per se.*"

"I wasted half an hour this morning trying to tell a staff member from Social and Anthropological Questions what she could easily have found out from reading the Staff Regulations. That Miss Delbanco who used to be in Conservation of Rural Communities and is now in Urban Welfare. A Subsidiary C, if you please, and wants a promotion to Specialized Two."

Glendenning laughed. "Talk about the Distant Prospect of Eton College."

Bekkus succumbed to smiles. "Well, I can't help laughing. But it isn't funny."

"What did you tell her?"

"I told her, 'My dear girl, *read* the Staff Regulations.' Of course it's that old business of being in a post that's over-graded. Claims she's been doing the work for X number of years, why can't she have the grade. Exactly the opposite, obviously—the post was upgraded for reasons of geographical distribution, and only rates a Subsidiary C. If everyone got the grade of the post they were in, we'd have a nice situation, I must say. In any case, the Director-General's circular specifically specified that assignment to a Specialized post does *not* imply entitlement to the grade. Why don't they read what's put in front of them?"

"How did she react?"

"Oh—she's a conflicted little individual. When I notified her of non-entitlement she said—in a voice that was supposed to create some effect or other—that it was about what she'd expected." Bekkus smiled again. "You can imagine how far that got her. Precisely nowhere. I said—with a smile, you know—'You know, Miss Delbanco, that you can always leave the Organization.'"

"How old is she?"

"Around forty. Maybe a bit more."

"Well of course. There you are."

Bekkus uncrossed his legs. "Oh, it's all in the day's work, I suppose. We're here to do a job and this is how it gets done. But the time it utilizes is unbelievable. Unbelievable." He took his document back off the desk. "Ah well, back to the salt mines. You think this should go under Mohammad, eh?"

"I do."

"And just forget the Mecca-nized part?"

"And the Scek."

"Thanks for your help, Clifford. I appreciate it."

Glendenning raised his hand in farewell, and completed the gesture by taking a paper from the top of his tray. "Anytime."

"Have a good day."

The paper that Glendenning had taken up was a letter to the Organization from a private person. Like most such letters, it was addressed to the Director-General of the Organization by name. It was written by hand on lined paper, and asked for assistance in augmenting the education of the writer, a resident of a village on the upper reaches of the Limpopo River. Below the carefully formed signature, there appeared the word "Help!"

Glendenning drew a heavy breath. Because he was associated with the aid programs, he received all manner of misdirected communications. How many times had he not instructed the Central Registry to send such letters—of which there were hundreds each week—direct to the appropriate officer in the Fellowship Division? Tearing a sheet from the block beside him, he drafted the routine response.

Dear Sir,

Your letter of 6 March addressed to the Director-General has been passed to me for reply. I regret to inform you that, in accordance with the legislation governing our existing aid programs, applications for study grants cannot be considered by this Organization unless forwarded through the appropriate ministry of the government concerned.

Alternatively, may I direct your attention to the manual "Paths to Learning," issued by the Research and Amplification of the Natural Sciences, Arts, and Culture Commission, an agency affiliated with this Organization, which lists fellowships and scholarships available under numerous international programs. A copy of the most recent edition of this manual (RANSAC 306/Ed.4) may be consulted in your local public library.

With good wishes for the fulfillment of your aspirations, I am

Yours sincerely,

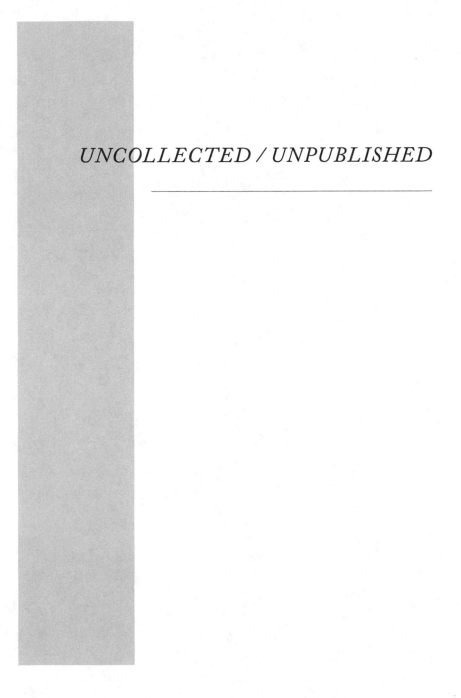

UNCOLLECTED / UNPUBLISHED

WOOLLAHRA ROAD

Ida was supposed to be having her nap, but when she heard a horse and cart coming down the street she got off the bed and climbed on the window seat to look out. The milkman came in the morning, and it was too early in the afternoon for the baker; a cart at this hour could only mean a hawker—and, sure enough, it was a man selling clothes props. The decrepit cart was laden with saplings of eucalyptus, roughly stripped and forked at one end.

"Props for fourpence." The horse dawdled down the road, pausing at each gate. "Props for fourpence." Nothing moved in the street, not even a dog. The day was hot and very dry. The prim gardens, the lank gum trees were deaf, motionless. "Props for fourpence." The cry was growing fainter.

The child, bored, went back to fetch a paint book and her doll, Rosie, from the crumpled pink coverlet. Returning to the window, she took up a crayon and did a little more work on a house she had been drawing. She added a plume of smoke to the chimney, because, although she could not remember ever having seen a smoking chimney, her picture books were full of them. Here in Australia, it seemed to have been summer all her life—breathless, burning days of drought. The pictures of smoking chimneys were like the snow scenes that arrived on cards from England each year during the Christmas heat wave—brief representations of that other, authoritative world where seasons were reversed (it was implied, correctly), and where children wore gaiters and mufflers and lived indoors.

The front garden, which the window overlooked, was on the shady side of the house, but even there the soft turf had died in the drought and been replaced by crisp, resistant buffalo grass, which also grew on the more exposed sides of the house. The steps were bordered with pink and blue hydrangeas, and with beds of fuchsia and daphne. Palm trees stood on the lawn. At the end of the short drive were red hibiscus and trees of wattle and frangipani. At the side, a wall covered with wilted Dorothy Perkins roses separated this house from the Armstrongs'. Sometimes the Armstrong boys, Rex and Leslie, came to play. Rex was eleven and enormous, and quickly got bored with Ida because she was so little. He wore gray knickerbockers, and a blazer with a crest, and a straw boater circled by a broad, striped ribbon. The Armstrongs had kept Rex in a good school—"in spite of everything." The Armstrongs had lost all their money.

It was 1935, and Ida was four years old.

She would have liked to go into the garden, but her mother would be annoyed if she didn't sleep, and in any case the back of the house was more amusing. The back garden was huge, and had beds of flowers and vegetables and an orchard. A swing had been built in the orchard, and if you were swung high enough you could touch the mandarin trees by extending your feet. Beyond the orchard was a field of high grass forbidden to children because of snakes. The snakes occasionally came into the garden and had to be killed with a heavy stick that was kept in the garage for the purpose. The grass of the field was cut down from time to time by Alfie, the man who did the garden, and lost cricket balls would turn up then, or an old kite, or singed rocket butts left over from Empire Night. The grass was never burned off now, because of the danger of fire.

Even the orchard and the garden had their perils. There were bees in the grove of Buddleia. In the mornings, kookaburras perched on the lowest branches of the trees, looking for lizards or worms, and would burst out laughing right over your head. And there was a gray goanna, like a short, thick snake, harmless but horrible, that came to the kitchen door to be fed by the maid, Marge, with raw eggs.

The perils of the back garden were so attractive that Ida turned her back on the window and slid down from the wooden seat. Taking Rosie up by one china arm, she made her way out of the room. The hallway was dark—blinds were drawn and doors closed at this time of day—and she descended the stairs carefully, grasping the rods of the banister with her free hand. From the foot of the steps, she went through to the back of the house, where a screen door opened from her father's study onto a glassed-in veranda.

It was hot on the veranda, but there sat her mother, in a blue dress, sewing. Her mother, who was dark and beautiful and very loving, had strong, impatient opinions, and a quick temper that flared without warning and was felt through the house. Ida was both afraid to be out of her sight and afraid of making her angry, and she creaked the screen door open and looked cautiously around it.

But her mother just smiled and let her come and sit on the polished floor beside her and play with the colored silks and reels of cotton in the quilted box. Ida lined them up in their varying sizes and then in their different shades, and when she tired of that she simply sat leaning against her mother's leg, rubbing with one finger the round button on the high-heeled shoe. The sun burned on them through the glass; her mother came here to sew because of the light, but she hated the heat, Ida knew. She couldn't breathe, she said, until the southerly started to blow in the evening—the cool south wind that reached Sydney from the sea. She couldn't bear to see the garden wither in the drought. One evening, she went out and watered the lawn, although that was prohibited because of the water shortage, and a passerby, seeing her with the hose, had shouted that he would report her to the City Council. Her mother threw down the hose in a fury, and came inside and said she was sick of the drought and the depression. When Marge told her it would get cooler soon, in May, she just shook her head and said she was homesick. On the study wall there was a photograph of a girl in a fur coat standing in snow, like the Christmas cards.

Jock, the Airedale, who was nosing about in the field, suddenly began to bark and came running up through the orchard. The abrupt activity shook the trees, or so it seemed, and sharpened the light. The shoe button shifted out from under Ida's finger as her mother rose to look through the glass of the veranda.

A woman had come round the corner of the house and was walking very slowly toward the back door. She was dressed in black and carried a large, square hessian bag that flapped, almost empty, against her thigh. Her slow, slow walk carried her past the flowers and the vegetables and the barking dog, but she didn't look about her. By her face and her figure she was not old, but her walk was old. Her feet moved painfully on the smooth flagstone path. The uneven hem of her dress reached, in some places, almost to her ankles. She wore a round hat of black felt, crammed down on her head.

The kitchen door opened as she reached it, and Marge looked out. The dog slipped inside, still barking in little short puffs. The woman spoke, not accentuating her words with any movement, clasping the thick loops of the bag against her hip. Marge—short, plump, and fair—came out onto the step and closed the door behind her because of the flies. The voices came indistinctly through the hot glass of the veranda. In a moment, Marge opened the door again and both women disappeared into the house.

Ida and her mother had moved away from the windows; they heard Marge's step before they could sit down again. Marge appeared on the veranda, her face creased and uneasy. Ida knew, before she spoke, that her voice would be lowered. It was so low, in fact, that the child could scarcely hear.

"Walking all day," she said, "poor soul . . . this heat . . . she's looking for work" and ". . . children . . ."

Ida's mother stuck the needle into the sewing in her hand and put it down on the chair. Her face, too, was troubled. She went inside, through the study and into the hall, with Marge and Ida following, and down the corridor to the kitchen.

The woman was standing by the kitchen table, still holding her bag. She looked austerely at the group in the doorway. The skin of her face and arms was brown and dry, but she had young features and, under the battered hat, limp, dark hair. She didn't speak, but sat at the table when she was asked, and drank a glass of lemonade straight down without stopping. When she had done that, she seemed to sag in her chair; she propped her elbow on the table and her brow on her hand, and closed her eyes.

At the sink, the two women were slicing and spreading, and Marge had brought a jug of milk from the ice chest. Ida stretched her own elbow onto the table's edge, staring and wishing that the woman in black had not come. Her arrival had turned everyone silent and queer, and she did not look at Ida or speak to her, as women usually did, but sat there, almost lifeless, with the brim of her ugly hat lowered over her hand. After a moment, the child drew away and sat down on a box of groceries that had been delivered that day from Anthony Hordern's. Beside the groceries, Alfie had placed a shined pair of her father's shoes, and, putting Rosie down, she picked up one shoe and began to play with the laces. The heavy shoe slipped between her knees and distended the floral lap of her dress, but she pretended to be intent on it, hoping that when she looked up the woman would be preparing to leave.

Instead, her mother was putting plates on the table and a glass of milk, and the bowl of fruit from the dining room. No one paid any attention to Ida, even though she had dirtied her dress with the shoe, which she now tumbled back onto the floor. The woman began to eat from a plate of cold meat, with sharp motions of her fork and knife. She showed no sign of going away. Marge was making the strong tea, dark and bitter even when it had milk in it, that they had every afternoon, and a cup and saucer had been set on the table. Ida saw with relief that her mother's tea tray had also been laid—the tray with willow-pattern china and a plate of Arnott's biscuits that was carried to the back veranda every afternoon.

When the tea was ready, her mother filled the cup on the table and her own cup on the tray. In an undertone, she asked Marge to fetch some tinned food from the basement. Then she picked up the tray herself and went out of the kitchen so quickly that Ida, who was afraid of being left with the woman at the table, jumped up and scuttled out after her.

The dog, stretched out on a patch of uncarpeted floor in the study, scrambled to his feet as they passed through, and pattered onto the veranda. He and Ida were allowed one biscuit each from the tea tray—which always meant one more. Ida took up her position by her mother's chair, wondering if the ritual would restore their afternoon. But her mother was not thinking of her; she was frowning over the dishes on the little cane table at her side. When Ida looked at her, she handed her a biscuit absent-mindedly, and broke one in half for Jock, and sighed.

The mother and child might have been sheltering there, they were so still, when the kitchen door clanged at last and the slow, flat steps sounded on the path. The steps grew fainter, until they could not be heard at all, and Ida thought that her mother would smile now and give her the second biscuit. Even Marge was relieved, it seemed, singing in the kitchen a song she would not ordinarily have chosen: "K-K-K-Katy." She sang this only when she was unnerved, because it was disrespectful; Kate was the name of Ida's mother.

". . . the only g-g-g-girl that I adore," Marge sang.

Ida looked warily at her mother, who smiled at last—almost with complicity—and reached toward the plate.

The singing suddenly broke off. "Oh!" said Marge. "Oh, Madam!"

As her mother started up, Ida had once more the impression that the light changed. There was barely time to reach the doorway before Marge appeared there.

"Oh, Madam, please come!" she was saying. "That woman . . ." and they all hurried after her into the house.

The kitchen was orderly, the table cleared, instead of the scene of carnage Ida expected. You wouldn't have known the woman had been there. But where the shoes had lain, and the doll, there was nothing at all—just the shiny green speckles of the linoleum.

"Rosie!" Ida howled in rage and horror. "Rosie!" Rosie, at the moment, was shuddering along Woollahra Road in a hessian bag, jostled by a pair of shoes. Appalled, the child flung herself round to be comforted, and as she did so it occurred to her that now her mother would get really, terribly angry—even worse than over the business of the hose, angrier than Ida herself.

But her mother seated herself at the table, where the strange woman had sat, and lowered her brow on her propped hand. She did not utter a word.

FORGIVING

L ucas," she said, crossing the lawn and sitting down on the grass beside him, "they will never forgive us for this."

He was smoking a cigarette, the other hand gripping his wrist around his bent knees. "What we have to say to each other," he said, "is more important than going to a dinner party." He spoiled the resounding effect of this by asking, "What did you tell them?"

"I said that you were sick and I had to stay with you." She sat sideways, and the folds of her skirt almost covered her bare feet. "I don't think they believed me—I'm not much of a liar." She thought she saw his eyes widen, and flushed. She tore up a few blades of grass and rolled them between her fingertips. "The grass is quite damp," she said. "Perhaps we should go inside?"

"No," he said. "It's pleasant here."

The house, although built inside a wood, was on a gradual slope, so that their view was framed but not obscured by trees. Below the wood, cultivated land—scarcely any of which was theirs—stretched across a little valley and up the opposite hill. The few lights already glowing in the warm evening came from farms or from other summer houses, or belonged to cars that passed along the road at the end of the valley. Their own house, at their backs, was unlit, sharply white in the fading sunshine—a small Greek-revival house just large enough for two people. For years Lucas had talked of adding a wing so that their occasional summer guests might be more comfortable, but in fact the house could only be extended at the sacrifice of its proportions. The wing had stayed unbuilt and the guests continued to sleep in the living room, able to return to town as soon as possible. Kate and Lucas had no children.

"Yes, it is lovely this evening," she agreed, enlarging his more moderate remark. She waited for him to speak again, but he only threw the end of his cigarette into the grass. "Should you do that?" she asked. "Is it safe?"

"You just said the grass was damp," he pointed out.

She thought, dejectedly, that a sudden conflagration would at least divert him from what he was about to say, but the moments passed with no delivering outbreak of flames, the cigarette having disobligingly fizzled out in a patch of clover. She wished she had brought a sweater for her bare shoulders, but did not like to go inside for one now. She changed her attitude and sat, like him, hugging her knees. "Let's hope they won't drive over to see how you are, and find us sitting out here."

Again he did not reply, and she was left to feel that her remarks were received as crude attempts at appeasement—which they were. She looked at him, and he lighted another cigarette, throwing the match away with a certain insistence. Then he said, "I just can't get used to it."

She said, cautiously, "I'm not quite sure what you feel."

"Well, I feel—all the classic symptoms, I suppose." He made a brief ironical movement with his shoulders. "Like the deceived husband in a play. I keep telling myself that after all it doesn't matter, you didn't mean it, it's only what I've done myself, but I still can't get used to it."

She curled her toes in apprehension. "From what you said this morning, I take it you don't intend to do anything about it?"

"*Do* anything? What should I do?"

"I mean," she said, knowing he had understood her, "that you don't intend to leave me."

"It doesn't seem on that scale, does it? From what you tell me. What was it you said it was—an aberration?"

"An incident."

Without turning to her, he suddenly burst out, "Ah, Kate, how could you?"

Twisting her fingers together around her knees, she said in a small, gruff voice, "You leave me alone too much."

"It's not *my* idea, for God's sake. What can I do, if they send me on these trips? It's the way I earn my living, after all." ("And yours" fitted neatly into a small pause.) "I don't choose it."

"You might be less enthusiastic about it. I mean, you could—*object* more."

"There wasn't anyone else who could do this last trip."

"You were away for two months," she said.

"Well, one doesn't go to Africa for the *day*, you know." He stopped, surprised to find himself in a defensive position.

She said, seeing this, "I'm not justifying myself."

"Hardly," he replied, ungenerously.

"Lucas," she said, not daring to touch him, but laying her hand on the grass between them, "you are right to mind. I would hate it if you didn't, and I'm terribly, terribly sorry. But it was just silly, that's all. It didn't *matter*. Please don't think it mattered."

"That seems, somehow, to make it worse." He drew on his cigarette. "Yes, I do mind. Of course I mind. I mind like hell."

"Don't," she said.

"What did you expect?"

"In the first place, I didn't think you'd—know," she said, barely hesitating to make the correction. "And then, I suppose I thought you would be more—philosophical about it."

"I can only say that you have a curious idea either of philosophy or of me."

She laid the side of her head against her knees. "Lucas—don't be so cold with me," she said. "Please don't be." The darkness was coming down quickly and she could hardly see him now: he was a black, self-contained shape, a ship exuding smoke and showing a single light. "We talk like a couple of stage Englishmen. I would really rather that you hit me."

"Don't be melodramatic—you know you'd have a fit if I hit you." He did agree, nevertheless, that his idea of acceptable behavior had left him no way of dealing with such a discovery.

A mosquito was biting her ankle; she felt that at this juncture she had no choice but to disregard it.

He went on. "It must make a difference."

"Everything makes a difference."

Annoyed by the solecism, he said, "Do you think I can ever be away from you again without thinking of this?"

She said, without spirit, "The other possibility would be not to go."

"You're unreasonable," he replied in a hard voice.

"In any case, it's not as though it had ever happened before. Or would again."

"I have no way of knowing that."

"Except that I tell you."

"Then why has it happened *now*? Kate, can you tell me why?"

The cars could be heard swishing along the main road. She put her cheek back on her knee and stroked her palms over the grass on either side of her. She said, apparently with total irrelevance, "It was my birthday."

"What?"

"I hadn't heard from you for weeks. And it was my birthday." She sighed. "That's all. I know it doesn't help."

"A form of celebration, I take it?"

She turned her face away.

After a moment he said, "The photograph you sent me, then—he took that?"

"What photograph?"

"A photograph taken up here. On your birthday, you said."

"Oh. Oh, yes. . . . I'm sorry. Yes."

"Kate," he said, aghast, "don't you have any sensibilities at all?"

"Well," she said helplessly, "you kept asking for a photograph."

"I hardy imagined you would go to such lengths to obtain one. . . . How *could* you send that to me?"

She made an ineffectual gesture toward him. "It was the only one I've ever liked." Her voice, inexcusably, carried the suggestion of a smile.

"It didn't look a bit like you," he said crossly. They sat for a while

without speaking. Presently he said, with an air of monumental acceptance, "Perhaps this is the customary thing. Perhaps one has no right to
ask loyalty."

"Perhaps one has no right to *expect* it," she said. "But I think one must
ask it."

He was silent again, making it clear that she had forfeited her right to
adjudicate human behavior. He could tell, from the interruptions of her
breathing, that she had begun to cry. He said unyieldingly, "Now Kate,
pull yourself together," and added, as though tears were by nature frivolous, "this is serious."

"Yes, I'm sorry," she said, not raising her hands from the grass but rubbing her tears off on her skirt with motions of her head. "It's only because
I'm tired. I couldn't sleep last night. In fact, I felt quite shaky all day."

He doubted this, but dared not say so. Once, years ago, he had expressed skepticism about an illness of hers, and she had promptly and
irrefutably fainted, in a shop; since then she had been, in this respect,
unchallengeable. Now, however, having dried her eyes, she began to cry
all over again and with such a suppressed, pathetic sound that he could no
longer ignore it. He said, in a milder tone, "Kate, please stop."

"I'm sorry," she said again, "but it's the way you speak to me."

"But, dear," he protested, with a sense of injustice, "I can't pretend this
is nothing. I'm only trying to make you understand how much it matters
to me."

She looked up at him in the darkness. "I can't help feeling," she said,
and again he could hear her smile, "that you might have accomplished
your object with a quarter of the exertion." She gave a sharp sniff. "I don't
have a handkerchief."

"Nor do I. We'll go in, in a minute." He put his cigarette out carefully
in the damp earth.

"Lucas," she began, "if it would help—I can tell you how it happened."

"Please don't," he said, his voice rising again. "I couldn't bear to know
any details."

She was silent, and then said, "How strange—it's *so* what a woman
would want to know. Isn't that interesting?"

"No," he said, but almost laughed. They were quiet for a while, and when he next turned his head he said, "Kate," sharply, as if she might have disappeared in the meantime. "Let us go in." He got up quickly and, feeling for her hand in the dark, helped her to her feet. He could not embrace her so soon without diminishing the significance of all he had said, and he let her go abruptly—thinking (mistakenly) that she would not have detected the passing of his anger. They stood for so long, however, facing each other, unseeing, that he was obliged either to speak or to take her in his arms, so he said into the darkness, "About the letters—I probably should write more."

She touched his hand lightly. *"Don't."*

"No, really, I think you have a point."

"Lucas," she said, "I'll cry again." He put his arm about her shoulders and they crossed the lawn awkwardly, holding each other and out of step. "Be careful," she said. "I left the watering can somewhere round here."

"What a dark night," he said, as they went up the path to the house. They stopped and stared at the sky. "Perhaps it'll rain. I'm glad we didn't go out to dinner."

They walked on. They had almost reached the door of the house when she stood still again, within his arm, and said, "Lucas—what did you mean when you said that it was only something that you'd done yourself?"

COMFORT

L ovely," Morgan said, leaning down from the landing with his hand on the banister.

"What is?"

"You, on my stair."

"Oh." Lucia laughed. As she came to the last few steps, she halted and extended her hand, not in greeting but so that he might pull her to the top—which he did. "So many *steps*," she gasped, pausing on the landing. "Morgan, why don't you *move*?"

"I like them," he said. "They keep away all but the intrepid."

"I'm not intrepid."

"So you hardly ever come," he said, and smiled. They were standing outside his open door. "I would kiss you, but I could never get under the brim of that hat."

"I'll take it off in a minute," she said. "I mean—I'll take it off *anyway*."

He touched her elbow. "Come in. Mrs. Fanshaw's here—it's her day. If you'd only rung up yesterday I could have put her off."

"Well, I just suddenly wanted to *see* you. I haven't seen you since before I went away." Lucia lowered her voice. "Lord, do you still have Mrs. Fanshaw? Marvelous name. Like an eighteenth-century courtesan."

"Which she probably was." Morgan closed the door behind them and called out, "Oh—Mrs. Fanshaw. Miss McKitterick's here. Will we be in your way in the living room?"

Mrs. Fanshaw appeared in the bedroom door, tall, queenly, with a lacy cap of curled white hair. "Not," she said, "at the mo."

Lucia was pulling a pin out of her straw hat, and turned her head sideways to murmur a greeting.

"Morning, Madam," Mrs. Fanshaw said, only just smiling back. "Well, sir, in a little I might come and finish in the kitchen, if that won't bother you. I won't be more than five minutes, at the outmost." She often improved upon shopworn phrases in this way.

"Fine," said Morgan. He followed Lucia into the living room. She sat on the sofa, her discarded hat on one side of her and Morgan on the other. She shook out her fair hair. Her dress spread about her in flowered folds.

"You're quite brown," he said. "Where did you get that?"

She looked at her bare arm as if she had never seen it before. "I can't be. The weather was very bad till we got to Yugoslavia."

He was silent for a moment. He wondered how he could ever have imagined that she had taken the trip alone. "Weather's been remarkably good here," he said.

"Oh, this morning was glorious. If I hadn't been feeling so utterly—demoralized, I would have walked through the Gardens."

"How did you come, then?" He had a sensation of evading the issue.

"In a taxi."

"You could have taken a No. 29 and got off at Palace Gate."

"Well I didn't."

"Will you have some tea?" He got up and went into the kitchen, which opened off the living room. "It's all ready." He brought the tray out and put it on a low table in front of her. "I'll see if there are some biscuits around."

She heard him opening cupboards in the kitchen. She looked about, at the handsome old furniture, which had belonged to his mother, at a wall of sagging bookshelves and a litter of papers on shaky little tables like the one before her. The teapot and the pitcher, silver, were magnificent; there was an enamel saucepan of hot water, cups without matching saucers, and a single spoon. "What about sugar?" she called.

He came back holding a tartan tin and a glass bowl half filled with encrusted sugar. "Will you pour?"

She had to use a fold of her dress to protect her fingers from the heat of the handle. "But in Yugoslavia it was fine," she said. "The weather, I mean. Don't you have a strainer?"

"God no. Of course not."

"Oh, Morgan, why don't you get *married*?" She handed him his cup.

"Cheaper to buy the tea strainer," he said.

"*Seriously.*" She gave him a swift glance.

He drank his tea. Finally he set his cup down and stretched a little. "Oh well," he said. "*Non sum qualis eram*, and all that."

"Oh, Morgan," she said again, but with a faint commendation, as if he were a child who had given the correct reply.

"However," he continued at once, as if she must not get up her expectations, "I'm not going to blow my brains out, or anything like that." There was another pause, and he added, "What a dated expression that is. It sounds as though it would have to be done with a fowling piece."

They both laughed.

What now? thought Mrs. Fanshaw, entering with a duster in her hand. She never comes here, that one, without she wants something—it stands out like a needle in a haystack. "I think you've got the worm in your chest, sir," she said.

"Oh yes?" Morgan inquired politely.

"There's every sign. On the sides, and around the handles." She shook her duster out the open window with a sort of flurried determination, as if she were signaling to the enemy. Her cap of feathery hair and a coating of white face powder that had lodged in her eyebrows contributed to an air of having been herself improperly dusted. "Better watch it. Once it gets in, it spreads like wild flowers."

"Really?" said Morgan. Why on earth doesn't she shut up and go into the kitchen, he wondered.

"Oh, certainly. Hand over foot," she said. She noted Morgan's hand, which touched the sweep of Lucia's dress, while Lucia, unconcerned, looked at Mrs. Fanshaw over her teacup. Heartless, Mrs. Fanshaw observed to herself; heartless. "I'll put those biscuits on a plate." She picked up the tartan box. She went into the kitchen and closed the door.

"It's really too bad," said Lucia, "poor old thing. Imagine having to work at that age, going on one's knees to scrub, lifting furniture about. What a shame. Good strong face she has, too. Nobody's fool."

Morgan settled back with his cup. "Well, what's your news?"

"Oh—no news, I suppose. Really nothing to tell you." She poured hot water into the pot—cautiously, for the saucepan had no lip. "In fact . . ." she said, and hesitated.

Mrs. Fanshaw reappeared. "Must have been here for years, this tin. It's a regular Pandora's box—you'll never get it open."

"We'll do without, then," Lucia said.

"In fact?" Morgan prompted her, when they were alone again.

"I was going to say that I only seem to come here when I want something."

"You name it," he said, hoping it wouldn't be money, for he didn't have any at present.

"I meant—comfort. All that."

"Not much of that around here," he said, indicating the room. "Of comfort no man speak."

"I meant the other kind."

"Anything new?" he inquired.

"Oh no. It wasn't a success, this trip. It was awful."

"Even in Yugoslavia?"

"Most of *all* in Yugoslavia," she said, rather sharply.

"I only thought—because of the weather . . ." Then he said, "Why don't you leave him, I always wonder?"

"Because—" She took out a handkerchief and wiped her eyes. "Because, if there's any possibility of its coming right, I don't want to add to the waste in the world."

Morgan sat holding his cup and looking unhappily into it. "Tea all right?" he asked.

"Oh, divine," she said, but with a suggestion of not allowing her attention to be diverted.

She was always using drastic words like that, he thought: divine, gorgeous, ghastly. If, on the other hand, she had something serious to say, it came out offhandedly—"a bit annoying," "rather boring"—which was just as exaggerated in its own way. He sometimes wondered hopefully whether these mannerisms would have irritated him if he had had to live with them; and could never sufficiently convince himself that they would.

"Of course," she continued, "it may never come right. In which case it would be better to stop now, as you say. Some kinds of persistence are just stupidity. I mean, it just eats away all one's self-respect, don't you think?"

"Well," he said, "one should not worry about what one cannot change." He intended this injunction for himself.

"Isn't that exactly *why* one worries, though? Because one can't change it?"

"Doesn't it work at all, then?"

She had put down her teacup and was absent-mindedly fluting the folds of her dress. She said, "He isn't kind."

"Not kind" he understood to be something quite distinct from cruel, something perhaps even less desirable: it implied having understood the principle of kindness and having rejected it.

"He keeps telling me," she went on, "that he hasn't promised me anything. I sometimes think, don't you, that that must have been the first thing Adam said to Eve in the Garden of Eden?"

Morgan smiled. "Aeneas says it to Dido," he said.

"And then he arrived the other night in a fearful state—terribly abusive."

"You mean—he was drunk?"

She nodded solemnly. "Titus Andronicus, my dear."

"Well, I'm sorry," he said helplessly.

"One doesn't have to behave like that, does one? Even if one doesn't feel—deeply." She opened her left hand so that it extended in his direction. "I mean—I am not like that with you, am I? Just because I don't . . . ?"

"Oh no," he said.

"And you don't mind my coming here like this?"

He took her little hand, but without looking up and with an air of capitulation. "Oh well," he said.

"It isn't awful for you—to see me, I mean?" Her head was bent toward him with a certain insistence.

"I love to see you." After a moment he added, "It is awful, yes."

When she said his name, he was obliged to raise his eyes.

"Morgan," she said, her fingers resting in his, a pearl ring on her smallest finger pressing into his palm. "Does it hurt you very much, then?"

Looking into her face, he thought that this must always be a rhetorical question. He looked away. For the space of a second, he closed his eyes.

She sat back, withdrawing her hand. She put away her handkerchief. Shaking her hair again, recrossing her legs, she seemed to revive. After a moment, she asked, "Is there any more tea?"

He poured it in silence, and chipped out a little more sugar from the petrified bowl.

"Well, I feel better," she said, "for seeing you. You're so *good*, Morgan. Such a comfort. I think I should come here all the time, just to get renewed. A sort of purification—like the lustrum."

"The lustrum was every five years," he said with a smile.

"Which reminds me—I must watch the time. I have to be somewhere for lunch."

"Oh? Where?" he asked.

She put down her cup. "Now, you're not going to give me dreary directions about the buses again." She looked around for her handbag. "Do you have a mirror?"

"In the hall," he said.

She gathered her things together—her hat, her gloves. He pushed the table out of her way.

"I look hideous," she said, putting on her hat before the mirror. "All this business is making an old woman of me."

He watched the back of her head. He stood very still, like a person who in a great defeat somehow maintains his dignity. He said, "You look splendid." It was the most fitting word he could think of.

"You're a pet to say so." She let him hold the door for her and went out onto the landing.

"I'll come down and put you in a taxi," he said.

"Oh, don't do that. There are heaps of cabs in the High Street. Really—I'd rather go alone."

She stood with her hand on the railing, her foot on the first of the carpeted stairs. She did not want him to know where she was going—after what she had said about giving up, about being reasonable. All that was perfectly clear to him. Light shone through her golden hat, on her brown skin. There was a smell of floor polish and, very delicately, of her perfume. Faint sounds of the street came up to them and, on the floor below, a gramophone was being played quite loudly: Beethoven was worrying about what he could not change.

"Mind the stairs," he said.

"You *are* sweet, Morgan," she said. "To cheer me up."

"I haven't done anything."

"Well—I do feel better, though. It was so soothing—being here, sitting on your sofa, drinking tea—"

Reaping havoc, Mrs. Fanshaw added to herself, passing through the hallway behind them.

"Yes," said Morgan, leaning over the banister once more as she went, far too quickly, down his long flight of steps. "You look quite restored."

OUT OF ITEA

The road from Delphi to the sea is one of the safest roads in Greece—that is to say, it is possible, even on its worst bends, for two cars to pass without one of them necessarily falling into the ravine. It is a well-surfaced, well-traveled road, bounded by rocks, shrubs, and pastures, which descends first to a brief plain of olive groves and finally to the little harbor of Itea where a ferry departs every so often for Patras in the Peloponnesus. By car, the road from Delphi to Itea takes about twenty minutes; by bicycle at least twice as long.

In spring the olive groves are drenched with their pale, prolific flowering, and the port of Itea—which consists of a cluster of sun-colored, flat-roofed cubes—is as busy as its temperament will permit it to become. The handful of cars lined up to take the ferry have interesting number plates and their foreign owners sit under the thatch awning of the waterfront café awaiting their turn to drive aboard. They may have quite a while to wait—for the boat, in accordance with the Greek nautical tradition, is not likely to leave on time. However, they need not be bored and do not seem to be—they have only to look to be entertained. The café looks on the tiny port and the tiny port looks on the sea; and the sea, on all sides, reflects capes and mountains, rocky or grassed, wild or cultivated, all with that legendary significance that in Greece seems to be not merely in the eye of the beholder but some knowledge possessed by the landscape itself. Behind Itea, if they turn their backs on the sea, the waiting tourists can look up at Parnassos or at the peaks above Amphissa, or retrace with their eyes that road that winds back up to Delphi.

When the ferry blows its whistle, there is a hasty gathering of newspapers and cameras. The travelers stub out their cigarettes and call for the bill, which by now most of them are prepared to recognize as the *logariasmos*. They need not hurry, though they do not know it, for the whistle is only the signal for putting on board three trucks loaded with bales of wool. It also brings out of one of the square houses the captain of the ferry, in a white cap, white shirt, and shorts, who sits down in the café, on one of the chairs vacated by his passengers, and orders what seems to be his breakfast. In the hot sun the passengers wait by their cars while planks are laid from the wooden pier to the iron flap of the ferry. The trucks are guided aboard—with some difficulty but little excitement—and the handful of foreign cars now follow.

The first car is a red Triumph with an Irish number plate, whose owner pulls a face when he realizes that he is to pay for the privilege of being first on board not only by being last off but also by being wedged between two of the wool trucks, one of which is shedding, in a light breeze, wisps of wool from a torn bale. The Irishman, who—like most Irishmen who own red Triumphs—looks like an Englishman, is young and good-looking and, since he eventually manages a short laugh at his wool-gathering predicament, appears to be good-natured. The beauty of his wife (who had laughed earlier and longer) is reminiscent of the twenties: her dark-red hair curves in to her cheeks, and her build is willowy. She wears a great straw hat, a pink shirt, and cerise trousers, and she fairly springs up the ladderlike stairs leading to the upper deck.

In the next car, a Volkswagen, are two American women—certainly teachers, possibly college professors. The stocky one, who is driving, fits the car efficiently into a square of the deck and even exchanges a few words of Greek—awkward Greek, self-conscious Greek, but Greek—with the seaman who is waving the cars up the ramp. Her friend, the lanky one, lifts an immense woven handbag from the back of the car and checks the necessities for the crossing—sunglasses, a thermos, post cards, a note-book, a phrasebook, and two crushable cotton hats that have followed their destiny. These ladies wear seersucker dresses that have dripped and are dry, and canvas sneakers over white socks. Up they go, enthusiastic, purposeful, to the passenger deck, where they find for themselves, injudiciously, a place in the sun.

The next car has a Greek number plate. It is a hired car from Athens with a more or less uniformed driver and a Greek woman guide in front, and a couple, who seem to be Danish, in the back. The driver parks carefully in his assigned place, then leaps out to help his passengers. The Danish couple and the Greek guide speak French among themselves. The Greek lady is pleasant, handsome, middle-aged, and wears that slightly sad look of misplaced cultivation that guides inevitably acquire. Her hair, iron gray, is tied up in a loose knot; her cotton dress is dark blue.

Her clients the Danes are elegant, sympathetic, refined. The lady wears her graying blond hair in teased, fashionable curls. Her white piqué suit has been ironed that morning, and her nails painted the night before. Nothing could be fresher or more welcome on the deck of a ferry than she. She carries in her arms a big bouquet of the thyme whose purple flowers can be seen on all the surrounding hills. She is charming and gay and greets the deckhands in French, as if they were part of international society. (Her husband is about to correct her when one of them returns a courteous "*Bonjour.*") The husband is of middle height and middle years; his yellow hair is thinning, his well-made body thickening. His face is unlined, but experienced, amused. He wears a white shirt and linen trousers, and carries his jacket on his arm. He has the personableness of intelligence, and the little party is no sooner on deck than he resumes his discussion with the guide.

Now comes a Greek farmer with a boy of about ten, wheeling two loaded sacks in a handcart. Now a wiry sunburned woman with a chicken in a wicker basket, a frail elderly couple with a clumsy bundle wrapped in cloth, and four young people—three girls and a youth—in dark clothes, possibly on their way to a family funeral. These people are soon deployed throughout the ship—leaning on the rail near the cars or spreading their parcels over benches on the upstairs deck, or strolling about to chat with the crew. The whistle is blown again, and the green water around the ship is lightly churned.

The captain leaves his table in the café without paying (can there be such a thing as an account at the Itea café, or is it possible that he owns it?), and strolls toward the pier holding his folded newspaper. Like some martinet, some stickler for punctuality, he takes out a watch and chain as he walks along, glances at it, and snaps it shut. (Is this to confirm more precisely the extent of the delay?) As he pauses to put it away, two figures appear behind him where the Delphi road joins the waterfront. Since they are on bicycles, they soon draw almost level with the captain, but politely do not pass and allow him to board his ship alone.

These new figures are singular enough to attract a little attention, although their type is familiar in spring and summer on the roads of Europe: a boy and a girl—he about twenty, she perhaps a year younger, each with a plain pedal bicycle to which is strapped a heavy pack. They are both short, fair, and neatly built. A tiny Norwegian flag has been painted on the boy's bicycle. He wears a bleached khaki shirt, khaki shorts rolled up an inch or two, and leather sandals with rope soles. His legs and arms are fuzzed with ginger and deeply sunburned to a peeled and blotchy red. His face is reddish brown except at the hairline and disfigured by an uncertain ginger beard.

They wheel their bicycles on board. The girl is wearing a loose yellow jersey, above which the back of her neck shows crimson, and a limp cotton skirt of red and blue flowers. On her limbs the down is blond. Her arms are as crimson as her neck, but, since her legs are scarcely pink, there must be a pair of blue jeans somewhere in her monstrous pack. Her hair has been cropped almost as short as her companion's. On her feet are roughly made sandals of a very old design—an open casing laced together over the instep with thongs that continue halfway up the calf and tie there.

Among the cars and trucks they find a place to put their bicycles where they can be seen from the deck above. The girl's pack is the same size as the boy's and must, by the look of it, weigh about thirty pounds (one imagines some misguided pact of equal responsibility), and rummaging in it she produces a paper bag spotted with grease and a clear plastic bottle of water. A frying pan has been strapped to the side of her pack—the sole token of her sex. The pack is closed again and the boy leads the way to the upper deck, where they seat themselves in two canvas chairs just vacated by the American ladies, who have gone into the shade of the wheelhouse.

The iron ramp of the ferry has been cranked up, the whistle blows a third time, and the ship is under way. A small group has somehow collected to wave them off, and in the café the waiter stands among the empty tables shading his eyes. The suns shines, the breeze strengthens, the wool floats more thickly down. On deck the foreigners look back to Delphi, where the ruins are visible only for a moment in a curve of the hills.

"He was changed into a dolphin, you know. Right here. That's where they get the name. Delphi." The stocky teacher is the bossy one.

"Who?"

"Apollo. For heaven's sake."

The younger one is writing in a notebook. "I'll put it in at the end. How do you spell Oedipus's father?"

The Irish couple have taken a bench for themselves, and even have a small cushion covered in imitation leopard. They sit sideways looking out to sea, their knees companionably touching, their *Guide Bleu* warping on the seat between them.

"What were the Mysteries of Eleusis?"

"Nobody seems to know." He is more serious than she.

"Maybe that's the point." She brings a pink scarf out of her pocket and ties her hat on under her chin. She looks back at the mountains and sighs. "Wasn't Delphi *divine*?"

He smiles. "It's nothing if not that."

"Is that the Castalian spring? That groove to the right?"

"No—I don't think we can see it from here. Don't you remember, we had to drive farther up the road to get to it."

"Oh yes." She recites:

> *"A little Learning is a dangerous thing;*
> *Drink deep, or taste not the Castalian spring."*

"That's the *Pierian* spring," he corrects her, and they both burst out laughing. They turn their attention back to the deck. Like all travelers in Greece, they have run into some of their fellow tourists before today—on the Acropolis, was it, or behind Herodes Atticus?—and have already exchanged nods and smiles with them this morning.

Delphi disappears. The chauffeur of the Danes' car arrives on deck with a steward. The steward sizes up the situation, then goes back for a collapsible table which is set up for the Danes' lunch. "*Parakalo*," says the stocky teacher, rising to her feet, and soon there are tables for the teachers and the Irish couple as well, and a boy who speaks only Greek is taking impossible orders for lunch.

The Danes and their guide are in deck chairs. They have brought books, and their books are in earnest: *Die Griechischen Altertümer, Le Trésor de Sifnos, Alexander's Path; their Guide Bleu* has been warped for years. Before lunch the party has a glass of retsina apiece, and the guide talks to them continually, pointing from time to time.

"And there is the spot where Byron landed." She says it in English, in honor of the occasion—not loudly but in the slightly oratorical manner of guides, so that the Irish couple and the stocky teacher turn to look, and the chauffeur comes over to the rail. There is a sloping headland, a bay, another tiny port.

"He landed there," says the teacher to her friend, who has not heard.

"Apollo?"

"Byron," she says, but as if the confusion were understandable.

Only the Norwegians have shown no interest. They sit together with their hands linked, their feet on the lower rung of the rail, and look at the sea. Once they look at each other. A look such as that, though it passes between two people in a fraction of a second, is seen by everyone and is unforgettable.

Without speaking she releases his hand and brings the crumpled paper bag up from beneath her deck chair. In the bag there is a newspaper parcel and she unwraps this, spreading the paper over her knees. Pairing what she finds inside—two small loaves stuffed with cheese, two boiled eggs, and several tomatoes—she is calm, engrossed, more mysterious than Eleusis, more romantic than Byron. He reaches over to eat from her lap—from the little table made by her spread knees and the sheet of paper covered with Greek characters and centered by a photograph of King Constantine.

They have been sailing for some time in a more open sea. Coming upstairs with a loaded tray, the waiter does a little dance on the deck to steady himself. There are omelets, plates of goat cheese and cucumbers, and unmarked bottles of retsina, and a thick tile of bread is laid beside each plate. There are even paper napkins, which presently blow overboard.

The boy, who has finished his last tomato, is the more genteel of the pair. He gathers together the eggshells and bread crumbs and puts them in the paper bag, which he sternly prevents her from throwing into the Gulf of Corinth. The waiter takes it away and they resume their positions, lightly holding hands. In a moment the girl is asleep, her shorn head tilted back, her pale gorge prominent in her sunburned neck.

It is impossible to be unmoved by their presence, by their absence. They have everyone's attention to some degree, though no one can command theirs. The guide nods toward them with her melancholy smile. The Irishman, having completed his meal, lies down on a bench with his head in his wife's lap. The Danish lady touches her husband's hand. The ferry splashes its ungainly bow against wave after wave, and on all sides of them—for all the while they have been in sight of the Peloponnesian shore—can be seen the disarming shapes of the Greek coast, sometimes steep, sometimes low-lying, not always readily imposing, for this is an Oriental idea of a coastline rather than a Western one. For the space of a minute, heavy rain falls from the blue sky—the sea is freckled with it, it splashes over the deck, on tables and empty dishes, but no one stirs. The Norwegian girl opens her eyes but doesn't move, and in a moment the rain is behind them.

"Patras," says the chauffeur, and once more the passengers are brought to the rail. Patras, the substantial town fixed in an arc of the oncoming land, is their destination and they cannot disregard it. They have chosen to come to this shore and they line the rail like a little group of immigrants, wondering what life it will offer them even temporarily.

"Missolonghi," the man says, pointing farther and in another direction. There is a tremendous headland, cliffs, some flat land.

Only the Norwegians still watch Patras.

Standing beside the boy's chair, the stocky teacher tells him, "Missolonghi. Where Byron died."

He gives a careful smile. Turning to his companion, he translates, "*Byron døde der,*" but one senses that he does so merely from politeness.

She is bending forward in her chair to dry her face with her skirt. She looks up, smiles and nods, and says, "Thank you," gravely as if to a child.

The guide sits down again with her Danish friends and spreads out a map of the Peloponnesus. "Olympia," she says—for they are all headed for Olympia: it is their reason for landing at Patras—"is on the border of the district of Arcadia."

The ship slows down. They are nearing Patras. The town looks hot and slow. Above the waterfront there are hotels, terraces, a garden, a gas station. The harbor is empty except for a few caïques, a tanker, and a tug or two. An exchange of whistles brings the ferry almost to a stop. It glides toward the pier, covering the last quarter of a mile so slowly that the passengers go back to their seats and the guide resumes her lecture.

". . . was the site of the Games, which took place every four years regardless of the political relations of participants. In those days"—she shrugs—"they suspended the wars for the Games. Now they suspend the Games for the wars."

The teachers and the Irish couple eavesdrop—one never learns so much as from another person's guide. The Norwegian girl stands up at last and leans on the rail, but the other travelers are losing interest in her: she is all very well, but they have come here for the real thing—art, history, truth—and cannot afford to be sidetracked.

The boy is first down from the deck. He squeezes among the cars, the girl following, and reaches the bicycles just as the boat touches the pier. They have disposed of their paper bag and have nothing to repack. They wheel their bicycles forward a yard or two, exchange a few words. The girl lifts her head to look at Patras and laughs.

There is something drastic about the arrival of a ship against a dock—even if it is simply the ferry from Itea against the pier at Patras—some sensation of adventure, almost of rescue. A definable episode is completed, a less definable one begins. Chains are rattling, ropes creak around bollards, and there are the ritual shouts of "Oi! Oi!" that presumably give guidance to those concerned. By the time the flap of the ferry is let down, all the passengers are on the lower deck—those on foot preparing to walk to their destination in the town, those with cars repacking their belongings. The cars are too hot to enter, and their owners stand beside them in the sun.

The cyclists are first off. The other tourists must wait—for one of the wool trucks is to be allowed off before the cars—and they watch the two figures weaving up the short rise that leads from the pier to the main road. At last it seems possible to talk about them.

The Danish lady laughs, brushing the tough spines of the thyme from her white jacket. "But such discomfort! Such discomfort! At my age—unthinkable . . ." She pauses, but her husband doesn't smile or reassure her. It is not the moment for jokes about age.

He says, "We will overtake them in no time."

The stocky teacher has put on her sunglasses. "They took so little interest. One can't imagine why they come to Greece."

Her friend's imagination may be less deficient, for she looks vague. She says, "I expect we'll bump into them in Arcadia."

The Irish couple slide into the scorching seats of their car. "This bloody wool," he says.

Still looking at the road, his wife asks him, "But what will they *eat*?"

"Tomatoes."

"Where will they sleep?"

"Together."

"One could give them a lift perhaps?"

"With those *bicycles*?" he begins in halfhearted horror, but then says, "No. No. Let them alone." A signal is made for the cars to move on, and he starts the engine. "They're having the time of their lives."

THE EVERLASTING DELIGHT

To a foreigner there is something not quite credible about the stillness of the Italian countryside on a July afternoon. Even an American woman who had spent, as Mrs. Olivia Drew had done, a year in Italy doubted whether this suspension—it almost seemed—of life itself could be a habitual state of affairs, and she looked about her at the deserted plain as if to say, "You can't mean this." There was not a car to be seen except her own, not a soul, not an animal on the road or even in the driveway through whose gates she ultimately drove.

When she first lost her way on the mountain above, Mrs. Drew had seen a pair of woodsmen among the trees and stopped to ask the way. *"Per Sant'Andrea, come si va?"* But these country people had never heard of the village for which she was headed, though she knew it must be nearby. It was one of the woodsmen who had directed her to the house on the plain below, pointing it out from the spur where she had stopped the car. She could inquire there.

It had seemed so far off. "There's no house nearer than that?"

No, that was the house where she could be directed. *"Il Conte,"* the woodsman said, pronouncing it *"Honte"* in his regional voice.

She had set off down the mountain, on a road of red dust that changed, from time to time, into loose pebbles or into an arrangement of stone slabs whose central prominence made her afraid for the axle. She was sure, at first, that some house or village would turn up before she got all the way down. But no, the track wound onward, downward, losing sight of the villa below but always, she knew, approaching it. The woods were very close on each side of the car, and birds sang at her open window. An occasional overgrown stone wall suggested that this land had once been cultivated, and she caught a glimpse, through trees, of a solitary ruin— the stump of a white stone castle, half covered with ivy. The single tiny clearing she came upon, however, was made around a monument, and she slowed down to read the inscription, so strange did it seem to find oneself addressed in that lonely place. A simple slab surmounted by a cross, the monument bore nineteen names in alphabetical order and a brief legend to the effect that these men ("*martiri*"), executed here by the Germans in 1944, had comprised the Resistance of the villages that circled the foot of the mountain.

As she drove on, the Conte's villa came into view again. She could see, still farther off, clumps of stone houses, a Romanesque campanile— villages as distant, as tentatively suggested, as in a seventeenth-century painting. The nineteen honest men from these towns of the plain weighed on her heart as she came down the last loop of the mountain road.

Now the road improved abruptly and she passed quickly into the open plain. It wasn't until she entered the open gates of the villa and found herself in a short, shaded driveway that she recalled how early it was. She hoped the Conte took his afternoon nap in some lofty chamber, far from the reverberations of his doorbell. Perhaps a servant would come out to meet her so that she need not even ring. It was no time of day to pay a call.

Parking the car under the trees, she opened the door, swung her legs to the ground, took out her mirror and comb. When she looked again at her watch, it was still no more than three o'clock. She closed the door with a warning slam, and walked through the garden to the house.

She saw at once that this was no ordinary villa. Or, rather, that it was singular just for being ordinary in a part of the world where every country house is distinguished. One could not have said, for example, that the house was ill-sited; it simply had no site—as if on this unexpected plain, between so many inviting elevations, its owner had jabbed a finger and said, "I'll have my house there," with no reflection whatever. Moreover, it was a new house: though built in the Florentine manner and stuccoed the usual light pleasing yellow, it was certainly no more than fifty years old. And it had, of all things, a prosaic, comfortable, almost suburban porch fitted into its main façade—a porch that had nothing to do with noble loggias or spacious terraces and in which a fringed, swinging garden seat had been installed. This seat was littered with magazines.

Mrs. Drew turned to look back at the garden she had come through. Pebbled paths led to a large pond, almost a little lake, but here too something was peculiar. Although its form had been prettily reproduced from some old design, the pond was disproportionately shallow; at present, though half full, the water made little more than a deep film, clustered with rubbery foliage. Around it, the garden was extensive, well tended, and, even on this hot afternoon, brilliantly alight with flowers.

The doorbell was of the kind that draws out from the wall on a handle—the handle in this case being a flowered ceramic one. Olivia Drew heard it ring inside the house, but this sound was followed by no other. Rather than ring a second time, she wondered whether she might simply drive on to one of the villages she had seen. She stood on the porch, undecided, her eye wandering over the scattered magazines with their cover photographs of royalty, posed and deposed. There was a full ashtray on a wicker table, and a loop of narrow purple ribbon.

She was about to go down the steps when she noticed, on the wall of the porch facing the swing seat, an engraved plaque:

THIS HOUSE WAS ERECTED IN 1928
BY FEDERICO GASPARINI-BONDI
AND HIS CONSORT MARIA LAURA
TO ENHANCE THE YOUTHFUL JOYS
OF THEIR CHILDREN AND FOR
THE EVERLASTING DELIGHT
OF THEIR DESCENDANTS

Everything about the little plaque was as charming as its message. Each of the marble corners had been lightly scrolled; the lettering was elegant, and surmounted by an incised decoration of leaves and tendrils. It provided, Mrs. Drew thought, a smiling counterpart to the sorrowful monument she had just seen on the mountainside.

She was reading it over, and wondering whether "delight" was in fact the best way to translate *diletto*, when a quick step sounded and the door opened.

The man who stood there gave no sign of having been roused from sleep. That he was a servant was evident only from his way of holding the door as if it were his responsibility rather than his property. He was trimly dressed in light clothes. His face was dark, blunt but not ill-natured, and he had a deep scar on his cheek—a semicircular scar as precisely inscribed as one of the curved decorations on the marble plaque.

She begged his pardon. She had lost her way up there on the mountain. Did he know the village of Sant'Andrea?

He knew two of that name. One was in this direction (he pointed so vaguely that she was reminded of her conjecture about the siting of the house), and the other was in that.

They were both silent, confronting this information. Then he stepped back and went on courteously, "Won't you come in? A glass of lemonade—"

She thanked him, but she must get on to Sant'Andrea. She was going to visit friends there. If she could telephone, perhaps?

Inside the house, a man's voice called out. "Fulco! Someone lost? Bring them in."

Fulco said, again motioning to her to come in, "*Il Conte.*"

A woman called from upstairs, "In the *salotto*. It's cooler there. I'm coming straight down."

"*La Contessa.*"

Mrs. Olivia Drew did enter the house, but hesitantly, feeling that there had been a mistake, that some other lost traveler was expected. Ringing steps approached her from the back of the house, and lighter ones down the curving staircase at whose foot she found herself. Nothing about her presence in this unknown house could justify an eager reception; waiting there, she felt sure to disappoint.

They appeared at the same moment, the Conte short, stout, and twinkling, his consort taller only by her coil of faded hair, fragile, dressed in gray. Before she had properly presented herself, Mrs. Drew had been conducted from the stairs to a doorway, and before she had properly told her story she was seated on a sofa and lemonade had been sent for.

"I really must get on—my husband expects me back in Florence this evening. I drove out to meet these friends, you see, and got lost coming over the mountain. The village isn't on the map, and I relied on someone being able to tell me the road."

"It's not a village at all." The Conte slapped the arm of his chair. "Not the Sant'Andrea you're looking for. It's an old estate with an enclave of houses round the main building."

"My friends have rented a house for the summer. I don't even know the owner's name. The house is called—"

"Il Palazzolo."

"How ever did you know?"

The Conte and his consort exchanged a gleeful smile. The Contessa explained, "There's only one house there it could be—"

"And that's my cousin's! He always rents it out to foreigners for the summer. Keeps him there in comfort for the rest of the year." Now the old man slapped his bald head in dismay. "Wrong thing to say. I beg your pardon."

The lemonade was brought by a brawny country boy wearing white cotton gloves. Leaning back on the sofa, which was covered with a pretty chintz of lilac flowers, Mrs. Drew looked about her. Since this could not, in the circumstances, be done discreetly, she said aloud what she was thinking. "What a charming room!"

Like the house itself, the room was not splendid. It was comfortable, even lovable, a room of armchairs, of small tables and small objects, of flowers and photographs—of photographs above all. Young people, swimming, riding, skiing; formal portraits of babies, snapshots of children playing with animals; a boy being presented with a heavy book; a shy girl in the tight-waisted, long-skirted dress that in 1947 was known as the New Look. There were houses, gardens, parties on terraces, groups on beaches, a couple in a gondola. On some photographs the written messages were so long that they disappeared into the frame; other pictures had been mounted in pairs or as a series.

"These are your children?"

The Contessa did not at once respond, but leaned over the back of the sofa where they sat and handed Mrs. Drew a youngish woman in a garden chair. "This is my daughter." After a moment, she added, "She lives in Argentina. In Buenos Aires."

"Does she come here? Do you go there?"

The Contessa put the photograph back. "Her husband represents an Italian company there. She comes—yes—every four years, for a few weeks. They've been out there for eighteen years."

The Conte said, "At first they thought they would be sent home after a few years—so we didn't go. And now we're too old, it's too far."

"And—this is your son?" Mrs. Drew put down her glass and took up a picture from the table beside her.

"No. No. That's my grandson, my daughter's boy." The Contessa smiled. "Nearly two meters tall."

"Something in the food out there," put in the old man. "All so tall, so stringy. Something in the food." He took on the peculiarly serious look Italians assume when delivering lay opinions on scientific subjects. "*Non ingrassa, ma fa crescere.*"

The old lady got up suddenly and came back with another photograph, of two young men in a sailing boat. "Our sons," she said. She sat down again and looked at her husband. "They both died in the war."

The Conte made a movement as though to reach out and touch her. "One died in the war. The other—"

Across the room his wife returned his gesture with her fingertips. Husband and wife seemed, still, both so spirited that this grief would have to pursue them to the end of their lives in order to crush them completely. "The other," she explained, "was missing, then a prisoner. He did come back from the war, but within six months he was dead of cancer. I still feel he died from the war. I can't help believing that without the war he would be alive." She leaned back, pressing her hands together in her lap, not resigned to being so sad.

The old man said, "My dear."

The Contessa touched her guest's arm apologetically. "You mustn't think we make everyone sad with our story. I keep the photographs here.

I like to have them out, and we're only here in the summer, when hardly anyone visits us. In our apartment in Perugia I keep very little from the past—except furniture, of course. So much furniture, from both our families. Now some of it is here, upstairs, but this house was never intended for antique furniture."

"We had the idea, when the children were babies, of making this house for them." The Conte lifted his hands to invoke the surroundings. "We have land here, and there was another villa that belonged to us, a mile or so away, now sold. But this was to be their house. No antiques, nothing to spoil, nothing to get scolded about. No cliffs to fall off, no pond deep enough to drown in. Everything easy, nothing intimidating. Just for children—ours and theirs."

"What a sweet idea. What a sweet house."

"It *is* a sweet house," the Contessa said. "I was worried, while it was being built, in case it mightn't have a nice nature when it was finished. Because houses have that too, like people, something they're born with; things happen to them later, of course, but good disposition is more mysterious. This one turned out well. It really is *simpatica*."

Mrs. Drew put her hand on the chintz cushion beside her, a departing gesture. "I must be going."

"Not a bit of it," cried the Conte, twinkling up again. "You'll be too early if you set off now—it's only twenty minutes from here. Take time to get your breath back and we'll send you on your way. Look, I'll have Fulco telephone. It must still be the same number as my cousin's, I've got it here." He snatched up a leather address book from a pile of albums, opened it on his knee, and pulled a monocle from his pocket. "Here we are. Oh no, no, that's another cousin. Yes, here it is."

Mrs. Drew smiled at him. The old man was like Proust's duke, with all his cousins. He was also irresistibly kind. While the telephone call was made, she described her journey down the mountain.

"It was a woodsman who pointed out this house—the villa of '*Il Honte.*'" She reproduced the Tuscan pronunciation with a smile.

"I sometimes think," said the old man, "that that chap in the poem of Catullus, who pronounced his 'c's as aspirates, must have come from hereabouts." He broke off to declaim, "'*Chommoda dicebat, si quando commode vellet dicere*—' But forgive me, you were telling us about your drive down the mountain."

"It was beautiful, really. So solitary, except for the woodsmen, and so silent, except for the birds. There must have been hundreds of birds singing beside the car all the way down."

"There are *upupe* all over that mountain."

"The striped one that looks like pieces of other old birds put together? Yes, I saw him. Pheasant, too—a lot of pheasant, mostly female."

"There used to be boar up there, and deer, in the old days. Now only pheasant and hare. It doesn't look it, but it was an inhabited place until fairly recently—there are overgrown paths that used to lead to farms. The farms are all derelict now, abandoned, everyone gone to the towns. It was too hard a life, you know—water's the great difficulty, and then no electricity, and so cut off in winter. No one wants to do it these days."

"I didn't see a single building—oh, except a ruin, but that was no farm. More like a castle."

"That's Montevecchio. That belongs to us. It was a marvelous place for picnics when the children were little—battlements, towers, and a great stone staircase leading to nowhere. No one really knows when it was built, only that a noblewoman fortified it and lived there with her retinue in the twelfth century. A queen, the people round here will tell you, but it was actually an exiled Lombard countess. In the days when we used to go up there, there was still one noble room intact, almost like a throne room, with a stone dais at one end and curved capitals on either side of the door—perhaps that's where the legend came from, about the queen. Fulco tells me it's all ruined now—young people drive up there on Vespas at the weekends and pull it about, carve their names and heaven knows what else, and the weather does the rest. It isn't safe, either, these days. The grass there is full of poisonous snakes—as soon as people leave the land, the snakes come back."

"I thought of getting out to look at it, but I was worried about the time, and then the road was difficult just there. In some places—but of course you know—there are big stones, almost like rocks."

The old people smiled at each other. "So what are they, then"—the Conte lifted up his finger in a classroom attitude—"those big stones?"

"Not—Roman road?"

"Of course it's Roman road! An old, old road that existed before the Cassia was built. La Via Romea, that's what it's called, La Via Romea. This is ancient country round here, though not much digging has been done. God knows what's underneath. Before the war we found an Etruscan tomb right here in our garden. The government sent someone to look at it—he nosed around, made off with the loot, all that. There must be other tombs, cities perhaps, who knows? Once in a while someone comes across a piece of a pot or a weapon. There was a lot of fighting over this area. Though I suppose," he added glumly, "one could say that of any spot on earth."

Mrs. Drew said, "It's serene enough now."

The Contessa shook her head. "Not for much longer. They're building a highway—you can see it from the upstairs windows, coming closer all the time. It'll pass by about half a mile from here. A link to the Autostrada. It's called—" She appealed to her husband.

"La Superstrada," he said solemnly.

"*Ecco. Superstrada. O Dio*, it's all very well building these new roads, but the way they speak about it you'd think it was an act of Divine Creation. A cousin of ours was here last month, talking as if no one had ever seen a new road before. 'The future of Italy is in these roads,' he kept saying. Well, the past of Italy is in the roads too—they made roads from Rome to the ends of the earth. Now they're at it again, that's all."

"Something for the road, that's it!" The Conte leapt to his feet. "That lemonade doesn't do anything for you. A drop of something stronger, to give you courage for the journey?"

"No, really not, thank you."

"Well, you're right, it doesn't give you courage at all." The old man flopped back into his chair. "When our daughter went out to South America for the first time, in '49, we decided to have a bottle of champagne always at hand on a table—in an ice bucket, you know, with a couple of glasses. The idea was to cheer ourselves up from time to time." He made one of his absurd, endearing gestures of total capitulation. "And it didn't help at all! Not at all!"

Mrs. Drew put her hand out once more on the cushion beside her. "What pretty material."

"Those are my colors," said the Contessa. "Lilacs and lavenders and blues. I found the material in Florence in the Via Tornabuoni. I loved it so much that I sent some to my daughter, but the sun must be different there, for it faded immediately."

"*Ma che dici?*" her husband asked indulgently. "How can the sun be different?"

"I mean—the light must be stronger. Or her chairs were more exposed." The old lady's mouth drooped at the thought of the life she would never even have a glimpse of. Then she turned to her guest. "Let us show you the rest of the house."

Upstairs the rooms were again large, cool, and pleasant. The old couple led their visitor through two or three bedrooms and a room with a piano before the Conte paused at a pair of double doors in a delighted certainty of surprising her. Throwing the doors open, he preceded Mrs. Drew across the room and opened the shutters.

"My bedroom," the Contessa said.

The room, in contrast to the rest of the house, was richly furnished with eighteenth-century Venetian pieces. Commodes, chairs, tables, fantastically contoured and painted, stood around the walls, and between the windows an immense mirror, perhaps eight feet tall, mistily reflected the splendid bed that took up half the room. A vast canopy, containing a smaller, bell-shaped canopy of the same material, was supported by twisted and gilded posts and descended in scalloped hangings drawn back with gold silk cords. Canopy, hangings, and bedcover were all of the same peacock-blue and gold embroidery.

"It's never been restored." The Contessa lifted a fold of the curtains to show the work. "The other pieces have been touched up from time to time, but the bed never."

"This is the furniture you spoke of, from your family?"

"This is the bed I slept in as a girl." The old lady hesitated.

"But we bought it only last year!" the Conte finished.

His wife smiled. "You see—I was brought up in a big house." She named one of the great villas of the Veneto. "It had a famous series of these beds that were commissioned from embroiderers in the seventeen-fifties—a red one, a rose one, a gold one, green one, and so on, in connecting rooms. Seven in all, for the seven children of the house at that time. The villa was sold by my brother before the war, and sold again a few years ago—I knew all that, naturally, but I hadn't been near the house for thirty years. Then, last year, my husband and I were in Venice and went by chance to a furniture exhibition at the Palazzo Rezzonico. There were exhibits of rooms from various periods—you know the sort of thing—and all at once I came through a doorway and found myself in my own room, with this bed and furniture I hadn't seen since I was a girl."

The Conte held up his hands. "What a scene!"

"Nonsense," said the Contessa, smiling still. "Only a few tears. But it was too much. I'd given up even my memories of that time, and there was the room come to find me. We discovered that the present owner of the villa had sold off all the other beds years ago, and this was the last one. So we rescued it. We couldn't afford the rest of the room—besides, I already had these other chests and chairs from the time of my marriage—but I got my bed back again. There was no room for it in our place in Perugia, so we broke our rule about this house and made a Venetian room here." They walked around the bed; with its enclosure of draperies, it was like a small chamber in itself.

The bedroom opened on the far side to the landing of another, smaller staircase.

"We can go down to the garden this way, through the chapel," the Conte told Mrs. Drew, leading her down. "Then you can see the house from the other side."

The chapel was tiny, full of flowers.

"The Mass was given here regularly," the Contessa told her, "when we had a real staff, and *contadini*. The chapel is so small that half the congregation had to stand outside, around the door. When our daughter was married here, the guests stood right up to her elbow."

There were two memorial tablets, one on each side wall. Mrs. Drew, glancing away from this terrible symmetry, met the Contessa's eye.

The old lady nodded. "My elder son was killed in Greece, in 1941." When her visitor was silent, thinking of the other, rougher tablet on the mountainside, she went on, "Yes, the campaign of Italy against Greece—you're thinking, What could be worse?" She repeated, after a moment, "What could be worse?" The Conte went across the room to unbolt the doors into the garden. A shaft of hot light struck the travertine paving where they stood, and the Contessa said in a low voice, "The following year, our other son was reported missing in North Africa. We did everything to get news of him, things one could never imagine oneself doing. I went down to Rome. Through my mother I had a distant connection with the Pacelli family, and I used this remorselessly to get help from the Pope in finding out if my son was alive. When we discovered he was a prisoner, I made more trouble to have parcels sent to him, badgered people to get letters through. You think yourself incapable of behaving in this way, but when your child's life is involved you find you can do anything." Now she did turn away, and they walked slowly out into the garden. The Contessa took her guest's arm, not for support but with an air of giving encouragement. "Anything at all," she said.

"I'll get Fulco to bring the car round," the Conte said. "He can dust it off a bit for you." He disappeared around the side of the house. They were standing at one end of an *allée* of immense lavender bushes in full flower.

"Do you like it?" the Contessa asked.

Mrs. Drew smiled with pleasure. "I've never seen anything like it," she said. "Can we go down a little way?"

They strolled along together between the double row of bushes, whose scent and color were so deep as to give an illusion of shade. Every bush was filled with the whirring of bees.

"It makes the finest honey of all." The Contessa stopped to break off a faded sprig or two. "The flowers are past their best now. At the end of June it was marvelous—so beautiful that I wouldn't have exchanged it even for the avenue of lemon trees they have at Montegufoni. There are some new plants here—the bushes get tired after a few seasons and have to be renewed. But we should have shown you this garden from above—it should be seen first from an upstairs window, because of the patterns of the flowers and the boxwood. We designed it all so carefully, long ago, and it's only now coming to perfection."

The Fiat, driven by Fulco, appeared at the corner of the villa. It had been cleaned off on top and looked like some humped animal that had waded in red dust up to its haunches. When they walked over to it, Mrs. Drew saw that someone had put, on the front seat, half a dozen small gauze bags of lavender, tied with violet ribbon.

"A little souvenir," the Contessa said, taking her hand.

The Conte gave directions. *"A destra, a sinistra, poi dritto.* Then you come to a tiny track of stones, and you think, It can't possibly be this— and that's how you'll recognize it, because that's it!"

Mrs. Drew laughed. The Conte kissed her hand. She got in the car and leaned on the window sill, thanking them. "I've loved seeing your house," she said.

"If you come this way again," the Contessa told her, "be sure to let us know. We're here until September. It's too far from Perugia to come for weekends, but we spend the summers here now."

The Conte smiled his permanently rueful smile. "So it does get some use, after all."

THE STATUE AND THE BUST

C an you all hear me?" the teacher was asking, not because the group was large—there were only nine or ten girls—but because of the traffic roaring through the square.

"Yes, Miss Ingram." One or two girls at the rear muttered, "Yeah, yeah," in long-suffering undertone, but only to be funny, Michele supposed, since they looked reasonably contented.

Michele was sitting on the steps of the Hospital of the *Innocenti*. He had parked his car in the square while he did some business in Via de' Servi. Returning to the car, he had seen the group of girls enter the piazza, and had sat down on the steps to watch. He judged them to be about fifteen or sixteen years of age. Their summer dresses, too short for Florence, agreeably revealed long arms and legs. They all wore the same kind of sandal—bought, possibly, on a group excursion to UPIM. One girl was very plump, another had freckles, another carried her arm in a sling: after a few moments, he could tell them apart quite easily. Sitting there in the sun, he dwelt disinterestedly, like an artist, on the texture of their hair, the tones of their flesh, the curve of lip or shoulder, the waists sketchily defined by the shiftlike dresses. The color of the eyes was in every case concealed behind dark glasses; it was as if some custom, the converse of wearing the veil, compelled them to hide their eyes.

It was the teacher, however, who interested him, and this was more of a mystery. She was about thirty, short but upright, holding her head high, like a small, crowded flower that tries to get its share of the sun. As he watched, she hopped up a couple of the shallow steps to command the girls' attention. She wore a dress of blue cotton with fine white spots and carried a huge straw bag over her arm and a guidebook in her hand. With the girls there, it was hard to tell what she looked like; the fact of their presence gave her an air of maturity she might not have had on her own.

What was curious, though, was a radiance, something singular she carried about her as ostensibly as her handbag, something quite unconnected with her looks. She had an unusual voice, too, pure, measured, distinct, and the quality of this seemed detached from what was said.

"The Piazza della Santissima Annunziata," she was telling them. "We'll be going into the church in a moment. Right now we are standing in front of the Ospedale degli Innocenti, a home for foundlings since the fifteenth century." It was odd the way the words rang out, clear and fully formed but with that guidebook flatness. He could tell her Italian was terrible from the way she pronounced the names.

The girls' attention wandered from her. So, for the moment, did Michele's. He looked around the square as she pointed out the delicacy of the arcades, the Della Robbia decorations, the place where the curtains of art parted, letting in a shaft of countryside; but he was only thinking, What an idea, using a place like this for a parking lot. He groaned over the cars, forgetting how glad he had been to find a wedge of space here for his own Seicento.

"I want you to notice particularly," the teacher said, and Michele came to himself with a start, as if he had been in class, "the statue of the Grand Duke Ferdinand I, at this end of the square."

Michele had been looking at this statue, where it rose above the crouching cars, and thinking that it was an inferior piece of work to have been so prominently placed and that even the greatest sculptors had moments of mediocrity. Trust a foreigner to single out this for special attention, leading up to it as if it were the most significant thing in the square, simply assuming that, since it stood in the loveliest piazza in Florence and was old, it must automatically have artistic importance. But no.

"This statue is the subject of a poem by Robert Browning. Yes, Cecilia, I know it's hot. It's just as hot for me as it is for you. We'll go into the church directly. The poem—the poem is called 'The Statue and the Bust.' Does anyone know it?"

Michele was fascinated to observe the change in her as she said this—her resolute, instructive manner falling away and being replaced by an emotional stillness of breast and shoulders, a voice tremulous with feeling. It was not that she had lost her composure; whatever moved her expressed itself out of private, contained reserves.

"It is the story of a love affair supposedly conducted between the grand duke and a noble lady who lived in the palace just to the right of the statue." The guidebook closed in her indifferent grasp as she recounted this matter known by heart. "You will see that the grand duke's head is slightly turned in that direction. The legend is that they met only once, but that for years afterward the duke went past this house each day and the lady sat in the window to exchange a glance with him. After many years, her looks no longer being what they were, the lady had a bust of herself in youth placed at the window, so he might see that as he passed each day, rather than her aging face. Subsequently, the grand duke placed the statue here, where it might always look at her."

The girls were enchanted. So was Michele. So, he noted, was the teacher, turned away now toward the corner of the square and pointing, like a statue herself, her arm outstretched and her head uplifted.

"Why didn't they get married, Miss Ingram?"

"That was not possible." She said this gravely, conclusively, declining to gossip on a circumstance so crucial.

"Which window is it, Miss Ingram, with the bust of the lady?"

"There's no bust. It's only a story. Browning made up that part after he'd seen the statue."

"Ohhh." Comically, they exaggerated their disappointment with long-drawn-out ohhs until she had to stop them.

"Can you say it, Miss Ingram, the poem?"

Michele saw her hesitate. She could say it, but didn't have the courage.

"Say it, Miss Ingram!"

"Say it," he added unheard.

She made up her mind. "It's too long." She smiled—she had a sweet smile—looking all around the group of girls as if her care for them went beyond safe custody. "When we go into the church," she told them, her voice leveling again, "you'll see a picture by Andrea del Sarto, a painter who was also the subject of a poem by Browning."

Michele grinned. So it turns out that the whole piazza belongs to this Robert Browning. Who would have thought it? He enjoyed the idea of this little woman trekking her literature around the world, imposing it on oblivious monuments. All the same, it was evident that, as far as she was concerned, Andrea del Sarto wasn't in the same class with the grand duke.

While they were still turned toward the statue, a man wheeling a barrow crossed the end of the square.

"Watermelon! Oh, Miss Ingram, may I have a slice of watermelon?"

"Oh, *please*, Miss Ingram?"

"Miss Ingram, I'm *dying*."

"Not so loud. All right, if you're quick. D'you have change? If not, be careful with the notes—the five thousand looks like the one thousand. Mind the cars. And don't talk to anyone."

They wagged away, one after the other, across the square, a line of bright pennants being run up like a signal over the paving stones. Miss Ingram had been standing in the same place, with her back to Michele, but all at once she turned and faced him. She walked to where he sat and went straight past him, up the steps, to stand in the shade of the portico. He twisted around to look at her. She had taken off her sunglasses and was rubbing them with a handkerchief. Older than he had guessed; not much younger than he.

She had not noticed him at all.

Michele wanted to talk to her, to speak English, to belong for a moment to that world where even children traveled easily and women quoted poetry. He cursed all his countrymen who had ever promiscuously accosted foreign women, beclouding what he conceived of as his serious approach to this one.

"The statue is by Giambologna." He got to his feet and went up to her.

"I'm sorry?" Her eyes were gray, enormous, unsurprised.

"I said, your statue—the statue of the grand duke, the one in that poem. Is by Giambologna."

She said doubtfully, "In the poem it says 'John of Douay.'"

"Is the same person. He was Flemish."

Standing down one step, he was exactly of her height. She had a full, smiling expression, suited to her voice. She had particularly lovely ears, small and close, looped over with strands of light-brown hair.

"You speak English well."

This open, easy way she had of talking, quite unflirtatious, interested Michele. He thought, You tell the girls not to speak to anyone, meaning men, and straightaway you speak to me; but he felt the emptiness of the charge. "I live one year in London, to study English for the hotel business. Instead, now I work for my brother. He imports foreign foods for the supermarket."

"Oh, a supermarket, even here?"

"Yes, the big one outside Porta Prato." He could see she didn't care, though—would not care even if he told her about the Chianti flasks sheathed in woven plastic, or the canned music played there all day long. He followed her eyes across the square to where, by the pedestal of the grand duke, the girls were arched over their crescents of watermelon, stretching their necks forward like ponies to avoid staining their dresses. "You come from London?"

"Yes. From Islington."

"There are some nice houses in Islington."

"Yes," she said, not laying claim to them. "Difficult to get to, though."

"The girls, too? From Islington?"

"Oh, no, they're from everywhere. America and England. One's from Kenya."

"You do this often?"

"No, only this time. It's because of the fifty pounds, you see."

"I'm sorry?" he inquired, emulating her.

"The currency restrictions. A private person can't spend more than fifty pounds abroad this year. I was saving it for Italy, but then I used it up."

"You went somewhere else?"

Her eyes went back to the grand duke. "Yes, to Paris for a week, in May. Unexpectedly."

"Well, that was nice," he said artfully. "Worth it."

What a lot I now know about you, Miss Ingram. That you came into this piazza because of that statue, that you know nothing about art, you like poetry, you live in Islington, and you have a lover who is either poor or stingy, who has been in Paris and is now in Italy. Since he quoted to you this poem, the lover is married and intends to stay that way. To hell with him and his poem.

"An undistinguished work," he suggested. "That statue. Unworthy of all this."

"I like it," she said serenely. "Because of the association, you see."

Well, it's frightening, Michele concluded, looking at her. Just when one thinks oneself most secret, one is most transparent.

About me, he went on to her, you might have noticed that I have bushy hair, speak English like a wop, wear a wedding ring, and carry a zippered brief case—might have noticed, that is, if you had taken the slightest interest. As things are, no one can reach you. In silence, he accused her: I have never seen anyone more in love in my life.

Her condition made her immune to any importunity, protected her as completely as if she had been carrying a child.

"Lucky to get you," he said. "These girls."

"They're nice girls," she said. "All they really want to do is go shopping," she added, as though to give an idea of their virtues.

"It could be worse."

She agreed. "I'm not much of a guide. I'm really an English teacher. I have to read up on it beforehand."

"That makes it nice and fresh."

It was delightful, the way she laughed with her whole face, exposing nice little teeth and quite a lot of her upper gum. "Look," she said to him, "I'm going to sit down here till they come back."

He stayed leaning against a column of the portico while she seated herself on the top step, arranging one knee demurely over the other in precisely the pose of the fresco she had mentioned, in the cloister of the church. He would have liked to make the comparison to her, but unfortunately that was another thing that had turned corny, telling foreign girls they looked like madonnas. In fact, this one was more vital, more resourceful than any madonna—more like some sturdy animal curled up there in the shade at his feet, the dots on her dress giving her shoulders a supple, speckled look, as if she would spring away at any moment.

Don't be too stalwart, he implored her; it's a terrible trap, that making the best of things. You could end up sitting in a window in Islington, turned to stone.

"Here they come." She did not stand up immediately. She stuffed her handkerchief away in the big straw bag and took out her sunglasses, then got to her feet. She went down one step, forgetting about him, then turned around. "Goodbye." A handshake never entered her head, but she gave him a curious, old-fashioned nod. "Thank you for the name."

"Name?"

It had already escaped her. "Of the sculptor."

"Oh. Now I'll always think of it as an English statue, anyway."

That touched her, he saw. She lifted her eyes for a second in the tender look she had given the girls, raised her hand, and walked away.

"How was it?" she asked the girls.

"*Super*, Miss Ingram."

"Mine wasn't. Nothing but seeds."

"Will it stain?"

"Do you have—now listen to me, all of you—do you all have your scarves for the church?" They started delving in their handbags. "Remember what happened at San Gimignano."

They remembered, all right, good little Protestants. "That priest was crazy. What a kook."

"First, we're going into the cloister, to see the painting I told you about. La Madonna del Sacco, which means the Madonna of the Bag." The girls collapsed into giggles. She opened the guidebook. "Don't be silly. There's a bag in the painting. It doesn't say why."

They crowded around to look at the reproduction. "Cripes, an old laundry bag."

"A laundry bag, yet."

They walked away toward the church, her clear voice calming the shrill cries of the group. Michele couldn't believe she would not look back at him, but she walked right across the square without hesitating, quite absorbed in what she was saying, only nodding to right or left as she spoke with the girls.

At the entrance to the church portico, she stopped and turned around, lifting her arm.

His hand shot up in answer, but she wasn't looking at him. She had raised her arm to shade her face. She was looking at the statue, going away from her with averted head, high above the cars.

Michele lowered his arm, feeling ridiculous. He strolled over, gave the parking man one hundred lire, and found his hot little car. "*Addio*," he muttered into the rearview mirror as he watched her disappear into the cloister, as heedless of his poetry as the statue had been of her own.

He reversed the car loudly, right up against the railing that protected the grand duke, and drove out of the square.

LEAVE IT TO ME

The question is," said Miss Helena Palmer, as they changed gear for the last long spiral of country road, "how would I have managed without you?"

The young man at the wheel thought the question quite otherwise, slowing down as he asked the air, "Is this it, then? Is this it?"

His young wife beside him pointed out a signpost beyond. "Of course it is. Look, it says." They drew up to the notice; there was the name of the proprietor of all that land, and who knew what else besides, surmounting a prohibition against hunting. "The house must be up there, over the curve. You can see where the avenue begins."

"Good for you," her husband said, accelerating again, "spotting that." Though in fact the notice could not have been missed, its white paint now luminous in the setting sun that was throwing up from the landscape all manner of objects—a dovecote, a scarecrow, a tractor—that would have been dormant in a softer light.

"Sorry," the girl, Marian, said as they drove on, remembering they had interrupted Miss Helena Palmer. Turning round from the front seat where she sat in her newly married fastness, deliciously paired, two to Miss Palmer's one, she put her bent brown arm over the back and gazed on Miss Palmer with superior happiness—quite looking out from the golden bar of heaven, as Miss Palmer put it to herself, though not ill-naturedly, wishing them both well.

"My thanks for giving me a lift. That was it. I'd have hated to pass through Florence without seeing the Fenwicks. But how to get out here, if it hadn't been for you?"

"It's not so far as it looks. All these curves make it seem a long way. Anyhow, delighted." And she really does seem nice, thought the young man at the wheel, a good old girl. A Raeburn, with her coloring, prim yet all aglow. What would the old thing be, fifty? He was an art historian, spending his honeymoon at Florence that summer, helping here and there with the restoration of flood damage.

The girl continued to lean her bare arm over the back of the seat, chatting with Miss Palmer, flicking back long gold hair with a smile that said, Aren't we young? Aren't we nice? Miss Palmer could not but agree.

"You look like the Blessed Damozel," she said, then regretted it, wondering if the girl might say afterward to her husband, "Think she's a bit dykey?" A single person was vulnerable, open to any accusation, never getting the benefit of any doubt. She studied the girl's face as it turned like a sunflower toward her. Would she be a loving wife, a laughing wife, or a dull, opinionated one? It was like looking at a newborn baby, trying to discover the resemblance that would later manifest itself.

"How lucky to be able to rent this." Marian was waving her other hand at the window. "A place like this."

Helena Palmer nodded. "And not just a matter of having the money either, or the year to spare; but the taste and enterprise to do it. Most people get fixed in their ways." She meant herself, fixed as an assistant curator at a museum in Boston.

"They come from Philadelphia," Marian said, as if that might have simplified the decision. Marian came from South Kensington and had never crossed the Atlantic.

"Besides, you know Jimmy's working here." She enjoyed referring to a Personage as Jimmy.

"On a thesis, is it?" Miss Palmer asked, and the two in front smiled indulgently: an American pastime.

"To be fair," the young man said, being fair, "it's actually part of the new book. Another sociological study. I liked the last one. Got something to say all right, has Jimmy." Here the gravel made a sharp turn that took them over the breast of the hill. Rounding the curve, the man at the wheel brought the car to a sudden stop.

His wife cried out.

Miss Palmer said, "Good God."

In surmounting the ridge they had come to the edge of a wide valley floored with fields and olive groves; but rising, on its opposite side, into a long, closely-wooded hillside. This far hillside stood against the lilac sky; seeming vaster than it probably was, as Florentine hills do. Through all its length it was a single sheet of flame.

At the turn the road widened, providing a shelf that was at present used as a lookout—two or three small Fiats were parked there, and half a dozen Vespas. Their owners stood in silence, or sat on the low edge of the retaining wall, staring out across the valley.

"Oh, Robin, I can smell it," the girl said. Some shift of the wind, or of their own awareness, had carried the smell of burning into the car.

"Hear it, too." The sound—a hissing, a crackling, a roar—was coming clearly across the valley.

"I saw the glow," said Miss Palmer. "And thought it was the sun."

Another Fiat now drove up behind them. "Let's get on to the villa," Robin said, and they drove again, parallel to the inferno. The two women stared at it without words.

The villa stood at the very peak of the hill. A walled courtyard in front was entered through an archway, on which there was a coat of arms, all in the same pale stone. As they came through, their host walked out of the house to meet them, waving, calling.

"Wonderful you could all come. Can you pull up by the oleander— that's just fine. Helena, great to see you." He was a wide man with a great jaw and hound-like eyes. His smile made an arc in his big face, the smile of the man in the moon.

They got out of the car and stood in a row, messengers at a play exuding their bad news.

Robin said, "You don't know what's going on outside your gateway?"

"A *fire*," Marian said. "The most terrible fire."

They walked back over the courtyard, out through the archway. "Jesus," the wide man said. "Oh Jesus, Jesus."

Below at the turn of the road the group watched on in silence, dispassionate as Orientals.

"We've been on the other side of the house all afternoon. No one told me. I've been working. Janet's been asleep. I saw a small fire there at noon. No one told me about this."

"Here's Janet." The wide man's slender wife was in the courtyard. Robin thought again how in Italy one was continually tempted to attribute faces to the painters—this one Manneristic, with deeply molded features, the eyes heavy-lidded yet cavernous, the hair swept back as if by a rush of air. With some, one could detect the hand of a master; with most it was merely "School of," or "After . . ." There was a lot of overpainting; and, once in a while, a fake.

"Isn't this horrible." Janet embraced them. "What a welcome for you. They just came to tell me about it." They stood with their backs to the house. The fire burned more and more intensely as the dark came down, and now it was spilling out in melted lights toward the valley, like a volcanic eruption.

"It's not like a forest fire. It's like the sack of a city, the burning of Troy." It was true. The black towers of cypresses, the arcs of umbrella pines against the sky made up a fantastic architecture which, moment by moment, the flames consumed. One hissing column of fire, driven upward in a series of small explosions, could be heard over all the rest, a single instrument from the frightful orchestra. Like the opening of a new movement, there was thunder far off in the east.

"Alessandro says there was rain at San Donato this afternoon."

"Too much to hope—"

The thunder was over them now. The heads of the group of watchers below had turned in their direction: one of them sat in silhouette, with palm extended.

Miss Palmer said, "I felt—"

"So did I. Oh God, if only it would."

They implored the sky. Large drops fell sparsely on the gravel. And that was all. Where the sky had been dark, the stars came out.

"Let's go in. There's no use standing here." Janet took Helena Palmer by the arm. They turned their backs on the fire. "How nice you look."

Jimmy thought, walking behind them to the house, how nice they all looked—the women in smooth pale colors with summer-colored skin and shining hair. Robin tall and serious. Jimmy liked good looks, good taste, good will. He liked the way he had arranged life, including as much of these as possible.

"I like your villa," Robin said. "A beauty."

"We live on the other side, mostly," Janet said. "It gives onto the garden. But of course this is the front." A servant held a door, they passed through. "The façade is after a sketch by Sangallo. Then it got the usual going-over later on."

They sat in a red-tiled, white-vaulted room, around a low table of drinks.

"So awful," said Miss Helena Palmer.

Jimmy poured gin and tonic for her. "It touches on what I'm writing just now. The Italian sense of responsibility. Or absence of it. In our countries, a fire like that—you'd have the fire brigade out in a minute, the whole countryside would pitch in. Here, everything is personal—if it's their family or their lover they might help out, but no civic responsibility whatever. Even if the *pompieri* were called, they wouldn't show for hours. Look what happened in the flood—official negligence all over, the Premier didn't even visit the city after the disaster. And if you ask a Florentine what he thinks of it all, he'll shrug and say, 'What do you expect?' The point is, you *must* expect—you must demand—that the state and the communities take their responsibilities seriously. But no—here everything is personal."

"Well at least that's something," his wife said. "We tend to load onto the community the things that should be personal. Isn't one always hearing at home, 'That's not my problem'?"

"Oh come on. Every country has its version of that expression. Come on now. Come off it. Don't they say in France '*Ce n'est pas ma responsabilité*'?"

"In England we say 'That's not my affair,'" Robin said. "In fact, after 'Trespassers will be Prosecuted,' it's our favorite expression."

"All right then, what *is* it here?"

Jimmy twisted the stick round in his drink, his elbows on his widely spaced knees. He grinned, the man in the moon. "I'll tell you what it is, the Italian version. It's '*Ci penso io*'—'Leave it to me.' Those words, they're the kiss of death. That's the way the brush-off goes round here: 'Don't worry, I'll take care of it. Leave it to me.'"

They all laughed. He went on, "This is the weekend, you see. There are lots of fires at weekends in this dry weather—not all this bad, naturally, but bad enough. Every Sunday you hear of an *incendio* somewhere in the vicinity. Picnickers leave campfires, drop cigarettes. And then there's the hunting season—which opened last week, end of August."

"I hate the hunting," Janet said. She had lain in bed that morning listening to church bells through the sound of shots.

"Oh, those cars," cried Marian. "Coming out here this evening, so many cars on the road, just festooned with dead animals and birds."

"*Please.*" Jimmy touched her arm. "Lay off that. We're having pheasant for dinner."

"We are comfortable here, yes." Janet turned her head to ask the servant for bread, illustrating her point. "The house is lovely, and the modern things all work besides. And plenty of water, which is almost never the case in these places."

"I was going to ask," Miss Palmer said, "supposing the fire brigade *did* come, how would they get water to put the fire out?"

"You beat it out," Jimmy explained. Why won't she let it drop? "You need as many men as you can get to act as beaters and to dig fire-breaks. You'd be amazed how quickly they can beat it out. I've seen them."

"There's a house," Janet said. "On that hillside. Right at the top."

Robin helped himself to the wine. "Perhaps it's a chapel."

"Would that make a difference?" Marian asked. "I mean, might it be uninhabited?"

No one answered. Somebody said, "This bread needs salt."

"They never put salt in the bread in Tuscany."

"And this is your own wine, is it?"

"The wine and the oil, both. And the vegetables. In fact, just about everything's from our own land this evening."

"All the lower part of that hillside is olive groves. Where the fire is."

"I tell you, Janet, it could be put out almost instantly. All you need is enough people."

There are five of us, Robin was thinking; six with the man who is waiting on us. Oh, but the clothes, the hair, the painted fingernails ... the talk. People who talk like this don't fight fires, everyone knows that. . . . And then, is it true—can one even get near such a fire as that?

I mustn't be the one to say it, Miss Palmer began, or concluded, to herself. It was this spinster business again—a single woman was so vulnerable, likely to be dismissed as hysterical, deranged. It might even be true. In any case, in the end they probably wouldn't let me go—the men would have to go alone. It would be like agitating for a war in which one was going to have a protected occupation.

"Do you think *anyone's* there?" This was Marian again. "Couldn't it just keep spreading? I'm not thinking about us. I only mean—might it?"

"I've asked Alessandro to telephone our *fattore*—the man who manages the land for the owner. He may have heard something."

This made it possible to get to the cheese. Which was also from the estate.

"They've seen too much, and that's what it comes back to. Been through too much. Too bloody fatalistic altogether. I've written about this. And will write more."

"They have seen the righteous forsaken," said Miss Helena Palmer.

"That doesn't authorize them to forsake everyone in sight. They won't even lift a finger to help themselves."

"Look here, though, Jimmy, isn't that exactly what we enjoy? After all, we can't have the lot"—Robin moved his elbow to say, The wine, the oil, the oleanders, and the sketch by Sangallo—"and then denounce the temperament that produces it."

"A package deal, eh?" Janet smiled.

"Oh, don't misunderstand me," Jimmy said—thinking this an unfortunate phrase always, but repeating it just the same. "Don't misunderstand me. Listen, I'm mad about the Italian temperament. I adore the Italian temperament. All I'm saying is, the Italian temperament—mentality, if you like—is like a big rich cake, with a slice missing. And that slice is the sense of responsibility. Well, what about it, Alessandro?"

The servant came to the table speaking quietly, and began to remove the plates.

"So there you are, the *fattore* knows nothing. He thinks maybe the hunters started the fire to clear the underbrush, and then it got out of control."

No one believed this. It would have been too perfect. Janet put her napkin on the table. "Let's have coffee in the other room."

"In Sicily, when it's very dry, the fires start by themselves," Marian said. "I saw them last summer, when I was there with Mother."

"Spontaneous combustion."

"You see, it's this very chapter I'm working on right now. There's the matter of the Catholic upbringing, too, the Catholic conscience. Ultimately God is responsible for everything. Big deal."

"Like the fall of Constantinople. Everyone was in the churches praying when they should have been manning the ramparts."

Miss Palmer stirred her coffee and heard examples. She listened to dates and names—Massimo d'Azeglio, Mussolini, Matteotti. She thought, If he recites enough of these facts we will in some way feel better about sitting here drinking coffee while that fire rages outside. Why? However, she was calm now, seeing that no one was going to do anything. It was the suspense that had been unnerving, the sense of choice; and the same calm was settling on the others. Only Jimmy struggled to make sense of himself. In that case, Miss Palmer wondered, is he the one who minds most, in spite of everything?

Jimmy said, interrupting himself in mid-recital, "Let's take a look at the fire."

They were in no hurry to do so, conscientiously putting out cigarettes, setting down brandy glasses. There was of course something obscene about the fire regarded simply as a spectacle; yet it was there, sooner or later they would be drawn back to it.

"Marian, you had a sweater."

"It's in the car."

I shouldn't have said that, thought Helena Palmer, about the righteous. It sounded straight out of the Bible Belt. It made sense, but it didn't sound right. Oh, one has to be so careful.

Now here is what I meant about Italy, Robin wanted to say, stepping outdoors among the jasmine and the lemon trees in tubs, and tasting the thin scorched scent that embittered all the others. There is always some question or other.

"I hope the tortoise isn't about," said Janet. "I don't want to tread on the tortoise."

"A tortoise, how sweet."

"Only a little one. But forty years old. He was wounded in the war by a piece of shrapnel."

"Ours or theirs?"

"Oh, how can you ask?"

The light from the house scarcely reached to the gateway, which they walked under to darkness, their footsteps hesitating from stone into gravel.

Below, one car remained at the turn of the road. It was occupied by a pair of lovers.

The tail-light of this car was turned on, a tiny stroke of red. Where the fire had been there was nothing but the dark. If they stayed there long enough looking out into this darkness they would eventually be able to distinguish the outline of a hill, like a great wave against the sky. But their eyes were unused to the night, after the lighted house; and as it was they could do no more than sense the hillside's charred presence, there where they had seen it in flames, as they stood in a group outside the gate—the two couples clasping hands; and Miss Palmer with her arms folded over her breast, not in judgment but because the night had turned cool.

SIR CECIL'S RIDE

The taxi might have been out of control, rattling off down the mountain, rounding the curves by luck. Constantin stood putting the change away, filthy little tickets of money that he buttoned in the pocket of his shorts. A dark-green Humber that came whirring sedately over the pass hesitated alongside them offering wordless rescue—the car itself raising eyebrows at two Europeans on the roadside in the heat. (This driver was white, coming up from the club at Deep Water Bay.) The second car slipped over the precipice with finality, like an emissary that has offered terms and been rejected: let battle commence.

"You wanted to walk," Constantin said. "And now we're going to walk."

It was not that she wanted to walk but that she wanted to be with him on the Sundays he spent walking. He knew this, and supposed he was challenging her to confess it like a fault. "It is here," he said, and they turned off the Magazine Gap Road onto a shoulder of gravel. There was an opening in scrub, then the path. There was even a lettered sign—three English words set on a tilted post, in soil so dry you might have lifted the pole out of the ground like a dead plant.

His finger prodded a skyline. "Our path goes right across that chain of hills." She could see it zigzag, disappear, flick out again. "And comes down at Repulse Bay." The names were often like this—combative, ballistic: Magazine, Repulse. It was a fact, universal, of colonial life.

He took her wrist and swung it lightly, let it go. The girl ambled contentedly, relieved of the dis-ease of being where he was not. Only too glad to have left, because of him, the green, ordered side of the island where the city was a plaster lozenge in long agglomerations of Chinese towns, and habitation seethed in a snake dance along the shore. To have left the sister who said, "You're daft," sullenly, from bed, as she pulled on sandals, tugged at mousy curls, dropped the comb in her pocket as sole equipment for the journey. In the bedroom windows, vegetation was as dense on slopes and heights as tenements were below, the tropics terraced around irruptions of pastel villas that climbed into humidity—pale houses ripped open by looters during the Japanese withdrawal, some scaffolded, others already restored.

In the city you might glance up any teeming street of stairs to find jungle at the top in a green overhang. The passageways of steps that led up from Queen's Road were stacked, like shelves, with merchandise—whole walls of print materials in bolts, looped-up cascades of plastic handbags, Niagaras of colored belts, rafts and wheels of paper flowers for funerals, everything your heart could desire from UNRRA supplies to ivory penknives, table napkins from Swatow, and trays from Amoy stenciled with vermillion dragons. Ascending like an offering, all this branched at last into extravagant green leaf.

Her checkered dress had exhaled its last breath of starch in the boiling cab. She had no hat and as she walked her eyes squeezed up against the sun. She had not learned to wear sunglasses, was always taking them off to see the colors. He kissed her salty wrist and again released it. He said, "I am too young to be involved with women half my age." Constantin was thirty-six.

He would explain to her about the path. Constantin knew all kinds of things, every thing. "It was an early governor who laid it out. Just as you wanted to walk, he wanted to ride. The roads of the island, such as they then were, palled. In any case, roads take the shortest route. By winding round and round these hills you get an illusion of distance, as if you were not on an island. Thus Sir Cecil rode."

The girl saw the track winding round and round. "All this for his recreation." In the tone of her parents. "Hundreds of coolies laboring for months."

"Or a handful of overworked ones, mostly women. He would have told himself it served some larger purpose. That is generally the way."

"Now it is," she said. "In those times they didn't bother."

But she did not know Sir Cecil's dates.

"You think hypocrisy is new?"

"Only with regard to empires."

How could she talk of the past, who had no past to speak of?

The bay appeared on the left—or, it would be, west. Warships idled—a dove-gray carrier, a cruiser, sloops. All movement there came from merchantmen, ferries, junks, and from a Sunday line of little yachts racing out past Ly-ee-mun. Between island and mainland a concrete sea shone like an aerodrome on which the craft sped or stayed. For the yachtsmen it would be green water, ruffling the hull and cool-rushing through the fingers you trailed over the side. At Ly-ee-mun, where the girl once sailed with Freddy from the Secret Service, the water was deepest, and deeply blue. Freddy flung overboard the crusts of their sandwiches, saying, "Bong appitee, fish." She had watched the receding bread briefly inflate, almost expecting the snapper or garrupa to rise to it, like carp. Freddy was lovable. It was Constantin she loved.

The underbrush became an occasional roasting bush, became strewn rubbish, fell away entirely. They had come now to the start of silence, where none of the road noises could follow and no sound lay ahead, not even an aromatic rustle in shrubbery. The scene enlarged to receive them, as they matched to it their pace, their solitude, their expectations.

It was less like land than a monstrous topography involving the emotional language of maps—faults, depressions, relief; it might have been a chart layered in colors of intensifying aridity. The hills were empty everywhere, scarcely prickled with growth: naked, like flesh—no, like hide, or like some unsociable material, canvas, calico. It was the cadaver of a landscape, making you realize how upholstered, how nourished and overfed were hills elsewhere.

In fact you would have said a zone, not a country, a geology still simmering on who knew what banked fires. It was cracked and gashed to the bone, it was scooped and seamed by landslips or the rains. The valleys were ravines, dried watercourses, moraines of tumbled stone. And the sky, all sun, was crowded with mountains, clear of birds. No living sign, no indication of humanity—not even of human error.

He and she might have been first in this convulsed desert, but for the path.

The path narrowed, intent and serious. It was beaten earth, merely, and small stones. He had said, "Our path"—yet no route had ever more conclusively rejected possession, association. Except in regard to Sir Cecil.

She saw hillsides passing, and felt that he and she made their way up and down and put the appalling scene to some purpose. He, as if from far off, watched the pair of them creeping among all this obduracy. The hills of the mainland, on which at times he walked, were redder still, less tufted even than these of the island: the real thing, the hills of South China.

He said, "I have just a memory of the gorges in the north. I was—what—two, not even three. It is hard to impress a baby, but even a baby was impressed. When we came out of Russia it was across Siberia and down those gorges." Constantin was safely British now, and had a passport. He had gone to schools in England and been brave for England in the war, and the least they could do was make him British: this least they had done. In the nature of things he could never be English. But a passport cannot be overestimated when you have passed your childhood stateless in Shanghai.

Constantin, securely British, remained foreign in ways that, giving intense pleasure to the girl, displeased in other quarters. He spoke the Shanghai dialect and had a Cantonese teacher twice a week. These were only some of his excesses. He could sing, for instance, and in French; had given her a copy of the memoirs, newly published, of Benois, from the bookshop in Ice House Street. In German prison camps, after Arnhem, he had translated Novalis to pass the time. None of this was usual, and some of it—though not the part about the book—had been reported to Whitehall, Eyes Only, in the pouch.

The back of her neck absorbed heat defenselessly, though it was up to her to have brought the hat.

The sea surfaced again, as a modesty piece in the cleft of two brown hills. It was mineral green below an aberrant cloud—green of the jade that would be sold everywhere in the city except at the best jewelers, who, to a European clientele, showed no jade except the rarest: to them, Dakotas flying out of Rangoon and Saigon brought cargoes of diamonds, emeralds, amethysts, all that. Nor did they show much gold (which otherwise was everywhere, too, mostly in teeth but also on pens, watchbands, bangles, and the rims of spectacles, and wadding up hailstorms of cheap jade rings in Queen's Road windows); but had, each, an elderly Sikh with turban and rifle on a cane chair at the door: a cigar-store Indian.

So the girl reflected—feeling, all but seeing, the ring on her finger as she walked and looked at the green sea. One of the tacking yachts came into view; and went about, as they watched it—doing just for them its solo turn on jade sea. They saw it pause, shake its white self upright out of its element; saw the sails briefly flail and slacken, the boom swinging in a panic of independence, at an utter loss, until it leaned, once more triangular, with its other shoulder on the wind.

Freddy of MI5—or 6, or 7—was a good sailor, no shouting, content to munch sandwiches and come in last.

They had arrived at a ramp of stones, down which they slipped and slid, reaching the bottom with a thud and a short run. She supposed the horse—Sir Cecil's—had managed this with its usual aplomb. She began to understand why Sir Cecil rode.

"That's the last we'll see of the sea," said Constantin, as if they were embarked on some endless journey to the interior. He said these things and they were always true. People would look at him in the street, curious that authority should inspire no fear.

"Granite and erosion," he observed of the land in which they were now locked. There was grandeur in this bleached place where even the least of the hills strove, in its outline, to become a mountain. Not to the girl, with her undeveloped sense of such beauty—it was one of the things he hoped to change in her. The feeling for nature, when it comes strained through literature, is too luxuriant, too soulful: *vieux jardins reflétés par les yeux*—too much of that.

"Say some lines to me, Elizabeth." You could open her at any page.

Total recall, but of some previous existence—the virtuoso performance of a singer who otherwise knows not a word of the language. She had begun at the end, looked up the last chapter of experience, and how would she ever work her way out into this incarnate present?

The dress was soaked right round its checkered middle. The girl touched her burning hair and the tendrils at her ears, wet as if she had been in the sea. She did not mind all that much his wanting to change her; it showed a stake in the outcome. Without change, there was the threat of the colonial dames, their baffled sexlessness, their eternal deplorings, the life is artificial, is artificial. Scheherazades of endless grievance—the No. 1 Boy who took opium, the amah who boiled my pink shantung, the cook who, though recommended by Mildred at Jardine's, had done something peculiar with the New Zealand lamb.

Hand in hand they slithered down another declivity, then passed singly along a ledge. Mountains parted to admit more mountains, and again the path ran jaggedly ahead at apparent random, as if a child had scored the map. Rocks were jumbled like stale cake: up through your shoes they tingled with noon, and in the worst of them grooves had been chipped so that the beast, or person, might make his way across.

The girl wondered about Sir Cecil, who rode in white, whose white sun helmet, and perhaps breast, were looped with gold; who sought and created such arduous silence in which to hear stirrups chinking, hooves ringing, and the heavy breath of horse and man.

Not necessarily of the prevailing view that to proceed at all was to be in some form of flight, she yet perceived that Sir Cecil might have sought distraction here from possibilities that were almost infinite: a wife, silently aggrieved or harshly vocal; the lack of any wife; bereavement, separation, perversion. Remorse was perhaps expiated, or reflection developed, in these lone exertions. Such things passed in her head like scenery, with (the wife theme being dominant) a shiver of long skirts, a flickering of high-boned collar, and Chinese boys in pale gowns and slippers plying punkahs in darkened rooms. While the rider, erect, deliberate, moved on through vacant summer with something like purity.

Sir Whatsit, the present governor, had been in prison like everybody else. Receptions had now resumed at Government House—tastefully modernized by the Japanese during the governor's absence, though with the doubtful addition of the pagoda. Invitations arrived tactile with gold, everyone attended. Nobody went to the camp at Stanley, far out at Tai Tam, where names and deaths were scratched around disintegrating walls, along with the calendars of Xs which in their beginning had no known end. No man or woman released from there could get the tongue around such reality. After a lifetime passed in denouncing the artificial, actuality had stunned them trivial forever. The sentences beginning "When we were in Stanley" all ended with the tale of weevils in the rice cake, or the loss of the hoarded shoes. There had been breakdowns since, but not anyone with backbone.

The War Crimes people gave parties that lasted all night. Opposite the cathedral, Japanese prisoners were kept in enclosures behind the barracks, waiting for the War Crimes to get to them. Their prisoners, our prisoners, it was catch as catch can. You walked past the wire, the prisoners were hanging about, suspended for the enactment of justice. In autumn they were let out on the road an hour or two each day to rake the leaves. They wore olive fatigues and were under guard of a sentry—who would be a boy of perhaps eighteen, with yellow hair and glasses, or dark hair and pimples, himself barely out of custody from home or school. The trees behind the barracks had great red flowers in spring: Flame of the Forest, Constantin said.

"How long were you in prison, Constantin?"

"One hundred and sixty-six days, all perishing cold." The khaki shirt stuck wetly to his back, the black hair wetly to his head. "Also thirty days of prison hospital." A swatch of flesh was missing from his leg, leaving a purple cavity along the shinbone. Once he had drawn a map for her, like an old soldier, marking in the north bank of the Rhine, a bridge, the Polish brigade, the First Airborne Division. He had told her that the colonel's head was blown off while they stood together, and how he had lain for days untended in an upper bunk in a shed for captive wounded. All this was decently enclosed in war; it was like delivering a string of obscenities as polite conversation. The immense indecency of war he kept, a colossal secret, to himself. Folding the map he had laughed and said, "A thin red line of heroes," sounding like Freddy. He had kept folding until the map was small, and made this joke and pressed it into her hand.

At Government House they were wearing braided uniforms and suits of white duck, and in the evening scarlet cummerbunds and decorations. They were wearing long kid gloves that buttoned back to expose the fingers, and hats with veiling stirred by ceiling fans. The girl stood there on platform soles holding a glass while Princess Elizabeth became engaged six thousand miles away, or India became a nation, or a viscount with protuberant eyes was passed from hand to hand. She sat on a gilt chair while a Georgian poet told a carefully selected audience about light in poetry, on his way to Japan; and was later unsuccessful in obtaining his book from Kelly & Walsh in Chater Road. A colonel of the Inniskillings in a saffron kilt had taken her aside—"I'd like to tell you *my* little jingle"—but her apprehensions were unjustified, as it was only about the typhoon season:

> *June, too soon;*
> *July, stand by;*
> *August, it must;*
> *September, remember;*
> *October, all over.*

He told her that a great liner had nosed its way into the post office in the typhoon just before the war. And that the last typhoon had halved the sampan population which, don't misunderstand me, was in any case getting out of hand.

From the windows of all this you could see China across the bay. You were in the Far East; you were so remote from the familiar that your immediate surroundings were described as Far.

She turned to discover the distance they had come, but the hills were mirrored behind as ahead, disclosing nothing. The morning sense of putting the earth to their purpose shriveled to the ache of a remembered gaffe, ludicrous as having brought the comb. There could be here no human disturbance of the slightest significance. To detonate the scene would be to impose on it the same aspect as before. Without birds, there was not even the sort of tension into which a shot might be fired.

The day that India was independent, cannon were fired in the afternoon.

Up on the tennis courts at May Road, people stopped playing and said "India," and "I only hope they have the sense," and it was the same at the golf clubs with the lovely names, "Shek-O," "Fanling," where men called Tug and Taffy and Bongo leaned on their niblicks, fatalistic for the first time: "Who knows?" Certitude belonged, like the crimson carpet in the Peninsula Hotel, to the great Before-the-War.

"In motion," Constantin said, "there is a salutary exhaustion. It drives out the devil."

Constantin came and went in civilian dress to Nanking, to Harbin, to Kwangchowan, about the King's business—for, with the passport, he had acquired a king. He told her, "Going to China does not give importance; one becomes less important the farther one gets into China." He returned, put on his uniform, and sat down to write the long reports that, coupled with his trip through the gorges and his accomplishments, gave displeasure. "What are you telling them?" "The inevitable, Elizabeth." A fat man came from London with displeasure plain on his plain face. The truth can only be told, like poetry, to a carefully selected audience; that was part of the indecency of war, of peace. If he were to marry the girl she would have to know of his despair over this. They would talk about it beforehand as something central to their domestic lives, like income or birth control.

"Love," he said. "I have not been in love since I was your age." He might have added, "Until now," but had a moral obligation not to do this. Or persuaded himself of these larger considerations: that is generally the way. He must not match, from knowledge, the immeasurable solemnity of youth; he would be vigilant. The price of vigilance is eternal liberty. All the advantages being nevertheless hers, unrealized, even the intensity with which she trots along, two steps to his one. Montaigne playing with his cat wondered, Is she the plaything or am I?

The girl's thoughts were all of marching—of route marches, forced marches, marches bearing packs and rifles, boots, boots, boots, the Children of Israel, the retreat from Moscow. A sense of proportion lightened the step only briefly: reasonableness, like the fatalism of the taipans leaning on their niblicks, could not be sustained. Napoleon had in any case ridden—like Sir Cecil. It was stupefying to think that Sir Cecil had done this repeatedly.

A shadow at the limit of vision resolved itself into spars of growth—a blur of hot bushes, not beautiful enough for a mirage. A dried, greenish stain spread with slow precision at the rate of their approach. I can do this, the girl promised herself, neither slackening nor accelerating the automatic placing of her feet, not taking stock of her sunstruck body nor in any way threatening by disruption of gait or posture her ability to arrive. There would be the descent to the sea, still, and the last slopes leading down to the hotel there. The arcades and awnings of the hotel veranda cast their hallucinatory shadow before: thirst escaped at last from agonizing confinement, overwhelming her in reckless foreknowledge of dripping tumbler and slaked throat. Imagination ran riot over orangeade and ginger beer.

She was proud not to have complained, to have swallowed without comment the stuff about salutary exhaustion. But, now the enterprise was assessable, she did marvel that this had been done to her. If I had collapsed, if there had been an accident . . . With a taste of repugnance, she thought how he had said, "You wanted to walk." She hoped he was not going to give her grievances against him; she hoped, if so, she would not nurture them in the local tradition of the everlasting wrong.

The degree of thirst was a new experience, reductive as pain. Soldiers in the desert passed round a flask to wet their lips, not taking more than their honor-bound swallow—she had seen Gary Cooper in *Beau Geste*. He and she could have brought the flask, at least. Another black mark for Constantin, who, knowing every thing, had known how far, how hot.

Fronded trees showed themselves, thinly inclined, congregated in search of shelter rather than to furnish it. It was the place where a watercourse had been channeled down. As they came up they could see the stream falling on a cement conduit and disappearing under a causeway. The causeway was formed by a kind of concrete coffin graven with the imperial imprint: with medieval crest, the motto in French.

"You're mad!" Constantin shouted as the girl knelt to drink—striking up her cupped hands, splashing water over her dress and tears into her eyes. She plunged her forearms into the slide of water, defiant, as if they too might contract typhoid there, or dysentery, or blackwater fever. She sat to take off her sandals that unclamped themselves painfully, the buckles branded grittily onto the instep. Each foot, when washed, instantly dried. He sat down under the trees, trees in name only, the trunks slender as bamboos, and watched her doing this. At her age there was beauty even when looking a sight. Beauty all-powerful, and as vulnerable as her blistered neck.

She sat near him in the shade of strange afternoon. He had taken off his shirt. Touch was unthinkable, she could scarcely bear the pressure of clothes, she had spread her hands wide on the grass of the oasis. There was the mottling light, the shine of water, and the sound. There was the life—of beetles, butterflies—renewed in these leaves and grasses. There was the glow of reflected, unremitting day; and the spell. One would have thought it necessary to conjure up such fullness, to coax or dramatize it into expansive being. Its having sought them out here, taken them unawares, a million to one, imposed a decent silence, a tribute already shaped with remembrance.

Ludicrous, if you thought about it, this squatting on the ledge of a great rock in the China Sea. Yet he looked on in silence at her outspread arms, her sunburned leg and checkered dress, her shoes capsized on the coat of arms, her tender neck.

Soon it would be as before; he would get up and put on his shirt—and at length did so. He washed in lethal waters; he brought her shoes. He took her hands and pulled her to her feet, and put dry lips to her salty hair. He said that they could not stay there forever. There was untruth in this: something would stay, and he could not, putting on his shirt, make it all as before.

They were out of this in a hundred paces, and stood again on a long spine of the rock. Where there should have been a prospect of the sea, and the grand staircase of fields descending to it, there was the tin sky, the carcasses of hills. Far, far off, at many miles, there was the winding incision of a path—some other path, not conceivably theirs.

Constantin said, "We've come damn nearly halfway."

The girl had always held disappointment to be the cruelest sensation, mocking you back into childhood. And now this landscape reeled with disappointment, was disappointment brutally incarnate. She tried—on her tongue that had become, quite simply, thirst—she tried the syllables "I cannot." But did not speak them—and in this place tears evaporated before they could be shed. Reasonable comparisons were long since gone, nothing whatever being relative to the present case. There was no holding this fire in the hand by thinking on the frosty Caucasus.

She thought on Sir Cecil, who rode while others walked and was cruel to animals.

They had ceased to sweat. Her arm where it emerged from the sleeve was aged and crumpled, like the shredding worst of the paper money you reserved for the Kowloon Ferry. When the path was plain before them she would shut her eyes now on rings of purple that remained as rainbows beneath the lids. Her steps, no longer regular, no longer an even two to his one, blundered into him. "Sorry." She had a pebble in her shoe, and shook it out in walking rather than ask for quarter. Constantin walked straight and strong, driving out the devil, and paused only when she had fallen far behind. She would come stumbling up, asleep; they would resume. He had seen a lot of this in the army, the sergeants shouting "You, there!" He said without rancor, "Pull yourself together."

She flashed awake. "Shut up."

He laughed. "When I was a sergeant, I was obeyed. More so than when I became an officer." Constantin had been commissioned in the field during the Italian campaign. A signal had been delivered; he had been told to join the officers. "Which meant, one left the shade of the tree where one was, and crawled on one's belly to another tree to join the brass. This was in the Alban Hills."

She dreamed a classical landscape, wooded; an ellipse of lake in an emerald valley; the cool shade of the Italian campaign. Anger withered like everything else, and she kept pace.

You had to remember that the rains fell here, the unimaginable rains. There were months when the rains fell every day, rain or shine; they could fall in bright sunlight, and this scene of dehydrated clarity could not be exempt. The rain collapsed on you, there was always more where it came from. Thus it fell without any sense of release on either side. One must believe in rain here too, sluicing out primeval sediment from crannies, rinsing stones down streaming canyons in a wash of mud.

It was as if the island were leading a double life. The rains belonged on the green, other side, where mildew was a topic, whole lives were lived around mildew and the houses had electric hot rooms for leather and wool, and chintz chairs were put out in the sun on a dry day like a row of invalids, and there were few dry days. The rains were part of all that, like the invitations on which the gilt lettering might be read like Braille, and the salad being washed in permanganate, and the black taffeta New Look of the French consul's daughter; people shouting "You're mad," "You're daft," "You, there," at any exercise of will.

Sir Cecil might have rode in rain, oblivious; but for them this place was dry for a lifetime. It was a dust in which you might have come upon the bleached skeleton of a horse—the jawbone and smooth sockets, the serried ranks of phantom teeth.

That the earth should be so indifferent, or malevolent—the earth you had scarcely begun to harm.

Constantin said, "It is no use having expectations. We will know when the end is near."

The knowledge would come in shifts of air and changes of soil, from smells of plants and of the approaching sea—atmospheric matters apparent, also, to Sir Cecil's horse in its time, pricking its ears and picking up its feet and quickening its dank sides. The end would have come from such things as these, even before the scrub began again—a bristle, a tussock, a clump, a scrabbling of cover out of which hills less and less rekindled.

As to other forms of knowing, it was clear that knowledge ought to arise from, and in atonement of, a degree of suffering otherwise monstrously or comically useless: the raw material having been provided, it was the supposed duty of experience to make order of itself in such a way. That no such duty was recognized except by herself, that no abstract, mechanical process stood ready to perform its mitigating service, began to be realized by the girl and to threaten her with new, immeasurable labors. Nothing at any rate could be expected promptly or directly. Even immediate perception ran the risk of foundering in its impending reclamation by human systems, drowned in the relief of normalcy, submerged ignominiously in the very ginger beer.

"This is the last ascent." Not comfort or a concession, it was information. When he got home, exorcised, he would calculate miles exactly on a map. He would enjoy his bath, his dinner. Today of all days, might believe himself in love.

The final pass was banked with a parapet of stones. Downward, the track innocently altered character, disappearing briefly into undergrowth and emerging already charged with rural purpose, quite at their service. They leaned on the stone brink of all this change.

She saw the sky emptied of hills at last, vertiginous, and the great sea. The valley at their feet swelling with colors and fertility, scalloped with crops, with the cream-green gardens of the hotel and the curve of white sand. She looked out to promontories, inlets, and the turreted folly of a billionaire. In the foreground, people were painted in attitudes of exertion or repose. Trousered in black, women flowed through fields, rhythmic to the bamboo on their shoulder. Under a circlet of straw, a man rested, fatalistic, on a hoe; and presently ran his comb through the landscape's hair. Cars sent up spangles from the shore, there were umbrellas, there were beach huts woven like kraals. Mothers who could turn any beach to Brighton fidgeted on deck chairs and called, high-pitched, for Ronnie and Tess to make it their last dip.

How they pretended they had been at it all the time, that nothing had happened. How swiftly they took up their positions.

In the arc of new-peeled sky and late ocean, the dark innumerable islands extended far out toward Lantau. Like flung stones—or as countries might look, set on the curve of the earth, if only you could see the globe entire.

"The whole world before you," Constantin was saying.

On the hotel terrace someone would be bringing a telephone out of doors. Important messages would be carried on salvers by Cantonese in white jackets, in the wake of the trays of all-important drinks. A young woman walked, stately, with a flowered parasol, while colonels told about typhoons and a golden spaniel gasped beneath a chair.

If you could see the globe entire.

Winding round and round one gets the illusion of distance, as if one were not on an island, the filament going back to there and forward from here at apparent random. She knew she would not marry this man, and that it would come about in grief not to be mastered in advance, endurance enlarging as the earth raised the stakes. And that for the present they would proceed on false assumptions—assumptions shed in her huge fatigue, like arms and equipment discarded on the march, which, whether recovered or regretted at some later stage, had become an intolerable encumbrance in extremity.

She now drew away from the balustrade of stones. On the terrace below, Sir Cecil swung down into the throng of waiting houseboys saying Master, and, crop and helmet in hand, walked up the steps into the world. Above, like the ship they had seen pause on the morning sea, she stood up out of her element, in helpless independence, before turning, as she must, along the unmade furrow of some other course.

LE NOZZE

W hat did we say? Forty-nine by twenty-two?" He held the measuring rod open in his hands.

She had brought the stepladder from his kitchen and was clearing the top shelf of a closet. She looked down at him. "And thirty-five inches high," she said.

At a corner of the room where a bookcase now stood, he measured a space where her chest of drawers might be placed.

"It's like the first act of *Figaro*," she said. "All this measuring."

"Only—that's for a bed."

"A chest of drawers might be even more symbolic—don't you think?"

He was writing numbers on a piece of paper. "No," he said.

She smiled into the closet. She began to sing, "*Cinque, dieci . . .*" She stopped.

"Don't stop."

"I can't really sing."

"What's that got to do with it?"

She dropped a pile of magazines onto the floor. "Heavens. I'm getting so dirty. This dust—I don't know what your maid's been doing."

He had gone on his knees. "I suppose these books will have to go.

There won't be anywhere else for them, after your things have been moved in."

She dropped another magazine onto the heap.

He added, "It's a shame."

"It wasn't my idea," she said faintly, "to . . . move my things in."

"No." His head was lowered into the corner. His voice smiled. "It was my idea. One of my better ones."

"*Venti—trenta* . . ." She had found a shoebox of bills and was looking through it. "I was allowed to sing in *Pinafore* once, at school."

"What were you?"

"Oh—just a sailor. At school I was always A Sailor. Or An Onlooker, A Bystander. When we did *Julius Caesar* they let me call out 'The will! The will! We'll hear the will!' Things like that."

"Doesn't sound like you," he remarked. "Especially that bit about the will."

"I suppose all these are paid?" She showed him the box.

"Of course."

She replaced it on the shelf. "Once, when I desperately wanted to play Pocahontas, they made me An Indian."

He was examining the books on the shelves. "That was a pity."

"Yes. I had just the right hair for it. And I so wanted to get rescued by Captain John Smith."

"It was the other way. She rescued him."

"Oh well. It comes to the same thing."

He sat back on his heels. "But she married John Rolfe."

"What a lot you know," she said.

Finding that she meant this, he remained silent.

"The chest could go in front of the books," she suggested.

"It would make the room too small. No—I'm afraid there's nothing for it but to get rid of them."

He doesn't have to make such a point about it, she thought. "It does seem a waste," she said. "What are they?"

"Nothing special. Books I had at college." He pulled one or two half-way out. "*The Decline of the West. Green Mansions.*"

"Oh, that's so sad," she said.

"Which?"

"*Green Mansions.* Every time I read it I want to sit down and cry."

As if she reads standing up, he thought.

"What's this?" She held up a scroll enclosed in a cardboard tube.

"Let's have a look." He got up, dusted his knees, and came over to her. "Oh"—he handed it back—"it's a certificate for crossing the Arctic Circle."

"Good God."

"I went to Alaska one summer, when I had nothing better to do."

"That would be the reason, naturally."

"It was extremely interesting," he said aloofly. "Overpowering natural phenomena. Vast areas quite untouched by Man."

"Poor darling," she said. She waved the scroll over her head. "All hail Caesar . . ." She put it back in the closet. She placed her hands on his shoulders. "You'll never have to go to Alaska again," she said.

"Unless," he said solemnly, "we decide it's all a bad idea."

She smiled. "If that's your attitude, you shouldn't go round measuring people's chests."

"I never measured anyone's chest but yours." He reached up to take her in his arms. "Come down, O Maid, from yonder mountain height."

"I'm too heavy for you."

He lifted her down.

"I'll put dust all over you."

He kissed her.

"I'll make some tea. In a minute."

"I've made out a list of places we could go." He put his cup and saucer on the coffee table and brought a folded paper out of his pocket.

"Let's see." She lay down on the sofa with her head in his lap and held the paper before her eyes.

He spread her hair over his knees. "In the Bahamas," he said, "you have to be a resident for eighteen days."

She studied the typed page. "Banns is spelled with two 'n's."

"Is it?" He plaited the ends of her hair. "What are you smiling at?"

"At how nice it is."

"What is?"

"That I got to be Pocahontas after all." The list wavered, then collapsed. "What *are* banns, anyway?"

"I think that's when people get an opportunity to hold their peace."

"Sounds a bit like asking for trouble." She reached out to put the list on the table. "We might change our minds at the last minute."

"Might we? Why?"

She squinted up at him. "Oh—you might discover you didn't like the color of my eyes, or something."

"I don't think that could be the reason. We'll have to think up something else."

She rinsed the cups under the tap. "This china," she said.

"What's wrong with it?"

"It doesn't look like you."

"I think it's rather pleasant—that pattern of bare branches."

"It looks like a diagram of the central nervous system. You know—like those advertisements for headaches."

"Advertisements for headaches?"

"For aspirin, then." She held a saucer up to her forehead as an illustration.

He said seriously, "Nina helped me choose it." He had been involved with Nina when they met.

She washed off another dish. "This plate has a crack in it." She set it down on the sink. "Not that you'd notice, with that design."

He lifted it up, with an air of taking it into safe custody, and dried it. "You never understood about Nina," he said. "I needed time to work that out."

"All I knew was"—she set the last dish on the draining board—"I wasn't staying around for any blinking Judgment of Paris." She began to wash out the sink.

"I didn't feel like Paris."

"Who knows what Paris felt like?"

He held a glass up to the light. "Whatever became of the apple, after it was awarded?"

"Don't know. Unless that was the apple that What's-his-name threw to Atalanta. Where do these spoons go?"

"In the middle drawer. What *was* his name?"

"Menander."

"No—that's a poet. Meleager."

"Of course."

"It's like a game of catch—this apple getting chucked about in history. Paris—Meleager—Adam—William Tell . . ."

"Newton," she said, surprisingly. She took the dish towel from him. "I think that's everything."

"Not quite."

She put her arms about his waist, the dish towel clasped in her hand. "Did you finish measuring the chest?" she asked.

"Yes—that's the perfect place for it."

"I'm so glad." She leaned against him. "It all makes me nervous sometimes."

He held her tightly. "I wouldn't worry about that. It's enough to make anyone nervous."

After a moment she lifted her head. "Was that the same Paris who got Helen?"

"Why, yes," he said. "Wasn't she his reward—for choosing Love?"

THE SACK OF SILENCE

M rs. Peale. Can you hear me?"
    "Wait till I turn this off. Now."
        "That noise. Whatever is it?"
"The Hoover was running."
"How's that?"
"I said, I was running the vacuum."
"Not that. Outside. Listen." Rosie leaned over the banister.
"Oh, it's the bee, dear."
"Bee nothing. A thousand woodpeckers working on tin."
"The working bee. You'll see if you come down." Mrs. Peale opened the front door. "Hammering nails into the elms. The whole town."
"For heaven's sake."
"You make a circle of nails round the trunk of the tree. It's supposed to stop the elm disease."
"I see."
"Didn't you get the circular? And they came round, too, door to door. But then, you didn't get up here last weekend."
"No, that's right, we stayed in town."

"Nice when you can come up here weekends and be quiet. Don't trip on the cord."

Rosie closed the front door and crossed the hallway. "Some coffee, if it's ready?"

"Thanks, but I've got the kettle on for a cup of tea. I'm going over to make cookies for my daughter's boys when I'm finished here."

The percolator was drawing great labored breaths, like a patient in anesthesia.

"Must be growing up now, Mrs. Peale. They're older than Teddy."

"You remember them, they came by at Halloween."

"I don't think I saw them."

"Oh, they were here all right. You must remember. One was the devil and the other was a skeleton. You gave them a bag of marshmallows."

"Of course." Rosie stood at the kitchen window, drinking coffee. The kettle shrieked.

"Breast high." Mrs. Peale poured.

"How's that?"

"The nails. They're driven in at breast height. Special nails, from Peru."

"From Peru. Fancy that." Well, of course—tin mines, Incas, all that: Why not?

"Yes, Peru, Illinois. If you'll leave that cup. I was just turning on the dishwasher."

Upstairs, Rosie had forgotten to make the beds. She pulled the sheets down, then up again, and thumped the pillows. The dishwasher pounded below, cars swished on the highway. Mrs. Peale turned the vacuum on again. The furnace started up with a gasp and throbbed lightly and quickly through the floor and walls, as if the house had had a bad fright.

All the time, Rosie thought, silence is being broken.

The silence, first broken when Rosie started school, was until then a long afternoon passed in gardens, or on beds where she held a doll and charted shapes in figured wallpaper. At school, however, her train of thought had been permanently disrupted. Voices, there, were sharp, always questioning, always demanding an answer—as if they, not she, were in need of an education. To the question "What does that make?"

she had replied, "Four," and surrendered forever. Later she came up with other answers—"The Great Fire of London," "The Treaty of Utrecht," "Dryden"; or "I don't know"—this particular answer was not unrelated to silence. She recited out loud the fruits of others' silences. There were questions that gave answers, replies that were merely questions—a chain reaction of interrogation that sputtered along for years.

During that time silence was tolerated only when it had official sanction: "Silence, girls," someone said loudly. One developed the ability to stare at a page, even to read, without breaking into one's state of mind. Each November a morning assembly began with two minutes' obligatory silence—the only silence into which no girl ever managed to giggle, growing up as they were in the shadow of the Great War and the Great Depression, and some baffled sense of shame that two such events had been allowed to come about.

Mrs. Peale turned off the vacuum. Rosie sat on her child's bed. Her flesh tingled with the blows of the hundred hammers on the Peruvian nails. Two minutes' silence. Why two minutes? Was that as much as anybody could be expected to stand, thinking about the First World War? Ought it to be cumulative, if intended as a tribute to the dead? In that case, by now should we not be permanently dumbfounded, speechless with horror?

But that wouldn't be silence, then, not really, Rosie thought in all fairness. The front door opened, and closed with a tight thud. "Well, darling," said Rosie.

"Sitting here. Thinking what?"

"How do you know I was thinking?"

"Just a clever guess."

"It was about the sack of silence."

"Sack in what sense?"

"Sense of ransack. Plunder. I read it in a poem. How our generation

> *watched with mixed feelings*
> *the sack of Silence, the churches empty, the cavalry go.*

The cavalry's rather stretching it, all the same."

"I do remember horses, though, in towns."

"Well, so do I. Pulling drays. Clydesdales with huge furry feet. Always in pairs. The horses, I mean. What good times we had before the Industrial Revolution." Rosie leaned back, her hands clasped round her knees. "Where's Teddy?"

"With the Dunstans' boy. Playing Blast-Off."

"Listen, you heard about these nails."

"Not only. I was roped in. Have to hammer some right away so we can hold up our civic heads."

"They're from Peru."

"There must be mines, then, in that part of Illinois. Wasn't that where the Lead Rush was?"

"*Lead* Rush? As if a gold rush isn't ignominious enough."

A man's voice cried out, "*Inner peace, inner peace—*" It roared up at them, frantic. "*No other way—*"

"Bishop Sheen's got turned on."

"I said she could, she asked me as I came in."

"*Inner peace—*"

"I'm afraid it'll frighten Teddy."

"Not after Blast-Off. Nothing could."

"I heard the cardinal this morning. He was in the lilacs."

"Frightened out by the nails."

They were silent. Rosie said, "Where have we been silent?"

"Not here." He raised his voice to be heard above the noise from below. "Not much in town, either."

"Where, then?"

"Segesta, Olympia . . ."

"Bassae, Volubilis, Tarquinia." Rosie on her wedding trip had made the circle of the Mediterranean. "Ruins mostly. Places where the noise has had time to die down. The tumult and the shouting dies; if you live long enough. Woods at the foot of Stratton Mountain."

"That's not ruins. Not Vermont."

"No, but there was so much snow. Snow gives a sort of age. Silence is white."

"Silence is golden."

"There are leaden silences too."

He stood up. "On to Peru."

"I actually heard the silence once. One night, in a garden."

"How was it?"

"Earsplitting." Rosie stretched out, her arms behind her head. "Do I give them tea when they reach this end of the green?"

"Lord, must you?"

"That's what I'm asking."

"Play it by ear. I'd lie doggo if I were you."

Lying doggo, Rosie heard him go downstairs. Outside, he called, "Teddy. Teddy." Certain voices, certain sounds—music, laughter, the sound of the sea—were not infractions; had their own component of silence. Just as one spoke of silence as part of a natural condition: "I kept silent," "I remained silent." How many voices there had been—beloved voices, voices one had ached for, calling one's name, reading aloud on summer evenings, voices with inflections, accents, silences of their own. And all the other voices—impersonal, resentful, furious—and the metallic disturbances of office life: the clash of filing drawers, typewriters, telephones, buzzers, voices shouting "Going up," "Going down," "I won't stand for this" . . . So-and-so was a big noise, someone else a pipsqueak. And how many cars, trains, planes, loudspeakers, transistors—

"Going, Mrs. Peale? I'll be right down."

"I'm off now."

"See you next week then."

"All being well."

In the living room the television had been turned down but not off. A pair of figures capered through a mime about breakfast food. You should be able to cover it, like a parrot, when you want it to be quiet, thought Rosie, twisting the switch and causing the mummery to be sucked back soundless into a pinpoint of white light. The dishwasher changed gear and dried up. The heating, like the Hoover, had long since ceased to run. Rosie lay down on the sofa with her book.

"Well, for crying out loud. Hiding in here."

"Mrs. Lauder. I thought I heard the knocker. Come in. Mr. Lauder."

"Quiet as a mouse, while we were hard at it. But we won't squeal on you."

"Tea and cake?" said Rosie.

"Perhaps a shot," said Mrs. Lauder, "of something."

"Mr. Lauder?"

"You'll have to roar." Mrs. Lauder leaned over, put her hand on her husband's knee. "Dad. Have you got it turned on, Dad?"

"Not so loud," the old man said.

Rosie splashed whisky into glasses, pierced at breast height by a high whistle as Mr. Lauder adjusted his hearing aid. "Soda?"

"A dash for Dad. Rocks for me. Last night, then, you arrived?"

"Late, yes, from New York."

"I wouldn't live there if you paid me." Mrs. Lauder clashed the ice about in her glass. "We like a quiet life."

Rosie shouted, "Crackers?"

The old man shook his head, tapped his ear. "Makes a noise when I eat."

"Everybody's hammering away," said his wife. "It's a scream. Even the General showed up and pounded for a while: just a couple of small trees, nothing to shout about."

"And does it help the elms?" Rosie inquired. "Honestly?"

"Oh, they certainly say."

"That big tree, for instance, at the end of the green."

Mrs. Lauder reflected. "That's a maple."

Rosie objected, "But it's got a disease."

Mrs. Lauder drank, swallowed, shook her head. "Strangled root."

"Unsound," said her husband.

"Oh, fairly crying out for attention. No one talked of anything else at the cocktail party. Going to crash down one of these days."

"Hits the spot," the old man said, holding up his glass.

"It's been reported. But you have to din it in."

Rosie siphoned more soda onto whisky. "Now what's that? That noise?"

"The Big Vac, that's what it is." Mrs. Lauder listened. "Must have reached the Russells' property. You'll be hearing plenty of that this fall. I promise you."

"A machine for the leaves, is that it?"

"Why, just fabulous, the way it sucks them up. Whoosh, and it's all over. I'm saying, Dad—the Big Vac."

"What a difference. Eh, Mother?"

"Something," said Rosie, "that one doesn't hear of in New York."

"New York," the old man said. "I wouldn't live there if you paid me. Too much racket."

Mrs. Lauder broke a cracker in two. "Then you zoom back on Monday?"

"Early," said Rosie.

"Racket in both senses," the old man said, with a gust of laughter.

"Uh-oh. Get a load of that. Sounds like rain, Dad."

Rosie went to the window. "Teddy. Teddy."

A voice called to her, "Bang bang. You're dead."

"Children," said Mrs. Lauder.

"Teddy," Rosie said.

"Nice. But not restful. What are you *doing*, Dad?"

The old man had taken off his hearing aid to examine it. He fumbled with the lamp beside his chair.

"It's a pull, Dad. *A pull, Dad* . . . That's got it. . . . Just listen to that. Thunder yet. We'd better be whizzing along."

"Which way do you go?"

"Turn up Roaring Brook Road, and shoot straight across from there. Home before you can say Knife. Come on, Dad. Snap out of it."

"Lightning," said Rosie, at the door. "Why don't you wait?"

"Thanks, but no. Got to whip up something to eat. Friends said they'd call."

"Listen to that, though."

Mrs. Lauder waved. "The thing is not to get rattled."

"Rosie."

Rosie ran downstairs.

"Didn't you hear me?"

"I was running Teddy's bath. How did the nails go?"

"Those nails. What were the Lauders doing here?"

"Whooping it up. Oh—listen."

"Let it ring."

They sat together on the bottom stair. The furnace shuddered. There was honking on the highway, and a scream of brakes. Rosie said, "Bang bang. We're alive."

"What's going on out there?"

"The Big Vac."

"You haven't told me about the Lauders."

"They wouldn't live in New York if we paid them."

"Useless to offer, then. What did you say?"

Rosie said, "I held my peace."

EDITOR'S NOTE

This collection brings together Shirley Hazzard's published and unpublished short fiction—twenty-eight stories in all. The book is divided into three sections, keeping together as a group her two early collections: the first ten stories are those collected in *Cliffs of Fall* (1963), followed by the eight stories from *People in Glass Houses* (1967). Of these, all but one were originally published in *The New Yorker* ("In One's Own House" first appeared in *Mademoiselle*). Of the final ten uncollected and unpublished stories, "*Le Nozze*" and "The Sack of Silence" were found in typescript among Hazzard's papers, which are now held at the Rare Book and Manuscript Library at Columbia University in New York City. The remaining eight stories in the final section were published between 1961 and 1974, again, mostly in *The New Yorker* ("Forgiving" was first published in *Ladies' Home Journal*, "The Statue and the Bust" in *McCall's*, and "Leave It to Me" in *Meanjin*), but have not previously been collected.

Alongside these twenty-eight stories, it should be noted that, across her writing career, Shirley Hazzard also published sections of her novels as stand-alone pieces: four chapters of *The Transit of Venus* (1980) and two of *The Great Fire* (2003) appeared between 1976 and 1990, and *The Evening of the Holiday* (1966) was first published as a long short story in 1965, all in *The New Yorker*. These have not been included in the present collection.

BRIGITTA OLUBAS